THE GOD PEAK

ALSO BY PATRICK HEMSTREET

The God Wave

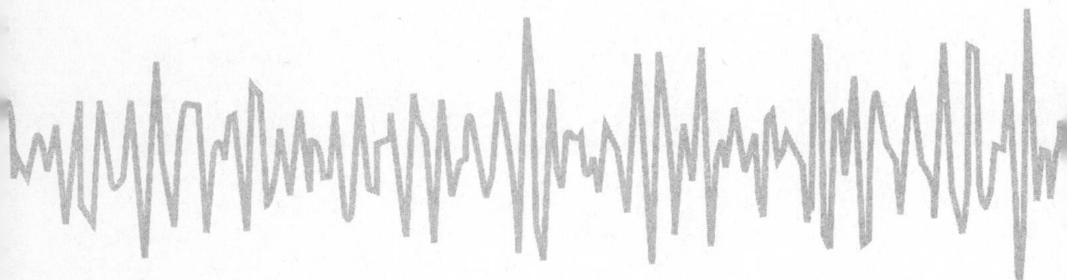

THE GOD PEAK

Patrick Hemstreet

HARPER Voyager
An Imprint of HarperCollins*Publishers*

This is a work of fiction. Names, characters, places, and incidents are products of the author's imagination or are used fictitiously and are not to be construed as real. Any resemblance to actual events, locales, organizations, or persons, living or dead, is entirely coincidental.

HarperCollins books may be purchased for educational, business, or sales promotional use. For information, please e-mail the Special Markets Department at SPsales@harpercollins.com.

FIRST EDITION

Designed by Michelle Crowe

Library of Congress Cataloging-in-Publication Data has been applied for.

ISBN 978-0-06-241956-9

17 18 19 20 21 LSC 10 9 8 7 6 5 4 3 2 1

For Seth

CONTENTS

CHAPTER 1—Hall of the Mountain King 1

CHAPTER 2—Under Mount Olympus 22

CHAPTER 3—Spin 42

CHAPTER 4—Breakout 63

CHAPTER 5—Aftermath 75

CHAPTER 6—To See the Wizard 89

CHAPTER 7—His Peculiar Talents 105

CHAPTER 8—Catching the Wave 122

CHAPTER 9—Silent Running 143

CHAPTER 10—Inside Joey Blossom 158

CHAPTER 11—Black Ops 168

CHAPTER 12—Requiem 188

CHAPTER 13—Councils of War 195

CHAPTER 14—Beneath the Surface 213

CHAPTER 15—The Loyal Opposition 222

CHAPTER 16—Emergence 240

CHAPTER 17—A Kingdom Divided 249

CHAPTER 18—Best-Laid Plans 262

CHAPTER 19—Of Gods and Men 276

CHAPTER 20—Adepts 295

CHAPTER 21—Rage 305

CHAPTER 22—Olympus Fallen 320

CHAPTER 23—Moving Heaven 334

CHAPTER 24—Midnight 349

CHAPTER 25—Going to Ground 356

EPILOGUE 361

ACKNOWLEDGMENTS 365

THE GOD PEAK

Chapter 1

HALL OF THE MOUNTAIN KING

Chuck Brenton woke up every morning in a room overlooking an anonymous and arid landscape of scrub and grass before going off to work in a science fiction story. The lab in which he had an office and in which he did his research had the gleaming, sanitized look and feel of something from a futuristic film. The light was pure and seemed to come from every direction at once; the air was unscented and could be heard gently sighing through filters and baffles on its way down from its desert source.

He wished it were not so sterile. He was allowed early morning and evening visits to the deck overlooking the striking glacier-carved canyon and sagebrush-covered hills. If the light was just right, he could catch the sparkle of sun on the ripples of a nearby stream or see the snowy summit of a mountain range to the southwest. The air outside had a purity to it—a dry, winey perfume that was intensely pleasant—that was in direct contrast to the canned breaths he felt like he was taking each second inside. Chuck wished he might be allowed to go walking out there, but that was not on their hosts' menu of choices. He did his exercise by walking the extensive warren of hallways that connected different parts of the Benefactors' domain (the Center, they called it) or on an elliptical machine in the ground-level gym.

Their lab—which they thought of as New Forward Kinetics (or "NeFK" in their robotics expert Daisuke Kobayashi's acronymic vocabulary)—was a wonder of stainless steel, Plexiglas, and pale quartz. It was more or less an attempt (and a successful one) to re-create and expand upon the work areas they had left behind at their original facility. The central core of the lab was a work area in which Dice could have fielded a team of twenty robotics engineers if he'd had them at his disposal. There were tool racks and worktables—everything Dice had had in his previous workshop and more. Except, of course, red glowing exit signs above randomly located steel doors.

At one end of the room was a testing facility with a large, square workout mat for Chen Lanfen, a series of machine bays—some already equipped with robotic arms and objects—and an art studio for Mini. At the other end of the room was a cluster of computer workstations, only two of which were in use by Chuck and his protégé, Eugene. Around the perimeter of the room were several offices that—though their walls were translucent below and transparent above—offered some privacy to the inhabitants and which were virtually soundproof when the Plexiglas doors were closed.

The world Chuck shared with his colleagues and friends (he had stopped thinking of them as "staff" long ago) was circumscribed, guarded, and carefully monitored. As long as he was hip-deep in his work with human kinetics, he felt almost normal. Work did that—gave him a place to train his eyes and mind so that he didn't think about what had become of his house, his furniture, his garden, let alone what was happening inside and around a mountain on the other side of the continent. At least the pragmatic issues were being taken care of—he knew, for example, that his mortgage was being paid out of the Benefactors' apparently deep pockets. And as for the other members of his team, they were all renters; their apartments had been cleared out and their belongings either ferried here (wherever *here* was) or put in storage.

Except for Mini.

He glanced over at her now as she did a graceful series of dance moves that caused a flock of delicate rainbow-hued sprites to appear as if tossed from her open hands. That seemingly effortless harnessing of her nimble brain's zeta waves had earned her the affectionate title "Butterfly Sorceress." The title was attributed to Euge but seemed to appropriately sum up the group's affections for Mini.

Minerva Mause had been living in a college dormitory when Kristian Lorstad had rescued Chuck and his team from entrapment by the shadowy paramilitary organization that called itself Deep Shield. At twenty-one, she was very connected to her parents and still spent summers at home. Covering all of her bases had posed the most difficulty for the Benefactors, but proved beyond doubt that it was not only their pockets that were deep. As far as her family, friends, and professors knew, Mini had taken a one-semester break to do research with Forward Kinetics—the company she worked for—something that required the signing of a nondisclosure agreement. On the surface it was crazy, she was so close to finishing her degree. But this job, the "zeta-ing," this is why she went to school in the first place. She was on the cutting edge, a novel form of human expression; she was on the crest of the wave. She got to that point without having to finish her studies; college could wait while she carried on in her dream. The position required much travel as well. Her family would get postcards from various locations. What helped sell this so easily was that her many friends had already seen how immersed she had become in a job she'd never spoken of and a boyfriend they'd never met. If her e-mails were few and far between, it was understandable. Chuck's family and her own had been friends for decades; her parents trusted that all was as it should be.

That trust weighed on Chuck. For perhaps the hundredth time, he wished that he hadn't involved Mini in Forward Kinetics, then tried to set aside his pointless sense of guilt by reminding himself of an ageless allegory by Jalaluddin Rumi: poor, crazy Majnun, separated from his beloved Layli, was pursued through the streets of the city by night watchmen, cursing their heartlessness . . . until his wild flight led him directly to the garden in which Layli dwelt. If one could see the end of a process at the beginning, the poem instructed, one would have a completely different understanding of its meaning.

That was the spirit that Chuck tried, with varying degrees of success, to bring to his understanding of the role Kristian Lorstad and the secret organization he represented were playing in his life and the lives of his colleagues. Still, he had been both grateful and disturbed when he'd entered his spacious room at the Center to find all of his clothing and personal effects—including his entire library, movie collection, and his home computer. All had been carefully moved here from his house in Silver Springs, Maryland. He knew from talking to them that everyone else on his team had had a similar reaction.

"They even had my workbench laid out with the little squirrel bot I was tinkering with at home," Dice had told him. "All the tools. All the parts. Every last screw. Laid out just as I left it—only here."

And that question still lingered: where "here" was—they still weren't certain, and Lorstad would say only that they were "somewhere in the western United States."

For Mini, that astonishing relocation had been of paintings and sketches and figurines from her corner of the art studio at school. For Lanfen, it had been her workout mats, her gi, and her collection of martial arts weapons. For Eugene, it had been his personal laptop and library of science fiction, fantasy, and scientific literature.

Chuck had taken the Benefactors' attention to those details as a gesture of respect and an indicator of his team's value in their eyes, but it had also impressed upon him that this was not a short-term relocation. Their "we mean you no harm" demeanor might be a pose. He suspected that if the renegade black ops unit calling itself Deep Shield had gained control of their fate, they might have disappeared permanently. With the Benefactors, there was no telling. They were a riddle, wrapped in a mystery, inside an enigma, or however that Churchill quote went. Chuck had wondered many times in the past week if his desperate phone call to Kristian Lorstad had pulled their chestnuts out of the frying pan only to deposit them in the fire.

"Dr. Brenton."

Chuck looked up over the monitor of his workstation in their shared main lab to see Lorstad watching him. *Speak of the devil.* It was eerie the way the man could enter a room without drawing attention to himself. He projected an aura of mildness and calm, but his pale eyes were vivid and sharp and missed nothing.

"Have you thought any more about my question?" he asked.

"I've thought about little else since you asked it, frankly." Chuck glanced down at Mini's MRI that he'd been studying.

Lorstad rounded Chuck's workbench and looked over his shoulder at the images. "That's Mini, isn't it." Not a question.

"Yes."

"Mm. This was when she was manifesting her sprites." He pointed. "Interesting the way the activity seems spread out across the receptors as if . . ."

"As if the zeta pattern is generated in a field instead of in an isolated location?" Chuck finished. "Very."

Lorstad sat down in the seat next to Chuck at his workbench. "Given this increasingly general activity, does that suggest anything to you about the formula for generating zeta waves?"

Chuck grimaced. He hated—no, too strong a word—he *distrusted* Lorstad's quest for formulas. It reminded him too much of his erstwhile partner, MIT mathematician Matt Streegman.

My deceitful, manipulative partner, who is still in the clutches of Deep Shield . . . if not their back pocket.

But Matt and Deep Shield were—presumably—thousands of miles away, and Lorstad was right here. So he focused his attention back to the immediate . . .

Threat? Is that the right word? Either way, he was wary around him.

"It suggests that any formula I might arrive at is going to involve more than simply stimulating this or that portion of the brain."

"That goes without saying, Doctor," Lorstad said patiently. "*We* have a formula for that sort of process. But it has limitations."

Chuck turned to look at him. "You mean the Benefactors have a process? You've mentioned that before. Can you be more specific?"

Lorstad stared at him a moment longer. Long enough that Chuck thought he would not answer the question.

He seemed to come back to himself from a mental distance, took a deep breath, and said, "I can. In fact, I think I will show you. All of you."

He looked back over his shoulder at the other people in the lab. Mini was dancing in a cloud of surreal butterflies and birds and sprites. Lanfen was going through a series of kung fu moves, supplementing her muscle control with her kinetic talents and seeming to float as if in lower-than-normal gravity. Euge sat at his laptop, matching EEG output to MRI results, while Dice and his borrowed assistant assembled a robot for Lanfen to work with.

Dice looked up from his robot. "All of us what?" His face was drawn, his complexion more gray than golden. Of all of them, he had left the most behind: his fiancée, Brenda. She was still in the outside world and, while Lorstad had repeatedly told him she was safe, Dice—no less than Chuck—was distrustful of anyone with the power, the resources, and the sheer networking ability to do what Lorstad had done over the last week and a half.

Once bitten, twice shy.

"I need to show all of you something that I hope will help you understand why your work in kinetics is so important to us," Lorstad said, "and to the rest of humanity. Please, come with me."

Dice looked skeptical, so Chuck nodded at him in assurance he didn't necessarily feel himself. *But anything we can find out now can only help us understand what the hell is going on here.* He started walking with Kristian.

Lorstad led them out of their lab and into the huge main hall of the Benefactors' underground facility. Of course, Eugene had dubbed it the Hall of the Mountain King within hours of their arrival. It was a long, cavernous space with a brightly lit floor level populated by about two dozen pleasant but curious people working at computers. They were arranged in groups by discipline or task, according to Lorstad. There were large LED displays on the curving walls over their workstations that showed maps and tactical information on the places around the world the Benefactors were watching, for whatever reason.

Of those, Chuck and his colleagues only knew that the splash of yellow near the east coast was a similarly hidden installation beneath another mountain that had lately belonged to Deep Shield. Now it was held by three of the most powerful people on the planet—Sara Crowell, Timothy Desmond, and Mikhail Yenotov. They were an architect, a game developer, and a construction engineer, respectively. *Were* being the operative word. Because now they were something . . . *more.*

People who could do terrible things if they quite literally set their minds to it.

Like Lanfen and Mini, they were Zetas—humans who had trained their brains to produce zeta waves and to use those kinetic impulses to manipulate their environment. They had so far driven Deep Shield from their own base, grounded all military aircraft worldwide, and threatened to do more in the pursuit of world peace. Whatever their agenda, what was clear was that only another group of similarly talented and skilled individuals could hope to take them on.

Chuck rejected the scenario that they intended to destroy the world. He knew them; he had trained them. Tim was antisocial and isolated, but Sara and Mike were both intelligent, moral people. Yes, they'd expelled the forces of Deep Shield violently from their mountain base, but what choice had they been given? They would not be made slaves, and Chuck—having fled across the country himself—could certainly respect that. But it still created a problem in which two men and one woman had the ability to hold the world hostage.

The solution to that problem was to go to Pennsylvania and contact the Zetas, he was sure of it. He just had to convince Lorstad and his associates of that.

Lorstad led his guests to the end of the great central hall where there was a bank of three elevators. They entered the one farthest to the left and went down. Chuck tried not to show how much that startled him. He had thought the floor their lab occupied was the lowest one in the facility. He glanced sidewise and caught Lanfen and Dice looking back at him. Clearly, they had also noticed the anomaly. Eugene and Mini seemed to have eyes only for each other.

"Get a room," Dice muttered, and Chuck almost smiled for the first time in days.

Lorstad, of course, didn't even react.

"The area you're about to enter," Lorstad finally said, "is off-limits to all but a handful of our staff. It must remain so."

"How did you cue the elevator to go down?" Dice asked. "There's no control on the panel."

Lorstad gave the robotics engineer a significant look with a lift of his pale eyebrows. "You do the math," the look said.

"Oh, yeah. Duh," Dice murmured and pointed at his own head. "You're one of us."

The look Lorstad gave him at that statement was impenetrable. Chuck did not even attempt to decode it.

The elevator doors opened onto a broad corridor identical to the ones on higher floors except for the color of its walls. These were pale green and seemed to glow. There were doorways at long intervals along both sides of the corridor. Lorstad led the way briskly out of the lift. About twenty feet down the hall, he hesitated momentarily, then turned to a door on the left. The flat panel retreated into the wall, admitting the group to a chamber unlike any they'd yet seen.

It was large, dark, and had, as its centerpiece, a pair of what looked like—

"Sensory deprivation tanks?" asked Eugene. "You're not planning on putting us in there, are you?"

Lorstad smiled. "Dr. Pozniaki, I have no desire to put you into sensory deprivation units. My hope is that *you* will enable *us* to get out of them."

"Wait a minute," said Euge. "Wait. You're telling me this has something to do with how you guys learn to use your zeta-like abilities?"

Chuck grasped immediately what Lorstad was showing them. "You program your abilities from the outside," he murmured. "Using these."

"Yes. Using SDUs and binaural beat therapy—or a combination of binaural beats and timed flashes. The subject is immersed in the tank, where they are exposed to these stimuli, enabling them to achieve a state of being in which the . . . well, the spirit or soul, perhaps, actively functions in the absence of physical distraction. It learns to extend itself outside the body. To detach from the body and to act without it. To then manipulate the body and other physical objects or processes."

Chuck found himself nodding. "Yes. Yes, I've followed the research LaBerge did at Stanford. It was fascinating. In fact, I came close to moving in that direction with my own research, but it never occurred to me that prolonging lucid dreams could lead to . . . to what it is we—I mean, the Zetas, do."

Lorstad tilted his head to one side. "It's not a long leap from lucid dreaming to out-of-body experiences, Doctor. And once one begins to study the implications of an OBE, well, those implications are stunning."

"Astral projection," murmured Chuck.

"Oh, c'mon!" Eugene protested. "Are you saying that what Mini or Lanfen does—or what any of the Zetas do—is a form of astral projection?"

"Isn't it, though?" Lorstad asked. "Your Zetas, as you call them, can reach beyond their physical reality to manipulate external objects." He turned to look at Mini, who was circling the immersion tanks, her eyes as big as half-dollars in the muted light of the room. "Mini, here, projects objects that exist only in her mind out into the so-called real world, where they take on the appearance of being real. What is that, if not a form of astral projection?"

"Astral projection," said Lanfen quietly, "is a projection of the self."

"Astral projection," said Eugene, mimicking her quiet tone, "is a myth."

"Then what is it we all do?" Lorstad underscored his words by turning to look at a lighted control console along the wall. On a sloping panel, a fader moved and the ambient light in the room increased. It decreased again with a concomitant downward movement of the fader. "Or at least what some of us do."

Eugene frowned and cut a swift glance toward Mini. "It's just . . . that whole astral thing. It sounds so . . . unscientific."

"So does saying we're made of star stuff," said Dice wryly. "But it happens to also be true."

"Maybe it's just the terminology that's bothering you, so how about we stick to 'out-of-body experience'; does that sound a bit more scientific?" Mini joined with a grin and tilt of the head.

"When you're in this state, what happens?" Chuck asked, ignoring the asides. "Guided meditation? Mental suggestion?"

"Guided *exploration*—or perhaps, observation—is more accurate. And, yes, suggestion. We come here"—he reached out to lay a hand on the closest tank—"to immerse ourselves in our selves. To reopen neural pathways and retrain our minds to their higher functions."

"I don't understand," said Lanfen. "You mean, you *lose your abilities* over time? How can that be?"

Lorstad smiled crookedly. "You find that strange? We find it strange—and immensely hopeful—that you have learned to achieve zeta states and capacities in such a way that mere practice makes perfect."

"There's someone in there."

Chuck turned at the sound of Mini's voice to see her staring down into a port in the lid of the farther of the two isolation tanks. The expression on her face wavered between horror and fascination.

"It's Alexis," Lorstad told them, moving to stand next to Mini.

Chuck followed. Through the port, he could see the woman floating in a thick liquid—almost a gel—that was tinted turquoise like the water in some ornamental fountains. She wore a form-fitting dry suit and her face was half-obscured by a helm that included black goggles that wrapped around to also cover her ears.

"How long will she need to be in there?" he asked.

In answer, Lorstad glanced at a display built into the curving side of the machine. Chuck assumed it showed Alexis's vital signs and probably other information as well, such as the temperature of the solution she was floating in.

"She went in at ten P.M. last night. She should be emerging in the next half hour or so."

Chuck glanced at his watch. It was nine thirty in the morning. "That's a long session."

"Yet short compared to the hours spent there during the initiation process."

Mini turned to look up at Lorstad, a frown creasing her brow. "You mean she slept in there?"

"Not slept. The binaural tones put her in a state of deep meditation. But the flashes are to keep her from entering REM sleep."

Chuck nodded. He now understood why the Benefactors were so eager to find an alternative to their process of "learning" to produce psychokinetic abilities.

A chime sounded in the chamber, echoing strangely off the walls. On the console a light flashed. A moment later a pair of technicians—a man and a woman—entered the room from an entrance obscured by Alexis's SDU. They hesitated when they saw the group standing between the two tanks.

"Good morning, sir," said the woman with a deferential nod to Lorstad. "Will you be staying for Ms. Bruinsma's emergence?"

"I think not, Dr. Pence. We'll leave you to your ministrations." He started to turn, to lead Chuck's team from the room, then paused. "You haven't met our guests. Dr. Dana Pence, Niles O'Hare, these are Doctors Charles Brenton, Daisuke Kobayashi, and Eugene Pozniaki, Ms. Chen Lanfen, Ms. Minerva Mause. Ladies and gentlemen, Dr. Pence and her assistant are members of our staff here at the Center."

There were murmured greetings all around. Chuck felt awkward. There was a strange tension in the room that he couldn't quite fathom. He pondered it as they made their way back to the elevator. Just before they entered, he paused and gestured back down the corridor.

"How many of those immersion units do you have?"

"Twenty. Only half of them are used at any given time. The others serve as backup and emergency units."

Chuck frowned, doing the math in his head. "You have

about—what—eighty to one hundred people working here at the Center—"

"Closer to one hundred fifty if you include the maintenance and housekeeping crew."

"That's not nearly enough SDUs for that many people."

Lorstad blinked, then laughed. "Only a fraction of the people here use the units, Dr. Brenton. There are perhaps twenty of us here at maximum at any given moment. Right now, for example, there are only eight."

"'Us?'" echoed Eugene, just as Dice asked at the same time, "Eight of what?"

"Eight Learned. Eight like me."

"And Alexis," added Chuck.

"Yes. The others—the staff—are . . . well, they're normal." Lorstad's gaze skimmed Eugene's and Dice's faces.

"Mundanes, you mean," said Dice.

"Muggles," said Eugene, "like me."

Lorstad shook his head. "I'm sorry. I don't understand the references."

"No," said Euge. "You wouldn't."

"Ah."

Lorstad led them into the elevator and back up to their lab, where he excused himself, but not before he had fixed Chuck with his piercing gaze and said, "You understand now why it's of great interest to us that we learn to employ our talents as you have. I would therefore like to begin undergoing your training process as soon as possible. And I would encourage you, Doctor, to put all necessary effort into formulating what best ensures success."

Chuck nodded and watched Lorstad leave the lab, the semitransparent doors gliding closed behind him. He was still nodding thoughtfully when the others surrounded him.

"What was all that about?" Dice asked him. "What makes our machinery so much better than theirs?"

"REM sleep, for one thing. When they're in the tank, they can't go into REM sleep. That severely limits how often and how long they can enter the state necessary to . . . recharge or retrain themselves."

"I don't understand," said Mini. "Why would they avoid REM sleep? That's where lucid dreams are born."

"Yes, but if you're going to take *conscious external* control, then you have to be in a waking state. It may be a meditative state or an altered state of some sort, but you are awake, not sleeping. During sleep, all the activity is interior, and the whole point of their therapy is to cause it to manifest in the outside world by intention."

"Why is that a problem, though?" asked Mini. "I mean, why is avoiding REM sleep a limitation?"

Eugene answered her. "If a human being goes too long without REM sleep, they lose the ability to function mentally. Eventually it can lead to psychosis and even death."

"Then why risk it?" Mini asked.

"Because their tech *does* work," said Chuck. "It's just inefficient. They'd have to spend far longer in the tank than was healthy to maintain their abilities at the levels Mini and Lanfen do naturally. And it's not just the REM sleep problem. They'd have to be catheterized repeatedly, kept on antibiotics—plus, their muscles would atrophy over extended periods. And yet, how much would we risk for our abilities." Now that Chuck had developed his own zeta waves, he found it hard to imagine going back. Mini nodded at that, but still seemed unsure.

"But why?" she asked. "Why are they so dependent on the machines? I mean why doesn't the—the charge last?"

Chuck shrugged. "I'm not sure."

"I think I might know," murmured Lanfen. Her dark eyes were solemn as they met Chuck's. "Lorstad said it: they learn to work *outside* the body. Detached from the body."

"And you don't?" asked Euge.

Lanfen shook her head. Chuck realized that he and Mini were echoing the movement. He stopped.

"I can't speak for Mini," Lanfen continued, "but when I'm . . . practicing kinetoquism I'm projecting *from* the body, but I'm still attached to it somehow. Anchored."

"Yes," Mini agreed. "Me too."

"When I—when we—stop projecting, we're recharging naturally, without even thinking about it. Our meditative state is self-generated and our capacities are rooted in our *selves*, in our consciousness; it recharges via the physical generation of energy. What they're doing is actually cutting them off from a natural energy source and creating a dependency on those machines."

"Yeah," said Eugene quietly, "and muggles like me."

LANFEN EXECUTED A BACKWARD DOUBLE somersault and landed lightly in an office chair she pulled into her path kinetically while in flight. Her workout complete, she let her momentum carry her chair over to Dice's workbench. The robotics expert and his newly minted assistant had been working for hours on the robot that Lanfen had already decided would be dubbed Pippin.

Yes, she knew it was silly to name a machine and to get attached to that machine—which she had signaled she meant to do in the very act of naming it. But it was what she did. Her laptop had a name—Carter, after a favorite TV character played by a favorite actress. Secret agent stories were something she enjoyed losing herself in, and the post–World War II setting was the icing on the cake. Her motorcycle had a name—Bruce, just because it seemed like a Bruce. She wondered what had become of Bruce. The last time she had seen him was when she'd tucked him into the storage unit at her apartment complex.

She pulled her mind away from her possibly irretrievable life and watched the two men working over Pippin now; she was fascinated by the process of assembling the mechanical frame around the thick cable of spinal column. Dice's assistant, Joey Blossom, was a young Shoshone-Paiute Indian. He wore his hair long, and braided while he was in the lab. Lanfen had learned that he was from the Duck Valley reservation near Owyhee, Nevada, and had been assigned to the lab because of his background with computers and electronics. He had a master's degree in computer science and a trade school diploma in electronics and, until he had gotten his job with the Center, had been gainfully employed installing and maintaining the computer system in the Sho-Pai community center in Owyhee. He'd left a high-paying job at a top laboratory to return home to the reservation, to Owyhee, to his family. That might or might not mean the Center was close to the Duck Valley reservation, though the topography looked right for that part of the country.

One thing was obvious—Joey was good at what he did. So much so that, after only a few days of working with him, Dice trusted him with some of the more exacting work on Pippin's wiring harness. Dice could be awfully discriminating as to who touched his toys, so this was a glowing testament to Joey's skill.

Joey glanced up at Lanfen as she rolled to a stop near the workbench. She sensed equal parts curiosity and unease. Considering whom he worked for, she doubted the unease was caused by her abilities. She smiled at him. He did not smile back.

"So," he finally said, when he had a momentary lack of wires in his hands, "you're a martial arts expert."

"I am a practitioner of kung fu, yes."

"Pretty impressive, what you were doing there. All the acrobatics and the—the psychokinesis."

"Lanfen prefers to think of it as kinetoquism," said Dice. "Sort of a takeoff on ventriloquism. Instead of throwing her voice, she throws her self."

"Her *self*?" Joey repeated, looking at her more directly.

"My consciousness. My spirit. I extend it to manipulate the environment."

"You believe in the spirit? But you're a scientist."

She laughed at that. "No, I'm a kung fu practitioner. Dice and

Eugene and Chuck are scientists. I'm pretty sure Chuck believes in the spirit, too, though." She turned to Dice. "So, when do you think you'll be done with my little droid friend, here? I'm bored and lonely and tired of dancing without a partner."

Dice grinned at her. "Whiner. You have rolling chairs. Maybe we could bring in the flight cases from the Brewster-Brenton unit and you could roll those around, too. Maybe have kinetic races."

They had been able to smuggle a Brewster-Brenton Brain Pattern Monitor with its kinetic converter out of their old lab, along with a Brenton-Kobayashi Kinetic Interface (BKKI, aka "Becky"), but they'd been forced to abandon Lanfen's robot companion, Bilbo. He was still stored (*imprisoned,* she thought) in the bowels of Deep Shield's underground facility in the Michaux State Preserve in Pennsylvania.

"You didn't answer my question: how long before Pippin is ready for his trial run?"

Dice glanced at his watch. "I'd say at least another hour. Longer, probably." His stomach chose that moment to growl loudly and he grimaced. "Well, then there's that. The spirit is willing, but the body requires food."

Lanfen hopped up from her chair. "I'll run down to the canteen and grab you guys some lunch. What do you want? Sandwiches? Salads?"

Joey blinked. "*You're* going to get *us* lunch?"

Lanfen shrugged. "Why wouldn't I? Soup? Duck confit? Filet mignon?"

"Now you're just being mean," said Dice. "Tuna fish sandwich for me if there is such a thing in that gourmet hot spot. And some milk."

"Tea is better for the soul."

"Not sure I have one."

"Joey?" She looked to Dice's assistant.

"Same here, only I'll take a water."

"Okay, a couple of tuna sandwiches, one milk, and a water—

oh, and two souls." Lanfen smirked, then saluted and went off to fulfill the orders. She did so in a perfectly nonchalant manner as to assure Joey she did not consider him *less than.* She stopped off at Chuck's office first to see if he wanted anything. He was sitting cross-legged on the short sofa across from his desk, pen in hand, frowning at a pad of paper in his lap.

"Wow, that's old school," she said, leaning against the doorframe.

He blinked and looked up at her. "Oh, uh, yeah. When my thoughts are sluggish, I go into troglodyte mode. Helps . . . sometimes."

"What's the problem you're working on?" Lanfen wandered into the office and sat down next to him on the sofa, peering at his pad of paper.

"Lorstad asked me to see if I could come up with a formula for what we do. A sort of overarching equation of the elements of success."

"Do you even *do* math?"

He laughed. "Of course, I 'do' math. If you're going to go into the sciences—any of them—you have to have a working knowledge of higher math. Although, I have to admit, that's more of a Matt thing. I'm really missing him right about now." He hesitated, bouncing the tip of the pen on the pad. "He wanted to come in, you know."

"Come in? You mean, he wanted to come *here* with us?"

"This was before I called Lorstad. Matt reached out to me to let me know what was happening on his end. He wanted to know where we were so he could join us. I talked him out of it. Said we needed an insider on that end."

Lanfen read his face. "Mmm. There's a big fat *but* in there somewhere."

Chuck nodded, staring down at the notations he'd been noodling. "I didn't trust him, Lanfen. I thought maybe he was going to sell us out. After all, he knew better than anyone that without us, there *is* no Forward Kinetics, no remote robotics program, nothing for General Howard to use."

"Tell me you are *not* feeling guilty about this." Lanfen grasped Chuck's upper arm in a firm grip. "Chuck, for God's sake, that's absurd. He *did* sell us out. He lied to you—to all of us. We were worried about getting asked out on a date by the military, and it turns out he'd already accepted a proposal of marriage. I don't blame you for not trusting him. I would have made the same call."

He looked over at her. "First of all—*ow*! You've got a strong grip. Second, really? You think I was justified in being that cautious with Matt?"

She nodded, letting go of his arm. "Yes. Absolutely. So, don't second-guess yourself. If you need help with your math, ask Dice."

"Dice has enough on his plate."

"Yes, but he can still help. Anyway, speaking of plates, I was just on my way to the canteen to procure some sustenance for the geek squad. Want something?"

Chuck took a deep breath. "Yeah, a break from this." He tossed the notebook and pencil over onto his desk and quirked an eyebrow at her. "Mind if I tag along?"

She savored the momentary curl of warmth the thought of his companionship brought, then hopped up from the sofa. "Never. Besides, my food-juggling skills are severely limited."

"Huh. I seriously doubt that." He trailed her from the office, falling into step with her as they entered the long central cavern where the Center staff worked, then turned right toward the canteen and staff lounge.

"So, talk to me about this formula of yours," Lanfen said. "I saw a bit of it: *N* plus *C* plus *R* plus something, something . . ."

"Oh, yeah. I was just toying with elements that go into a successful growth of zeta capacities: natural inclination and/or desire, plus concentration, plus repetition. That's what I've got so far. And I'm not sure if natural inclination is necessary. I mean, clearly it's helpful to have the natural talent and the desire. Maybe both. But it may just be more a matter of aiding the learning curve than being a binary obstacle."

"Well, if it helps, I'd define natural inclination as a combination of talent *and* desire. But I see what you mean. It's hard to pin this stuff down."

"Exactly. Especially since we still don't know if some people just can't do it at all. Anyway, I thought I said I wanted a break from—" He jerked a thumb back toward his office.

Lanfen grinned sheepishly. "Sorry. Food first. The formula can wait."

"Don't let Lorstad hear you say that. I think to him this formula is some sort of grail. To me, it's just an aid to facilitate ideation. We already have a repeatable process. That's what matters."

"Yes, but it's a process that, right now, depends on you, Dice, and Eugene. And Lorstad wants to be first in line to be the next to experience that process."

"Yes. The first of many. Well, of about twenty to thirty individuals, he said. I guess Benefactors will be jetting in from all over the world to get zeta training."

Lanfen shook her head. "That seems so . . . inefficient. There are a hundred people here who could benefit from our training. You can't change the world if you limit the next stage of evolution to a handful of elites."

Chuck didn't answer, but she knew he was thinking the same thing.

"EARTH TO BLOSSOM." DICE SNAPPED his fingers to get Joey's attention back on the task at hand. The guy seemed unable to keep his eyes from wandering after Chen Lanfen as she left the lab with Chuck.

"Oh. Sorry. I just . . . She . . ."

"Yeah. She's all that," Dice agreed, grinning.

"No. I mean, yeah, she's beautiful and amazing, but that wasn't what I was . . ." Joey leaned across the workbench, lowering his voice. "*She's* bringing *us* lunch?" he said, putting the same inflections he had on those words earlier. "Why would she do that? She's a Mindbender, right?"

Dice laughed. "A who? A what?"

Joey reddened. "Sorry. I shouldn't talk about them that way. The Benefactors. You won't tell Lorstad—"

"Hell no. I mean, *hell* no, I won't tell on you and hell no, she's not—*we're* not—part of the Benefactors. Lanfen and Mini are just people who have learned to use a set of mental muscles that most people don't know they have."

"I heard a rumor," said Joey, "that your people don't tank. I wasn't sure I believed it. But you're saying it's true."

"'Tank'? You mean the immersion therapy? No. We don't do that. You'll see when we start working with Lorstad."

Joey let out a sharp bark of laughter. "Fat chance of that happening. He's not going to allow a plain old vanilla human being in the room while he's becoming even more godlike."

"Yeah, well, he's not going to have much choice. There have to be plain old vanilla human beings in the room to run the equipment. You may be one of them."

That raised Joey Blossom's eyebrows. "Really? Well, if you can swing that, I'd be much obliged. I'd love to see what it is you guys do with all your tech."

"That will require us to actually complete this robot," Dice told him. "Can you handle adjusting the optics?"

"You bet," Joey said, his normally stoic features seemingly lit up, and he bent to his task.

Chapter 2

UNDER MOUNT OLYMPUS

Mike Yenotov watched the blood pressure cuff inflate, grunting when it hit its max and began to deflate. The LED screen of the little machine ticked off the numbers in time with a soft, repetitive beep. Blood pressure looked good. So did his wound. It was scabbing over cleanly with no sign of infection.

He tried not to think about how he'd sustained it.

Mike pulled off the cuff and returned it to the basket below the blood pressure monitor. The machine rolled away from him to stand against the wall like a silent sentinel. He looked around the infirmary with its pristine surfaces and wondered how long it would stay clean. Even down here there was dust and he wasn't sure his kinetic abilities ran to vacuuming.

Stupid. Thoughts like that were stupid, irrelevant. Dust was the least of his worries—*their* worries. He shared this domain beneath the mountain with Sara and Tim. Sorry—*Troll*. Regardless of what he called himself, those two were his only companions at the moment. They were—or rather had been—his . . . colleagues. He couldn't think of either of them as friends. Not now, at any rate. Maybe even not before all this. But now, they were . . . he wasn't sure what.

Partners in crime, maybe.

Dust might not be an issue, but other things were. Take those full-spectrum light bulbs that Deep Shield had everywhere. They allowed the staff to live underground for extended periods of time without the medical problems that came from long-term lack of exposure to sunlight. He assumed that there were replacement bulbs and other supplies somewhere down here, but they hadn't found them yet. Of course, he was the only one who'd even thought of looking for anything beyond food, water, and a way to wash bodies and clothing. Sara and Tim were focused on the outside world—specifically, on ways to control it. Mike, trying to think ahead, had constructed an observation deck on the eastern slope of their mountain home—just in case.

He slid off the exam table, wincing a little at the pain in his rib cage, and considered raiding the canteen for something to eat. Or maybe doing another inspection tour. He knew what he was doing. He was putting off going back down to "ops." If he went back, he'd have to deal with Sara and Tim's outrage. It wasn't that he was bothered by anger—he'd worked with too many foremen to worry about being yelled at. But a Zeta's outrage . . . that could be toxic. He wondered if they weren't poisoning each other, creating a sort of feedback loop that just fed and fed on itself. They were furious at General Leighton Howard for his assault on their position. Furious at the military establishment he represented. Furious at whatever politicos knew of and sanctioned Deep Shield's operations.

Mike was pissed off, too, but not so much at that stuff as at the hijacking of his life—of all their lives. As he saw it, the whole damn mess was a cascade of what-the-hell-did-you-expect? What the hell had Howard expected when he'd essentially made them prisoners in his secret mountain military base? What the hell had the Zetas expected when they'd exiled the general and all his crew to the outside? Of course they were going to try to get back in. Of course there were fail-safes and self-destruct plans and booby traps. Of course the general was going to try to limit their access to the outside world.

As per usual, thinking about their current situation gave Mike a headache. He wandered into the dispensary where medicines and other medical supplies were kept in a locked cage. The door to the cage lay on the floor where he'd flung it the first time he'd accessed the dispensary's stores. He started to reach for the dial at the top of the ibuprofen dispenser—a device that reminded him of a gumball machine—but the bandages over his wound pulled. So he reached for the dial kinetically; it was second nature at this point. He just visualized a hand turning it, and two tablets dropped into the little plastic tray on the front of the machine.

He tossed back the pills and followed them with a swig of water from a water dispenser. (*How soon before we run out of water?*) A crackling sound came from his shirt pocket. He gave it a thought, switching the walkie-talkie on.

"Yeah?"

"You get lost, Micky?" Tim asked.

"Changing my bandages."

"Sara wants you back down here. She's getting ready to call Howard. Figures you oughta be in on the conversation."

Conversation. That was one word for it. More like ransom demands. Sara had, just that morning, crashed a small regional banking system in the Midwest as a sort of demo—a moderately destructive reminder that, though he'd clipped their wings somewhat by restricting their access to cell towers, there were still things she could do beyond the halls of Deep Shield's ex-HQ. Howard would have to be an idiot to think she wouldn't employ every resource she could to achieve her goals. It must totally burn him that the communications and computer network he'd worked so hard and so secretly to build was now being used against him.

Whatever they want to call this next phase in the discussions, he definitely needed to be there.

"Yeah. I'm on my way," Mike said.

He shut off the walkie-talkie and took a deep breath, reminding himself that Sara's goals were his goals. He just wasn't sure about her means of achieving them. He shook himself mentally for that. Everything they'd done had been defensive, he told himself. Everything. They just wanted a better world. A world where men like General Leighton Howard and organizations like Deep Shield were not allowed to exist.

He remembered pictures in the Bible storybooks he'd read as a boy. Lions and lambs playing nice. Tanks rusting in junkyards. Orchards full of fruit being harvested by smiling families dressed like they were on holiday. He didn't take those images literally, as he had when he was a kid, but he still wanted that world in which lions and lambs just got along.

Problem was, he didn't feel so much like a lamb anymore.

He retrieved a couple more ibuprofen and popped them into his shirt pocket. Well, not *his* shirt, really. The shirt pocket belonged to whoever's uniform he'd borrowed a piece of.

He wondered if it had been one of the soldiers who'd died in the assault on the mountain. Odds were pretty good.

Mike shook off the image that conjured and headed down to the operations theater. On the way, he passed by a series of long, narrow rooms in which Deep Shield had stored row upon row of robots built expressly for remote manipulation. He had tried to count them manually at one point, only to give up when he reached five hundred. There might be many times that many in this warren. He had no idea. What he did know was that they would never rust. Steel and titanium and aluminum didn't. He wondered how long it would be, though, before their wiring harnesses desiccated in the dry air. It almost didn't matter. The Deep

Shield guys had built them with servo mechanisms and a rudimentary AI because their Zetas hadn't known how to manipulate the bots directly. He and Sara and Tim did. The wires could all disintegrate and they'd still be able to make use of the robot army.

Except that they wouldn't. That would be his personal part of their endgame, he decided—destroying every last one of those war machines. Well, maybe he'd have to let Tim take down a couple hundred. The thought almost made him smile.

He entered ops quietly and slid into a chair at a console near the back of the room, angling a glance at the faraway ceiling. The place had a state-of-the-art fire suppression system. In this room alone, there were enough nozzles to flood the place. He wondered what effect all that water and fire retardant would have on General Howard's metal army.

"Where the hell's Mike?"

Mike jerked his head up and peered at Tim through the muted light in the room. The overhead lighting was dimmed in favor of bright, full-spectrum LEDs that lit the workstations the Zetas had appropriated. The kid was sitting in a pool of light about four feet in front of him at another console with his Converse-clad feet propped up on it, his face bathed in a rainbow of radiance from the lights on his control panel. Sara was pacing back and forth beneath the wall of tactical and real-time displays at the head of the room. Mike glided his chair forward on silent casters and tapped Tim on the shoulder.

The younger man yelped, twisting so violently he pitched himself out of the chair and onto the concrete floor.

"Son of a bitch, Mike! What the hell'd you do that for?"

Mike shrugged. "Just letting you know I was there. Thought you heard me come in." He thought nothing of the kind, but he wasn't about to admit it. Tim had always rubbed him the wrong way. He'd come to view him with a sort of annoyed fondness, but under their present circumstances, there was less fondness and a lot more annoyance.

"Bastard," mumbled Tim.

Mike raised his head to see Sara regarding both of them with impatience. "I'm here, boss lady. What's the plan?"

"The plan is, we're going to issue some demands to General Howard. Demands that he will disregard at his peril."

"Okay. What demands?"

"First of all, that they stop trying to pry us out of this mountain. Second, we hear from your wife and kids that they're okay, that they're not being harassed in any way—"

Mike felt as if someone had poured ice water over his head. "My family is in Canada."

"Yes, and if I were Howard, I'd be looking for a way to extract them."

"The Canadian government isn't going to just give them up. My wife's got dual citizenship."

Sara crossed her arms over her breasts and gave him a look that was almost pitying. "Mike, Howard has no real authority in the American government or the military. His extraction would not go through diplomatic channels. He'll probably just send one of his black ops teams . . . if he has any left."

Mike stood slowly. "The hell he will! That son of a bitch *touches* my family and I will end him."

"And that is something that I want to impress upon our dear general. *You* need to communicate with your family and your family needs to remain free."

"Canaries in a coal mine," Mike murmured.

"What?"

"My family. You're saying they're like canaries in a coal mine. If they get locked down or fall silent, you'll know Howard's plotting something."

Sara stared at him for a long moment, then said, "I suppose it would have that advantage, Mike. But I care that your family is an obvious point of leverage. We need to do what's necessary to keep them safely out of harm's way. I'm sure you agree."

"Sure I agree."

"Then we're in accord. I also want Howard to get the *real* U.S. government involved. He's a traitor. He has no authority to be speaking on behalf of the government or the people of America."

"Howard is scum." Tim had climbed back into his seat and resumed his casual pose.

Sara ignored him. "I'm sure you'll agree we need access to the real power, Mike."

Tim snorted. The sound echoed harshly in the cavernous room. "I'm pretty sure that'd be the heads of multinational corporations, who are just as scummy as Howard, in my book. Man, but I'd like to take those jerks down."

Sara cut him a swift glance, a Mona Lisa smile on her face. "You'll get your chance. I did some snooping in Howard's private files. He's beholden to a number of multinationals who have interests that his little robot army were intended to serve. They'll no doubt be asking him embarrassing questions about how that's going."

"So," said Mike, "what are you going to demand?"

"Access to the Oval Office and the Pentagon."

Mike laughed. "Like that's gonna happen. Like you said, *he* doesn't have that access to give."

Sara's smile became a grin. "We'll see." She opened a channel to the Deep Shield camp at the foot of the mountain. "This is Sara Crowell," she told the tech who answered. "I want to talk to General Howard. Immediately."

Tim snickered, then cupped his hands over his mouth and called out in a high, singsong voice: "Paging Leighton Howard. Will Leighton Howard please report to the principal's office?"

Howard was there so fast, Mike imagined he must have been standing right next to the communications console.

"Howard here," he identified himself.

Sara got right to the point. "By now you will have ascertained that none of your attack forces survived the attempt to kill us and that you are unable to detonate the charges you intended to destroy this mountain. And you will have gone to Mike Yenotov's house and found it empty."

There was a moment of silence, then Howard said, "Yes to all three. But you should be warned that we know where Yenotov's family is. We traced them to Ontario."

Mike tensed.

"And *you* should be warned," Sara said, "that if we do not hear from Mike's wife in twenty-four hours and continue to hear from her on a daily basis that she and the kids are *still* in Ontario and free—well, let's just say you really wouldn't like the consequences."

When Howard didn't answer, Sara continued. "Now, I think we're clear that you're not getting back in here by force and that you are not going to be able to trigger your explosives. Are we indeed clear on that, General?"

"Yes." Howard ground the word out between his teeth. Mike was convinced he could literally hear the man's molars chipping.

"Wonderful. So, here's what I want. I want to talk to the president. In fact, I want a direct line of communication."

"That's—that's impossible."

"Why? Because she still has no idea that the little snafu in Pennsylvania had nothing to do with hackers or cyberterrorism? Because she still doesn't know it was connected to military bases going dark all over the world? Tsk, tsk, General Howard. You're withholding information from your own commander in chief."

Silence again. Mike exhaled sharply. He admired the way Sara could peg this guy, but it infuriated him that this traitorous jackass would try to maintain his authority in the face of what the Alpha-Zetas had already proven they could do.

"Or maybe you don't consider the president your commander at all?"

More silence.

"Maybe," he said aloud, "he needs a reminder of what the stakes are, Sara."

Sara glanced back at him over her shoulder, then turned to Tim. "Tim, pick a corporation. A corporation that's monkeyed with people's lives—maybe they've gobbled up little independent companies, stolen their tech, and then fired all their employees. Or maybe they've polluted the natural resources of the people living downstream from their facilities. Or maybe they've sold defective equipment to the military—the real military. Think about what you'd like to do to that company's resources." She hesitated, smiled, and said, "Then do it."

"Hot damn!"

Tim swung his feet down from his console and rotated his shoulders as if to loosen them. Then he looked up at the set of displays that covered the front wall. On the central one, a map of the United States appeared, but a map that showed not highways or state boundaries but the unbounded filaments of the national telecommunications system. Grinning from ear to ear, the programmer lit up several hubs on the map in lurid red. A second later, traceries of equally bright green began to flash and pulse like lightning.

"Very Christmassy, Tim," Sara said. "Can you describe for the general what you're doing?"

"I'm moving financial resources, General. Some of them are going into my personal coffers—think of it as a commission. But a lot of it is going to where I think it would be better spent."

"Going from where?" Howard demanded. "What company or companies are you attacking?"

"Oh, I'm sure you'll hear about it in the news, dude. And given the twenty-four-hour news cycle, I bet you'll hear about it pretty quick. Hey, you can blame the same cyberterrorists that you blamed for the 'Battle for Olympus.' Did you tell the president that you'd taken care of that?"

"Oh, no, Timmy," said Sara, her voice cool and sweet. "He hasn't told Madam President a damn thing. But he needs to. Don't you, General Howard?"

"I don't think you understand, Ms. Crowell—"

"I don't think *you* understand, General Howard. If you don't put us in touch with the POTUS, we're going to continue to pull things apart. And we're going to figure out how to get in contact with her ourselves."

The man laughed. He actually laughed. "I'm sure you and your friends are clever enough to figure out how to contact the president, but I doubt you'll be able to convince her that you're not just some nutcase who's not even living in the real world. Remember, all this stuff you do is completely unknown in the White House."

"Well, it won't be for long, now will it?" Sara broke the connection kinetically, drawing a finger across her throat in a gesture that graphically relayed her contempt for the man she had cut off. She swung around and glared at Tim. "If he tries to reestablish communications, just ignore him. He clearly needs to stew for a while. Mike, how long is your mental reach?"

"How long do you need it to be?"

"Can you reach D.C.?"

Mike considered that. "If I have a line of sight, yeah."

She moved to the console he was seated at and perched on the edge of it. "Okay, so let's say I can isolate surveillance cameras in target areas—show you what I'd like you to manipulate."

"If I can see it, I can work it."

"You seem pretty sure of yourself, Micky," Tim said, pivoting in his chair.

"I am, *Timmy*. What's the target?" he asked Sara.

"Let me find one for you," she said, and turned to look at their windows on the world. "And Timmy, I'd like you to start thinking of some interesting viruses."

MATT STREEGMAN STARED AT THE man sitting across from him in his office at Forward Kinetics with a riot of thoughts having a melee in his head. What finally came out of his mouth was, "Why didn't you ask me this before?"

General Howard's graying brows lowered in obvious displeasure. Which was saying a lot since they had been set in a perpetual scowl since Chuck and his team had bolted. Matt was surprised the man hadn't keeled over of a heart attack by now and was sure his stomach lining must have been eaten through.

"I'm asking now," the officer said. "Help me understand these—these people. How do I communicate with them? How do I control what they do?"

"They're not controllable. No, wait. Let me be very specific: *you* can't control them because they will never give you the opportunity. They don't trust you. They no longer need to trust you. The time for trying to understand them was back before you tried to force them to do your bidding. You treated them as if they were machines that you just had to understand well enough to make use of. Or even as soldiers that could be ordered about and wouldn't question your authority. Either way, they were never human beings to you."

"Were they human beings to *you,* Streegman? Weren't they just a product?"

Matt had to acknowledge that there was some truth to that, sad as that made him feel. "Touché. Although, to be fair to myself, I'd have to say I thought of them as . . . students or—"

"Specimens?"

"Proofs of concept. They were never intended to be the product, General. I wasn't selling *them.* I was selling potential. I was using them only to show you what your own people could achieve. You're the one who changed the game."

"No, your lame-brained partner did that when he took his crew and bolted."

Matt shook his head and sat back in his office chair. "Look, Leighton, you can argue all day about causality. But in the real world, you'd lose that argument. I understand why you took some of the security precautions you did, but you went to lengths you didn't have to and, more to the point, *shouldn't* have gone to. Replacing our grounds crew with agents? Firing our administrative staff? Bugging our offices, our homes? Putting tracers on our vehicles? You started treating us like we were . . . dangerous."

Howard's broad face reddened. "Dammit, Streegman, they *are* dangerous. You made them that."

"No, General. Again, you're not seeing the whole picture. *You* made them dangerous. You cut them off from the real world and tried to intimidate them. When that failed, you tried to destroy them. If I'd had any idea what sort of outfit Deep Shield really was going in, I'd never have gotten into bed with you in the first place. But I was drunk on my own sense of accomplishment. And I was greedy and stupid. Chuck was right to do what he did. It was the only thing he could have done."

"This debate," Howard said, rising from the side chair across from Matt's desk, "is getting us nowhere. We need to get those people out of that facility and we need to do it immediately. Do you know what Sara Crowell just demanded of me?"

Matt shrugged.

"She demanded that I get her in touch with President Ellis."

Matt chuckled. "She demanded that you out yourself, you mean. That you humiliate yourself and probably get yourself arrested. I'm willing to bet that Sara finds your behavior treasonous and she's thinking the POTUS just might agree with her about that."

"I can't 'out' myself, as you put it."

"You mean you won't. How highly you must think of yourself, Leighton, to imagine that your reputation, even your *life,* is more important than the lives already lost through your . . . patent evil. More important than the lives that potentially could be lost. More important than a full-throated revolt that devastates this nation's economy and infrastructure."

Howard's lip curled. "I never took you for a bleeding-heart liberal."

"Oh, cut the crap, Leighton. I never took you for a coward. But that's what you are—a greedy, self-absorbed coward. Hiding behind your soldiers and your well-funded 'programs' and the people who are bankrolling them. Do you think those people are going to continue to support you when you show up on the evening news?"

"Where the hell do you get off calling me—"

Matt stood, slamming his hands down on the top of his desk. "I can call you a greedy, self-absorbed coward because it takes one to know one! Now, if you really want my advice about how to handle the Zetas, do what they want. Go to the president and explain to her what's happened. You can blame me, if you want. I'll be your mad scientist—or mad mathematician—whatever. Just do it before more people get hurt."

Howard didn't reply. He fixed Matt with a look that would have been lethal if Howard himself were a Zeta, and strode out of Matt's office. Mere minutes later, Matt heard the chopper lift off from the parking lot and collapsed back into his chair. He was like Howard in other ways, too, he mused. He was every bit as hoist by his own petard.

"I HAVE THE PERFECT TARGET." Sara sat down next to Mike at the console he'd adopted as his station in the ops theater and at which he had been trying to figure out how to run a trace on his family. That wasn't really his forte—working with electronic signals and networks—but he hadn't wanted to ask Tim or Sara to do it. They were both occupied elsewhere.

The central display at the head of the room switched from its view of the Deep Shield installation at the foot of the mountain to a vastly different and very familiar scene. The Washington Monument, dominating its end of the National Mall. The morning sun illuminated the construction equipment and scaffolding that surrounded it. Two huge cranes stood like twin sentinels to either side of the obelisk. There was a crowd gathering on the grass and paths around the structure and news trucks had congregated along the closest curbsides.

"What's going on there?" Mike asked.

"The upper stories of the monument have gotten a fresh cladding of white marble *and* the capstone is being replaced with one covered in gold, if you can believe it." Sara gestured with one hand and the view moved closer to the base of the building. "See? That's it there in that heavy-duty sling. Today at noon, it's supposed to be lifted to the top of the structure by one of those cranes and nudged lovingly into place, while officials sing George Washington's praises and mouth the wrong words to 'The Star-Spangled Banner.'"

Mike sat up straighter. "What do you want me to do?"

"I want you to start the festivities a little early."

"But . . . all those people. If I screw up, somebody could get hurt."

Sara rested a hand on his shoulder. "Mike, you worry too much. I'll call Howard, tell him to keep an eye on the proceedings at the monument. He'll move people out fast, I'll bet."

"How? You keep saying he's got no authority—"

"But he does have connections. Trust me, Mike."

He was getting tired of people saying that to him. His trust had gotten him locked inside this mountain with these two. Yet he took a deep breath and said, "Okay. What do you want me to do?"

"Work the capstone's crane. Give that archaic status symbol a nice little crown."

Mike frowned at the crane, let it fill his vision, then his thoughts. He felt its gears and drivers and mechanisms. He tasted the vinyl air in the cab and smelled the steel and lubricant. "Okay. Sure. I can do that."

"Great." Sara stood and the communications channel to Deep Shield crackled to life.

"I need to talk to Howard," she told whoever was minding the store.

"He's on his way in."

"Put me through to his cell phone. I know you can," she added when the guy started to protest. "Don't stall me, soldier."

"Just a moment."

In mere seconds, Howard's voice came across the connection. Mike imagined he heard relief in it. He was sure that wasn't going to last.

"Ms. Crowell. I have a proposal to make."

"Really? Does it involve me talking to the POTUS?"

"It involves you getting to keep the mountain. Or leave it if you'd rather. You may go wherever you like in the world. Anywhere. We won't follow you. We won't approach you. We won't attack you. Just go wherever you would like to go and do whatever you would like to do."

"What we would like to do, General, is put an end to war. That means putting an end to your asinine plotting and manipulations of people's lives. So, here's my counterproposal. You get me in touch with President Ellis and you confess your part in this *and* the parts played by any associates or aiders and abettors you have in Washington, and then *you* disappear. We won't follow you. We won't approach you. We won't attack you. Same deal you offered us."

"That's unacceptable."

Sara glanced from Mike to Tim, who had taken a break from whatever he was doing to monitor the interaction. "How did I know you were going to say that? General Howard, as you may be aware, there is a special ceremony taking place at the Washington Monument today. I recommend that, when you get back to your base, you grab a TV or surveillance feed of the area around the monument. I'll supply one if you can't get it."

There was silence on the other end of the line. "What are you planning? What do you think you can do—?"

"Pretty much whatever we want. Whenever we want."

"I'm arriving at the base now. Let me—I don't—" He cut off from his end.

"Wow," said Tim, winding a lock of his riotously curly hair around one finger. "You really rattled the guy. I think he's about to implode."

"We'll see."

"How long are you going to wait?" Mike asked.

Sara made a face. "He just got there. Give him five to assess the situation. Another five to contact someone in Washington. Maybe ten to actually get something to happen."

"Get what to happen?" asked Tim.

"We'll know it when we see it," Sara said. "*If* we see it."

Roughly fifteen minutes later, something changed in the feed they were watching. Police cars appeared at the periphery of the camera's eye, and officers began to move into the crowd, directing people away from the base of the monument. Then the view leapt to what was apparently a television feed. A reporter, microphone in hand, waved her crew back, glancing over her shoulder at the monument and its attendant cranes.

"I don't know," she mouthed. She said more, but it was lost on Mike.

Sara made a frustrated sound and audio kicked in.

The reporter tapped her earpiece. "They're just telling us to fall back to the truck. Maybe a terrorist threat? I don't know. Back up. Back up. But keep filming."

"Now, Mike," said Sara softly.

Mike already had the feel of the crane. He'd worked one like it before. Knew it. It fit like a glove. He willed the engine to life. The operator—who could be seen in the TV camera's view standing on the crane's treads—reacted by climbing into the cab. Mike ignored him. There was nothing the man could do. Ultimately, even turning off the engine wouldn't stop Mike; it could only slow him down a little. He worked the controls with ease, lifting, turning.

He grunted as he felt some pushback. It was the operator, trying to stop the crane. The guy gave up after several tries and left the cab. He scrambled down from the huge tank treads and ran toward the camera, joined by a group of his fellows who had been on or near the scaffolding.

By the time Mike had lifted the capstone clear of the ground, the area around the base of the monument had cleared. Mike watched the progress of the capstone in its sling, rising toward the apex of the structure it was designed to top. Sunlight flashed like fire from the gold overlay. It was like a phoenix, Mike thought. It was a symbol of American greatness and it would help them wrest power out of the shadows and restore it to the democratically elected leaders—and to the electorate itself. To people like him, like his family. Folks who gain a skill, get a job, and contribute. People who have but one ambition, to create and maintain a home for their family. The people who are always pawns on the chessboard and invariably hurt when people like Howard meet and plan nefarious schemes in dark, smoky rooms.

No more.

Mike had gotten the capstone within twenty feet of its resting place when Sara bent and spoke into his ear. "Break the damn thing."

What broke was Mike's attention. He let go of the crane and the slow rise of the capstone stopped. The sudden change caused it to swing and tremble at the end of its thick cables.

"Break—what?"

"The damned obelisk. Break it. Bash it in with the capstone." Sara's eyes were bright with zeal, and there was a fine dew of perspiration on her lip and forehead.

"You go, girl!" whooped Tim.

Mike ignored him. "Sara, do you realize what you're asking me to do? This thing has been standing since the nineteenth century.

It's a symbol of this country's founding and first president. You're an architect, for God's sake. How can you—"

She grasped his shoulder. Hard. "It's become a symbol of power, Mike. The power of the privileged over the disenfranchised. Of the strong over the weak. Of male dominance over everyone else. We need to break it. Don't you see? We need to force Howard's hand. If we make this public of a display, there's no way he can keep his damned secrets."

Mike glanced at the screen.

No more. No more secrets.

He saw that, since the crane had stopped moving, the construction workers and some police officers were making their way across the grass back toward the monument. He gritted his teeth, put his mind back to the task, and pivoted the crane to the left so that the capstone swung out over the approaching men and women.

Several of the ancillary displays in the operations room had come online now. They showed a close-up on the driverless cab of the crane, the empty scaffolding behind it, and stunning footage of the gleaming capstone swinging at the end of its tether.

Like a priest's censer during Mass, Mike thought. A prayer sprang to his thoughts: *Please, God, let no one be hurt.*

Mike reversed the movement of the crane's long arm, the capstone following on its trailing arc. The crane's arm cleared the naked top of the monument, but the capstone, dangling tens of feet below, crashed into the marble sheathing like some bizarrely shaped wrecking ball. Marble shattered, crumbled, and fell, larger chunks tearing away pieces of the scaffolding and carrying it along on their plunge to the ground. Mike could hear the sound of people shouting and screaming now, their voices bleeding through the open TV audio feeds, overlaid with the excited commentary of the reporters on-site.

"Again," Sara said.

Mike swung the crane back, realizing that a new sound had entered the mix—the sound of helicopter rotors.

"Holy shit!" cackled Tim. "It's a gunship! It's a damned gunship! An Apache Longbow. I've digitized those babies. That is one badass machine. With Hydras or Hellfires, I bet—missiles, to you noobs. That'd be ironic, wouldn't it, if they start shooting at shit and bring the whole thing down into the reflecting pool?"

"I seriously doubt if it would reach the reflecting pool," said Sara blandly.

Mike ignored all of it—the copter, the crowd sounds, Tim's exclamations of amusement—and swung the crane back toward the monument a second time. Tim got his wish—the gunship opened fire on the empty crane cab, though only with machine guns. As might be expected, the bullets merely ricocheted from the metal surfaces and sent those closest to the crane into full retreat.

The capstone struck the northern face of the monument a second time, ripping away more scaffolding and bringing down an avalanche of stone. The topmost part of the tower seemed to shift slightly.

"That's it," murmured Sara.

The helicopter gunship had not given up, though. It circled the crane, angling south and changing its orientation, looking for a clear shot. Even Mike suspected the thing carried Hellfire missiles, but it was hard to imagine the pilot might be persuaded to use them. What could he possibly do that would not cause even more damage than Mike could?

A shot of adrenaline coursed down Mike's spine. What if the idiot pilot *did* fire a missile at the crane from that oblique angle? What would happen to the people clustered around the fire trucks and police cruisers on the avenue just to the east?

Mike did the only thing he could think of: he reversed the crane and cranked it into as swift a 360 as he could. The capstone, beginning to slip from its damaged sling, flew around, centrifugal force pulling it away from the center of the spin. At the end of its pivot, the crane's long arm collided with the second crane in a scream of metal on metal. Its flight interrupted, the capstone tumbled erratically at the end of its cables. Now, finally, it slipped from the sling and hurtled toward the monument's southern flank. The cables and sling, freed of the capstone's weight, backlashed like a flail and clipped the hovering copter.

The capstone smashed into the monument, crushing the scaffolding on its northern side and loosing another cascade of stone. The copter slewed wildly, its missile systems belching flame as it attempted one last Hail Mary against the rogue cranes.

It didn't have a prayer.

The Hellfire missile instead glanced off the roof of the crane's cab, skipping like a stone on a pond before it was fully armed and striking the monument roughly thirty feet above the base and exploding. The cranes were enveloped in a cloud of debris and smoke amid the cacophonous sounds of shredding metal and shattering stone. The top of the obelisk shuddered and settled and then, like a great tree felled by Paul Bunyan's axe, it began to topple . . . toward the road behind it.

Mike reflexively reached out with his increasingly developed sense of the atoms that made up the world and applied as much force as he could to check the fall. He exceeded beyond his wildest expectations. As if a giant's hand had slapped it aside, the towering structure shuddered again and swayed back away from the crowds and the emergency vehicles and the media crews. It even missed the helicopter as it fell due west.

"It's pointing right at the Lincoln Memorial!" crowed Tim. "Dammit, but you're good, Micky! Man, you can plan my castle assault any time." The programmer jumped out of his chair and did a celebratory jig. Mike put his head down on his console and tried not to notice that when Tim danced, something in the shadows danced with him.

Chapter 3

SPIN

"This is amazing footage, Cos. It's damned hard to edit it, though."

Regina Price was on her second pass through the destruction of the Washington Monument and she was still shaking. They'd gone live with the feed on WHUT, as had every other station serving D.C., but she already knew she and Cosmo had something special—something few if any other teams had. Now she was trying to get it into a format suitable for their evening news programming.

"I wish I could take credit for it," Cos murmured.

She shot the cameraman a weird glance. "Cosmo Hernandez, in the five years we've worked together, I have never known you to exhibit false modesty."

"I'm not being modest, falsely or otherwise."

"Yeah, right." Regina followed the camera eye practically into the empty cab of the crane. "Oh, I've got to use this zoom here. You bored right in on the cab. It's killer."

Cos was silent, but she heard him shift away from the door of the editing suite. "I mean, that showed great instinct," she told him. "I bet everyone else was panning back for the big picture, but I think you got the money shot. Hell, I think you got all the money shots. It still freaks me out that the cab was empty. They're already speculating about that online. You know, was it robotics, or RC, or just whacked machinery?"

When he didn't comment—something so un-Cosmo-like that it was cause for alarm—she glanced back over her shoulder at him. He looked . . . uneasy. Spooked, even.

"What is it, Cos? What's wrong?"

"I didn't shoot that footage—exactly."

Now he had her entire attention. "What are you talking about? Of course you shot it. It came out of your camera."

"Reggie, when that whole thing started, I was just getting set up. I had the camera pointed roughly at the grandstand—yards away from the monument—and I was noodling with the focus." He paused, looking even more deeply uncomfortable than he had before.

"Cos . . ."

"I didn't swivel the camera to the crane, Reg. It swiveled itself. I know it sounds weird and crazy and delusional, but the camera moved of its own accord and it executed that zoom without my intervention."

Reg turned back to the computer on which she was editing the raw footage. "That's impossible . . . isn't it?"

"Yeah, you'd think so, wouldn't you? But then you'd think a crane going all rogue like that on its own would be impossible, too."

Reggie was used to the cameraman pulling jokes on her, but she didn't think this was the case now—she'd never seen him this solemn. Besides, it was nowhere near April Fools' Day and the situation was far from humorous.

"Look, Cos, if this is some attempt on your part to inject humor into an otherwise terrifying situation—"

"No. And I have evidence that's not what I'm doing if you

need something beyond my word. When I stepped out a minute ago I called a buddy of mine at WETA. He says the same thing happened to him. He finally ended up pulling the camera off its stand and hand-holding it."

Reg was struck by that. "You didn't do that—why?"

"After we pulled back, I—I guess I wanted to know what my ghostly cameraman was after. So I set the stand down and just watched. And that may be why I got all the money shots. Because whoever was really driving my rig—"

"Knew what they were aiming at," Reg finished with him.

The two were silent for a moment in which Reggie felt as if many tiny ants with very cold feet were hiking across her shoulder blades. She finally got her numb lips to move.

"Who do we call? And don't say Ghostbusters," she warned, raising a fist in mock threat when he opened his mouth.

He smiled wanly, running a shaky hand through his hair. "Now who's trying to inject humor into an otherwise terrifying situation? Maybe we—I dunno—maybe we call the State Department?"

"Hey, guys?" One of their interns—a long-haired blonde Cos referred to as Galadriel—popped her head through the door. "Um, the station manager needs to see you, pronto. He just got a call from the State Department."

"MADAM PRESIDENT, THEY'RE READY FOR you in the Sit Room."

Margaret Ellis was out of her chair before her chief of staff had even finished the sentence. She was more than ready for the Situation Room. She would go in and pull her close advisors around her like a blanket, like armor—both. She knew that many of the presidents who had faced crises before her had been skeptical of the people who met them in the Sit Room—distrustful, impatient, disrespectful. She was none of those things. These people were her best defense against partisan crap, self-interest (enlightened or otherwise), and hubris. Her eleven-year-old son called them her Wizard Council. They were like that at times. She hoped this was one of them.

"Did we get all the pertinent video from the media?" she asked her chief as they walked.

"Yes, ma'am. Everything we could find." He seemed about to say more, but didn't.

She glanced at him sharply. "What is it, Curtis?"

"There was one video feed that surpassed all the others for sheer . . . effectiveness. I watched it as it streamed down. This is not your garden-variety terrorist action."

That raised Margaret's eyebrows. "Is there such a thing as 'garden-variety' terrorism?"

"I mean terrorism in which you can actually *see* the terrorists."

That sentence made her cheeks feel as if they'd been touched by an icy wind. "I heard the early reports . . . which is not to say I believed them."

"Believe them."

They reached the Sit Room and Curtis carded the door open. Margaret entered, feeling as if she actually did enter a congregation of wizards. These were intensely bright and expert people—each with his or her own realm of expertise. Mostly, they had learned, during the first term of Margaret Ellis's presidency, to work well within those realms without trespassing on each other's goodwill, while avoiding the age-old problem of empire building. Now, well into her first term, they normally functioned like a well-oiled machine. She noted a problem with that dynamic immediately:

Whatever this situation was, it wasn't normal.

Everyone at the long, oval table stood. Margaret seated herself next to the chairman of the Joint Chiefs of Staff—Navy Admiral Joan Hand.

Hand nodded. "Madam President. Mr. Chamberlin. We have the video from WHUT cued. This first piece is the one that is the most troubling."

It was and it wasn't. Yes, certainly, the sight of the empty crane as the construction crew fled the area was disturbing. So was the seemingly purposeful movement of the huge machine. As much as she wanted to, Margaret could not make herself believe that there was not deliberate intent behind its behavior—that this was not just a malfunction. Yes, all that was "troubling"—to use Joan's completely inadequate word. But the image that Margaret knew would be seared into her mind was the sight of the Washington Monument—a national fixture since the 1800s, a symbol of the greatness of America—toppling, headless, amid a billow of smoke from a U.S. missile.

Friendly fire.

She closed her eyes and still saw the fall of the obelisk. She suspected she'd see it every time she closed her eyes from now until the day she died.

"We were damn lucky," Curtis murmured.

Margaret opened her eyes and turned to look at her chief of staff. He looked approximately as shaken as she felt.

He met her gaze. "We're damn lucky that we got the warning in time and no one was killed. If it had happened during the ceremony . . ."

On Margaret's opposite side, Joan Hand leaned forward, frowning. "Yet it *didn't* happen during the ceremony. *And* we received a warning. Which makes the new video that just surfaced a bit anomalous."

Margaret swung around to face the other woman. "What video?"

Joan Hand nodded at the media technician seated at the far end of the table before a large LED display. The display came to life again, this time with an interior view of a dimly lit room in which a man in the flowing garments common in the Middle East addressed the camera. The voice-over claimed, in stilted, deadpan English, that the strike on the "heart of the beast" was the work of Al Sabbah, the terrorist group known as *The Morning,* and that there would be more such events in the near future.

"Who's the speaker?" Margaret asked when the screen had gone black again.

Joan slid an iPad toward her. "He's an Al Sabbah lieutenant who calls himself al Hajj Mahmoud abd-al Qadir. He rose to prominence about four years ago in Iraq and served as mouthpiece for the Iraqi Al Sabbah affiliate. He's a Sunni. A scholar of the Hanbali school of jurisprudence. But he's also Western educated. Attended the London School of Economics. He hasn't been heard from for several years. In fact, there was some speculation that he was dead."

Margaret gave the man's dossier displayed on Joan's iPad a quick once-over.

"Is that why you say this is anomalous?" Curtis asked. "Because he's been lying low for so long?"

"No, because of what I said before: we were warned of the attack in advance and it didn't happen *during* the ceremony. If it had, hundreds of people might have been killed or injured. It's not like Al Sabbah to pull their punches. We have a team of experts going over this video right now to verify its legitimacy and check the provenance of the accompanying Facebook and Twitter posts."

Margaret nodded. "I'd like to speak to the journalists who captured the footage of the incident. Curtis, if you'd arrange that . . ."

"Of course."

"So we don't think it's Al Sabbah, correct?"

"No, ma'am," said Admiral Hand.

"Well, if it's not Al Sabbah, then who is it?" Margaret asked. She expected no answer and got none.

"HOLY *SHIT*!" EUGENE SAT UP straight at his workstation, barely able to comprehend what he had just seen. He had headphones on; his exclamation was significantly louder than he'd intended.

Dice, Joey, and Lanfen looked up from their work on Pippin, and Chuck, who had been working in his office that morning, got up at once and came to the open door. "Euge, what is it?" he asked.

Eugene turned to look at him, blinking as if he'd just surfaced from sleep. He pulled his headphones down around his neck and pointed at his computer screen. "This news report. Someone just blew up the Washington Monument."

That brought Chuck out of his office, and pulled Dice, Joey, and Lanfen away from the new robot and lured Mini from a painting she was working on—applying color without brushes and sometimes without pigment. They all moved toward Eugene.

"Blew it up?" repeated Dice. "As in terrorists?"

"Well, no—actually it looks like one of our own attack copters blew it up but . . . wait—watch this." With the others forming a tight knot around his chair, Eugene reran the video, which he'd found as the result of a Reuters news flash.

They watched. When the camera zoomed in on the rogue crane, revealing that the cab was completely empty, Mini gasped and Dice murmured, "Oh my God. It's them. It's gotta be the Alphas."

"What are they saying this was?" Chuck asked. "Is there anything beyond the news flash?"

"Let me see if I can find anything," Euge said, and attacked his keyboard, wildly tapping search terms into the address bar of his browser. He hit enter and got a 404. "What the hell? I lost the Internet!"

"What seems to be the problem?"

They all looked up to see Kristian Lorstad watching from the open door of the lab—his face, as always, inscrutable and placid.

"The problem is," said Eugene, "I just lost my Internet connection!"

"The problem is," said Chuck, "the Alphas are going public."

"What makes you say that?" Kristian asked.

Eugene just gawped. *Is this guy as cut off from reality as their location implied?*

He pointed at his computer screen. "Rogue machinery taking out the Washington Monument? Haven't you seen this?"

"We are . . . looking into it. Please, Dr. Pozniaki, don't let yourself be distracted by outside events. The Alphas—as you call them—cannot be allowed to deflect us from our purpose."

"'Deflect us from our purpose'?" echoed Chuck. "I thought our purpose was to rein them in. Neutralize them—and I don't mean that in the military sense. Keeping this sort of thing from happening *is* our purpose."

Lorstad glanced down at the pale quartz flooring, his lips pursed thoughtfully. After a moment, he looked up again, meeting Chuck's gaze. "Our purpose, Charles, is to evolve. To correct the flaws in humanity by transcending them. In that context, the loss of a national monument is a minor development. Wouldn't you agree?"

Chuck shot Eugene a frowning glance, then rounded the workstation to stand toe to toe with their host. "No, I do not agree. The Alphas are clearly exercising an unprecedented level of direct control over mechanisms far beyond their base of operations. If they can reach the Washington Monument, they can reach into the White House, into the halls of Congress, into the Pentagon. And not just by following available electronic pathways. I doubt that crane was on any computer grid. Do you even understand the implications of that?"

Lorstad's face registered mild comprehension. "Of course. Trust me, Charles. The Center is completely off the grid. The Alphas cannot reach you here. They don't even know where 'here' is."

"Neither do we," mumbled Dice.

Lorstad glanced at him over Chuck's shoulder. "Which is for your own safety and well-being, Dr. Kobayashi." He changed the subject. "How close are you to having a workable machine for me to learn with?"

"We're ready anytime you are, Dr. Lorstad," Dice told him. "We have a simple drive bot for your first steps and a human analogue ready to go into testing for when you've mastered the simple mechanics."

Lorstad nodded. "I'm pleased. May I assume I can start my journey as early as tomorrow?"

He looked to Chuck, who nodded mutely, his face set in an expression Euge recognized as a cover for frustration.

"Wonderful. Now, I need to borrow Mini from you for a bit, if I may."

Euge started to ask what he wanted to borrow her for, but realized that would only make him look like an overprotective boyfriend. That was an impression he wanted to avoid; he didn't want either Lorstad or Mini to see him in that light.

I don't have to like it, though.

Mini, being Mini, simply asked, "Oh? What for?"

"First," said Lorstad, smiling at her amiably, "I'd love to see what you're working on in your studio . . . if I may, that is."

Her face lit up in a way that always made Eugene's heart do funny things in his chest. He hated to admit even to himself how it disturbed him to see that light shine on another man. He bit down hard on his personal angst and said nothing.

"Of course you may," Mini said and moved to show Lorstad her studio.

Chuck raised a hand to stop them, though. "Kristian, wait. Are you responsible for cutting us off from the Internet? Was that intentional?"

"Charles, I assure you, it is best that you do not let the outside world in. No good can come of it. Believe me, we are adequately shielded from any attempt the Alphas might make to get to you here."

"That is not my concern, Kristian. My concern is for the people who may be caught in the path of whatever destruction they mete out. There were tourists, news crews, workmen, and law enforcement officers in the National Mall when that"—he made an emphatic gesture at Eugene's computer—"happened."

Lorstad tilted his head, a slight frown knitting his brow. "And if you are aware of everything the Alphas are doing? What then? Do you have the capacity, now, to do anything about it? Are you actually prepared to *confront* them?"

Chuck reacted as if Lorstad had punched him in the gut. He flinched visibly and took a step back. "No," he said, his voice muted. "No, we don't. We're not."

"Neither are we," Lorstad told him soberly. "Which is one reason I wish to begin my own education as soon as possible. I've also identified others whom I would like to begin the Zeta program."

Chuck merely nodded. Lorstad escorted Mini to her studio at the far end of the room, glancing back over his shoulder with a puzzled expression. Eugene was the one who was puzzled, though. *What is with the guy, anyway? Does he really not understand our resistance to being cut off from the world? Blind and deaf to what the Alphas are doing?*

"He doesn't get it," Chuck said softly. "He either doesn't understand what they can do or simply doesn't care. I can't decide which is worse." The Center was beginning to slowly tighten the noose in a very Deep Shield manner. No—he couldn't believe that; these were scientists after all, not soldiers. He prayed he was right.

"Doomsday cult," said Lanfen.

Everyone turned to look at her.

She shrugged. "Look at them—self-contained little universe, the glorious goal of human evolution on the horizon. At least that makes them different from Howard and his band. But they may be resigned to the idea that some old stuff has to be destroyed in order to make way for the new stuff. They may even welcome the idea."

"We talking about Sara and the boys or our hospitable hosts?" Euge quipped.

"Welcoming a new, better world doesn't require being callous about a potential loss of life in the old one," said Chuck grimly.

"There wasn't any loss of life in Washington," Euge was quick to point out.

"This time," said Chuck. "There was no loss of life *this* time." He glanced around at the others and took a deep breath. "Back to work, everybody. Lorstad is right about one thing: if we aren't ready, willing, and able to do anything about the Alphas, we can't waste time obsessing about what they're up to. We need to *make* ourselves ready."

Everyone went back to what they'd been doing except for Eugene. He was watching the pair at the far end of the room, backlit by the magnificent "wall of light" the Benefactors had constructed to shine on Mini's studio space. Lorstad was manifestly more interested in Mini than he was in Lanfen or even Chuck. The question was, of course, *Why?*

MATT STRODE INTO LEIGHTON HOWARD'S office at the Forward Kinetics campus and thrust his iPad at him. "This was the Alphas, wasn't it?"

Howard didn't even look at the video frozen on a frame that showed the top of the Washington Monument bowing toward the Lincoln Memorial like a priest at an altar, wrapped in a cloak of smoke and debris. "What do you think?"

"The newsfeeds are saying it was Al Sabbah. That Al Sabbah took responsibility for it."

"I have no control over what Al Sabbah decides it wants to take credit for."

"I suppose you think that buys you some time? It won't. Not with Sara. You cannot stonewall her. She will just do something bigger and badder. Go to the president now, for God's sake. This is the golden opportunity to get her to believe you. Take me with you. I'll sell her on the truth—"

"You are dismissed, Dr. Streegman."

Bullshit.

And then it dawned on him that he didn't need to just think it.

"Bullshit. You can't dismiss me. I'm not one of your grunts. You cannot hope to stay dark any longer."

Howard looked up at Matt over the lid of his laptop. "You have no idea what I can or cannot hope, Doctor. I gave Ms. Crowell and her associates one of the items they asked for. I gave them the whereabouts of Mr. Yenotov's family and pulled my assets back. They're now in touch. That will buy us time."

"Time to do what?"

"I really can't discuss that with you, Streegman."

Matt muzzled his desire to throw his iPad at the man's head and left the office. God, but this was a wretched situation. He had no way to contact Chuck—no idea where in the world Chuck was. No way to contact the government without being discovered. He was like a rat in a maze of dead-end corridors.

Maybe, he thought, *I should try to find a way to reach Sara.*

Howard was in contact with her on a fairly regular basis. Maybe there was a way he could piggyback some sort of message on the general's signal without being caught. The Alphas might be monitoring the outside world in ways he possibly couldn't imagine. Clearly, they had appropriated television signals. If he was going to reach them, he had to think outside the norm. With that in mind, he retired to his own office to think and plan. He knew he was being monitored, so he took the precaution of making notes in a small three-ring notebook that never left his pocket. The notes were in a code he'd developed in college so he could make observations without other students being able to read them. Only two people knew that code—he and Lucy. He'd shown it to her when they were both seniors at MIT. They'd used it to write love notes to each other.

When she'd lain dying in the hospital, destroyed by a neurological disorder that was as much a mystery today as when she'd contracted it, she'd tried to communicate with him using that code. Only then, he hadn't known it; Chuck had ferreted it out.

He wished for the thousandth time that his wife had lived long enough for Chuck Brenton and his brain wave theories to come into the picture, then realized—also for the thousandth time—that were it not for Lucy's death, he never would have gone into partnership with Chuck or founded Forward Kinetics in the first place. There would have been no Brewster-Brenton Brain Pattern Monitor, no Brenton-Kobayashi Kinetic Interface, no Streegman Kinetic Converter, no conversion algorithm . . . and no Zetas.

"DO YOU SPEAK GERMAN?" LORSTAD asked as they walked the corridor of the secret lowest level.

Mini started to wrinkle her nose, then caught herself. Since forging a relationship with Eugene and taking on a full-time job with Forward Kinetics, she had become hyperaware of those little personal habits of expression, dress, and speech that made her brothers and father ruffle her hair and tease. Were she alone with Euge, wrinkling her nose might elicit a smile or a kiss; in context with a professional team of scientists or with this very proper, vaguely European gentleman, it just made her feel like a child in the company of an adult.

There were two things she had never realized before she fell in with Chuck Brenton's crew of misfits. One was exactly how much her father's and brothers' views of her had molded (or maybe warped) her self-image. The other was how good it felt to fit in *somewhere* without being like any of the people around her.

This brought her to another jarring realization: she hadn't thought about "fitting in" for some time. She found herself studying Kristian Lorstad and wondering what it was about him that made her suddenly self-conscious. A second later, as she met his gaze, she knew the answer: *he* was studying *her*.

"German?" she repeated. "No. I speak French fairly fluently, though. I did a term abroad in Lyons. But my attempts to learn German were failures. Too many pronouns."

He tilted his head in that characteristic way that reminded her of the family cat, and she felt the weight of his regard. Should she not have made light of the German language? But he only smiled and said, "Just so. I asked because of the painting you showed me—the fairy Valkyrie. She reminded me a bit of you."

Mini laughed. "You're the first person to make *that* connection. She is sort of me. The way I see myself on the inside . . . I guess. Soft and tough. Gentle and strong."

"In armor made of crystal."

"I can't see myself in metal armor."

"Neither can I."

Lorstad stopped before the immersion room he had shown them before. The door opened automatically to admit them. Music began to play softly from unseen speakers. Mini knew it well.

"*The Magic Flute*!" she said. "I love this opera."

"As do I. The computer plays it because it is also my favorite and is what I choose to surround myself with when I immerse. The 'Queen of the Night' is my favorite of the arias. 'Der Hölle Rache kocht in meinem Herzen,'" he said softly, then translated, "'The vengeance of hell boils in my heart.'"

"Is that what that means? I knew it had something to do with hell. Violence and vengeance wrapped in beauty . . . It's like *them*, isn't it? Like Sara, Mike, and Tim with their zeta powers. The powers themselves are a thing of beauty, but instead of using them to create beauty, they use them to pursue vengeance."

"Which you cannot understand," suggested Lorstad.

"Oh, no. I *understand* it. I just reject it."

He seemed surprised, looking at her in a way that made her feel like a specimen under a microscope. "'Vengeance is Mine; I will repay, saith the Lord'?"

"Even God doesn't mete out vengeance," she said. "He metes out justice. There's a difference. But, honestly, I don't think we human beings are quite capable of justice ourselves. We only imagine that we are."

"That is certainly true, Minerva. And it is why the Benefactors exist. With your help—with Charles's help—we will create a new humanity that is capable of justice."

"I hope you're right." In an effort to escape Lorstad's disconcerting gaze, Mini moved to peer into the immersion tank nearest her. To her relief it was empty. "It feels . . . strange to think of being so in charge of our own evolution, but I guess we have been for a long time. We just haven't done a very good job of it. Too lazy. Too selfish. Too unaware of our own reality."

"You are a very perceptive young woman, Minerva." He moved to stand next to her. "One inclined to deep thought. Perhaps you might consider an immersion session yourself? I think you would find it deepens the effects of meditation exponentially."

Mini considered it—for an instant—and then rejected it. The very thought of being in that tank filled her with dread. She shivered and stepped back from the machine, shaking her head. "No. I couldn't."

He was studying her that way, again—she could feel it, though she wasn't looking at him.

"There is nothing to fear."

"Yes, there is. Remoteness. Being cut off from . . . everything. Everyone." She glanced sidewise at him and saw that he was smiling at her indulgently.

"I have always found that one of the richest pleasures," he said. "To be alone with the music in my head, weightless, disembodied, unique."

I am not you, she thought, but did not say it aloud.

He guided her through the immersion process anyway, describing in some detail the various stages of it, the exhilaration he felt during the out-of-body "walks" he had learned to take. She recognized his intent: even though she had told him she didn't want to undergo immersion, he was trying to sell it to her. She felt a tingle of irritation at the spin exercise, because it reminded her so much of other situations she'd been in, in which someone was trying to convince her that she didn't know what was best for her or what she wanted. The counselor who'd tried to steer her into commercial art (because surely she wanted to make good money); the guy who'd tried to get her into bed with him by mansplaining that she just didn't get that pairing love with sex was hopelessly anachronistic (he'd actually used that word, too)—when that didn't work, he'd told her he loved her. His final bid was a failed attempt to ply her with booze.

What would Lorstad tell her, she wondered, to try to get her into that tank?

MARGARET ELLIS KNEW SHE SHOULD eat the sandwich that the Secret Service operative had just set on the table between her and her chief of staff. She could feel her blood sugar ebbing but her stomach was tied in knots. The Al Sabbah video was legit, to all appearances. The thought of a terrorist organization being able to stab at the heart of American identity in the cradle of its administration made Margaret sick.

Most troubling was the fact that no one had seen anything. There had been no suspicious activity near the monument. None. None of the agencies involved in the massive manhunt had discovered anything after the fact, nor had they seen anything leading up to it—not even cell phone traffic. This act of terrorism had occurred as if in a vacuum. No leaks, no chatter, nothing until the warning less than half an hour before the attack. The denizens of the Sit Room had been monitoring security traffic all morning and there had been nothing but a handful of false leads.

Margaret pinched the bridge of her nose with one hand and reached for the sandwich with the other. Her eyes were on a computer display that showed the area around the wreck of the Washington Monument. It was crawling with investigators. They were especially concentrated around the crane and were disassembling the engine and hydraulics, looking for sabotage. There was no doubt they'd find something. The crane had clearly been under the control of an outside party.

She shifted her attention to the Apache. It was inarguable that their own helicopter gunner had brought the obelisk down. That was troubling enough. But the kid had a clean record of exemplary service and was a devout Methodist with no Islamic connections. Most disconcerting was that the gunner claimed he had discarded the idea of using a Hydra on the crane because of possible damage to the monument. He was devastated by what he saw as a failure on his part.

Margaret was fairly certain he'd had nothing to do with the behavior of the crane.

"You know," said Curtis, chewing on his own sandwich, "we've already started getting people asking when we're going to rebuild."

"Mm. No surprise there. I bet we've also had the requisite number of conspiracy theorists who claim the White House is at the bottom of it."

Curt smiled wanly. "Conspiracist *Clue:* President Ellis in the National Mall with a rogue crane."

The sandwich tasted like sawdust. Margaret chewed and swallowed anyway.

The door to the Sit Room opened and Admiral Hand reentered, her jet-black brows drawn together in a perplexed frown. "Madam President, there's someone I think you should talk to. I took him to Curtis's office."

Curt frowned. "Who is it, Joan?"

"A student from Maryland State who says the Al Sabbah video we've been shown is a fraud."

"What? Our experts—"

"Apparently don't read lips."

Two minutes later, huddled in Curtis Chamberlin's office, sandwich forgotten, Margaret leaned against Curt's desk and looked down into the terrified eyes of a college junior whom Joan introduced as Keyvan Tahir. The young man was nearly trembling and his knuckles were white as he gripped the arms of his chair.

"Tell the president what you told me," Joan said quietly.

"Well, I was watching the replays of the video on CNN," Keyvan said, "and my roommate asked if I could please turn down the sound because he was trying to study. When I did, I realized that the man in the video is not saying what the audio claims he is saying. I think it's an old video, because the man in it is talking about an attack on a school in Mosul."

"How . . . ?" Margaret started to ask.

"I told you," Joan reminded her. "Keyvan reads lips."

The young man nodded. "I lost my hearing when I was three and didn't get it back until I had a surgery in sixth grade. I learned to lip-read Arabic and English—my grandparents didn't speak much English back then."

Margaret stood and held out her hand to the boy. "Thank you, Keyvan, you've just done your country a great service. If you don't mind, there are some other people I'd like you to talk to about this."

He shook her hand solemnly. "Yes, ma'am. However I can help. There is one more thing. I mean, it's sort of subjective I guess but—"

Margaret stopped him. "No, please. Tell us whatever you feel might be meaningful."

"Well, I grew up around a lot of people from Egypt and other Arab countries who speak English as a second language. The guy in the voice-over . . . he didn't sound like a native Arabic speaker to me. I think it was someone faking an accent. It was good, but it didn't sound authentic. That's just my opinion, but—"

"Keyvan," said the president, "right now, I trust your opinion more than I trust my own ears. Thank you." She looked at Joan Hand. "Admiral, would you set up a briefing for the Joint Chiefs and DHS personnel and have Keyvan repeat what he's told us? If you think it might be helpful, perhaps he could sit with your analysts and review the video. Then we need to start this investigation all over again—from a completely different angle."

"Yes, ma'am." Hand rose and escorted Keyvan from the room. She turned back at the door long enough to give Margaret a significant look. "I just might offer Mr. Tahir a job when he gets out of college."

"That might not be a bad idea."

"Back to the Sit Room?" Curtis asked when the door closed behind the admiral.

Margaret shook her head. "Can't spend all my time in there, Curt. Neither can you. I need the congressional leadership in the Oval Office as soon as you can arrange it. This damned thing isn't what we thought. And we need to find out exactly what it *is* before something worse happens. Have you scheduled a meeting with the news team?"

"Tomorrow morning—"

"I need to see them now."

Curt nodded and reached for the phone on his desk.

"Curt." Margaret looked down at him, her arms wrapped around herself. "Is this connected to the cyberattacks on military facilities? Is this . . . part of a bigger plot?"

"I don't know. It could be someone—a homegrown terrorist group even—taking advantage of the current tension to make a move. But . . ."

"But what, Curt?"

"That this is the work of some patriot group coming down from the hills seems an outrageous conclusion at best. This is also way beyond our wildest projections on Al Sabbah's capabilities. The tech, the funding behind this . . . it's going to take some looking."

Margaret folded her hands, leaned back, and sighed, speechless, yet poised, as fear pressed on her chest.

Half an hour later that fear was underscored. Margaret had two media journalists from WHUT in her office—Regina Price and Cosmo Hernandez. What she was hoping to get from them were their personal impressions of the action they had recorded on the National Mall. She got far more than that. By the end of the story they told her, Margaret's blood was thoroughly chilled. She went into her meeting with the congressional leadership feeling as if she had just walked into the middle of a Dan Brown novel.

She did not waste time with pleasantries, but sat the congressmen and congresswomen down around the coffee table in the center of the Oval Office and said, "Al Sabbah had nothing to do with this. The video was a hoax. Right now, we have no idea who did this, how they did it, or why they did it." She took a deep breath, gazing from one stunned face to the next.

"Now I'm going to tell you something even more disturbing."

LEIGHTON HOWARD SAT AT HIS desk at Forward Kinetics, staring at the blinking light on his phone and procrastinating. He did not want to take this particular phone call. He knew pretty much exactly what he was going to hear: It was taking too damn long to get this thing under control. It was becoming public. The president was aware of the anomalies. It was only a matter of time . . .

He took a deep breath. It wouldn't do for him to lose his temper with the man who thought he was calling the shots for Deep Shield. He picked up the receiver. "Howard," he said. Crisp. No-nonsense.

"What the hell is going on over there? I just got out of a meeting with the president in which she informed congressional leadership that your Al Sabbah red herring stunk to high heaven. Then she shared some eyewitness testimony that made my hair stand on end. Ghosts in the machinery. Cameras shooting whatever the hell they wanted. Missiles firing on their own. This isn't what we signed up for, Howard. You promised advanced weapons technologies, not . . . whatever this is."

Howard thought quickly. "I suggest you ask Madam President if she's thought about how we're supposed to fight an enemy like this one. Ask her if she's considered if our current level of technology is adequate to fighting invisible terrorist operatives."

There was a long silence on the other end of the call. Howard waited tensely.

"Are you saying this was a ploy to make kinetic tech more palatable to the lady in the White House?"

"If she's at her wits' end and you offer her a solution . . ."

"How'm I supposed to make a robot army a solution for—"

"You're the senator," said Howard. "Politics is your job. Mine is to wrangle the tech and exploit the military applications. I believe I've done that."

In the end, the senator could not disagree, and Leighton Howard went away from the call knowing he had successfully dodged a bullet. But there were more in the chamber, and he also knew that it was time to go back on offense if he was going to avoid those, too. He called for his chopper to be readied and headed back to Pennsylvania.

Chapter 4

BREAKOUT

"Al Sabbah? Is this Howard's idea of a joke?" Sara was livid, pacing in front of the bank of screens that served as the Alphas' windows on the outside world.

Most of them showed breaking news reports on the aftermath of the destruction of the Washington Monument. Endless reruns of the available footage and live feeds of the investigators who had swarmed the National Mall. The hashed and rehashed video of some Arab guy (at least Mike assumed he was an Arab) claiming the act against the "beast" for Al Sabbah.

Apart from monitoring the news, several of the displays showed feeds from the surveillance cameras Howard had installed all over his downslope base. Tim immensely enjoyed turning the general's own resources against him. The screens that had earned Sara's anger, though, were the endless loops of the Al Sabbah functionary claiming credit for the attack on one of America's most beloved symbols.

Mike wondered that the concrete floor beneath Sara's feet

wasn't smoking or—given the direction of her particular talents—that the video screens weren't melting.

"He's a chauvinist, Sara," said Tim. He set the bowl of chili he'd been eating on his console, dislodging several empty soda cans that clattered to the floor. "He thinks if you're beautiful and female, you must have a head full of air. I've been monitoring some back channels out of D.C., and I've been hearing the word *hoax* a lot over the last couple of hours. There's this thing I've been working on, too—burrowing into Howard's communication channels. He's got 'em isolated pretty effectively—he's not using so much as an inch of public circuitry for access—but because he's got cameras halfway up the mountain, and those cameras are linked back to his camp, I can do this."

He snapped his fingers and one of the big screens at the head of the room showed an external view of the woods. The view swiftly leapfrogged down the mountain until they were looking at the perimeter of the Deep Shield camp.

Sara stopped pacing. "You got us his video feed. Good work, Troll."

"Better than that, Fearless Leader. I think I can use *this* to infiltrate their main communications system and give us access to outside phone lines and carrier waves."

"How soon?" Sara demanded. "How soon do you think you might be able to get me direct access to Howard? Right now we're dependent on that landline to even talk to the bastard."

Howard's cutting them off from communications channels after their decisive taking of the mountain was galling to Sara and Tim alike. Mike thought it was odd that two people so capable of manipulating electrons and reality hadn't come up with an alternative way to extend their reach. Sara and Tim were still somewhat limited in their direct manipulation of mechanical things. He wasn't. It was ironic, really—he was limited by line of sight (mostly, anyway); Tim and Sara were limited by electronic connections through which they could "see" in ways Mike could only imagine . . . but he could imagine them and had little doubt that in the future he'd be able to manipulate mechanical devices he couldn't see through the same conduits they used. He'd already made a few strides in that direction, very quietly. Mike opened his mouth to say that they weren't really that hamstrung, but stopped himself. He wasn't sure why. Instinct, maybe. It seemed to him that it might pay to have some secrets of his own.

He realized that Sara had turned to face him and was watching him intently. It was creepy.

"Mike, if you can see targets in their camp—mechanical targets—can you affect them?"

"I don't see why not."

"I want to send General Howard a message. Timmy, get me into Howard's office."

"Uno momentito," Tim murmured.

A handful of seconds later, they were looking at the inside of the general's camp office—a single-wide, full-length trailer. The viewpoint suggested that the surveillance camera was located above his desk in one corner where the wall met the ceiling. The trailer was empty at the moment. Howard was wherever he was when he wasn't there—probably Forward Kinetics.

"Micky," Sara said, her voice like acid, "make something bad happen to the stuff in that trailer."

"Sure." Mike rose and moved to stand closer to the screen, focusing on it until the trailer's contents—a desk with a comm unit atop it, a couple of side chairs, a conference table—were all he could see. He started with the desk, wiping it clean with a stroke of thought. Everything atop it, including the "squawk box," went flying. Then he flipped the desk over, hurling it into the conference table, which tumbled into the trailer's far wall.

"Wish we had audio," said Tim. "That must sound awesome. I'm working on it," he added hastily after another of Sara's looks.

Mike spared a glance for the neighboring displays. "I think we've got their attention." In the yard of the compound, in the mess, and in several of the hastily assembled barracks, troops were suddenly on the move. Mike waited until a handful of them approached the trailer before he began to pummel the walls with invisible fists.

Atoms were manipulatable; the only difference between solid and not was atomic density. If you knew that, you knew how to make bad things happen. Sift through the clothing racks of quantum superposition and pull down phenomena as you chose. Mike, who hated violence, who had never—up until this evolutionary leap of faith that Chuck Brenton and his machines had made possible—so much as punched a pillow, took all the hostility he'd been collecting for the last several months and pounded it into the atoms in that trailer. The walls deformed as if a herd of invisible, gravity-defying buffalo were tap-dancing on them. The floor rippled and folded. The whole damn thing rocked.

Tim let out a hoot of celebration. "Yowza! Go Micky, go! Rock 'em, sock 'em Alpha *dude*!"

Mike ignored him, pouring more of his anger into the assault on this metal proxy for General Howard—the man who had destroyed his world, separated him from his family, from his life. The door of the trailer flew open and an armed soldier appeared in it. He wasn't there long; one of Mike's kinetic punches flung him back into the yard. In the next seconds, the front wall of the trailer was torn by a barrage of machine gun fire.

Mike sucked in a startled breath and shook himself free of his fugue. He glanced at other camera feeds that Tim was getting from Howard's camp, looking for the soldier he'd unwittingly sucker punched. Was he all right?

"Where is he?" he mumbled. "Where'd he go?"

"Who cares?" crowed Tim. "Hot *damn* that was a fine display of Alpha attitude. *Alpha*-tude!" He came to his feet in a capering jig that reminded Mike of that old Danny Kaye movie—*The Court Jester*—and offered Mike a high five.

Mike returned the gesture automatically, but he was still watching for signs of the soldier.

"Good job, Micky," said Sara. "That ought to get the general's attention. I imagine we'll be hearing from him shortly, and when we do, Tim, I'm hoping you will have found a way to get us full access to that camp. I want every electronic connection in that place under our control."

Tim grinned. "As you wish, my queen. I am working on it even as we speak."

"Why?" Mike asked. "Doesn't look like he's going to go to the president anytime soon. I mean, if he was the one who planted that Al Sabbah video, it's pretty clear he's still hoping he can get back in control—"

"I'm going to give General Howard an ultimatum, Mike. Either he goes to the president now on bended knee, or we show our hand, using him as an object lesson."

"What do you mean, an 'object lesson'?"

"I mean—"

Whatever Sara planned on saying was drowned out in a sudden spate of invective from Tim, which was drowned out in turn by the installation's perimeter alarms.

"What the bloody hell? What the fracking bloody hell! Are they *crazy*? They've got to be fracking crazy!"

Sara and Mike both swung to look up at the screens. It took no more than a glance to see that the camp was being mobilized. Every man they saw was scrambling into combat gear, while armored vehicles and howitzers were being stripped of their camouflage. But that wasn't what Tim was exclaiming over. Several of their own video feeds showed incoming air strikes. There were jets coming at them from four directions—a dozen, total. They were miles away still, but no less deadly for the distance.

As they watched, the lead jet in each formation fired its missiles.

Sara let out a snarl of rage. "Damn him! Mike, bring them down."

Mike looked at the missiles. He had no idea where they were in relation to ground zero. They were just things in the air.

"I need a tactical display, Tim!"

"Just bring them down!" repeated Sara.

"Not if I don't know where they're going to fall, dammit!"

"There!" shouted Tim. "There's your tactical!"

Mike followed his pointing finger to a feed that showed a tactical display of the area. The missiles were still inbound and still outside the park. The entire wildlife refuge had been evacuated and cordoned off, allegedly because of toxicity in the lakes. He would have to time this perfectly so that the missiles would fall inside the park where they were unlikely to cause the death of innocents—but not so close to the mountain that they'd cause more damage to the Deep Shield installation. He had no doubt they were "bunker busters." Leighton Howard knew better than anybody the extreme force it would take to bring down Olympus.

"Mike, what the hell are you waiting for?" Tim demanded.

"He's waiting for them to enter the evacuated area," said Sara. "Shut up and let him concentrate."

Tim subsided and Mike focused his entire attention on the incoming missiles, vaguely aware of Sara moving to have a murmured conversation with Tim. Mike took the missiles two at a time, mangling their innards with a thought and crumpling them from the inside out. They tumbled out of the sky in ragged pairs. Not all of them exploded—apparently their controllers had not wanted them to arm until they were on top of their target.

The missiles "magically" malfunctioning didn't deter them, however. The planes veered off and circled for another pass. Mike shook his head. Wasn't that the textbook definition of insanity—repeating the same process and expecting different results?

But that was just what the jets did; they ran a second pass and fired all their missiles simultaneously. He brought them down just as before. This time they all exploded.

"Timmy-Troll," Sara said softly, "can you charge the wires?"

"Let's see."

The monitors inside the Deep Shield camp showed nothing at first, and it took Mike several seconds to grasp what was happening. The first indication that something was wrong was fire. It broke out in the ruined trailer, in the mess tent, in the barracks. It sprang from floors, from walls and ceilings. Tim had somehow charged every wire, every electrical cable, with sizzling power. The shielding superheated, the plastic jackets melted, and anything in contact with the wires burned. The soldiers reacted by fleeing, naturally. As the surveillance feeds from inside the buildings failed, one after the other, they gathered in the center of the camp, weapons useless in their hands.

Tim was laughing. "Lambs to the slaughter," he snorted, glancing up at Sara. "Watch this."

Something rose from behind one of the large barracks tents. Something that Mike realized he'd been seeing out of the corner of his eye for days, lurking in shadows. It was—or it appeared to be—a minotaur. A ten-foot-tall, morning-star-wielding, armor-wearing minotaur, literally snorting fire and billows of red smoke. It strode toward the center of the camp, whirling its oversized weapon over its head. The spiked ball at the end of its chain was bigger than a man's head. Tim bellowed and the thing opened its mouth and bellowed with him. They couldn't hear this—only see it—but that meant what followed took place in an eerie silence that made it all the more terrifying.

The first man to hear and see the minotaur shouted and reflexively turned his gun on it, rattling off a silent barrage of machine gun fire. The minotaur opened its mouth wide in a roar and whirled the morning star threateningly above its titanic head. More men fired on it . . . from every side. Mike swallowed, sweating, trying to get his mouth to move—to make Tim stop. He couldn't. And for reasons even he didn't fully understand, he gave up trying.

Soldiers fell, brought down by friendly fire from only yards away—only feet away—for as solid as it looked, their bullets passed right through Tim's creation to find live targets on the other side.

Tim generated several smaller creatures and sent them into the chaotic melee. Hideous, misshapen things out of video game nightmares. They threatened and loomed and swung their battle axes at the soldiers and seemed to land blows—albeit light ones. Mike didn't know if Tim was pulling punches or simply lacked the zeta craft to make the blows completely solid. The soldiers shot at these creatures, too, and tried to bayonet them when they got close.

More men fell.

The last man died trying to escape the massacre. He ran, tripped attempting to dodge the imaginary morning star, and fell onto the bayonet of a dead comrade.

Only one camera was functional now, and Mike was fairly certain that was because either Tim or Sara had found a way to affect it independently of the network. That camera faithfully recorded General Howard's expression as he entered his ruined camp moments later. Trailers and tents still burned; men lay dead or dying. The air was filled with smoke.

Tim's creatures were gone, leaving no evidence they'd ever been there. To Leighton Howard it must have appeared that insanity had overtaken his men and they had killed each other in a violent fugue. He made a slow circuit of the camp, moving like a sleepwalker or a zombie, his face slack, his skin gray. Tim swiveled the camera to follow him. The servos must have made some sort of sound, for the general turned to look directly up into the lens.

"Heh. Now he gets it," said Tim, then affected a gravelly murmur. "'Yes, young Skywalker. Only now, at the end, do you see.'"

Almost as if he could hear the taunt, Howard moved toward the camera, stepping over bodies, drawing a handgun as he moved. He stopped before the tree the camera was affixed to and aimed at it point-blank.

"Go to hell," he mouthed and fired.

"Well, dammit!" exclaimed Tim. "That was rude. Now we don't get to see what he does next. Do you think he'll mount a one-man attack on us?"

"I don't know, but I want to find out," said Sara. "Mike!"

He looked up at her, realizing that he'd slumped into a console chair without knowing it. He cleared his throat. "Yeah?"

"How many bots can you manipulate at once?"

"A couple of them, maybe."

"Send them down the mountain. I need to see what he's up to."

"Sure." Getting such a simple order from Sara was almost a relief. Mike started to reach for the nearest bots kinetically, then decided he wasn't ready to show Sara he was no longer strictly limited to line of sight if he knew the mechanism well. He pulled himself to his feet and headed for the nearest robot storage area—the War Chest, Tim called it.

He got two of the lightweight ninja bots out of their charging stations and sent them out of the facility through a narrow access tunnel that served as a back door. He had them both "pill bug" and sent them careening downhill toward the burning wreck of the Deep Shield camp. He returned to the control room then, so as to keep an eye on them through the external surveillance system.

The moment before he lost sight of them—probably a quarter mile from the camp—he popped them both upright, fired up their onboard optics, and put them into a fast jog. Sara grabbed the video feed via more mundane means and fed it to their displays.

Mike thought about going into VR mode but decided that as important a breakthrough as that might be for him, he had no desire to witness the devastation Tim had caused as if he were there. He sat down at his station in the rear of the ops theater and watched the displays.

"Man, this is taking too long," Tim complained. "Even at a run, they're taking too long to get there. Can't you make them fly or something?"

"They're not built to fly." As soon as the words left his mouth, Mike realized that he was limiting his own thought. What, after all, was the difference between packing atoms together to create a solid "punch" and packing them to make a solid object glide along an invisible "slide" to a target location? Mike did not try this now, however. He was fairly certain that any failure that resulted in it taking longer to get where they were going would send Tim into some sort of tantrum. He settled for giving the bots a bit of an assist so that they ran like cartoon characters in bad animation, sliding along the uneven ground several feet with each step.

Sara turned to look at him oddly, but he ignored her. He was as eager to find out what Howard was doing as she was. The two bots broke through the perimeter of the camp into a pall of billowing smoke. Mike set one unit up as sentry and took the other slowly between the still-burning wreckage, its optics sweeping the area. Camouflage-covered bodies stained crimson with their life's blood lay everywhere. The audio feed sent back the crackle of flames, the sighing of wind, and the creaking of tree limbs. Jarringly, Mike could hear birdsong. He ignored it, making his way to the center of the devastation, to where they had last seen Leighton Howard.

He was still there. He lay on his back at the base of the tree with its mangled camera, a neat—if bloody—hole between his brows. The gun was still attached to his left hand by its trigger guard.

"Now that," said Tim, "is some seriously poetic justice."

"Except we needed him to *figuratively* fall on his sword," Sara said.

"You guys," Mike said, panning the robot's gaze away from the dead officer, "we have a more immediate problem."

"What?" Troll asked.

"The forest is burning."

AERIAL RECONNAISSANCE SHOWED THAT THE fire was fanning out from a clearing at the southern skirt of Pine Flat. Fire Captain Bert Cross suspected campers, though as close as the source was to an old firebreak road, it could have been someone tossing out a cigarette butt, or even a vehicle backfiring. Not likely at this time of year, but possible.

While the planes dropped borate retardant on the fringes of the fire and forestry copters dispensed vast buckets of water from the nearby reservoir, Captain Cross drove up the firebreak with a train of three off-road engines and an EMS vehicle.

"You know that clearing didn't show up on the last satellite maps I saw!" The driver of his vehicle—Sergeant Robert Apatow—shouted above the engine noise. "Someone carved that out in the last four months or so."

Cross gave him a sidewise glance. "I hope that doesn't mean we're going to be dealing with a meth lab or a bunch of squatters."

"Well, whoever the hell they are, I hope they got out before—"

"Yeah." Cross finished his thought with a word, watching the GPS screen.

"We're almost—" Apatow broke off to peer over the steering wheel and out the driver's side of the front window. "Is that a helicopter?"

It was a helicopter. It sat just south of the firebreak in a clearing barely big enough to hold it. It was small, dart shaped, camouflage painted, and mostly covered with a leafy net.

"Bob, can you get us down there?"

"Sure thing. Looks like the road picks up again on the other side of the chopper pad. I hate to say it for a number of reasons,"

Apatow added, steering the truck off the main firebreak and along a track that skirted the helicopter's clearing, "but I have a bad feeling about this."

Whatever bad feeling his sergeant might have had did not prepare Bert Cross for what they found at the end of the one-lane dirt road. When the trucks pulled to a stop, the two men found themselves looking out on an abattoir. The broad clearing was ringed with charred and half-destroyed tents and a trailer that looked as if something immensely powerful had escaped from inside. Within that circle of destruction was a scene more horrific than anything Captain Cross had seen in his twenty years in the service: dead soldiers lay everywhere—shot, gored, some burned by the fire that had apparently started in some of the tents and marched away up the hill, urged on by the prevailing winds.

"Jesus," breathed Apatow from beside him. "What do we do, Cap?"

"You deploy the water trucks and soak the northwest perimeter of the camp, then cut a firebreak. If the wind changes, the fire could turn and head back down toward Fayetteville. I'm going to call this in to the state police. We need help here."

Apatow nodded, flung open his door, and started to climb out.

"Bob," Cross said, "tell our guys not to touch anything in or near the camp, okay? This is either a terrorist action or a crime scene and we do not want to mess with it. This is way above our pay grade."

Bob Apatow nodded again, swallowing loudly enough for Cross to hear. "Yessir," he said, and climbed down from the truck. Cross reached for the radio.

Chapter 5

AFTERMATH

Matt couldn't have said exactly when he realized something at Forward Kinetics was "off." He was in his office indulging in escapist algorithms when he realized that the building around him had gone dead silent. He looked up, listened intently for a moment, then glanced at the clock on his laptop. It was two minutes past the hour, yet he hadn't seen the regular security patrol go by his office. He got up and wandered out into the hall. All he could hear was the quiet exhalation of the HVAC system and his own breathing.

He stood in the hall for a moment, then started down toward the robotics lab. When he was about as creeped out as he could be, feeling as if he'd wandered onto the set of a postapocalyptic film or an episode of *The Twilight Zone,* he finally heard the sound of voices from the direction of the lab. He got to the door as Brenda Tansy and Phil Rath emerged, looking just as perplexed as he felt. The rest of the robotics team was right behind them, reminding him of a bevy of quail venturing out onto an empty road.

They all stared at each other for a moment, then Bren said, "Where are all the Deeps?"

Matt glanced up the hallway toward the conference room that had been the nerve center for Leighton Howard's operations. "You mean the resident Men in Black, I assume. I have no idea. I just noticed that the regular detail hadn't wandered past my office door . . . and that the place was quiet as a tomb."

"They were in there," Phil said, gesturing toward the conference room with his chin. "One of them came in and called out the two guys that are usually stationed in the lab and then it just went all quiet."

"Well, let's take a look around," Matt proposed. "See what there is to see."

What there was to see were the handful of civilian employees wandering through a structure that every single member of the Deep Shield administration and its security details had abandoned. There were no Deeps anywhere on-site, their computer equipment was missing, and a quick scan of the parking lot revealed that all their vehicles were gone.

At the end of their extended search, Matt gathered everyone in the lunchroom and assigned himself and their admin, Ventana Salazar, to make a series of phone calls to numbers that had previously connected them to the people charged with overseeing their work. Matt tried the number he had for General Howard several times. It didn't even ring.

By late afternoon, no one had attempted to contact them. Matt sent everyone but Brenda, Phil, and Tana home with instructions to stay quiet and near a phone for the next couple of days.

"Do we come into work tomorrow?" one of the robotics crew asked.

"Are you working on something that makes you *want* to come into work tomorrow?" Matt asked in return.

Phil Rath answered for the entire team. "Weaponized shit? I think I can speak for us all when I say, 'Not just no, but *hell* no.'"

A round of "hear, hear" rippled through the small assemblage and Matt smiled. Cut from the same rebellious cloth, this bunch. When the last of the crew had trickled out of the cafeteria, Matt turned to Phil, Bren, and Tana—the people he thought of as his command staff . . . or the people he thought of as that after the original people had abandoned him—and said, "I don't know what's happened, but it looks as if Deep Shield has gone into hiding. I think I should contact the government."

"What part of the government?" asked Brenda. "After all this with Deep Shield, who can we . . ."

She couldn't seem to pull the trigger on the last word, but they all knew what it was.

"Trust?" asked Tana.

"Well, yeah . . ."

"Chuck had a friend at the FBI he contacted," Matt said. "I might be able to get the name."

"Can you contact *Chuck*?" Brenda asked. Her blue eyes were wide and hopeful. Wherever Chuck was, so her fiancé, Dice, might also be.

"I was able to contact him through social media as of two weeks ago. He's been monitoring LinkedIn. I can get a message to him—maybe. If not that, then I figure the Department of Homeland Security."

They parted reluctantly, as if they were all that was stable in a world that seemed to have gone pear shaped. Maybe they were. The last thing Brenda said to Matt was, "If you get hold of Chuck, please ask about Dice. Tell him . . . tell him I love him, okay?"

Matt assured her he'd forward her message and didn't feel the least bit inclined to tease. He thought about what he should do next, then sent Chuck a message on LinkedIn, before settling in to sip overcooked coffee from one of the pots that had been on all day. He was contemplating going over to Chuck's house when he heard someone come in through the foyer.

Correction—a whole lot of someones.

Should he get up and go look? Should he stay where he was? Put his hands on the table in plain sight? Hearing the tramp of feet in the hall, he rose and turned to face the door of the lunchroom, hands at his sides, and waited. He didn't wait long. In mere moments, a group of uniformed soldiers appeared in the corridor outside the lunchroom. They were armed and had their weapons combat ready. Matt stifled the urge to wave at them.

"Identify yourself, please," said a female soldier.

"Dr. Matthew Streegman. Could you return the favor?"

She didn't answer but turned her head and called back down the hallway. "Here, ma'am. It's a Dr. Streegman."

A moment later a woman in civilian clothes appeared in the doorway; the soldiers parted to let her through.

"Dr. Streegman," she said. "I'm Diana Maalouf from the Department of Homeland Security."

Matt let out a breath he hadn't realized he'd been holding. "Thank you. You've saved me the trouble of trying to contact you. Do you know where General Leighton Howard is?"

"General Howard is dead, Doctor. Are you an associate?"

He inhaled sharply. That explained the sudden evacuation of the offices. "Not a voluntary one, Ms. Maalouf—at least, not recently. I suspect that Howard's willing associates have all gone into hiding. They vacated the building this afternoon so quietly the rest of us didn't even realize they were gone. Ms. Maalouf, I would really like to tell someone what's been going on here—and what's going on in Pennsylvania."

The DHS agent gave him a long, searching look, then said, "I believe I can facilitate that, Doctor."

UNDER NORMAL CIRCUMSTANCES, MEETING THE president of the United States would have been nerve-racking, but something to celebrate. Under these circumstances it was nerve-racking without a damned thing to celebrate. Everyone around Matt was on edge; half the people—including the president—looked as if they hadn't slept in a while. He empathized.

He told them everything he knew about Leighton Howard and Deep Shield, including the horrific events when the Deeps had tried to get their mountain back. He knew nothing of what had actually transpired in the underground facility, only that of those who went in, not one had come out. There had been a cave-in deep on the main egress, but he knew that didn't account for all of the deaths, which told him something about the state of mind the Alpha-Zetas were in. It was easy to imagine the alienated Tim perpetrating the horrors that had popped out the gun turrets on the mountainside, but not Sara or Mike. Had the abilities their training had given them been too much for them to handle? Was it always true that absolute power corrupted absolutely?

Matt glanced up as the president's chief of staff cued the technician to begin running the video footage they'd obtained from what was left of Howard's base camp. When the minotaur appeared, Matt felt a deep, dark, slimy something trying to crawl out of the pit of his stomach. He forced it down. That had to be Tim. When the soldiers began firing at the mythical beast, succeeding only in slaughtering each other, he had to close his eyes. He opened them in time to see General Howard fire, point-blank into the camera lens.

"Where . . . where did you get this video?"

"It was on a memory stick from one of the few remaining surveillance cameras in the Deep Shield camp," said the navy admiral seated next to the president—an imposing Native American woman with eyes so dark they were nearly black and an impressive coil of midnight hair at the nape of her neck. "It's the only feed that shows what caused the slaughter in any detail."

"How did Howard die?"

The admiral exchanged glances with President Ellis, who said, "General Howard committed suicide. We found his body just below the camera we took the memory stick from." She leaned forward on the table and fixed Matt with a direct gaze. "Dr. Streegman, when you described what happened on that mountain earlier, I was inclined not to believe you. Then I saw this." She waved a hand at the video display.

Matt showed his palms. "I tried to tell Agent Maalouf . . ." He then shifted backward and folded his arms. "When they bugged out of Forward Kinetics, the Deeps took everything with them, including the video of their attempt to take back their facility. They kept their administrative systems very separate from ours. We had no access to any of their records; they had full access to ours."

"Dr. Streegman, what are we dealing with here?" the president asked. "What was that . . . *thing* that attacked General Howard's camp?"

"It was a . . ." He stopped to consider how to describe them. "The Zetas call them wraiths or golems. They're mental constructs—projections—the Zetas have learned to generate. Or, in this case, a particular Zeta. Tim Desmond. He was a game developer."

The president's chief of staff sat back in his chair with a gusty exhalation. "Wait. You're telling me that a paramilitary unit was massacred by a character from a computer game?"

Matt turned to look at him. "No, sir. They killed each other. There was nothing there to massacre them—which is a small mercy. But that may change. One of the Zetas—a member of the Beta team that disappeared with my partner—was capable of creating golems that were . . . well, that had some substance. That you could touch."

"How is that possible?" asked the president.

"Most of us—even crack scientists—can only passively observe quantum structures. As near as I can tell, some Zetas can actively observe and manipulate quantum structures. Tim Desmond can. Minerva Mause can. I'm pretty sure that's also what Mike Yenotov is really doing when he manipulates machinery—manipulating atoms, packing them more densely, exerting some force on them. I don't know how exactly, because I can't do it myself."

The president nodded thoughtfully. "So, there are three of these Zetas inside the mountain. They've obviously been successful in holding out against Howard's misuse of their . . . abilities. Howard is dead. Is it possible we could get them to come out?"

That was a loaded question. Matt wasn't sure how to answer it. "I think they'd like to come out. Mike has a family somewhere. I know he must miss them. But they had demands, President Ellis. Demands that I'm not sure you can meet. Maybe not even if you wanted to."

"What demands?"

Matt smiled wryly. "World peace. That's what they want and, where they're located and with their abilities, they have the capacity to bring it about—but not in any way you'd like. Remember that old biblical verse about beating swords into plowshares? If you and other world leaders are unequal to the task, the Alpha-Zetas may do it for you."

The president nodded. "The anomalous failures at the air bases. Yes. If they did *that,* then we have a problem."

He nodded again. "But that's not your biggest problem."

"It's not?"

"No. Your biggest problem is that these are *smart* people. They've killed . . . hundreds of men. Yeah, they were bad men. They were working against the good of the American people, against the good of the world, but they were people. You'd be bound by international and national law to consider the Alphas war criminals or thugs or traitors—to arrest them and indict them and put them on trial." Here Matt shook his head. "They are not likely to let that happen."

"We can't just kill them," said Ellis. "They're American citizens who—given your description of events—have been wrongfully imprisoned and even abused by a rogue paramilitary organization."

"And yet, they're now vigilantes. Waging their own war, usurping the people's prerogative to elect people to make those decisions," Chamberlin noted.

"I have to agree with your chief of staff," said Matt. "But I still think that's a technicality that I'm sure some politician could work around. This is something different." He looked at Ellis. "Madam President, this country has never faced anything like this before. I know these people. Up until they developed their zeta capacities, they were as normal as anyone in this room. Well, except for Tim, maybe, but that's a subjective judgment on my part. I guess what I'm trying to say is, I don't think you can go by the book on this one."

"Negotiate," said Admiral Hand. "You're saying we need to negotiate with them."

"Yes, and in good faith. No tricks. No promises you aren't able to fulfill."

"The United States does not negotiate with terrorists," Admiral Hand said.

"And that's part of the problem," Matt said.

"No offense, Dr. Streegman, but who are you to change a policy that has been in place for as long as this nation has been around?"

"No offense taken, because that's not what I'm saying. What I'm saying is the problem is you consider them terrorists."

"Aren't they?" the president asked.

"No—they're *another species*." He took in their shocked expressions, but felt he needed to press on. "And this is first contact."

The president took a deep breath and looked Matt in the eye. "Then it sounds like the first thing we need to do is find out what they want. Since you know them, I'd like you to help us do that, if you would."

Matt nodded. "I'll do whatever I can."

"YOU REALIZE, OF COURSE, THAT some elements within Congress are going to fight this tooth and nail."

Margaret looked up into Curtis Chamberlin's boyish face. She'd been on the phone for what seemed like hours, consulting with DHS, FBI, CIA, NSA—her mind was swimming in acronyms—and informing congressional leaders that they had just uncovered a clandestine paramilitary organization operating within U.S. borders. She'd had Curtis schedule a series of internal briefings for legislators and knew that Curt was right—there would be elements within Congress that would label the people holding the Pine Ridge facility terrorists and demand they be forced to relinquish it. This would be complicated by the fact that some members of Congress would be unable or unwilling to accept the reality of the situation, regardless of how many hours of video they watched or how many photographs they saw of the aftermath of Deep Shield's destruction or how many interviews they conducted with Matt Streegman.

There were still members of Congress who didn't believe 9/11 happened, either.

She rubbed her eyes, remembered her eye makeup too late, and swore softly. "I want to establish a timeline with milestones. We talk with these people in the mountain; we see what they want; we work toward some sort of . . . mutually agreeable accommodation. If that seems hopeless, then I'm willing to consider a military . . . option." She snorted. "I was going to say 'solution,' but to paraphrase a favorite old song, 'there is no military solution to our troubled evolution.'"

Curtis raised his eyebrows.

"The Police. 'Spirits in the Material World.'"

"Ah. Well, Madam President, your first congressional briefing is in two hours. Which leaves us some free time to figure out what to tell the public. The conspiracy theories are already in full swing."

"Of course they are." Margaret shook her head. "When are they ever not?"

TED FREITAG TOLD HIMSELF HE wasn't nervous. His constant toying with the ragged corner of his photo ID belied that. He stopped himself for the fiftieth time and considered what he'd do if the senator simply blew him off. Go home; go back to work at the Pentagon; forget any of this ever happened.

Yeah, that was good. Safe, even.

He had strong enough second thoughts about what he was doing to make him stand and glance at the door . . . just as Senator Roman Bluth stepped through it. Curiosity and annoyance warred in the legislator's expression.

"Senator," Ted greeted him.

"I don't have much time," Bluth told him. "I wouldn't be seeing you at all if my aide hadn't said you might know something about all this—" He waved at the window of his office.

Ted knew what he meant. "We have a mutual acquaintance—General Leighton Howard. I've worked with him over the years to provide intel that has proven invaluable to him . . . and to you, as I understand it."

"Intel?"

"Information that might normally have been collected by the Pentagon only to stay in the Pentagon."

Bluth sat behind his desk and waved Ted to a chair across from him. "Continue."

"My communications with General Howard were severed immediately after the—uh—the Washington Monument incident. I believe the parties that he was in negotiation with escaped his control."

"Obviously. Although, he was certain he could rein them in."

Ted took a deep breath. "I'm afraid he was unable to do that. General Howard is dead, along with everyone who was on-site at the Pine Ridge facility. Deep Shield was, for all intents and purposes, destroyed yesterday afternoon."

Ted watched the blood drain from the other man's face. It was an interesting phenomenon, really, and until this moment he'd thought it merely a figure of speech. Apparently not. The other man's obvious distress put him more at ease. He leaned back in his chair and crossed his legs.

"The general's units were massacred," he told Bluth. "The video taken by the forestry people and DHS of the aftermath is pretty grisly. It looked as if they'd killed each other. Had a friendly firefight. Howard seems to have committed suicide in the aftermath. It was . . . creepy. Probably the creepiest thing I've ever seen." He realized he'd been toying with his ID again and put his hand on his thigh instead.

"Why? Why would they kill each other? How could that have been related to Howard's project?"

Ted shrugged. "How much do you know about what Howard was doing up there?"

"How much do *you* know?" Bluth countered.

Ted just kept from rolling his eyes. "Look, Senator, we don't have the time or luxury of a Mexican standoff. I know about the Zeta program. I know that Howard basically took over an outfit in Baltimore called Forward Kinetics and appropriated their technology for military purposes. I know that you and Howard had been working closely on the project for political reasons—"

"My reasons for wanting to raise the sort of fighting force that Howard proposed have nothing to do with politics. They have to do with the current administration's weakness when it comes to national and international threats. They have to do with protecting this country from enemies I'm not sure Ellis is even aware of."

"Fine. I'm not going to argue with you, Senator. Whatever your reasons, I'm here to tell you that Howard and the greater portion of his military assets are gone."

"Then the Pine Ridge facility was destroyed?"

Was there relief in the senator's tone? Ted shook his head. "It's still in the control of the Zetas."

Bluth stared at him, face devoid of expression as he processed this. "You're telling me these . . . *people* caused mass insanity among highly trained U.S. military personnel—"

Ted raised his hand. "I didn't say that, Senator. I said, it looked—"

"What else could it have been? If not insanity, then what—mind control?"

Ted swallowed the sudden tightness in his throat. *Was* that *what happened? Had the Zetas—whoever and whatever they were—exerted some form of mind control over Howard and his troops?*

"You're telling me," Bluth went on, "that these people have control of a large, heavily armed installation."

Ted Freitag laughed as the absurdity of the situation hit him squarely between the eyes. "Senator Bluth, I think it's ridiculous to worry about them *having* weapons. They *are* weapons. And yes, it appears they are in control of the Pine Ridge facility and the wildlife preserve it sits in. And, as far as I know, we have no way of reaching them unless and until they want to be reached."

Bluth got up from his desk and paced the perimeter of his office. Ted watched him pace. After three circuits, the senator stopped and looked at him.

"What's left? You say these Zetas wiped out the units Howard had on the mountain. What didn't they get?"

Ted sat forward in his chair. "They didn't get Forward Kinetics."

The senator's face brightened. "Then we—"

"No—DHS is all over that. I heard this morning that they brought in one of the scientists behind the tech Howard was developing. But they *didn't* get his partner. Just before the situation at Michaux went south, the other scientist—Brenton—took off with half his team. Howard followed them to California, but they managed to slip away. They're still at large as far as I know."

"Those people are also Zetas?"

"Well, I think a couple of them might be. Howard gave me

five identities to keep an eye out for. You know, credit card use, phone records, Internet activity—that sort of thing."

"And?"

"Wherever they are, they are well and truly off the grid. The last credit card use for any of them was in the days prior to the Pine Ridge fiasco."

"What is your intention, Mr. Freitag? What do you plan to do?"

"My job. I'm a documentation specialist at the Pentagon. Nobody you would expect to have knowledge of this."

"Would you be willing to continue to moonlight?"

Ted shot the senator a speculative look. "You aim to put Humpty Dumpty together again?"

"If I can find the pieces. Howard must have had staff at Forward Kinetics. Can you track them down?"

"Well, I have the contact info of the guy who tipped me off. I can start there."

"And this Brenton and his people—can you find them?"

Ted laughed. "Senator, what did I just tell you? Even Leighton Howard couldn't find them."

"You're in a position—"

"I'm in an administrative position that allows me to see a great deal of the intel and documentation that passes through my organization. The only way I can find Brenton and his Zetas is if someone else finds them first—hopefully without realizing it."

Bluth returned to his desk and sat down behind it. He scribbled something on a piece of paper and handed it across the desk to Ted. "That's the number of a phone I used only for communication with Howard. Use it if you find out anything about anything. In the meantime, I'd like as much intel as you've got on any surviving members of Deep Shield and the Forward Kinetics people—missing or otherwise."

Ted stared at the paper, committing the number to memory. He then pressed it down to Bluth's desk with his fore and middle fingers. "Burn this. Incinerate or dissolve the phone this is connected to immediately."

Bluth reclaimed the scrap, tucking it into his pocket. He maintained a poker face while realizing this documentation specialist had just sent him to spy school.

Ted fixed Bluth with a speculative gaze. "Financial arrangements?"

"We'll work it out by phone. I'll . . . take care of you."

"*This* phone, a burner. It has only one number in it, and that connects to me." Ted produced a gray flip phone and placed it on Bluth's nicely polished desk precisely perpendicular to the edge. Bluth's desk intercom beeped just then. It was his admin with a call from the White House. He took the burner, stared at it a moment, then signaled Ted out of the room with a wave of his hand.

Ted let himself out.

Chapter 6

TO SEE THE WIZARD

The first thing Chuck did when he was finally able to get Lorstad to agree that he, at least, should be allowed access to the Internet was to check LinkedIn for messages. He'd made a logical case for it, arguing that someone on his team needed to monitor what the Alphas were doing to see if there was a pattern to their behavior and to assess whether it was escalating. Lorstad insisted that Chuck, alone, have that access. So he was the one to see Matt's semicryptic message, which he'd posted the day before.

You see the news? Big badaboom in Washington, courtesy of our friends in the Emerald City. If I may make an active quantum observation, it's quiet out here at the ForK in the road, now that everyone's gone. Deep in trouble, believe it or not. Miss you and the team. Wish you were here or wish I were there. Need to figure out next steps. Like Dorothy, I'm trying to figure out how to see the Wizard. By the way, a pretty blond lady says she loves dice. Weird, huh? Signed, Tin Man.

Chuck was jotting the first message down when the second one came in.

Ding dong, the witch is dead. Which old witch? The Wicked Witch of the East. Read the news. May have found a way to see the Wizard. Not some bulk-rate Wizard, the Powerful One That Uses Spears. Path leads through the Wild Hedges. Why am I talking like this? Not sure I need to, but you never know. What cat's got your tongue? Signed, Tin Man.

Chuck sat perfectly still for several long seconds, hands hovering over the keyboard. Then he glanced guiltily out through the lab into the main hall. This was insane. He was afraid to answer the messages. Afraid that he was being monitored and that Lorstad would catch him. Why should he be afraid? Matt was their mole, their man on the inside—or on the outside, depending upon how you looked at it. If the messages meant what they seemed to mean, Deep Shield was history and Matt had found a possible way to get to the Alphas.

He scanned the message again and the words *Wild Hedges* leapt out at him. He knew from the messages he and Matt had exchanged during his team's flight from Maryland that capitalized letters were to be taken as an acronym for something else. Hence, *ForK* was "FK"—Forward Kinetics. That made *Wild Hedges* "WH." There was also *Powerful One That Uses Spears*, "POTUS."

"White House, the president," Chuck murmured.

"White House what?"

Lanfen's voice from virtually on top of him made Chuck jump nearly out of his skin. He spun in his chair to find her perched—quite literally—on the arm of the side chair next to his desk. She was in a full lotus position, balanced on one hand, her arm extending down between her crossed legs. Beneath her, the rolling swivel chair did not so much as wiggle. As he watched, she grinned and lifted her hand to fold it into her lap.

She was floating. Above the chair. In the air.

"How are you doing that?"

Again, the grin. "Atoms, dear sir. See the atoms, manipulate the atoms. Gravity doesn't press so forcefully then. What about the White House?"

"It's in this message from—"

Lanfen's sleek, black brows winged upward and she put a finger to her lips, tilted her head to one side for a moment, and held very still. Chuck just watched, puzzled.

"Clear," she said after a moment, then said, "You were saying?"

"It's a message from Matt. Apparently, he feels he's still being monitored. Not sure by whom . . . wait, what do you mean 'clear'? Can you sense . . . ?" He gestured at the fire alarm out in the lab that they'd already ascertained was a surveillance camera.

"Surveillance devices, yes. I figured if Mike could do it, maybe I could, too."

"Mike could also block them," Chuck observed.

Lanfen smiled sagely, then asked, "Does Matt think it's the Benefactors monitoring him?"

"He doesn't know—"

"You know what I mean. None of us can assume that the only surveillance will be at his end. What's he say?" She descended silently from her lofty position and rolled her side chair over to Chuck's desk to peer at the screen with him.

"I think he's trying to tell me that . . . the Witch of the East—that has to be Howard, right?—is dead."

"Howard is dead?" repeated Lanfen. She was silent for a moment, then said, "He says 'Read the news.' Maybe he means that literally."

"Okay." Chuck opened a new tab in his browser and surfed to the Reuters newsfeed. He began scrolling down through the breaking news stories. And there it was. He clicked on the headline: *Michaux Forest Fire Follows on the Heels of Toxic Spill.*

Lanfen let out a slow breath. "Is that the Alphas, too?"

"Or maybe it was Deep Shield trying to get their mountain stronghold back." He went back to the LinkedIn feed. "Look. There are two messages here. The way I read them is that after the Washington Monument was destroyed, Deep Shield was in trouble. Not clear why or how those two things connect, but I could guess. It sounds as if he's also saying Deep Shield has left Forward Kinetics. See, he says everyone's gone."

"He wants to see the Wizard? Who's the Wizard?"

"Man—or woman—behind the curtain. I thought he meant the president at first, but the second message is clearer. Through the 'Wild Hedges'—WH—the White House—is the path *to* the Wizard; I think he means the Alphas. He needs to get into the Emerald City—the mountain—to talk to the people behind the Washington Monument incident. The Alphas."

"And of course," said Lanfen, smiling a little, "there's a message from Brenda for Dice." She looked at Chuck. "You're going to answer him, right?"

Chuck turned back to face his keyboard. After a moment of thought, he typed:

Saw the news. All fired up. Witch is dead? Did you mean that in the general and literal sense? Tell pretty blond lady we have her dice. Hope to return them to her at our earliest opportunity. Let me know how it goes with the Wizard. Signed, Cowardly Lion.

"Cowardly Lion?" asked Lanfen.

"Well, he signed himself Tin Man. I figure that makes me either the Cowardly Lion or the Scarecrow. The Cowardly Lion seemed more appropriate. I am the one that ran, after all."

Lanfen put her hands on either side of Chuck's head and turned him to face her. "Neither is appropriate. You're far from cowardly, Chuck. What you did saved all of us from . . . whatever it is the Alphas have been through, and you've already got one of the best brains I know." She hesitated for a moment, before quietly saying, "And one of the best hearts."

Chuck fell into her nearness, the dark tilt of her eyes, her spicy scent. He wanted to kiss her. She smiled and beat him to the punch, kissing him full on the lips.

In his glass-walled office.

Where everyone could see them.

He found he didn't care.

She pulled back a moment later. "Was that out of line?" she asked softly. "Did I read you wrong?"

He shook his head, savoring his very unscientific response to her kiss. "No. Definitely not. Not out of line. And you read me very well."

"Good. Now, are we going to go talk to Lorstad about this?"

There was something in her expression—in her energy—that brought Chuck into sharp focus. "You didn't just come in here to show off or kiss me, did you?"

She sobered and shook her head. "I've been edgy all morning. That 'someone just walked over my grave' feeling, you know? I figured, you're the one with the Internet connection. Maybe you could . . ." She trailed off. "That sounds silly, doesn't it? I probably just have cabin fever."

"No, not silly. I have to admit to some of the same antsiness. But here's the thing: if we go to Lorstad, he may just cut off our Internet access again. I'm sure he's monitoring it."

"Are you saying we shouldn't go to him?"

"No. I'm just saying maybe we need to think of another way of staying connected to the outside world."

As if following his train of thought, Lanfen turned her head to look out through the glass walls to where Dice and Joey worked to ready the system components for Lorstad's first session.

"Think we can trust Joey," Chuck asked, "or do I need to have you distract him while I talk to Dice? You could ask some questions about their modifications to Pippin."

Lanfen peered at the Sho-Pai engineer. "I think we can trust him. He's not exactly what you'd call a 'company man.' He tends to view Lorstad and the others as . . . well, 'other.'"

"The feeling is apparently mutual," Chuck observed. He thought back to their meeting with a half dozen of Lorstad's Benefactor cohorts. He hadn't felt that nerdy and out of place since high school.

"I was in the hospital for a broken wrist when I was in middle school," said Lanfen. "The result of a tactical error during a martial arts competition. When Lorstad introduced us to his friends, I flashed back to having my doctor come through my hospital room with a bevy of medical students."

Chuck laughed. "I was thinking the same thing. Not about being in the hospital, but that feeling of being . . ."

"An object of curiosity."

"Yeah. That." Chuck took a deep breath, let it out, and said, "Okay. Let's go talk to Dice and Joey."

Lanfen followed Chuck out into the lab to where Dice and Joey were bent over the new BKKI that Dice had laid out on one of his workbenches. The robotics engineer looked up as they approached and pulled off his safety glasses.

"What's up?" he asked.

In answer, Chuck handed him his iPad, which displayed Matt's LinkedIn messages. He frowned, reading the two texts from Matt. Chuck caught his reaction to Matt's reference to Brenda. All the tension seemed to go out of him in a rush. Chuck imagined he could almost feel it.

"She's all right," Dice murmured. "She's okay."

Lanfen laughed. "True love. We show him a dire message about the Alphas' activities and he focuses on the love note from Bren."

Joey looked from Lanfen to Dice and back again. "The Alphas—you mean those other Zetas—the ones that you think blew up the Washington Monument?"

Chuck nodded.

"What do you think this means?" Dice asked softly.

"I think General Howard is dead and that the Michaux Preserve is on fire and that Matt is in contact with the White House. He wants to get to Sara and the others. Talk to them. Maybe figure out what they want. I think Deep Shield has been knocked out of the picture."

Dice stiffened. "Then Bren's not safe back there. Lorstad needs to bring her in."

Lanfen took a step closer to the table and gestured at the interface cabling as if that were what she was discussing. They all did stuff like that. It was an adaptation to living and working under surveillance.

"No one's safe back there," she said urgently. "Not Matt, not anyone. I mean, think about it. The Alphas are cornered. They've already done some pretty serious damage—probably more than we know. It's not just a matter of getting Brenda out." She turned her gaze to Chuck. "I think we need to think of a way to get *in*."

"We need to talk to Lorstad." Dice all but growled the words.

Chuck nodded. "I agree. But we need to be prepared for him to—"

"To sermonize about us getting distracted," said Lanfen. "He's not going to like that we're focusing on this right as he's getting ready to start his training." She glanced at her watch. "In fact, he's due here in less than fifteen minutes."

"What Lanfen is leading up to," Chuck said, "is that we need to explore alternative ways of keeping abreast of what's happening outside these walls. You two have the skills to maybe accomplish that. Are you up for it?"

"Absolutely," Dice said without hesitation.

Chuck turned his attention to Joey. "You don't have to help

Dice if you feel it would put you in an awkward position. The Benefactors are your employers, after all. I promise we will do nothing to harm or even inconvenience them, we just—"

"I'm in," Joey said. "Hey, I live on this planet, too. Sometimes it seems like the Royalty forget that they share it with us."

Lanfen patted the wiring harness. "Better button this up. Here comes our student."

Chuck glanced out into the main concourse to see Lorstad approaching. Alexis was with him. It struck him just how like a gigantic fishbowl "his" lab was. He was relieved when Alexis separated from Lorstad as they neared the lab. She seemed uncomfortable with Chuck's team. The feeling was mutual.

"You'll talk to him about Brenda?" Dice asked.

Chuck did not miss the urgency in the younger man's voice and eyes. He rubbed at the bridge of his nose, massaging away a prickling sensation. "No time like the present."

Dice flipped his safety glasses back into place. "Then let's get this interface put back together. Give me a sign if you need me to stall."

Chuck and Lanfen met Lorstad at the door of the lab. "Before we begin your first session," Chuck told him, "there are a couple of things we need to discuss."

Lorstad's expression did not change. This did not surprise Chuck as much as it disturbed him. He described the intel he'd just gotten from Matt, explained the insecure position that put Dice's fiancée in, and ended with an appeal to bring Brenda Tansy to the Center.

"I'm not asking this merely on humanitarian grounds," Chuck added. "Brenda was Dice's brightest protégé and the head of the robotics team at Forward Kinetics. Having her here would increase Dice's productivity significantly. In the time it took him to create one remote unit, he could have done two or more. For you," he added, knowing this is what Lorstad would probably care about, "it would also mean we could work with your people in larger groups. And that, I assume, would aid all of us if the situation in the east continues to deteriorate."

Lorstad met Chuck's gaze at last. He had, up until that point, stood with a curious but distracted expression on his face, as if he were listening to music only he could hear. "You are unduly concerned about the 'situation in the east,' as you call it. Were anything truly dire to happen there, we would—"

Lanfen, standing shoulder to shoulder with Chuck, made an impatient gesture. "You didn't tell us about the fire at Pine Ridge. I'd call that dire."

Lorstad turned his imperturbable gaze to her. "A forest fire?"

"Please, we're not stupid. Chuck told you: it's more than a forest fire," Lanfen said. "It's part and parcel of what's happening with the Alphas. Weren't you listening? General Howard is dead and Deep Shield has been compromised or possibly destroyed—"

"Ms. Chen, calm yourself. Yes, things are in a state of flux at the moment. Yes, I understand your concern, not just for Ms. Tansy, but for Dr. Streegman and for anyone caught up in what is happening in proximity to the Alphas. But our best hope of dealing with them is to harness the power that you have discovered. To train up as many of the Learned as possible so that we may use our abilities without need for repeated immersions."

"We understand that," said Chuck. "But if we don't get a better idea of what's going on back east we will be in no position to seize opportunities to intervene when they arise. There's no reason not to do both at the same time."

"Charles, I assure you, I would recognize any opportunities—"

"No. I don't think you would. You don't know Sara and Tim and Mike the way I do—the way *we* do." He included the entire lab team in his gesture, and was absurdly pleased that the expression on Lorstad's face at last showed surprise.

"You believe you can assess the situation better than I can?" Lorstad's bemusement seemed sincere.

"Yes, I do. I've worked with these people closely over time.

I've watched them develop their zeta abilities. I've watched them interact with each other and interacted with them. I—or any member of my team—would be able to catch things I don't think even you could, regardless of how closely you've been watching us. Because you've been watching from the *outside*. We've all been on the inside. We need to know what you know when you know it, Kristian. You keep us in the dark at the peril of everything you're trying to accomplish here."

Lorstad raised a golden brow in as close an approximation of Mr. Spock as Chuck could imagine. "I will consider what you've said and I will take it to the Learned Council at my earliest opportunity. I will do this if you will continue to focus your attentions on quantifying how and why your process works and on making it work for us."

"You needn't even ask, Kristian," Chuck said. "In fact, I think we're ready to begin your first driving lesson." He gestured to where Dice and Joey were now attaching the neural net to the kinetic converter for Lorstad's first session. Stationed several yards away at the end of a slim fiber-optic tether was the simple rolling robot he was to work with—Roboticus Mark II. Returning to the hardwired system was something in the way of an experiment. Chuck had wondered if being able to visualize the movement of the signal from brain to bot was a factor in the learning process.

"Will I need that?" The Benefactor indicated the glittering cap of positron transceivers that would read his brain waves and translate them into impulses the machinery could act upon.

"We won't know," Chuck said, "until we start working with you. Besides, any data helps lead to your ultimate end goal."

Lorstad seemed to accept that and moved to seat himself in the chair Dice had drawn up next to the brain wave monitor.

"The Learned Council," Lanfen murmured quietly, as she and Chuck followed him across the lab. "That's new. Makes you wonder how big this organization is."

Chuck was definitely wondering the same thing, then focused on the task at hand.

They began working with Lorstad just as they had with Lanfen, Mini, and their other subjects, though with one significant change, introduced by the student himself.

"I have seen Ms. Chen working with her own powers in your lab, but only in small snatches. I would like a demonstration of her progress, if you please."

Chuck and Lanfen exchanged a glance, then Lanfen shrugged and asked, "What would you like me to do?"

"Several of our staff have reported seeing you doing a form of parkour that they find awe inspiring. I would like to see a demonstration of it."

Lanfen looked around the cavernous lab. "In here?"

"If it suits you. You have been practicing here, after all."

Chuck knew that Lanfen had also been practicing in deserted corridors, in her quarters, and on the balconies overlooking the rocky incline on which the Center's aboveground silhouette was perched. He had once observed her flipping herself from balcony to rooftop and suspected that she was probably capable of escape. He looked at her now, wondering if she would allow Lorstad to see the full scope of her abilities.

She met his gaze and shook her head slightly, then moved to the center of the long room, facing the backlit surface of Mini's studio wall.

"Hey, Mini!" she called. "Heads up. I'm coming through."

She started to run then, lightly, on the balls of her feet, floating down the broad central aisle. She gathered speed as she reached the far end of the room, then leapt gracefully into the air . . . and continued to run up the radiant walls to the ceiling. She kicked off from the top of the wall and went into an arcing backflip that caused everyone around Chuck to draw in a breath, Eugene to look up from his workstation with a squawk of surprise, and Mini to laugh in delight.

Suddenly, Lanfen was wearing a blazing pair of wings—half-angel, half-fairy—that dripped multicolored glory onto the floor below, where it pooled and faded. She carried the arc of her flight toward the distant ceiling, then turned a series of somersaults so fast that her body became a blur.

She burst out of the tuck position high in the air before descending, feetfirst, toward her audience. One hand moved as if beckoning to the people below and a workstation chair glided across the floor into the center aisle mere feet in front of Lorstad. Lanfen's descent slowed dramatically and she settled into the chair cross-legged. Her wings folded, then vanished.

"Ta-da," said Lanfen mildly.

Mini ran toward them laughing and applauding. "Lanfen, that was *wonderful*. I hope you didn't mind the wings."

Lanfen gave the other woman a brilliant smile. "Is that what that was? I wondered where all that light was coming from."

Chuck looked at Lorstad. The Benefactor spokesman was frowning thoughtfully, glancing from one woman to the other as if something in the display bothered him. Did he realize Lanfen was understating her abilities? Were they not as impressive to him as they were to his ordinary staff? Or was it something else?

"I am humbled. You did all of that—both of you—with these zeta powers you have developed?"

Mini nodded and Lanfen said, "Of course."

"And Minerva, how did you cause your wings to keep up with Ms. Chen's movements?"

Mini seemed surprised by the question. "I—I don't know. I just . . . I don't know."

There was a moment of uncomfortable silence, then Lorstad said, "I have a request to make of you both. I would like to have you examined by our doctors. Have them run some diagnostics—MRIs, whatever they feel would shed light on any physiological changes your growing powers may cause."

Both Lanfen and Mini looked to Chuck. He cleared his throat. "If the ladies have no objection, neither have I, but . . ."

"Yes?" Lorstad regarded him curiously.

"They received full periodic workups at FK."

Lorstad answered plainly. "We no longer have access to that data and new records must be created. Surely you understand that."

"Fine . . . but nothing invasive, right?"

"Drawing blood?"

"Is fine," said Lanfen—and Mini nodded. "It's for a good cause, after all."

Lorstad seemed happy with that and they went to work on his learning session, getting a baseline for his brain waves as a first step. They had a series of simple tasks set up that made use of their Roombot as well as some computer-based activities. Chuck explained the process, wondering all the while what had prompted Lorstad to inquire about physiological changes.

The session did not go well, though Chuck supposed in hindsight that he should have suspected it might not. The reason it did not go well was precisely why he'd expected it to go very right—he expected Kristian Lorstad to be well ahead of the curve when it came to kinetic manipulation. Far from facilitating his work with the kinetic interface, Lorstad's externally generated abilities impeded it. They interfered with his attempts to produce a clear, "unflavored" brain wave of any kind, let alone enter a gamma state. If he exerted any will toward something, his brain seemed to involuntarily draw on the powers it had been imbued with via immersion.

After two solid hours of trying to get Lorstad to consciously turn off his "power assist"—as Dice referred to it—the Learned leader pulled the neural net from his head and rose.

"This is futile. I would never have imagined that I would regret the powers I have striven so hard to acquire, but I do. I once read of a body of research on blindness demonstrating that, if a man has been sightless for as few as five years, when sight is physically restored, he will find he has lost the *mental* ability to see."

Chuck had, of course, read Oliver Sacks's study of the phenomenon Lorstad described and understood exactly what he was saying. "The brain has rewired itself," Chuck said quietly. "It's reassigned sight pathways to other things. But your 'power assist' is temporary. Once you've let it weaken—"

Lorstad's face went pale. "I cannot allow it to weaken to that extent, Dr. Brenton. I would be . . . helpless. Blind, deaf, crippled. I am even now nearing a scheduled immersion. If my powers have not ebbed sufficiently by now . . .

"No. We must find a way to work around this. I must either learn to control my autonomic responses, or you must find a way to neutralize them during this process. And," he added as he strode from the room, "you *must* determine what factors guarantee success in cultivating zeta powers."

"Kristian, there may be no guarantee—"

Lorstad stopped at the door and turned back to face them, his expression resolute. "I'll return tomorrow. I may bring another of the Learned with me to see if perhaps it is merely *my* peculiar talents that keep me from working with your machineries." He turned and was gone.

Silence wound its way among Chuck's team like a cat seeking attention. Glancing up at the fire alarm that wasn't a fire alarm, Chuck beckoned everyone into his office, where they sat around the small conference table.

Eugene was the first to speak. "Is that . . . ? Was he . . . ? That's the first time I think I've ever seen that man actually *verklempt*."

Dice nodded. "He was seriously disturbed."

"And frightened," said Mini.

Eugene glanced over at Chuck. "You see that coming, Doc?"

Chuck shook his head. "I did not." He leaned back against his desk, his eyes unfocused, his mind racing. "What if none of them can learn this without first letting go of their . . ." He struggled for a better term, then gave up. ". . . power assist? If they all have the same attitude toward being vulnerable that Lorstad does, they may never be able to learn our methodology."

Joey laughed. "That's damned ironic. The powers they're so proud of might be the one thing that keeps them from evolving away from needing to tank all the time. It might be easier for someone like me—" He stopped and hung on his own thoughts for a moment; Chuck was pretty sure he knew what they were.

When Joey spoke again, he confirmed it. "*Can* I learn what Lanfen and Mini do? What I mean, I guess, is *will* you let me learn it?"

Chuck dreaded the question. He dreaded it because he so much wanted to say yes and knew that if he did, Lorstad would consider it a form of betrayal.

"How would we do that?" Eugene asked. "I mean, you may have noticed that we sort of work in a fish tank."

"There are ways," Dice said, the wheels in his head clearly working frantically. "We have a portable Brewster-Brenton unit; Becky and the neural cap are small . . ."

"And," said Lanfen, "we have our own private exercise room that is *not* a fish tank."

Chuck realized he was shaking his head. "I don't think we need to go to those lengths. We start actively engaging in subterfuge, we *will* be found out eventually. We're not CIA material. I think we've proved that pretty effectively. We're scientists about to undertake an experiment that requires a baseline, after all. A normal human brain, untouched by either immersion tech or kinetic tech. We need a control. There's no reason why Joey can't be that control."

The whole team seemed happy with that idea—Joey first and foremost. A wave of something that was almost contentment seemed to infuse the air between them. Chuck certainly felt better now that they had a game plan. He understood the mechanics of that. His sense of autonomy and control had taken a severe beating since their involvement with Deep Shield and subsequent "rescue" by the Benefactors. And for the first time since they escaped from Maryland, he felt as if he had made an autonomous decision.

"His peculiar talents." Lanfen repeated Lorstad's words as they watched Dice and Eugene set Joey up with the neural cap from Chuck's office. "I wonder what they are."

Remembering the number of times Lorstad had seemed to move from one place to another without being heard or seen—including his initial appearance at Forward Kinetics—Chuck wondered if he didn't share some of Lanfen's propensity for extreme stealth or Mini's ability to blind someone to her real presence by creating a projection. Maybe Lorstad had some sort of cloaking talent.

"He seems to be really interested in what I can do," Mini observed. "Maybe he'll tell me what his 'superpower' is if I express interest in it."

"I'll show you mine if you show me yours?" said Lanfen, grinning.

Mini grinned back. "Something like that."

"Only if you're comfortable doing that," Chuck said. "I don't want to put you in any kind of jeopardy with him."

"He won't harm me, if that's what you mean. He . . . cares about me on some level. Maybe just as a scientific curiosity, but I think I'm important to him in some way." She hesitated, then added, "And he wants something from me. I don't know what, exactly, but something about *my* 'peculiar talent' means something to him—maybe to his whole organization. I don't know. It's just a feeling. I trust my feelings."

The words were uttered a bit defensively. Chuck put his hand on Mini's shoulder and squeezed.

"So do we," he said, and Lanfen echoed, "So do we all."

Chapter 7

HIS PECULIAR TALENTS

In Mini's mind, she was a secret agent on a fact-finding mission, or maybe Black Widow or some other agent of S.H.I.E.L.D. She kicked herself for that fantasy (how juvenile was that?), then kicked herself again for kicking herself. It was in her nature to fantasize—to play games with reality. It fired her imagination and inspired and informed her art. She more than suspected that if she shared her secret-agent fantasy with Chuck, he'd tell her to go with it.

And if she shared it with Eugene, his head would probably explode. The thought made her smile.

So, on her way to keep a luncheon "date" with Lorstad in the Center's five-star restaurant of a canteen, she marched into Chuck's office, where he and Eugene were discussing possible means of suppressing Lorstad's conditioning while he was connected to the Brewster-Brenton monitor.

"I'm off to play Natasha Romanoff," she said pertly, and grinned.

Chuck laughed. "That's a good way to think of it. Hold that thought."

Eugene frowned and his mouth formed a mutinous straight line. "Mini, this isn't a game. This guy . . . well, I think he has . . . expectations."

See? Laughter bubbled up in Mini's throat. "You think he has *designs* on me?" She made air quotes around the word *designs*.

Eugene blushed to the roots of his dark, curly hair. "I didn't say that. I just meant—what you said before—that he wants something from you."

Chuck glanced from one to the other, then said, "Euge isn't wrong to remind you to be careful. While they've been good enough to take us in, we're still not really sure what their motives are . . . or how long their goodwill is meant to last."

Mini gave them both an eye-rolling look. "Okay, Doctors Worrywart. I'll take all the precautions. But you know, I think what he seems to want most is for me to, I don't know, *approve* of what they do. The immersion, I mean. It's almost as if Kristian feels inferior. Or at least he's afraid that we'll *think* he and the other Benefactors are inferior because they have to 'tank' in order to exhibit their abilities."

That drew a laugh from Eugene. "Trust me when I say that *Kristian* doesn't have an insecure bone in his body. His air of superiority is—"

"Irrelevant," said Chuck. "Go on, Natasha," he told Mini. "Off with you. You have a mission to accomplish."

"Yes, sir." She gave Chuck a saucy salute, stuck her tongue out at Eugene, and went off to be a superagent.

EUGENE SLUMPED IN HIS CHAIR, watching Mini stride purposefully out of the lab. "Well, I managed to screw that up, royally. Now she's mad at me."

Chuck followed his gaze. "No, she's not. If she were mad at

you she wouldn't have stuck her tongue out. She would have just gone."

"You sure?"

"I've known Mini since she was a kid. Yeah, I'm sure. You're afraid of Lorstad's influence on her, aren't you?"

Euge sighed. "Is it that obvious? I just . . . I feel like the odd man out. I'm the only one on the team who doesn't seem to have any ability to do zeta. Mini . . . Mini is shaping up to have a really wonderful talent. Me, I got *bupkis*."

"Really?" Chuck asked with a quirk of his eyebrow.

"I mean, I've got nothing to offer *her*."

"How about the fact that you love her. That's not nothing."

"Yeah, but—"

"No 'but,' Eugene. I know Lorstad and his associates see some sort of line of demarcation between 'the Learned' and the rest of us. Mini doesn't. Lanfen doesn't."

"Yeah, but—"

"Euge . . ."

Eugene raised a hand. "I'm serious, Doc. You and Dice aren't full-fledged Zetas, but you at least got the damn training wheels off. I can't even make Roboticus shimmy without the spangly hairnet."

Chuck puzzled over that. It was true. Eugene could manipulate his favorite machineries relatively well for a novice as long as he was wearing the neural net. The moment it came off, or Becky was shut down, he was as unable as most human beings to manipulate his environment. There hadn't really been time to ask why and seek answers, but maybe there would be now, under the guise of working out Lorstad's problem.

"Well, you're ahead of the game then. Lorstad can't even make Roboticus shimmy *with* the spangly hairnet. At least, not without cheating."

That thought seemed to make Eugene feel marginally better. He sat up straighter in his chair and rolled it closer to the desk where his laptop sat, back to back with Chuck's. "That's true, isn't it? Maybe if we can crack Lorstad's code, we can crack mine."

Chuck gave up trying to convince Eugene that he didn't need to be a Zeta to win Mini's continued love and admiration, so instead he agreed that maybe their new line of research would yield fruit.

"This other thing Lorstad's got you working out," Euge said. "This hierarchy of requisites in zeta development—it's really related to this, isn't it? I mean, that's why he pushed you just now to keep after the 'formula,' right?"

Chuck sighed. "Right. And he seems unwilling to suppose that there might not be any such formula. Some things can't be quantified . . . or at least they resist quantification. This may be one of them."

"Ha. Don't let Matt Streegman ever hear you say that. He'd think that was next door to heresy." He paused to give Chuck a speculative look. "What if it *does* turn out to be one of those unquantifiable things?"

"I don't know. I'm not sure Lorstad would accept that."

"If we find a way to get around his problem, though, won't that answer his question about what conditions are required for zeta mastery?"

Chuck considered that. "It might. Or it might only answer *his* question—not *the* question. For example, his difficulty with zeta might be resolved by eliminating something he's *doing* rather than identifying something he's *not* doing. That doesn't answer the larger question of what conditions need to be in place in general to facilitate zeta mastery."

Eugene frowned. "Are you sure? I mean, we already discovered that one of the conditions needs to be the elimination of certain mental habits that get in the way of learning. What if the reason he can't even generate gamma waves and the reason I can't are actually the same—some mental habit that's getting in the way?"

Some questions, when asked, cause the universe to hold its breath. At least, that was the way Chuck experienced them. He thought of them as Absolute Zero Moments—moments when the entire creation seemed to slow to complete stillness and time simply ceased to exist. He found himself, now, in a breathless state of suspended animation, with the completely absurd conviction that Eugene was right. That led him to the next question: *If* he were right, what did it mean? Was there a singular mental habit that might result in both Lorstad's and Eugene's difficulties in creating gamma or zeta waves?

He thought back to the barriers the Deep Shield operatives had struggled to break through. Barriers that had to do not just with their military training, but with the mental and emotional conditions that had caused them to be particularly responsive to that training. One factor had been a certain linearity of thought—an orderliness that militated against spontaneity and multitasking. That, in turn, was rooted in an expectation that the world worked in a particular way—and not in a way that allowed someone to actively manipulate reality at the quantum level.

Faith, Lanfen had called it. Their early Deep Shield recruits had no faith that they could do what Lanfen and the other Zetas did. Their particular internal worlds did not operate that way, nor did their environment encourage them to imagine that they could.

Chuck peered at Eugene over his laptop display. Euge was notorious for his lack of self-confidence; that was his filter on what he could potentially do. Weren't Lorstad's externally conditioned talents also a filter that informed his sense of his own potential? A filter that led to a sort of conscious incompetence?

"What?" Eugene asked. "Is my hair sticking out all over?"

Chuck blinked.

"You're looking at me funny."

Chuck brought himself back to the problem at hand. "Your hair is fine—well, no, it *is* sticking up, but that's not what I was staring at you about. I was just thinking about—well, Lanfen calls it 'faith.' Maybe a more scientific way of putting it is . . . unconscious competence."

Eugene blinked. "What d'you mean?"

"Remember how Lanfen sort of tricked the Deeps into displaying their latent competence with zeta waves by distracting them? By causing them to—I don't know—forget to filter their behavior through their perceptions about what's possible? Each of us looks at the world differently and expects reality to behave in a particular way because that's the way it's always behaved. We have trouble coping when it doesn't."

Eugene went completely still, as if he were having one of those 'moments' Chuck had just experienced. As it often did, Eugene's brain took a hop, skip, and jump over the connective tissue of the thought process and landed on . . . "Wait. That would be an impediment to evolution, wouldn't it? If you keep expecting A to happen, then you're not likely to seriously entertain the idea that B can happen. And if B is necessary to reach the next level of evolution, then you're sort of screwed—evolutionarily speaking."

"Yes—except for those who can make that leap. They're the ones who move forward. So, how do we remove that barrier—that expectation?" Chuck asked. "Lanfen did it with the Deeps by involving them in a multitasking exercise that allowed them to forget, for a moment, what they expected they couldn't do. She . . . *surprised* them into moving from point A to point B. When Mini first exhibited zeta waves, she was skeptical of her abilities, too. We simply switched off the unit without her knowing it. She still believed she was being aided by the interface and had no reason to doubt."

Eugene snorted. "I get the sense that Lorstad is not so easily surprised."

"He was surprised at his lack of ability to work with the kinetic system without leaning on his 'learning.'"

"Touché."

"Maybe if we can't suppress Lorstad's talents, we *can* distract him from them." He got up from his desk, the idea settling more firmly in his mind.

"Where are you going?"

"I'm going to go chat with Lanfen. Why don't you play with this idea a bit more—see if you can't come up with some other possible solutions?"

"Chuck . . ."

Chuck halted and regarded his protégé over his shoulder.

Euge glanced around the room in tacit acknowledgment of the listening devices. "*Should* it be going well? I mean, should we have a breakthrough at this point?"

The elephant in the room. They had found themselves training clandestine special ops soldiers under Deep Shield. Now they were trying to unlock abilities in members of a cabal that was equally clandestine—if not more so.

Should it go well?

Chuck inhaled sharply. "For now, this is a good pace. If or when it's time to apply the brake . . . anyway just keep at it."

Euge nodded. "Actually," he said, glancing at the door, "I was feeling a bit peckish. Thought maybe I'd hop down to the canteen and grab a quick bite."

Chuck speared him with a look that could only be called *withering.*

"What?" Eugene asked, the picture of perfect innocence.

"Please, Euge. You're as transparent as our fishbowl lab. Do *not* do that. Mini would not appreciate being checked up on."

"Yeah. Yeah, you're right." Eugene looked impossibly hangdog.

"Besides," Chuck added as he exited the room, "hopping is very undignified."

"Oh! Oooh!" Eugene called after him. "You made a funny. A very lame funny. See me not laughing?"

SITTING AT A TABLE ACROSS from each other over lunch, Mini and Lorstad chatted about art and music—two areas in which they had much in common, though Kristian Lorstad did not, as Mini did, appreciate the visceral elegance of rock and roll. In fact, he found it strikingly odd that she could admire both Antonio Vivaldi and Joe Satriani and wax equally eloquent about the vocal talents of Leontyne Price, Tina Turner, and Ronnie James Dio. When she told him that one of her favorite musical collaborations was a live concert duet between Tina Turner and David Bowie on Bowie's "Let's Dance," he was struck speechless.

In that moment of awkward silence, the cheerful philistine launched her first attempt to find out more about their host and his compatriots.

"I guess you're not from around here," she teased. "You prefer European art forms with a rich history—symphonic, choral. I get it. I mean, you are from Europe yourself, right?"

He nodded, setting aside his fork. "I am. I was born in the Netherlands and raised there until I was fourteen."

"So how did you get to be part of all this?" Mini's gesture took in the entire underground facility.

He dabbed at his lips with a napkin, stalling, obviously trying to figure out how to answer without revealing too much.

Eventually he said, "I was born into it, actually. Most of us are. It is rare that a prodigy arises from a family outside of the Group."

Mini heard the capital G in that last word. "Really? So your mother and father were both . . . *talented*? I mean, they used the immersion technology?"

Something dark flitted through Lorstad's gaze—a momentary displeasure or pain, perhaps, like the tug of a scab on a half-healed wound. Mini put all of her senses to the task of reading the man sitting across from her.

"Yes. Both of my parents were of the Learned."

"Wow. Are they still involved with the Benefactors?"

"My father died some years ago. My mother is . . . no longer active in the Group. She left to care for my younger sister."

The mention of a younger sibling needing parental care prompted an immediate expression of dismay from the soft-hearted Mini. "What happened? Is your sister ill?"

Now Lorstad's face went through a series of minute but perceptible changes that Mini read in swift succession. She saw pain, anger, resolve.

"My sister . . . my sister was unable to benefit from immersion technology. The sessions unsettled her, caused her to withdraw. She had to be removed from the program and never developed any talent." He seemed about to say more, then shook his head. "It's ancient history to me. My mother is doing well, as is Anika. You have siblings, I believe."

Mini nodded, recognizing his attempt to shift the conversation for what it was. But that was okay—any good superspy knows they need to play the long game. "Two brothers. Quite a bit older. Very practical men with very practical lives."

"Ah. Not creative types like you."

"Nooooo, haha." Her face lit up with a genuine smile, rueful as it was. "I am unique in all my family. I was a sort of late surprise. A fluke."

Lorstad tilted his head with a smile. "I imagine you are. Unique, I mean."

She blushed slightly. "Thank you." Mini swallowed and hoped Lorstad didn't hear her breath quickening. For a split second she lost herself in his deep eyes and basked in the words flowing from his hewn jaw.

No.

Looking to now be the one to change the subject, she groped with her mind for a topic, then asked, "So, how old were you when you started your training?"

"Very young. Six, in fact."

"Six? My God, weren't you terrified?" The question was entirely sincere. The thought of climbing into one of those sensory deprivation tanks made Mini want to crawl out of her skin.

He shook his head. "Not at all. I regarded it as a great adventure. Besides, I had Alexis." He said that as one might say, *I had my teddy bear.*

"You trained together?"

"Yes. We usually train children in pairs, so that there is a link or bond forged between the two. We bolster each other's learning, we encourage each other, we monitor each other to make sure we maintain our health and well-being."

"You mean, you make sure you don't wait too long to—um—to immerse?" She really had to stop thinking of it as "tanking" or she'd slip and say it out loud to one of the Learned and insult them.

Lorstad smiled. "You were going to say 'tank,' weren't you? It's all right. We know the staff calls it that. It's petty, but doesn't anger us. Well, at least it doesn't anger most of us."

"So you and Alexis are a couple?"

"Not in the way you and Eugene Pozniaki are a couple. Although, certainly, that sort of relationship between two of the Learned is encouraged. There are not many of us in the world, even after several centuries, so the more children we can produce who share our susceptibilities, the better. I have to say, though, that given the fewness of our numbers, Dr. Brenton's methodology does rather open up the door to new blood."

There was something just a bit too intimate about his regard. It made Mini uncomfortable and brought heat to her cheeks.

"Why *are* there so few of you?"

He shrugged. "We do not always breed true. There are, in every generation, individuals like my sister, Anika, who simply are not successful in awakening their powers. In some generations, they outnumber those who *are* successful." He returned his attention to his plate and poked at its contents for a moment before saying, "If it's not too personal a question, may I ask how serious your relationship with Dr. Pozniaki is?"

Mini was silent long enough to make him look up at her. She gazed directly into his eyes so that he could not possibly mistake her. "I love him," she said bluntly. "He loves me. So, it's very serious."

"Ah," said Lorstad, looking away. "Yes. I see."

She felt a pit open in her stomach. It wasn't that she had feelings like that for Lorstad, but it just felt bad to see a man so obviously trying to mask his hurt—hurt *she* had caused him, even though it was through no fault of her own. It wasn't particularly fair of him to expose his emotions so baldly in front of her, but it didn't change the fact that he had, and—in doing so—she had been forced to shut him down. Putting it aside, Mini gently steered the conversation into a new direction, hopefully helping him save some face while also leading them to the place she wanted this to go.

"So, you have to immerse yourselves fairly often, then, to keep your abilities strong. Well maybe not you; you seem to be very skilled in all of this, if skilled is even the right word. I still can't help but wonder, though, isn't that inconvenient? I mean it must take a lot of discipline and just, I don't know, endurance."

"Not so much. At my level of experience, I must immerse perhaps once a week for several hours. But yes, when you first undergo the entrainment, you must spend significant time in the isolation chambers being conditioned to make use of your talents."

Mini propped her elbows on the table, put her chin in her hands, and gave him a look that her father had said could melt iron. "And what are your talents, Kristian? I've seen you move objects and you seem to be able to enter and leave rooms without being noticed. Is stealth your area of expertise? Some kind of psychonaut ninja?"

Now he looked coy. The smile lingered around his lips and his eyes said eloquently that he was not about to tell all. "Quantum physics is my area of expertise," he said, "as art is yours. But even with my understanding of . . . certain features of the physical universe, I am unable to do what you do. To create solid, programmable constructs so real as to deceive even our friends in Deep Shield—that, Mini, opens up a realm of possibilities that even as old an organization as the Benefactors has not been able to breach. Our talents, once programmed, do not grow—do not evolve. And if we do not return again and again for entrainment therapy, they deteriorate. I am hoping to have the results of the tests you and Ms. Chen underwent. You and your Dr. Brenton hold the key." A shadow touched his expression. "I hope he is able to determine how that key will unlock our full potential."

"He will," Mini said with complete conviction. If there were one thing she was sure of, it was Chuck Brenton's talent for finding answers. She smiled back at Lorstad and pondered her next question . . .

THE STRAINS OF *THE MAGIC FLUTE* submerged into a far simpler, more primal rhythm—a heartbeat, an ocean, musical breathing. His eyes played with the pulses and streamers of light fed to them by his blackout goggles. They sought patterns. The human eye—the human brain—always seeks patterns. It is a way of understanding the world. He used to try not to see them. He used to pull his eyes out of the seductive ebb and flow of light, then realized it was self-defeating. He was trying to establish control of his thoughts at too gross a level. With that wisdom, he learned to let his eyes roam where they would.

Was it possible that he now needed to attempt that control again? The thought escaped his grasp almost as soon as he had it. Deeper. His eyes sought to focus on different aspects of the projection—on the flashes of brilliance, then on the darkness opposite, then on the strands of colorful filament that wove among them.

Was darkness opposite? Was it not just absence? Were the flashes of brilliance revelations in photonic form?

He became intensely aware of his body and its shape and form as if his consciousness were pouring into it from the outside, filling it. With every pulse of light, with every beat of sound, he felt as if waves of sense lapped at his skin, but from the inside. His skin felt transparent. How could one feel transparent? He'd wondered that at first. Now he simply accepted that it was so. He floated. He filled with sound and swam in light. The pattern became a pathway. He followed it. It led out of the cave of the physical world and into a greater realm. He was looking down on himself in the tank; then he was looking down on the tank. The room was empty except for a technician checking his vitals on a monitor. He "saw" these things, but understood on some level that without rods and cones and retinas, he could not be said to see. He *perceived*.

The first time he had achieved this state—the out-of-body experience—he thought he had imagined it. His father had said nothing about it and he assumed, until he compared notes with Alexis, that it was just a flight of fancy. That was when he'd discovered that only some of the Benefactors had OBEs. He did. Alexis did. His mother had before . . .

He veered away from that train of thought.

He hadn't believed it. Had wanted proof. Alexis had given it to him by entering the Therapy Lab while he was in immersion and making a video of herself doing a series of things. When he'd come out, she had him describe what he had "seen" her do. Then they'd watched her video together.

Now he no longer doubted what he saw during an OBE. It was the OBEs, after all, that had begun him thinking about quantum entanglement, its application in the world beyond the immersion tank, and the lengths to which it might be taken. Kristian Lorstad had welcomed Charles Brenton's new technologies, viewing them as a way to extend and grow the powers of the Learned.

Now, as he perceived Brenton's team working with one of his staff and witnessed how easily that individual acquired the rudimentary ability to push the tiny robot around the room, to move a mouse pointer across a screen merely through the use of his very normal, very average human mind, he was no longer so certain of what zeta capacities augured. What if he were unable to ever learn to use his native, unenhanced abilities to do what he could now do through external conditioning? What if Brenton's technology did not grant him evolving powers, but robbed him of what he had? Robbed him of what made him Learned, what made him someone apart. Devolving . . . it was too much a price to pay if none of it worked. Then there was the unthinkable:

What if the Zetas thrived and made him and his society obsolete?

These ordinary people learned these amazing skills apparently through nothing more than practice. They did this in a fraction of the time it took him and his fellow Learned to achieve similar yet admittedly inferior results. And if more people than not can achieve the zeta state? What that meant for his society paled compared to the implications it held for humanity as a whole.

No. It mustn't happen that way.

He withdrew his consciousness from the kinetics lab and returned to revisit his conversation with Mini.

IT WAS DARK IN THE lab outside Chuck's private office—after hours for the Center staff. Even Eugene was gone—off to have dinner with Mini. Chuck stared at the screen of his laptop, focused on the scanned image of a human male in a virtual OR, brain exposed. He adjusted the neural net on his head and focused on the brain. This software with a VR helm and gloves allowed the clinician to pick up the model of the patient's brain and manipulate it, turning it, zooming in on parts of special interest.

This patient had suffered an accident that had taken his eyesight. When an operation had restored his sight some five years later, he had been unable to form coherent images despite the fact that his eyes were fully operational once more. Five years without sight had rewired his synapses. Based on the discussion with Kristian earlier, Chuck had pored over the man's MRIs and PET and CAT scans. With the virtual reality technology, he was now able to view the brain in three dimensions, and he had been able to see, in real time, how the organ had rerouted its signals to work around the missing sense of sight.

Yet even that tech had not allowed him to reach into the scanned brain mentally and attempt to return the synapses to their pre-accident patterns. Nor was there any surgical technique in either Chuck's experience or research as a scientist capable of that delicate an operation. But there was one thing . . . and he was hoping that zeta abilities might bridge the gap between knowledge and technology.

He knew what the pattern looked like in a sighted brain—knew which areas lit up, and in what order—as the mind worked at recognizing a face or a place or an object. It should be possible, he told himself, for one who understood the brain's currents to manipulate them, to guide the energies into particular channels, to order the sequence in which the synapses fired. So he held his patient's virtual brain in equally immaterial hands and imagined himself drawing a line for the neurons to follow—a circuit down which he wanted the impulses to travel.

The virtual synapses obeyed. The brain lit up in its proper sequence and the retrofit pathways were abandoned. Were this his actual patient, his brain would interpret sight again as it had before. The question before Chuck Brenton: could he effect such a change in real neurons and synapses as he had in the electrical impulses and photons of a computer-generated program?

Well, why not? After all, weren't photons and electrons and neurons all just units of energy? If you could manipulate one unit of energy, why couldn't you manipulate others?

For the second time that day, Chuck had an Absolute Zero Moment. He was a trained neuroscientist; he understood the minute workings of the brain and had built his career on its relationship to the human mind. He had now trained himself to manipulate units of energy, too, and matter was simply energy in a different form. Knowing that, what was there he *couldn't* interact with?

The thought was amazing, as were its possibilities, but just as quickly as it came, he was brought up short. *Fine, Chuck,* he thought, *but how do I prove that in a medical setting without causing someone irreparable harm?* Reaching into a brain or some other physical organ—even with invisible fingers of sense—was potentially dangerous. A sneeze, a stray thought, a moment of inattention could kill or maim. He recalled Mike Yenotov's early work with mechanical devices—especially the John Deere front loader—and remembered Mike's concern that he might lose focus, a potentially deadly event even when manually handling heavy equipment.

The explosive demise of the Washington Monument came unbidden to mind. Chuck had feared a deadly loss of focus—had worked hard with the team to figure out contingency plans for that—but not intentional mayhem. Had he misread Mike and the others? Had that potential for violence always been there, or was it merely the circumstances they found themselves in? He had to know, he realized. He had to know because all this was, in some measure, his doing. No, he didn't attack the monument himself, but he did open Pandora's box. Did the process of becoming a Zeta somehow alter their psyches? Would his companions be affected, Lanfen or Mini? He shook the thought away.

He stood and removed the neural cap from his head, only then noticing that he had never connected it to the kinetic interface. He flushed cold and hot in turns, realizing that he had taken a leap in his own evolution without even being aware of it—and yet didn't that in a way prove his theory of distraction he had discussed with Eugene? He set the net back on its stand with shaking hands. His first impulse was to tell everyone on the team. His second was to keep it to himself or to tell only Lanfen. For reasons he could not have articulated, he chose door number two.

Chapter 8

CATCHING THE WAVE

"We're back on the grid." Tim's voice held a note of wonder—or perhaps it was merely surprise. He hesitated, eyeing the display in front of him. "Well, at least we're connected to something outside this damned mountain besides TV broadcast feeds."

Sara and Mike both came to peer over his shoulder. The display showed the face of a young woman—a stranger. She was in air force uniform—pale blue shirt, navy blue tie. Her hair was pulled back into a braid. She was brunette and when she turned her head to speak to someone to one side, her delicate features reminded Mike painfully of his daughter, Darya.

"Doctor?" she said. "I have a connection, I think, but I can't see or hear anything. They're jamming from their end."

A man came into view—a familiar one.

Tim grinned. "It's Dr. Matt!" He cocked his head back to look up at Sara. "We want to talk to him . . . right?"

Sara nodded. "Indeed we do. Don't open us up yet, though. First—" She turned to Mike. "Get your bots ready for reconnaissance."

Mike returned to his own station and sat down. His bots were not only ready for reconnaissance, but they had been doing reconnaissance in the area of the destroyed Deep Shield camp since he'd deployed them. He'd used the opportunity to experiment with his own talents and realized something interesting—each robot, though they were supposed to be identical—*felt* different. He couldn't have explained that to anyone—maybe it was the personal touch of a single screw tightened more than another, or a wire soldered from a different angle, or a combination of thousands of those little things. But he knew it to be true regardless. There were four of them now, stationed at intervals down the mountain, and Mike had named each one. They were Anatoly, Boris, Zhenya, and Sacha. Sacha was his favorite, and was the one deployed farthest from the mountain peak to keep watch on the Deep Shield cleanup. So Sacha was the one he inhabited now—without even needing a line of sight. Now he just knew how the bot *felt*.

Sara went to stand before the massive bank of screens at the head of the big room and set most of them to show a huge visual of Matt Streegman and the room in which he stood. All except one. One, Mike noticed, showed Sara what Matt was seeing—her, standing at the front of the cavernous operations center in a pool of white light, her dark hair glossy, her face in dramatic shadow, wearing a black, formfitting jumpsuit.

She was impressive, Mike had to admit, and he more than suspected she even impressed herself. At the very least, she wanted to be sure she projected an intimidating image. Having lived with her these past few days, he wanted to assure her that she was definitely intimidating.

Mike kept ears on Sara's dialogue with Matt and eyes on the environment around the Sacha-bot. Sensors built into the robot's thorax and head told him that the ex–Deep Shield camp was sparsely populated by cleanup crews. His earlier observations had convinced him that their mandate was to return the area to something as close to its pre–Deep Shield appearance as possible, to make it appear as if the fire had spread out from a lightning strike or a simple campfire.

He moved Sacha closer and observed that the entire cleanup crew was composed of half a dozen guys with metal detectors going over the area where the bodies had lain. He wondered what had become of those bodies. Had they been buried anonymously? Returned to their families? Cremated?

He heard Sara laugh and realized he'd gotten distracted from her conversation with Matt.

". . . good to see me?" Sara was saying. "Why do I doubt that?"

"You shouldn't doubt it," Matt assured her. "I've been worried about you three. Howard had a stranglehold on Forward Kinetics. I can't even imagine what he must have done to you."

He looked older, Mike thought. Frazzled. Not surprising, considering that he'd been in the clutches of Deep Shield longer than they had. Why was Sara being so snarky with him?

"Not nearly as drastic as what we did to him, apparently," Sara said dryly. "The damn coward shot himself."

Matt snorted. "That surprises you? He put himself in a no-win situation." His face sobered. "He put you in a no-win situation, too, damn him. I hate how he treated you—like you were ordnance instead of human beings."

Mike couldn't see Sara's face—she had her back to him—but he caught her expression in the monitor she'd filled with her image. He saw the ripple of naked pain and anger that crossed her face—saw the softening in her eyes.

"Thank you for that, Doc," she said. "You're a good guy. So, where do we stand? I assume you've gotten the authorities—the real ones this time—involved in this?"

"Actually, the president came to me. Her administration had no idea what Howard was up to." His mouth twitched and one corner turned up in a wry smile. "Heck of a way you chose to shout 'We are here!' Sara. But it worked. You were heard. So, where we stand is, President Ellis wants to know your . . ." He glanced to one side as if conferring silently with someone before looking back at the camera. "She'd like to know your intent and your goals."

Sara cocked a look back over her shoulder, taking in Tim and Mike. "Our goals are simple: world peace, incorruptible governments and agencies thereof, safety, long life—"

"Not being thrown into prison," murmured Mike.

Sara and Matt both heard him and said, in perfect unison, "No one's going to throw you in prison, Mike."

The look on Sara's face, now turned toward him, told Mike she meant the words in an entirely different way than Matt did. She turned back to the screens.

"I'd say we need to talk at length," she said.

"With that list of goals, I'd say so, too. " Matt spread his hands. "Open up and let me in?" He grinned. "I come in peace."

Mike's view of the forest through the bot's optics was supplanted by a tiny minotaur waving its hoofed arms. "Got signal!" it said in Tim's voice, and indicated a direction by pointing with a miniature mace. Mike realized he was receiving intel about the location Matt's signal was coming from. It felt like a soft pulse of static electricity beating against his right arm—the robot's right arm. He turned Sacha into the signal and put him in motion.

"When can you talk?" Sara asked, adding, "You'll have to come alone."

"Obviously. As soon as I've been briefed." He glanced aside again. "Tonight? Nineteen hundred hours?"

"Agreed. We'll send you an escort. Mike . . . ?"

Mike nodded. "I've got a ninja bot coming your way, Doc. Don't let them shoot him, okay?"

"I promise they won't shoot him," Matt said. "It would be an exercise in futility anyway."

"Yes," said Sara, "it would be. I'm serious, Matt. When I said we wanted peace and security and an incorruptible government,

I was being perfectly serious. If I learned one thing from General Leighton Howard and his pack of mad bastards it was that this world needs saving and it finally has people capable of saving it."

She cut the link, but not before Mike saw the stricken look on Matt's face. The screens fell dark.

"Wow," said Tim. "It just hit me—we're superheroes. We're the Avengers and the X-Men all rolled into one. Aw, man! I guess that makes me the Hulk, right? I mean, I'd be Scarlet Witch except—y'know, girl. I guess Sara can be the Scarlet Witch. Black Widow is cooler, but no superpowers. And Mike, who will you be? I mean, you look a lot like Bruce Banner, but—"

"Iron Man," said Mike, wondering if he could think Tim to silence, and if he could do it without killing him. "I'll be Iron Man."

Sara cut across their conversation. "If you boys are finished playing make-believe, I'd like to sit down and come up with a coherent list of demands. We have an opportunity, here, to do some real good in the world. We should be ready to take it."

"You think they won't try to take us down?" Tim asked. "Win our trust by sending Matt in and then—boom!—try to blow us up or something?"

"They might. If you're afraid of them making Matt a suicide bomber, though, I think you can kiss that idea good-bye. Matt Streegman isn't the sacrificial-lamb type. But he might be a piece of a bigger plan." Sara slid into a chair and swiveled it to face the two men. "We killed American soldiers."

"Soldiers who were engaged in treason," Mike reminded her.

Tim snapped his fingers and pointed at Mike. "Yeah. We did the country a service and they know it. We took care of a problem they didn't even know they had."

Sara speared them, one after the other, with her pale, gray gaze. "*Someone* knew they had it. Howard wasn't bankrolling Deep Shield all by his lonesome. He was working with or for someone else. Someone with much more clout—possibly even political clout."

"Someone in the White House, you mean?" asked Tim, as if the sentence tasted like chocolate.

Sara nodded. "Or Congress. Or the Joint Chiefs. We don't know. Which means—"

"Trust no one!" Tim crowed.

"Trust no one," Sara agreed without even a hint of sarcasm.

The chill that swept Mike's body went all the way to the bone. He shrugged it off by focusing all of his consciousness on Sacha's tracking of the Wi-Fi signal from Matt's location. It was a strange sensation, feeling the signal as indescribable textures in the air, tasting it, smelling it, simply *knowing* what it was and where it was coming from. He immersed himself in the tingling awareness and tried not to think about trust.

WHEN KRISTIAN LORSTAD ARRIVED FOR his second attempt at learning to zeta, he had two of his fellow Learned in tow: the mysterious and aloof Alexis and a young Englishman he introduced as Giles Camden. Giles was one of the newest of the Learned and had only just crawled out of the tank after his first immersion. Eugene thought he seemed a bit bewildered.

Lorstad insisted that Alexis have the first try, so Eugene and Dice set her up with the rig just as they had their own Zetas in the earliest days of kinetic technology. The positron cap was on her head, cabled to the kinetic converter and thence to the Brewster-Brenton Brain Pattern Monitor and Roboticus Mark II.

Chuck described the principles on which the machinery operated—reading the subject's brain waves and converting them into discrete impulses.

"Those waves can easily move a stylus on a chart," Chuck told her. "So there's no reason they can't move Roboticus there. So, for the first trial, just concentrate on the joystick on top of the robot. It has a full three hundred sixty degrees of movement, but I want you to just concern yourself with back and forth right now."

"So simple?" asked Alexis. "I could take that device and throw it across the room."

"Yes, using your immersion-enhanced abilities. I want you to just use naked thought to move the joystick. Try to push it forward, please." Chuck's voice was gentle and his facial expression patiently neutral.

Eugene admired the hell out of the way he could do that. Chuck handled disbelief, arrogance, and outright mockery as if they were pleasantries. Euge wanted to snark back, despite the fact that he knew he wasn't good at it.

Alexis shrugged, closed her eyes for a moment, then opened them and focused her gaze on Roboticus. After a moment, her brow knit and her lips tightened. She gripped the arms of her chair.

"Don't try so hard," Chuck said softly.

Alexis glared at him, then back at the bot. It tumbled forward about five feet and ended up against a lab table with its little wheels in the air.

"This is ridiculous," she said. "You're asking me to ignore powers I have already developed. Let me use my learning."

"But that would defeat the purpose of what we're trying to do."

Before she could protest, Eugene interjected.

"You know," he said, looking at Chuck, "that might actually not be a bad idea, if only to establish a control among the—the Learned. I mean, maybe the abilities can be built up even with the power assist just through practice."

"Do you predict that it will?" asked Lorstad hopefully.

Chuck frowned. "No. I'd actually predict that as the Learned's enhanced abilities waned, she'd find it more difficult to do what would be easy at first attempt. But I'm willing to be proved wrong," he added at Alexis's sharp glance. "It's also possible that the abilities would strengthen with repeated use, though it might take longer than for a—uh—a nonimmersive talent."

"That's absurd," said Alexis. "There's no such thing as—" She cut off, her gaze flitting to Lorstad. "I . . . apologize. That was out of line. Kristian insists that your talents—if not innate—do not make use of immersion technology. I suppose I must accept that as fact."

But she didn't accept it as fact, Eugene was pretty sure. Her world was under threat. The typical first response to such a threat was denial. These upstarts had walked in and revealed that her years of submersion were essentially for naught. Not only that but the tanks may have produced inferior abilities across the board. Considering this she seemed to handle things with a fair amount of poise. She made repeated tries to not make use of her extended sense set but merely to operate the machinery via the homely activity of her imagination. Each time, though, the same thing: failure.

Not close.

No cigar.

No biscuit.

During a break, Chuck put Joey into the rig and got him to send Roboticus on a hesitant ramble up and down the center of the lab. Giles was next and managed to move the little bot in a timid, but straight, line. Chuck had probably intended these demonstrations to show Alexis what she could accomplish or to at least spark a sense of competition, à la "Anything You Can Do, I Can Do Better." But she just failed more her second time in the chair. Toward the end, Alexis simply began using her power assist to move Roboticus around the lab, almost certainly out of frustration.

It was a most entertaining display—especially the levitating and rolling across the ceiling and down the wall part—but it was next to useless in terms of what Lorstad wanted his people to learn. Well, at least where Alexis was concerned.

Euge gave Chuck a sidewise glance. He knew what he was

thinking: Her EEG is not very interesting. Sure it hits some gamma, but above that it really isn't that impressive. What exactly is the source of the Learned's power?

Chuck diplomatically assigned her the role of Control 2. Alexis's performance yielded no useful observable data. Her machinations were fun to watch but not very helpful to the cause as a whole. Joey Blossom would serve as control for completely untrained nonimmersive talents and Alexis would be control for immersive talents. Lorstad was not particularly pleased with this; he clearly wanted evidence or a harbinger that the full-fledged Learned could overcome their immersion training—or at least hold it in abeyance while flexing other muscles. That zeta abilities had eluded him and his co-psychokineticists so completely was beginning to grate and continued to confuse. This was more difficult than he imagined. Eugene had quipped that in order for the *Learned* to *learn* to induce zeta they would have to *unlearn* what they had *learned*. Lorstad agreed with his mildly humorous assessment, if not the jokey tone behind it. Regardless, he did not believe that instant mastery should be the standard, but surely a stronger beginning.

The whole session seemed like a fail for everyone but Joey and Giles, but by the end of it, Eugene had gotten further insight (he thought) into the Benefactors' issues with kinetic technology. He tried to articulate it during his debriefing session with Chuck.

"Remember what you said about confidence? That maybe I lacked confidence in my ability to develop zeta waves?" Eugene stood in the door of Chuck's office, realizing he also lacked confidence to advance theories about his ability (or inability) to develop zeta waves.

Chuck looked up at him. "I'm not likely to forget it. Why do you ask?"

After a moment of indecision, Eugene entered the office, closed the door, and came to sit in his habitual spot across the desk from

Chuck. He leaned both elbows on the desktop. "I think we nailed it—the Learned are suffering from the same . . . mental habit."

"Go on . . ."

"Now that I have seen more of the Benefactors' attempts . . . look, I was watching Alexis—her facial expressions, her color, her brain waves. She was frustrated, annoyed, dismissive. You heard her: she even doubts, deep down inside, that non-Learned can do what Lanfen and Mini do. Or that they should even *bother* trying. When Joey took a turn at the controls and got Robbie to take a walkabout, she was angry. And *that* was when she decided not to try 'our way' anymore."

Chuck nodded. "Yes, and?"

"I think she was angry because she felt suddenly inferior to a mere mortal—"

"Euge . . ."

"No, this is something we have to factor in. Alexis and her fellow Benefactors clearly feel a bit superior to the rest of us. No—that's wrong. Not a 'bit.' They feel *vastly* superior. Joey, to Alexis, is a—an ox. A lesser mammal. I doubt Alexis imagines that any naturally developed faculties she has in common with him—or with me—could allow her to do what immersion therapy allows her to do."

Chuck laughed. "Hard to imagine that the Learned suffer from a lack of confidence. Or a lack of faith. They seem pretty sure of themselves."

Euge gave him a wry look. "You know better than that."

Chuck's smile vanished. "Yes, I do. And I suspect your instincts are good, in this case."

"So, where does that put us?"

Chuck stared ruminatively out through the glass walls of his office at where Joey continued to work with Roboticus. "Focus on Giles Camden. If your thinking is correct, then what the Learned need to see is that one of their number who hasn't had his circuitry redirected by immersion therapy can make strides with kinetic training." He paused, then shook his head.

"What?" Eugene asked.

"We were right—we're no closer to being able to give Lorstad some foolproof formula for churning out zeta talents. It's not as simple as surreptitiously switching off the interface this time. You can't *make* someone have faith in their ability to do something. There's no pill or shot or vitamin we can give them to inspire certainty that they can affect the physical universe with their raw brain waves."

Eugene chewed on that for a moment, then asked, "How did *you* get that certainty?"

"I saw it work."

"You *theorized* that it would work first, *then* you saw it work. So you *suspected* it would work before you *saw* it work."

"Yes, okay."

"So," said Eugene, "maybe the question is: how did Lanfen or any of the other Zetas get that certainty? We basically took Mini's training wheels off without her knowing, but the others?"

"They had no idea what we ultimately wanted them to accomplish. In fact, I'd say *we* had no idea what we ultimately wanted them to accomplish until Mike showed he could manipulate machinery directly. They had no preconceived notions about . . ."

Chuck's voice ran down and stopped.

"So, maybe there's nothing we can do," Eugene said, reading his face. "We can't mind-wipe them and make them forget they know what we're trying to get them to learn. But that's nuts—they've *seen* it work, just like you and I did."

"No faith," Chuck murmured, his gaze unfocused. "No faith in humanity. No faith in *human beings*."

Eugene felt a thoroughly uncomfortable and slimy chill trail its fingers down his spine. "They think they're a different species already—is that what you're saying? Like—like they're from outer space or something?"

Chuck stood and started to pace—a good sign, Eugene thought.

"I don't think that's relevant," Chuck said. "That can be overcome . . . maybe. Hopefully."

He took a couple of strides with his eyes closed. "It's time to move on to Lanfen's misdirection techniques. Maybe we can force them to act unconsciously, instinctively."

"It's like the mom whose adrenaline allows her to lift the car off her kid. Right? It's like the brilliant things some people do when they're not thinking about it. It's spontaneous, reactive. Okay. Great. How do we get that to happen in the lab with Lorstad and Alexis?"

"Lanfen and I have an idea; I need to run it by everyone else, start implementation." Chuck, eyes wide open, turned on his heel and headed back out into the lab, calling, "All hands on deck! We have an experiment to design."

MATT TOLD HIMSELF HE KNEW the three people he was going into the mountain to see. He had trained them, worked side by side with them. They were colleagues, friends even. There was no need for nerves. No need for his stomach to be tying itself in knots.

He checked the receiver in his ear for the twentieth time as he moved to the outer perimeter of the reconnaissance camp, where the LED lamps ceased to shed their light. Due north. He stared up through the trees at the mountain. In the twilight it was hard to see the burn, though the smell of it was still heavy in the air.

There was movement in the brush to his right and a gleaming ninja bot glided out of the woods to train its optics on him. A knot formed in his throat and rolled down, hard and cold, into the pit of his stomach. He felt faint.

"Well," he said breathlessly. "Hello there."

"It's me, Doc. It's Mike," the robot said, then motioned to itself with one hand. "This is Sacha."

The fact that it was Mike, and the personal touch of his introducing the robot by name, made Matt relax. "Hey, Mike. You and Sacha are my escort?"

"Yeah. Look, we've got a lot of ground to cover—several miles. I figured I'd carry you. Unless they'd let you drive a jeep. The road's pretty torn up."

"Carry me," Matt repeated. "Sure. Why not. I've never gone anywhere by robot before." He picked his way across the clearing to the robot and stopped. "How do we do this?"

In answer, Sacha squatted slightly and made a ledge of its arms and hands. "Have a seat, Doc," Mike said.

He laughed uneasily, but turned and seated himself in the improvised chair. The robot straightened, lifting Matt easily from the ground, then turned and began a swift, ground-eating lope toward the mountain. It was exhilarating and made Matt experience the potential of these devices in a completely different way.

"Mike, this is incredible!" The words were whipped from his lips by the breeze of their passage. "Can you imagine what bots like this could mean for firefighters and EMTs? Can you imagine being able to go into a burning building or some other death trap and rescue people without risking the lives of the emergency workers? And the strength—a team of these things would be able to dig into debris fields and fallen buildings, rescue stranded hikers and mountain climbers."

"Yeah, you're right," said Mike's voice in his ear. "Funny, none of that stuff was on the short list of things you wanted to explore. Not enough money in it, Doc?"

Matt started to offer a sarcastic and angry comeback, but he stopped himself. Mike was right. He had been focused on where they could get the most financial support, but those ideas had all been in the back of his head. At least, they'd been on Chuck's short list.

"I thought we were working with the real government, Mike.

I thought they'd have more to invest than private parties. I had no idea what we were really dealing with."

"Yeah," Mike-Sacha said, "the devil."

"Can't argue with that," Matt said, and fell silent.

It took Sacha less than ten minutes to hike him up the slope and into a narrow cave. There he set Matt down on the sandy floor and moved to what looked like a blank wall of stone. "We're here," he told the wall. It vanished, displaying a thick metal door that slid to one side with a grinding sound that nearly made Matt want to scream. It was like a giant raking metal nails across a chalkboard . . . in a cathedral.

When the painful sound died, Matt found himself staring down the throat of a smooth stone bore that ran directly into the mountain.

"This isn't the main entrance." He looked up at the bot beside him.

"No," it said. "This is one of several secret entrances we've found since we . . . since we were brought here. The main way is . . . well, it's pretty well scragged."

Matt took a deep breath. "Yeah. I figured."

It took another five minutes to make their way into the heart of the mountain and up an elevator that shouldn't have been working—its controls were dark and dead. Matt was impressed.

"You doing this yourself?" he asked Mike's bot.

There was a slight hesitation before Mike said, "Yeah. Mechanicals are my thing, remember?"

Matt nodded, his mind already beginning to work on the mathematics of the situation. The Alphas were scared. Backs to the wall. Two formulas suggested themselves—multiply the fear, hoping it would drive them to surrender (not likely), or assuage it by talking up how important their future contributions to mankind would be.

That was certainly the option Chuck would take, and Matt

was astute enough to recognize that his erstwhile partner was a lot savvier about human nature than he was. But then he was unsettled by the question that popped into his head:

Are the Alphas still human?

THERE WAS STILL A BIT of weirdness to inhabiting a bot that Mike found disorienting. If he didn't focus tightly, the dissonance of seeing two versions of the world at the same time was dizzy-making. He was sitting at his console in ops; he was riding up an elevator with Matt Streegman—and activating the elevator and running the bot. Mike had always been pretty good at multitasking, but this was a new high. It was like that old circus trick of juggling mismatched objects—bowling balls, batons, and chain saws. He'd experimented with like objects, of course. He could handle about a dozen bots now if they were all the same type, but this was novel. He puzzled over how he'd done it and realized, again, the truth of that old adage that Necessity is a mother. If you needed to do something urgently enough, you simply acted . . . as he'd done with the focused objective of retrieving Matt Streegman.

It all seemed counterintuitive: focus more narrowly to broaden what you could do. And yet, here they were. They reached the ops level and stepped out of the elevator into the control room. Mike stationed Sacha at the rear of the room, before standing himself and turning to face Matt.

"Hey, Doc. Welcome to Olympus." He used the term ironically and got a perverse satisfaction at having beaten Timmy-Troll to the punch.

"Hey," said Matt, then looked past him at Sara and Tim. "Hi, guys. How're you holding out?"

"Very well, thanks," said Sara. She moved to meet him in the semicircular area framed by the curving banks of control consoles. She put her hand out to shake his. "Good to see you again . . . I hope. You have news from the outside world?"

Matt nodded. "I've spoken at length with President Ellis and the Joint Chiefs. I'm here basically to find out what you need from them to come out of the mountain and get back to your lives."

Mike's heart clenched in his chest at the idea of getting back to his life. "Hell," he said, "a plane ticket to Toronto would do it for me."

Sara gave him a look. "Down, boy. Remember, this isn't about us." She faced Matt again. "It's about the world, Matt. It's about how crazy and screwed up this world is because of men like Howard. Because of power-hungry tribal leaders and congressmen and prime ministers and ayatollahs. It's because those people don't care what happens to people who are not directly supporting them. What we need in order to leave here is the certainty that the president of this country will use our powers as a threat. All military activities will cease or we will act to stop them. Trust me when I say we can."

Matt took a deep breath. "Oh, I trust that, all right. You want the U.S. to what—weaponize you?"

Sara looked pissed. "Don't put it like that. It's not about us. It's about all the people who suffer and die because world leaders are consumed with greed and full of themselves. We want to go before the United Nations. The president needs to get them to call a special meeting of the Security Council first, then of the General Assembly. We'll put our proposition to them: if military aggression doesn't stop within a reasonable amount of time, *we will stop it*. That clear enough?"

"Yeah," Tim chimed in. "And if they need proof that we can, we'll give 'em proof. All the proof they'll need."

"Okay," Matt said, but he didn't look as if anything was okay. "How do you propose we proceed?"

"They send in some transport—drivers, unarmed," said Sara. "We leave here with an escort of ninja bots just to secure our safety. No tricks. No attempts to tranq us or kill us or render us unconscious."

"I'm pretty sure I can guarantee that," Matt said. "President Ellis and her staff have seen what you guys have done. She gets the picture. She also recognizes what a boon your abilities are to humanity and I think she gets that she can't do this by the old playbook."

"Just pretty sure?" asked Mike.

Matt turned to look at him—met his eyes. "No—I'm sure, Mike. Ellis is a straight shooter. She doesn't want to anger you, and she doesn't want to lose your talents to the world. She knows what she's got here. You three are unique."

"Unique?" Sara repeated, her eyes fixing on Matt's face. "What happened to the others? What happened to Mini and Lanfen? Where are they? Where's Chuck?"

Her fists were flexing at her sides and Mike sensed that she was getting revved up.

Matt raised his hands in a placating gesture. "They're safe somewhere. I've been in touch with them. I just don't know where they are—honest. If you come out of hiding, I think that will persuade them to come out as well."

Sara regarded him narrowly for a moment, then said, "You're wearing a wire, right?"

Matt hesitated, then nodded.

"Then Madam President has heard our demands. Talk to them. If we don't get out of here safely . . ."

"Admiral, you heard that?" Matt asked whoever was on the receiving end of his wire. "Okay," he said after a moment, then to Sara: "They'll send transport just as you asked. How many ninjas do you want to take?"

"Two for each of us."

"They'll send two Humvees."

"And don't imagine that by separating us, you can overcome us," Sara warned. "You can't."

"They won't try. And . . ." He paused to listen. "They're talking to the UN already."

Sara nodded and relaxed visibly. Mike felt the knot in his own chest uncoil. Maybe this would work out. Maybe he wouldn't have to spend the rest of his days hiding here or somewhere else. He hadn't been kidding about that ticket to Toronto, though. He'd gladly go back to his old life and never use his kinetic abilities again if he could arrange that. Maybe the Alpha Team didn't need to stick together.

The quiet of the ops theater was shredded by the sudden shrill buzz of a proximity alarm. "What the hell?" Tim jerked around to stare at the tactical displays at the head of the room. "That can't be the transport already."

It wasn't. It was a flock of drones flying low to the ground and approaching the mountaintop from a dozen different directions. The monitors showed them as tiny, darting ornithopters as they overflew the peak, scudding even lower to drop small, round objects—

"The air intakes!" Tim snarled. "They're dropping crap near the air intakes!"

"What sort of crap?" Sara demanded, as several of the objects exploded, tearing the camouflaged covers from the vents that brought fresh air in from the outside. Clouds of vapor settled into the open intakes.

Sara turned on Matt. "What is this, Matt? What are they doing?"

He shook his head, eyes wide with fear. "I don't know. I swear! It's not—it's not us. It's not the government." He spun away from Sara, putting fingers to his ears. "Someone's bombing us!" he shouted to his unseen listeners. "Someone's sent drones!"

"It's some kind of gas!" said Tim. "The assholes are gassing us!"

Sara flung herself at her console, system schematics appearing on the screen as fast as she could bring them there. "There! The ventilation system." She concentrated for a moment, then shook her head. "Electronic controls are down. Mike, you'll have to close them manually." Throat constricting from the very thought of breathing unknown chemicals, Mike hurried to peer over Sara's shoulder at the schematics. Shafts in white, a series of four doors in each shaft, shown in green. Green was open.

"Need the hatch design, Sara," he murmured.

She called it up. The hatches were irises. A series of irises—four at intervals along the shaft. Good forethought. He envisioned the shafts, the irising hatches. He felt them. Solid. Well lubed. He closed them one after the other, deepest to shallowest, not even considering what that would tell the other Alphas about the extent of his abilities.

"Wow," said Tim, shutting down the alarm's bleating. "That was close."

Sara looked at Mike over her shoulder. "That was impressive, Micky. You shut all the vents down at once. I had no idea you could do that."

"Neither did I," he fibbed. "Adrenaline is your friend, I guess."

Sara rose from her chair and turned to face Matt again. He had backed up against an empty station and was half-sitting on the console. He looked . . . scared. Mike had never seen Matt scared before.

"A better friend than some, I guess," she said. She advanced on Matt slowly, step by step, her expression unreadable. "Do you have an antidote on you, Matt? A gas mask? You're not the type to sacrifice yourself for the good of your fellow creatures, so I have to assume you either came prepared or the gas wasn't deadly."

"I told you," Matt said. "That wasn't—I can't believe President Ellis would do that."

"Even to send a message? Well, we'll just send one right back."

Mike realized what she was going to do only seconds before Sara moved. It was only a graceful gesture of one hand, as if she were reaching for something. In that simple action, she electrified the console Matt was leaning against—every metallic surface sizzling with blue-white energy.

He cried out once, horribly, and spasmed, static arcing between him and the console. His body was smoking when it hit the floor, giving up the aroma of cooked meat. Mike didn't make it to the head before he was sick.

"WHAT THE HELL WAS THAT?" Joan Hand stared at the live images from the recon teams low on the mountainside. "Where did those drones come from? I want telemetry, dammit!"

"Dr. Streegman's line is dead," said the communications technician quietly.

Margaret was pretty sure that meant Dr. Streegman was dead as well. She knew one thing and one thing only—somewhere in the nation she was supposed to be leading, there were people who did not want the Zetas to come peacefully out of the mountain and they knew, better than she did, how the installation was laid out.

"We need to find out who the hell ordered this attack. More important, we need to find the other Zetas," she said, her voice cutting through the chaos in the room.

"And we need to do it before someone else does."

MIKE HAD SACHA CARRY MATT Streegman's body out of the mountain and deliver it to the government communications outpost near the base of the slope. He had not wanted to touch the body, had not wanted to look at it. It was a caricature of the man—an empty, burnt-out husk from which the soul had been violently expelled. He'd read once that people who died that suddenly didn't even realize they were dead; their souls lingered helplessly at the place their bodies were killed, unable to move on. He wasn't sure he believed it, but even after Sacha left ops with the corpse, he felt Matt's presence—his last moments of fear and agony—like an accusation that hung in the cool air.

He said nothing to either Sara or Tim about how he felt. He

simply cradled the body in Sacha's steel arms and carried it to the bottom of the mountain. He meant to do it in remote mode until Sacha reached the spot Sara had designated the body would be delivered. He had not wanted to inhabit the bot on this grim journey. But when the time came, he made himself see through Sacha's optics, made himself speed down the mountain to the government camp, made himself own the death. He had believed Matt when he said he hadn't known about the chemical weapons someone had dumped near their air intakes. He even half-believed it wasn't the president who had ordered it.

As a boy, Mike had seen an old black-and-white movie called *The Day the Earth Stood Still*. The most vivid image he could recall from the film was the alien hero's robot, Gort, cradling his master's limp body after he had been injured by fearful humans. He saw that image reflected in the eyes of the soldiers he faced when he finally reached the government camp perimeter. He hesitated only a moment, then laid Matt down on the forest floor and stepped back.

"Give them the message," said Sara, close to his ear.

"This . . . this is what happens when people lie to us," Mike said stiffly. Then he turned Sacha on his metal heel and rolled him back up the mountain. The whole time, though, he couldn't help but wonder:

What do we do when we start lying to ourselves?

Chapter 9

SILENT RUNNING

"You look worried." Lanfen slid into the chair across from Chuck at the table in the canteen.

He glanced up at her. "Funny. I was going to say the same thing about you."

"Aren't we the observant pair. You first." She set her teacup down and broke open a warmed scone.

"Matt hasn't messaged me for days. Almost a week. Last I heard, he'd made contact with the Alphas and was going into the mountain to meet with them."

"You think—what?—that Sara and the others are holding him hostage or something?"

"Or that he didn't want to come out for some reason. It's just weird that he wouldn't ping me."

"Maybe he can't. I mean, they're still sort of cut off and—" She broke off, shaking her head. "Yeah, if they've got a line to the outside world, I have to think they've taken advantage of that to get a foothold beyond the mountain. I guess it makes more sense that they're not allowing him to communicate with the outside world, or that he's working something out with them." She blew out a gust of air. "It really sucks to be deaf, dumb, and blind, doesn't it?"

Chuck blinked at her. "Did you just say 'sucks'?"

She grinned. "I guess I've been hanging out around Dice and Joey too much."

He smiled at that. "So, you had something you wanted to tell me?"

She sobered suddenly, her face going with lightning speed from a smile to an uneasy frown. "When I was meditating out on the deck this morning, I noticed that there are security guards patrolling the slopes that weren't there when we first arrived. There are also cameras. I actually saw them putting in some of those during the night awhile back."

"How far back is awhile back?"

Lanfen grimaced. "The cameras went in not long after I showed off for Lorstad. I think he saw potential for escape. The security prowlers are new. In the last several days. I guessed maybe they're afraid I might take up desert parkour and run away or something."

Chuck felt his neck and cheeks grow hot. Did this increased attention to security have something to do with Matt going into Deep Shield? Did Lorstad figure he and his team might want to go back east to join him? Even if he had answers to those questions, though, the key thing was that the Learned clearly didn't trust Chuck or his team. "We shouldn't *have* to escape. We're allegedly here for our own protection."

"Protection at a price, Chuck. They want something from us. A formula. A path to success. The key to the universe. They know how much we're 'distracted' by what's going on back east."

"If Matt can't fix whatever went wrong with the Alphas, I don't see what good a formula is going to do the Learned." Chuck hesitated. "No, that's not true. I see that they think—or thought—that the combination of their conditioning with our training would be unbeatable. They could just squash the Alphas' rebellion."

Lanfen met his gaze. "What if they don't want to, Chuck? What if they really take this whole Learned versus Unlearned thing to heart? What if they don't care what happens to the masses of people in the world who aren't them or us?"

Chilling thought. "What makes you even think that?"

She leaned toward him across the table. "Do you know what they call their lab staff? The non-Learned ones?"

Chuck blinked. "'Our staff'?"

"Ha. Yes—but only in front of us. In private they call them 'the Profane.' I heard Alexis use the word a couple of times when she was talking with Lorstad after her failed attempt to use your tech. It bothered her that one of the 'Profane' could do what she couldn't. I don't like the sound of that."

"Neither do I," Chuck admitted. "But the staff have names for them, too, I'm sure."

"Yes. I've heard Joey call them 'the Royalty.' They sure act like that."

He had to admit she was right and that it didn't seem nearly as pejorative as 'the Profane.' It also really bothered him. If they considered their staff so completely "other" from themselves, then that same sentiment must apply to Lanfen, and Mini, and everyone else Chuck had led to . . . wherever the hell they were.

All of that added up to one thing: he needed to get a better sense of Lorstad's commitment to keeping them at the Center.

Or else he needed to figure out a way to get out of here—and soon.

"WE DIDN'T LIE TO YOU!" The voice was President Ellis's, filtered through the ops intercom system—which did nothing to diminish the stark alarm in it.

Mike trod the elliptical machine at a punishing pace. He was sweating, his muscles burning, and his mind still would not shut off. He had made the unwelcome discovery half an hour ago that repetitive physical action just left the brain alone to do whatever the hell it wanted, and his brain had fixated on Matt Streegman's death. Still, he pushed himself. The alternative was to listen to Sara's confrontation with President Ellis. He wanted no part of that, either, but his attention had been arrested.

Sara argued the improbability that the president of the United States didn't know what her own military resources were doing. It was a laughable argument under the circumstances. He had to believe Sara realized that, considering their experience with Howard, but was just playing hardball . . . or stalling to give Tim time to do what he did best—run rampant along electronic pathways. That was the plan, he knew: for Tim to establish unbreakable links with the outside world, something the president was making possible by using the communications camp as a relay station for her dialogues with the Alphas.

Fed up with the elliptical's inability to clear his mind, Mike hopped off the machine and left the gym, running. Maybe if he buried himself deeply enough in the corridors of Deep Shield (he refused to think of it as Olympus anymore) he could get lost or maybe find a way out that neither Sara nor Tim would notice. He stopped running when he reached the charging bays that housed the army of robots. There were almost a thousand of them, by his count, all shapes and sizes. Some of them were so bizarre he couldn't even guess what they were intended for. He felt most comfortable with the Hob-bots—the same basic model as Sacha and only a bit larger and heavier than the prototypes Lanfen had named Frodo and Bilbo.

Mike wandered into one of the bay-cum-labs and sat down on the edge of Sacha's charging station. The bot itself was up in ops at one of the stations Deep Shield had placed there in case the installation were overrun and they had to withdraw to the core.

He studied the remaining robots, familiar and friendly, and wondered how in God's name he had come to be here. How had what looked like a golden opportunity to rise above his career as a construction manager and structural engineer morphed into this? He was hiding in a mountain, fearful and feared, labeled a traitor—labeled a *murderer,* and in the company of other murderers. His family—the people he had worked so hard to protect—were lying low in another country, and there was every reason to believe his two children would grow up without him.

He didn't realize he was crying until the first tears dripped from his chin to stain his jeans. He was broken. So broken maybe his family wouldn't want him back if he *could* leave this damned place. He fell to his knees on the hard, cold floor of the lab and prayed.

MARGARET ELLIS WAS OUT OF her depth, and comforted herself that any president would have felt the same in this situation. The world leaders with whom she was meeting via a secure uplink and the physically present Canadian prime minister—Stephen Heaney—were similarly out of their depth.

Several were of the opinion that she should simply drop a tactical nuke on Pine Ridge Mountain and have done with it. She tried to make them understand that—besides the fact that she wasn't really comfortable with using nuclear weapons, let alone using them against her own people on her own soil—the people hiding in the mountain had proven their ability to knock just about anything out of the sky. She studied the faces of these national leaders—displayed in individual windows on the huge LED screen in the Sit Room—for any sign that they comprehended the situation.

It was perhaps human nature that some of them didn't . . . or didn't believe what she was telling them.

"If you are unable to handle the situation, Madam President," said President Valentin of Russia, "perhaps you should delegate to someone who *can* handle it."

She almost rose to that bait, but when you're a woman in politics—hell, a woman in general—you're used to men exerting their chauvinism and questioning your abilities. It was not a surprise it came from Valentin—he might have been just as belligerent with a male president, though she doubted it—and that made it even easier to dismiss as the posturing of a man who didn't want to emulate the time of Stalin, but the time of the czars.

"You've all seen the video of what these people can do," she argued in return. "Trying to sneak a nuke past them would be impossible, irresponsible, and possibly criminal. Besides which, it's not their fault they're in this position. They didn't set out to take over the world."

"No, it is the fault of rogue elements in your own military." There was a hint of smugness in that. *Asshole.*

"In times past," added President Kavan Isfahani of Iran, "were this situation to unfold on someone else's territory, you would simply send in drones or black ops teams or even bombers to take them out. You would not even bother to consult with the leaders of that country's government."

"You're correct. But this is not 'times past,' Mr. Isfahani," Margaret reminded him. "If anything, this is a future none of us ever even bothered planning for, let alone imagining. But it is happening, and *I* am the president you're dealing with now. And let me remind you all—once again—that the last attempt someone made to deal with the Zetas violently, using drone technology, was foiled completely. Unfortunately, it was attributed to me, though I had nothing to do with it. Nevertheless, it *failed* and resulted in the death of one of the co-creators of the Zeta program."

Margaret was still haunted by the image of the robot carrying Matt Streegman's ruined body out of the forest. She shook off the revulsion that evoked and pushed on.

"The takeaway from this, ladies and gentlemen, is that the

Zetas are expecting attacks and they are more than able to stop them. The attempt to drop chemical weapons on them was unsuccessful, but not disastrous for anyone but Dr. Streegman. What you're suggesting, Mr. President," she said, looking at Valentin, "even with a small, tactical device, is literally the nuclear option. In other words, the last possible thing we should consider." She could see he was going to interject, but she raised her hand to cut him off and pressed on. "One thing I don't think you're understanding is that these three are able to *control* matter. So, what if we send a nuclear missile at them, and instead of detonating or disabling it, they *commandeer* it? Then we have three of the most dangerous people in the world with a nuke in their back pocket."

Let him chew on that for a moment.

"They cannot possibly be that powerful, can they?" asked the British prime minister, Angeline Foley. "Yes, you've shown the destruction of the Washington Monument and the devastation done to the Deep Shield camp, but surely they're not—"

Whatever Foley had been going to say was cut off by the sudden appearance on the huge wall display of a minotaur in full 3-D, wielding a mace on a chain—no, a morning star. It appeared, first, in each of the individual displays that made up the larger unit, then it took over the entire screen so that it seemed to loom over the group in the Situation Room.

"Hello, humans." It addressed the gathered leaders in a young, male voice, completely ignoring the verbal expressions of surprise and annoyance from the assembled heads of state, who all apparently were being treated to the same view.

Margaret glanced down at the file in front of her. This was probably Timothy Desmond, twenty-six, game programmer. In the file photo, he looked like a college kid—mass of curly dark brown hair, saucy grin, watery eyes. Very different from the creature standing before them now.

"I suspect you're arguing over what to do about those damned weirdos in the mountain," he continued. "I mean, you guys are always arguing, right, so why stop now when you've *really* got something to bitch about? It must be nice, having all that time and power to not actually *accomplish* anything. We here in Olympus don't have time for bitching, though, so let's cut to the chase."

Margaret glanced sharply at her communications technician, but the young woman only shook her head and mouthed, *No control.*

No control. That was a pretty fair summing up of this entire situation.

"Here's what we want," the voice continued, seeming to come from the lips of the fantastical figure on the screen. "And you really ought to believe President Ellis when she says we will make it so if you won't. You will, quite simply, stop fighting your crappy little wars. Mother Russia will get her tentacles out of Ukraine and other territory she's got her eye on. Iran, you're going to stop underwriting terrorism. Britain . . . as you were, but you could send more relief to the Uyghurs. And China—you've got a lot of work to do. No more taking over random islands. And take better care of your people. No more jailing dissidents. We want them all released, pronto. Not to mention messing with Taiwan and Nepal. Or posturing with India. Speaking of which—India and Pakistan? Give it up in the Kashmir. Israel and Palestine, the time for dicking around is past. No more bombings in Israel. No more rockets into the West Bank or Gaza." The minotaur seemed to look around. "There's obviously more, but you get the idea: whatever violence there is in the world will stop now."

The Russian president was the first to react to this pronouncement. "We cannot simply stop—"

"Of course you can. That's what you don't seem to understand. *Of course you can.* You just stop. There—that's easy. Because if you don't, well, that won't be so easy. We'll have to do it for you and you won't much like our methods. I can pretty much guarantee that."

"What my esteemed colleague means," said the eminently practical German chancellor, Ruthven Salzburg, "is that there are governments and groups who are, shall we say, disinclined to peace. Governments and groups over whom we have neither control nor authority."

On the screen, the minotaur spread his beefy hands in a gesture of magnanimity. "Hey, that's what *we're* here for, guys. Handle your own shit first. Then you do whatever you can to convince these outliers that we are serious as hell and won't tolerate any dissension. Let them know the terrible consequences of disobedience to divine will."

The image on the screen changed suddenly to show a scene of such carnage and devastation that Margaret cried out—as did a number of the other statesmen and women online with her. She heard Stephen Heaney murmur "My God" and suspected it was a literal prayer.

The location seemed to be a vast cavern with a road running through its center. In the foreground were the twisted and crushed remains of armored vehicles, around and about which were strewn dozens of bodies in military camouflage. Blood and body parts were everywhere and smoke, steam, and dust rose into the still air. The destruction—the bodies, the ruined vehicles—stretched away into the distance, stopping at what once had been a massive steel bulkhead. It, too, was a wreck.

"This is what happens to the fools who challenge us," the minotaur said. "I hope you guys aren't fools. 'Cause, if you are, then you're gonna end up just like these guys. That's a promise." He chuckled. "So, you show your roguey buddies this video and any others you think it might take to persuade them that they need to beat their swords into plowshares and their tanks into theme park rides. And if they don't heed the warning, then you just stay out of our way and let us do what we do best—doing your jobs and stopping the bad guys." There was an odd moment of silence in which the minotaur looked over its shoulder, shrugged, and said, "Uh, someone else wants to talk at ya," before stepping to one side.

A woman appeared on the screen—like the minotaur, a rendered image, but to creepier perfection. She had a shock of red hair and was dressed in a formfitting black catsuit. She wore a half mask. Ellis almost laughed at the absurdity of it, indeed would have if she hadn't been privy to all that had been unfolding the last few days.

"What my impulsive friend has failed to communicate is that we have the means now to *know* whether you are complying with our demands. We have access to your worldwide networks, including many of the secret ones, and we'll soon have access to all of those as well. You have no firewalls we cannot breach and no communications we cannot surveil. Your rogue enemies are no less vulnerable than you are. Which means that we can also determine if they're failing to comply. To be clear, this is the opportunity you've all been looking for. We can solve these problems for you, and allow you to focus on actually helping your own people. But we're not going to sit idly by while you work so hard to destroy the world, which seems to be your primary purpose right now.

"Of course, we don't exactly trust you to do this rather simple request, but we're going to give you the benefit of the doubt for the time being. That said, we think it prudent to give you a deadline by which we expect any aggressions you are engaged in to cease. So, you have a month. That means if you've got troops anywhere that are not doing relief work, they will be withdrawn by one month from tomorrow. And don't bother trying to redefine 'relief work' to mask aggression. We know the difference, I assure you."

"Impossible!" exclaimed Valentin. "It would take months—"

"Hardly, Mr. President. You got them in place in less time than that. You can withdraw them at the same pace. Am I clear?"

There was silence.

"Am I *clear*?" the woman repeated, her voice a digitally enhanced roar that shook the room.

"Clear," said Valentin through clenched teeth.

"Good. As to the terrorist groups who are having a field day, their compliance date will be one month from the date the last of them is verifiably contacted with this information. We aren't monsters. We want to be fair. We expect you to contact those forces you can. Give them a chance. Then, if they don't comply, we'll contact all of them to make sure they truly understand the situation."

The back-clad figure knelt in the foreground, tilting her head to one side. "I understand how hard this is for you—taking orders from a complete stranger who looks like a damned cartoon character."

"Hey!" the minotaur objected.

She silenced him with a glance. "As hard as this is, defying us will be many times harder. *If* you defy us, your countries will all be rendered leaderless. I cannot overemphasize that your lives hang in the balance. Your lives . . ." She smiled. ". . . and your financial resources. Your *personal* financial resources. Our first act, if you fail to meet our expectations, is to take every penny you have—wherever you have squirreled it away—and redistribute it to the bank accounts worldwide with the least amount of money in them."

"Go, Sara!" the minotaur crowed, doing a grotesque bovine jig. Ellis actually blinked, to make sure this surreal image was actually happening.

It was.

The minotaur was dancing, and shouting, "Hit 'em where they live!"

"Down, boy," she said, still smiling, and rose. "Your clock starts tomorrow morning, nine A.M. eastern time. I like to sleep in." She made a cutting gesture at the minotaur and sauntered offscreen to the strains of the Police's "Every Breath You Take" and the amused laughter of the minotaur, who whipped his morning star over his head and then flung it toward the watchers. It flew from the screen into the real world, drawing a gasp from everyone watching.

Everyone in the Situation Room jerked back, the media tech actually throwing herself from her chair. The spiked ball whipped back into the screen with a metallic clank and the display went dark. A moment later, the faces of the world leaders appeared there again.

Margaret Ellis knew that the horror and confusion on their faces mirrored her own.

"SO, YOU THINK SHE'S JUST going to do nothing?" Ted Freitag couldn't keep the incredulity out of his voice.

Senator Bluth shook his head. "Oh, she's doing something. She's capitulating. She's betraying our country. Typical. This is why women shouldn't lead national governments."

Chauvinist, Ted thought. Aloud, he asked, "You mean the male leaders voted for more pragmatic options?"

"Valentin recommended nuking these damned terrorists."

"Oh, that's pragmatic as hell. Blow up a chunk of Pennsylvania. That ought to go down well with some congressional constituency."

Bluth stared out at Ted from his laptop display. "You mean to tell me you don't see the silver lining in this? The silver lining that totally escapes Margaret Ellis?"

"I've looked at the video from the meeting. I've read the written report. I see no silver lining, here, Senator. These Zetas think they're God, and might as well be, from everything I've seen come through my office. The world leaders at least need to give a damn fine appearance of compliance, wouldn't you say?"

The senator pulled a face. "*That's* your analysis? Freitag, I'm surprised at you—and a little disappointed."

Ted didn't really care what the senator thought, but he hadn't gotten to where he was by voicing such opinions. So he just sat there, stone-faced, while Bluth kept talking.

"This is a golden opportunity to get rid of some serious global headaches. I mean think of it—if Al Sabbah or some other terror group fails to comply, the Zetas take them down. Poof. Some major antagonists gone."

"You think?"

"I think. And I also think that by leaping to comply with the demands of these superhumans—I can't believe I just said that—Ellis betrays her weakness; she believes the United States is just like any other nation and must bend as other nations bend. We're *not* like other nations. We don't bend. We don't compromise. We don't obey orders from anyone else. That's what makes us America. We don't adapt, Ted. We make the other guys adapt."

Ted bit the inside of his lip to quash a smirk. "That your presidential campaign speech, Senator? I mean, Ellis is nearing the end of her first term, election's looming . . ."

"Part of my personal silver lining," the senator said. "Margaret Ellis doesn't see this as an opportunity to crush a few enemies and look presidential. I do."

"No, I think you're right. I think President Ellis sees this as a global crisis to be averted or managed. Or a problem to be solved. Women, huh? Can't look at anything realistically." He didn't even bother to throttle down the sarcasm. Bluth was a self-serving jackass, but he was a self-serving jackass who needed Ted Freitag's insider view of the intel that poured into the Pentagon day after day. He was also a jackass who paid very well. The great thing about men with the amount of hubris Bluth had is that they rarely heard anything they didn't want to hear anyway, so Ted was pretty sure his sarcasm was lost on the politician. "So, what's the game plan, Senator?"

Bluth rocked back in his chair, pondering possibilities. "I'll make a game—and public—effort to convince Ellis that she needs to stand firm in the face of these 'terrorists,' then I'll propose some alternatives to just rolling over and playing dead."

"Such as . . ."

Bluth smiled. "Such as fielding a special black ops team to go in and take these people out. It's time," he added, "to get the band back together."

"Deep Shield?"

"Deep Shield. You've had some luck tracking the remnants down—"

Ted raised his hand. "Marginal. I've located fifty people—all of whom were assigned to Forward Kinetics. You're going to need more than that to stage a coup. Or . . . a clever drone strike." Ted let that last comment sink in for a moment. "Ya know I could have been—"

Bluth reddened. "I'm sure you are familiar with the phrase 'need to know.'"

Ted knew he'd be stonewalled on that front. Still, Bluth had to understand the length of Ted's reach. Ted knew all about the ill-conceived failure of a drone strike the senator had cooked up. He most certainly was not trying to intimidate Bluth. He simply wanted to enhance his value. A set of eyes and ears positioned as Ted's were was worth a lot and that value could be progressively increased.

Bluth made eye contact, something he rarely did. "I'm not staging a coup. Ellis will be out of office in less than a year. That's just a fact—she is going to lose this election spectacularly. Let's face it: she and her party have run things into the ground. I just want to make sure the people know that *I* am the best alternative to rebuild. Reassembling Deep Shield will be part of that. I also suspect that rolling over and exposing our soft underbelly doesn't sit well with a great many military leaders. And with a bit of guided outside support—there are some countries that are particularly good on misinformation campaigns and cyberattacks that won't be tracked back to me—we can take advantage of their desire to *act*. I intend to use your fifty to raise up five thousand. Maybe more."

"Ah. Well, that means that if you become president, you'll have your own private little army. Careful there, Senator. Power corrupts. Or didn't you learn that lesson from your buddy Howard?"

Bluth's selective hearing kicked in to blot out Ted's admonishments. "I'm a third-term senator, Ted. I have a lot of friends on the Hill, probably more than Ellis." Ted understood this was as much a warning to himself as it was to Ellis.

Bluth continued. "The last thing Ellis wants to do this close to an election is lock horns with the Senate. The public will smell blood if even an ounce of dissent is hinted at. The American people will want a leader and a party that can actually handle things and unite our great government against a common foe. She'll be a symbol of disharmony and a president with far too many secrets."

"And you'll ride in on a white horse this November. You'll dump Deep Shield in her lap, dutifully informing the nation that these Zetas were created by our government on her watch. I get it. The thing is—why tell *me* this?"

"Because I have a little side project for you, Ted. But not here; we'll talk later. I can rely on you, can't I, Ted?" The question may as well have been *I won't have to kill you, will I, Ted?*

"Yes, sir, Senator."

Bluth smirked and dismissed him with his signature wave of the hand, leaving Ted to wonder if the extra money, no matter how considerable, he earned working for a Machiavellian bastard was worth the ulcer.

Chapter 10

INSIDE JOEY BLOSSOM

Chuck rested his forehead against the cool glass of the window and stared out across the desert landscape, which was still shrouded in the shadow and flame of early morning. He had risen and showered and gotten a cup of coffee from the seemingly bottomless pot in the gleaming, modern kitchen. Now, gazing at the peaceful scene he knew was hiding high-tech surveillance gadgets and armed guards, he had a most unwelcome realization: he did not want to go to work. They had scheduled another session with Alexis and Giles and he was dreading it deeply.

Giles was promising, but Alexis—who up until now had been convinced of her own superiority—was both challenged and challenging. Chuck reflected that the lifelong possession of a special ability or talent was seductive; it encouraged the talented to identify too strongly with their own ability, to define themselves by it. Alexis, in her mind, he suspected, saw her immersion-born capacities as who she was. Discovering that those capacities were incomplete or deficient in some way was clearly a rude awakening. All the more so when it also seemed that other, lesser beings could develop abilities every bit as special.

"Hey, you okay?"

Chuck turned his head just enough to see Lanfen watching him from the broad, open doorway to the kitchen.

"Yeah. I just . . . I'm just not really looking forward to—you know." He gestured at the floor, beneath which lay the iceberg vastness of the Center.

"If it's any consolation," she said, "I don't think Alexis is too keen on having another public demonstration of her basic human frailties, either. Not that she'd admit to having any."

"She'd see that denial as strength, I've no doubt." Chuck straightened from the window, shaking his head. "It's funny what we come to see as weaknesses. Just the very recognition that we have them, for example. That scares the socks off some people."

"Yes. And it sets them up for a fall."

"Fight or flight," Chuck murmured. "It's a catch twenty-two." He grimaced. "Listen to me—I'm speaking in aphorisms. I guess the coffee hasn't kicked in yet."

Lanfen came farther into the room. A cup of tea in one hand, she extended the other to Chuck. "Come on, Doc. There's no putting it off. Who knows—maybe today's the day that Alexis has a breakthrough."

"We can hope."

BUT IT WAS GILES WHO was the one to have a breakthrough. He was able to send Roboticus II on a wonky, wobbly tour of the lab floor and move a mouse pointer across a screen. This caused the young Benefactor to beam and made even Alexis smile—if you could call the brief lifting of the corners of her mouth a smile. She was eager to try again, herself, and submitted to having the neural net placed on her head without commentary.

That was where things went swiftly south. Alexis's use of her programmed abilities was reflexive. She could no more not use them than she could open her eyes and not see. After a ten-minute, white-knuckle struggle with Roboticus, she lost her temper and tore the neural net from her head.

"This is impossible!" she said and turned to fix Lorstad with icy regard. "I don't need this, Kristian. If you wish to continue this travesty, by all means do. I frankly have no intention of abandoning the Learning. I'm surprised you would. It was a gift from our families. Why would you toss it aside?"

"For the simple reason," said Lorstad, "that it is a weakness—a point of vulnerability."

Chuck was stunned by the admission. *He* certainly had come to see immersion therapy that way, but he was shocked to hear Lorstad put it into words.

"What if we were to be cut off from the immersion tanks?" their host went on. "What if our facilities were destroyed or inaccessible? What should we do then?"

"A weakness? This was a *gift*," Alexis repeated, rising, her skin flushing deeply red. "This was what our forebears intended us to be."

Lorstad moved to stand toe-to-toe with her. "No, Alexis. They intended us to *evolve*. The method isn't the gift—the *result* is. And right now, we are not evolving. None of us. You and I have been immersing since we were small children, as our parents did before us. Yet if we stop, the gift is taken away. It is not written into our DNA. Our powers are no more a reflection of our reality than a parrot's mimicry is a reflection of its native intelligence or comprehension of the words it speaks. The lab work we had done on Lanfen and Minerva confirms it: *they* are evolving; their brains are rewiring, changing—expanding. *They* are growing new mental muscles—new connections. *We* are using a crutch."

Stunned, Chuck sank into the nearest chair. How long had Lorstad been sitting on *that* last bit of information? Chuck had seen hints of neurological changes during their tenure at Forward Kinetics, but they'd never confirmed their depth or scope. He wondered if Lorstad would allow him access to the data.

To say that Alexis wasn't as interested in the physiological ramifications would have been a gross understatement. Her pale eyes blazed. "Parrots? You liken us to *parrots*? Then what are *these*?" Her gesture took in Giles and the members of Chuck's team. "Do you honestly believe them to be our *superiors*?"

"No. Not superior. But is it so hard to believe them our *equals,* Alexis?"

"They are in no way our equals," she practically spit. "Their powers must certainly be inferior, if a novice Learned can acquire them." She waved dismissively at Giles. "Perhaps this boy is resistant to immersion."

Lorstad hesitated, glanced at Chuck, and then said, "I took the precaution of terminating Giles's immersion sessions. He has not immersed for four days."

Chuck felt Alexis's reaction as a sharp tug at his heart. She stared at Lorstad in chill disbelief. "*What?* How dare you deny this boy his birthright? And for what—so that he can play with profane toys?"

She swung around, her arm outstretched, and made a slapping gesture at Roboticus. The robot flew into the air, tumbling wheels over crown toward the far end of the lab. Joey Blossom was standing in its path. It caught the Sho-Pai squarely in the ribs, lifted him from his feet, and flung him the length of the room.

The place erupted in a chaotic roil of sound and motion. Chuck's body seemed to move before his mind had formed an awareness that it was doing so. He ran the length of the room, fell to his knees beside Joey, and thrust the bot aside. The right side of Joey's rib cage looked like a half-deflated beach ball. There must be multiple broken ribs. Chuck was hit with a stark fear that one of them could have punctured the young man's lungs.

Riding a strong desire to undo the damage, Chuck lay a gentle hand on Joey's chest, calling to mind the virtual anatomies he'd been working with in the computer sims. In the moment he made physical contact, reality fell away. There was a bright flash of light, followed by the feeling of being sucked down a dark, twisting corridor.

Alice down the rabbit hole, Chuck thought.

In a heartbeat—the coincidence not lost on him, considering where his hands were—he was inside one of his simulations, surrounded by the digital representation of a human body. But there was something wrong with this body, obviously. On the right side, three of the ribs were broken and one pressed perilously against the right lung such that the tiniest movement of the body might puncture it.

Chuck became aware on some level he couldn't explain that someone else had laid hands on . . . on what? Where was he?

Didn't matter. He had to keep them from moving the body. How? All he could manage was a mental cry of warning: *Don'tdon'tdon'tdon't! DON'T MOVE HIM!* He imagined a charge of electricity surrounding him, pushing outward. The threat seemed to diminish—the other touches went away—and Chuck dove back into this new state of awareness. The ribs needed to be restored to their normal position and form, but that could only happen if he could exert pressure equally against every square inch of the underside of each rib . . . which he could do, of course. He just had manipulated his sims in that way. He imagined a pad of air sliding beneath the broken ribs and expanding, flowing into every irregularity in the broken bones. He imagined a lighter, but no less even, pressure against the outer surface.

As he guided the ribs back into position, he considered the question of healing. In time, the bone would grow back and mend the breaks. He didn't have time. He'd practiced stimulating tissue growth in his simulations. Now he set his mind to stimulating it in real flesh and bone.

As he worked, he monitored the body's vital signs—heartbeat, respiration, brain function. Irregular, but present—and there was a head injury. Bleeding.

Chuck was now completely in his element. Riding a surge of confidence, he inhabited Joey Blossom completely. It was both like and unlike the simulations he'd run time and again, but he knew what to do. He worked at the speed of thought, relieving pressure in the sagittal sinus, pinching off bleeders, rerouting blood flow, stimulating tissue regrowth and bone remodeling.

In a moment of epiphany, he realized he could adjust the inconstant brain waves by syncing them with his own. The heady exhilaration of that made him want to laugh like a child on a roller coaster. He stifled the desire, steadied his own brain wave emissions, and set his patient's to a meditative theta.

When he had completed his work, Chuck paused to assess, and experienced the most incredible sensation: he was in a cathedral with vaulted ceilings that opened to the night sky. He smelled sagebrush, heard the night birds. Was that what Joey was experiencing? Was it a dream? A memory? Chuck didn't have time to explore. He centered himself, feeling for the merely physical rush of air in and out, sensing the steady thrum of blood pumping through veins and arteries, the odd electrical thrill of synapses firing. He stayed with it until he knew that Joey's system was stable. There was nothing left to do.

Chuck felt a warm rush of satisfaction . . . that guttered when cold reality hit him:

He had no means of retreat.

He looked around, and there was nowhere to go. This was not a computer simulation. Nor was it an empty mechanism. This was a melding with another mind—another metabolism—and Chuck had no idea how to extricate himself safely.

Panic surged. His heart rate spiked. So did Joey's.

No, no, no, no, no. He couldn't let that happen. Moreover, he was uncertain if the vessels he had pinched off or mended would hold if Joey's blood pressure rose. He had to find a way out without putting that to the test.

Chuck calmed himself with a surge of will. Returned to a familiar mantra. His hand was still touching Joey's injured side. Could he backtrack along that channel if he *imagined* he could?

Almost the moment he had the thought, the connection was broken. Someone had moved his hand. In the welter of confusion that caused, Chuck somehow understood that he was no longer securely tethered to his own body. He was stranded inside Joey Blossom . . . and there was no way out.

AFTERWARD, LANFEN COULDN'T EXPLAIN WHEN she first realized something was wrong. Not with Joey—what was wrong with Joey was horrifically clear—but with Chuck.

He'd gone to his knees beside the Sho-Pai engineer, pulled Roboticus away, and extended a hand to the hideously broken rib cage. And there he'd frozen in an attitude of intense listening or . . . prayer, perhaps. In the seconds that followed, the others gathered around, Mini bursting into tears; Lorstad calling for the doctors to be brought; Giles rushing into the outer room; Alexis standing, immobile, her face a blank mask.

Lanfen and Eugene both reached for Joey's body to straighten it. Lanfen was repelled by what she could only describe as a mental shock, as if her questing hands had met with an electrical charge. Euge reeled back as well, their eyes meeting in a startled recognition that they'd shared that hefty charge of mental energy. It could only have come from Chuck.

Lanfen looked down at Joey's side again and failed to stifle a gasp of horror; the engineer's rib cage was reinflating, returning to its normal shape. She reached reflexively, but tentatively for his wrist, laying cautious fingers against the blood vessels there, feeling for and finding his pulse. It steadied under her fingertips.

She heard Lorstad bark something at Alexis in a foreign language—something that sent the woman storming from the lab. Lanfen looked back and saw the change in Joey's face—an indefinable relaxation of his features. And then . . .

Nothing.

She glanced at Chuck. His expression was intent, his brow knit, his eyes open but unfocused. And in those eyes . . .

Lanfen's pulse raced. She was suddenly and emphatically convinced that she knew what was happening inside Joey Blossom, and equally convinced that Chuck needed her help. She reached for Chuck's hand where it rested on Joey's chest, but Lorstad got there first and pushed both their hands away.

"The doctors are on their way, Dr. Brenton," he said, then frowned and repeated, "Dr. Brenton . . ."

Chuck collapsed to the floor like a marionette whose strings had been cut. The other members of his team reacted with inarticulate cries of fear and concern. Lanfen pulled him into her arms, grasped his hand, and set it gently back on Joey Blossom's chest. She spared only a second to say, "Everyone stand back," then closed her eyes and went quickly into the same prep routine she used to inhabit one of her ninja bots.

Then she dove into Joey Blossom's brain.

FOR ALL HIS PRACTICE WITH sims and bots, Chuck did not have Lanfen's experience with the very literal ins and outs of remote kinesis. Nor had he yet aspired to her ability to inhabit a mechanism and her own body at the same time. "Look before you leap" seemed the operative aphorism in this case, but if he had looked, Joey might be dead.

As it was, Chuck wasn't sure what would happen when the engineer regained consciousness. He was sure of nothing, in fact, except that he needed help.

So he prayed.

The prayer was wordless and came from the depths of his soul. He wanted nothing so much as to have not killed both himself and Joey through his instinctive but rash actions. He half-expected that the answer would be his own extinction and was surprised when he was suddenly aware of another presence *with* him inside Joey Blossom. At first, he thought it must be Joey regaining consciousness, and panicked anew. But he realized that he *knew* this presence well; it was familiar, comforting, and steady.

Lanfen.

How he knew it was Lanfen, he had no idea, but he *knew.* He also knew that she wanted him to put himself in her hands, to trust him in a way he had never trusted anyone.

He did it without hesitation or doubt.

She had somehow renewed the connection with his own body and brain and now walked him through his return. As she led him, she helped him understand that he needed to think about the physical connection as a pathway that could be followed. It wasn't, of course—not in any real sense—but Chuck knew that wielding zeta abilities was largely about visualization leading to actualization.

Follow me, Lanfen said, and he obeyed, treading a trail of light through a virtual wood. She led him to a bridge over a chasm and "told" him to walk back to familiar territory—back to himself.

Leap of faith, he thought, and stepped out of Joey Blossom and back into his own familiar turf.

He came to cradled in comfort and warmth, opened his eyes, and found himself staring up at Lanfen. She leaned over him, their foreheads touching, her silken veil of hair shielding their faces. He was stunned. Awed. It was more intimate than a kiss. More centering than a meditation.

Chuck took a deep breath that he was certain beyond doubt Lanfen breathed with him. "Thank you," he murmured.

"Welcome," she said.

She raised her head and the real world rushed back in with

all its sound and movement. Hands lifted him up, set him on his feet, sat him down. Doctors arrived from the medical wing with a gurney and a crash cart. Chuck watched as Dr. Pence worked over Joey, checking his vitals, sliding him onto a backboard and lifting him carefully onto the gurney before wheeling him away.

"Will he be all right?" Eugene asked.

Dr. Pence flashed him a glance and nodded. "I believe so. He seems to have sustained a mild trauma to the head and his right side. We'll do X-rays, CAT scan, MRI, and EKG, but his pulse is strong. What happened to him?"

Lorstad met Chuck's eyes briefly. "He was hit by a heavy, flying object. With that, to be exact." Lorstad gestured at the damaged robot.

The doctor opened her mouth as if to ask how that might have happened, then closed it again. "We'll be very thorough," she said, and followed the gurney from the lab.

Beyond the door of the lab, Chuck could see the Center staff clustered in little groups, watching Joey's progress toward the medical wing of the complex. Some of them had surely seen what had happened to their colleague. Chuck wondered what they would make of it.

Someone moved to block his line of sight. He looked up to see Lorstad regarding him with unconcealed—and quite intense—interest. No, more than interest—a dark, electric zeal. "Charles," the older man said, "what did you do?"

Charles had no idea how to answer that question.

Chapter 11

BLACK OPS

In all the time they had been at the Center, Lorstad had never before taken any of his guests into his personal sanctum. His spacious office was in the lowest level of the main house but had a large, oval window that overlooked the floor of the central cavern. It even afforded a partial view of Chuck's lab. He knew there were also electronic and perhaps extrasensory surveillance devices as well. He even knew where they were—Lanfen had shown him, having learned to sense them. She was teaching him to do the same.

Chuck read this change of venue as an attempt to both inspire and convey trust. Clearly he had been admitted inside the private workspace of the Benefactor leader with hopes he might reciprocate by divulging insights of his own.

"So, you have not been entirely honest with me, Charles." Lorstad sat behind a large desk of anodized aluminum, his hands steepled before him on the desktop. "You have been practicing your own kinetic talents. Talents that seem unique to you."

"That's not a fair assessment, Kristian. I never tried to keep it a secret. I've just been focused on your problem and only pursue my own pastimes after hours. And, to be fair, you haven't been forthcoming with me, either. If Alexis hadn't pushed the point, would you have told us what you gleaned from Mini and Lanfen's tests?"

Lorstad ignored his question to ask one of his own. "What, exactly, are your, ah, 'pastimes,' Charles?"

Chuck decided not to press his own question—for now. "I should think that was obvious. I'm a neuroscientist. I haven't participated in surgeries for several years, but I've been working with medical simulations to at least try to keep my skills up."

"What you did just now in the lab was no simulation."

"No. It was . . . potentially a mistake. I might have done Joey irreparable damage." *I might have done* myself *irreparable damage, too.*

"Instead, you saved his life."

Chuck looked up and met the other man's eyes. His expression was not quite dispassionate.

"I thank you for that," Lorstad added quietly. "Joey is one of our brightest staffers. I would hate to lose him."

"Yes, about that. Alexis—"

"—will not work with your team any further. Instead, I'm going to assign only novice members of our society to the zeta training and hope that, in the course of training them, you will find a solution to the . . . the problem posed by immersion conditioning. Now, I would like you to be candid with me, Charles. What did you do to Joey Blossom?"

"All right, but you need to be candid with me first," Chuck said, finding an opening once more. "Did you intend to let us see the data you gathered from Mini and Lanfen? Or was that yet another thing you didn't think we needed to know?"

Lorstad regarded him with a poker face that most certainly concealed frustration, impatience, and calculation. Finally, he said, "I intended to share the data with you as soon as I'd had time to . . . assimilate it and share it with the Council. My primary focus—and I think you will understand this—was what the data meant to the Learned. It was not . . . an easy thing to accept—that we are not changed by our technology in any permanent sense. But I would have shared the information with you. Now, tell me what I need to know. What did you do to Joey Blossom?"

"I stabilized him."

"You did more than that. His ribs were broken. You mended them. We all saw that. He is expected to make a full recovery in the course of the next several days. That is phenomenal. Miraculous, even."

Lorstad made a gesture at the wall behind his desk and a flat screen embedded in it came to life, showing a set of X-rays and a CAT scan. Joey's. Chuck was riveted. The ribs were not pristine—you could tell they'd been broken—but the remodeling was so complete that the breaks looked as if they had been suffered months ago.

He had done that. It was a sobering realization. He sat back in his chair and tried to take it in.

"How did you do this, and what part did Ms. Chen play in it?"

Chuck smiled briefly. "She saved *my* life."

"How?"

"Ask her."

"I did. She said only that she 'knew the ropes' better than you did. That you were like a child trying to ride a bicycle without training wheels, realizing only halfway down a steep hill that you still needed them."

Chuck's smile deepened. "She has a way with words."

Lorstad leaned forward and once more asked, "What did you *do*, Charles? How did you save Joey Blossom's life? Nothing your team has done so far showed any indication that you could . . . that you could inhabit another human being."

Chuck jerked his gaze back up to Lorstad's face. "What?"

"Ms. Chen inhabits her robots. I assumed that was the method you used as well."

And that's exactly what he'd done. He knew it now. He had

done it reflexively, instinctively. But he could not reveal that to Kristian Lorstad. The thought of someone like Alexis being able to reach inside another person and—

Chuck shivered. It was a thought that sent his mind into full retreat. He had considered only the benevolent medical aspects of the skills he was attempting to learn. Now he wondered if every miracle didn't have a dark side.

"No. I doubt it's possible to 'inhabit' another person. There's an intelligence there that's not present in a robot. Human beings are not machines. Besides, though I can move things around—remotely run software, manipulate objects—I've never come close to doing what Lanfen does when she inhabits a device. Inhabiting another human being . . . it's unthinkable. I'm a scientist, Kristian. I acted on a scientist's instinct. I tried to apply what I was learning in my sims."

"Without the use of your hands or surgical instruments. Without having to cut the patient open. Again, how?"

"I had a clear visualization of the affected areas." That much was true. "That enabled me to use my kinetic abilities to perform the necessary repairs. It was really just a matter of applying my knowledge of human anatomy with my zeta skills."

"Impressive. But what function did Ms. Chen perform?"

"She assisted."

Lorstad regarded him levelly. "You are being purposefully obscure, Charles. I beg you not to."

Chuck stifled a tickle of anger. "I guess I am being purposefully obscure. Damned frustrating, isn't it? Now you know how I feel shut up inside your big underground box with little idea of what's going on in the outside world because of your attempts to keep us focused."

"Ah. I see. Yes. Another exchange of information, then? What would you like to know?"

Chuck sat forward in his chair. "I've been in touch with Matt Streegman for some time—"

Lorstad's eyebrows collided over the bridge of his nose. "How? You have no access to e-mail."

"The Internet. He created a LinkedIn account with a fictitious name and we used coded messages in case someone was monitoring them." He ignored Lorstad's narrowing eyes and said, "Anyway, we were in touch when he suddenly went silent. He was trying to get to the government—the *real* government. He thought he'd made contact, was going to try to negotiate with the Alphas. Then he just stopped communicating with me. I thought maybe he'd managed to get inside the mountain."

Lorstad lowered his gaze to the top of his desk. Chuck had the impression of gears turning. "He did manage to get inside the mountain, yes."

Chuck exhaled. "All right. That's good, then. Isn't it?"

Lorstad met his gaze. "If I tell you what I know about Dr. Streegman, will you explain Ms. Chen's role in your treatment of Joey Blossom?"

"Insofar as I can," Chuck hedged.

"Your friend made it into the mountain safely. Unfortunately, he did not make it out safely. He was killed. Electrocuted, apparently."

Chuck felt as if the bottom had fallen out of his world. He fought vertigo, his hands gripping the arms of the chair as if he rode a roller coaster. He vaguely heard Lorstad speaking to him, vaguely saw his lips move, but the words were lost in the roar of blood in his ears.

"So you see," were the first words he consciously heard the Learned say, "there is nothing to be done. The Alphas are barricaded inside their mountain and seem unwilling to be pried from it."

"How do you know this?" Chuck asked, surprised at the rusty sound of his own voice. "How do you know Matt's dead?"

"I have means of surveilling the area. It provided me with a record of Dr. Streegman's body being carried from the mountain by one of the Deep Shield robots."

"You're sure he's—"

"There is no doubt, Charles. I'm sorry. But I thought Dr. Streegman had proven a traitor to your cause. Surely you didn't trust him."

"I didn't trust him, but he was my partner. My friend. He was also my only means of keeping track of what the Alphas were doing."

"I know what the Alphas are doing in a general sense."

"That's great, but you also won't tell us."

Lorstad shrugged. "It would serve no purpose at this juncture."

"For *you*."

"However you want to look at it," Lorstad said with a hint of finality.

Chuck sighed, but nodded. That was that, then. Matt was gone and they were cut off from the Alphas again.

"You were going to explain Ms. Chen's assistance to you. She is not a nurse or a doctor. She has no medical training."

"You pulled my hand away," Chuck said wearily. "Or someone did. Either way, it broke my contact with Joey, and that stopped my manipulation of his injuries. Apparently, I need the physical contact at this point in my development. Who knows, maybe I always will. Lanfen reestablished contact and kept any of you from breaking it again. Her function was to keep anyone else out of the operating theater."

"And that saved your life?"

Chuck groaned inwardly. He'd forgotten having already made that admission. Could he explain that away in some way Lorstad would accept as truth?

"That was hyperbole. When I broke contact with Joey's body, it somehow scrambled my synapses. I passed out. When Lanfen put me back in contact with him, it set everything to rights and I was able to complete my work."

Lorstad nodded. "I would like you to repeat that experiment under more rigorously controlled circumstances. Perhaps with a day or two to recover . . . ?"

Chuck could only stare at him. "It wasn't an experiment. It was an emergency measure precipitated by one of your supposedly superior comrades."

"It was an accident," said Lorstad. "Alexis didn't mean to harm anyone. She was frustrated."

"She was out of control." Chuck stood, put his hands on the gleaming anodized desktop, and leaned toward the other man. "Here's what I know, Kristian: power corrupts. Abilities like the ones we share can be a blessing if they're handled with care and compassion. If they're not, they are an unmitigated curse. Alexis isn't just frustrated, she's angry, and her anger turns outward. She shows no ability to empathize. She's dangerous, not just to . . . *Profanes* like Joey Blossom, but to anyone close to her."

"How do you know this?"

"How do you *not* know it?" Chuck turned on his heel and left Lorstad's office.

SO, THE PROFESSOR THINKS I'M *out of control, does he?*

Kristian raised his head. Alexis stood in the doorway of his office, her arms crossed over her chest, her thoughts dripping displeasure.

You eavesdropped, he thought.

She shrugged. *You didn't block me.*

He actually wasn't sure he *could* block her completely anymore, but he wasn't about to let her know that. *Do you care what Charles thinks?*

Strong negative.

Then why raise the issue?

She sauntered into the office, regarding him through hooded eyes. *Do you believe him?*

Kristian pondered how best to answer that question. He knew it to be loaded. *I believe that what you did betrayed . . . a lack of control and perspective. Not just the childish display of temper, but the verbal rant you indulged in after the fact. That could have been kept between us.*

She moved to place her hands on his desk and lean over it, very much as Charles Brenton had just done. A wave of scorn hit him like a hot, stinging spray. "I didn't *want* to keep it between us," she said aloud. "I *wanted* them to hear what I was thinking."

"Why? Whatever could be gained by making them aware of your . . . condescension?"

She glanced backward at the door and closed it with a thought before firing back at him.

Whatever could be gained by making them feel superior? Was that your gambit? The reason you pretend there are things they can do that we cannot? Did you expect your pet neurologist to work harder for you if he thought his training and technology would benefit us?

Alexis, I am not pretending. Everything I said in that room was true. They are evolving. We are not. Their synapses are being rewired, their chemistry rebalanced, their perceptions stretched and elevated. Perhaps we are the ones who are pretending to a status we do not deserve.

She straightened, eyes blazing. "I don't believe you!" she cried aloud. "I will *never* believe you! You are—are *smitten* by that girl. That child."

That child, as you call her, is a prodigy the like of which we have never produced even with the aid of immersion therapy. We play with atoms and electrons. We tinker with physical objects and energies. But not one of us can create semiautonomous entities. It is possible that Minerva might one day create autonomous entities—a form of life. It is imperative that she join the ranks of the Learned. This has nothing to do with me being "smitten." It has only to do with me being cognizant of her abilities.

Alexis smiled archly. *You forget, Kristian, how well I can read you. It galls you that she loves a mere man when you would offer her a demigod.* She swung around then, and strode from the room with jealousy radiating from every pore.

Kristian shook his head. He was beginning to think Charles's observations about Alexis had some merit. He was not jealous of Eugene Pozniaki; her read of him was full of her own projections. His entire dissatisfaction with the young scientist was that, of all Charles Brenton's comrades, Pozniaki was the only one who seemed to possess no talent for zeta abilities. That alone made him a poor match for such a vibrant talent as Mini. Charles, himself, Daisuke Kobayashi, or even Joey Blossom would make a better match. If the physiological and neurological changes the Zetas were undergoing were permanent, then it made the most sense to pair talent to talent.

That was not something Kristian thought he would ever convince the Zetas and their creator of, however. If they possessed one flaw, it was that they were simply too human.

THE RUSSIANS WERE PULLING OUT of Ukraine; Al Sabbah suddenly found itself unwelcome where it had before enjoyed much freedom to operate; Palestinian authorities unilaterally recognized Israel's right to exist within borders that would allow Palestine a contiguous area.

It was a good start, but it was a start that involved only those parties whose leaders had been firsthand witnesses of the Alphas' capabilities. Hamas was not impressed; North Korea was indignant and accused those leaders who had responded of rank cowardice; ISIS and similar groups were likewise continuing their operations confident that God was on their side.

The United States was tied up in democratic knots. The president and her team briefed Congress thoroughly on the situation, but Congress was divided in its response. A coalition of congressmen and senators—led by a Senator Bluth—insisted that the United States not "cave" to terrorist threats, but instead that she stand firm. They were not a majority, but had enough influence within the system to insist on making no military moves without more information—information that the president had no way to give them. The president was urged by her allies and confidants to humor Bluth and his gang for now. The upcoming election was, apparently, all too important. A major transition of power in the midst of this unprecedented crisis could present an insurmountable ordeal for the United States government and her people. The public must be soothed for as long as possible; the usual Washington infighting had to be mitigated for the sake of public trust. That all sounded wonderful, but hardly practical or realistic. She'd toe the line for now.

It was not unexpected, really, and Mike was relieved when neither Sara nor Tim seemed inclined to force the issue. The United States, Sara believed, would come around once they had witnessed what befell others who refused to comply.

The Alphas gave their first demonstration on the battlefields in Iraq where, when the Iraqis and allies stood down, ISIS thought it had been given carte blanche to take as much territory as it desired. ISIS forces had no more than begun a fresh offensive when every networked system in the so-called Islamic State disintegrated. Not, however, before destroying every connected component with showy finality. Every communications system shrieked deafeningly, then fell silent; every computerized weapon misfired in horrific ways; every supply corridor was disrupted. Planes fell out of the sky; radar failed; missiles exploded on their launch platforms. The jihadists were overrun with ifrits and djinn and several leaders were visited by the spirit of Muhammad, who sternly commanded them to lay down their arms while reminding them that "God loves not the aggressor."

Tim joked that he was probably in deep trouble for impersonating a Prophet while Sara contacted the leaders of the allied coalition that had been fighting ISIS and gave them permission to move in and mop up, after which they were to withdraw all but peacekeeping troops from the affected areas.

In the wake of that teachable moment, the war in Syria ended in strategic withdrawals on all sides and Hamas stopped firing rockets into Israel. Iran opened its prison gates and released every political and religious prisoner within. So did China. Even the drug cartels in South America became suddenly quiet and all but invisible. With that overwhelming proof of concept, three congressmen defected from Bluth's cadre. Sensing that momentum shift, President Ellis used executive powers to issue stand-down orders to American forces in Afghanistan, Iraq, and Syria. The Joint Chiefs found reasonable cause to curtail military action on several other fronts.

Bluth countered by accusing the president of outright failure to protect the American people and called for a removal of her executive powers. He began to hint that the Ellis administration's behavior with regard to foreign policy was being driven by timidity and fear of "special interest groups." Technically, he didn't really have a legal leg to stand on. But he didn't actually need one. Between social media and talk radio, he had all the outlets necessary to sow doubt and discord. Stirring the pot was all he needed to do at this point. Create chaos and fear and then present himself as a salve for the wound. The president's approval rating would plunge and then he could drop a little bombshell of his own courtesy of Ted Freitag's handiwork.

It helped that not everyone around the world was giving in. North Korea, for example, continued to bluster and bully, loudly threatening to invade her southern neighbor. The morning after the threat was made, though, the North Korean military woke to find that no device with a computerized component would operate. When the North Korean government expressed its outrage, it found itself dealing with a nationwide failure of its entire power grid and an infestation of ancient demons straight out of legend.

This was the case in other regions as well.

In Afghanistan, the leadership of the Taliban thought they had a golden opportunity to reinsert themselves into the government of the country by staging a daytime assault on the National Assembly offices in Kabul during a legislative session. They sent a convoy of more than a dozen military vehicles—including a tank—down Shura Street, blocked it to approaching traffic, and took over the forecourt of the Assembly building.

Watching an Al Jazeera video feed of the scene from the ops theater, Sara paced and considered options. She turned to Mike. "You have line of sight. What can you give me?"

Mike swallowed, wanting to say, cheekily, "I got nothing," but knowing she'd never buy it. "I can wreck the machinery—the guns, the vehicles. At least any that I can see."

"Do it." She turned to Tim next. "What about you? Your minotaur commander available to make an appearance with some of his cohort?"

Tim grinned. "You got it."

The minotaur that appeared on the screen in the center of the Assembly building turnaround was huge, and he had brought many friends. Some smaller versions of himself, some that looked like giant gargoyles. The minotaurs stomped among the vehicles, which—with Mike's urging—erupted in flames one after the other. They had only enough substance to swat small weapons aside, but Mike's internal destruction made them seem far more powerful. The gargoyles alit on ground and roof alike of the administrative building and deked the combatants into firing at them. They only appeared to have substance; as they had at the Deep Shield camp, the bullets went right through them and took out whatever or whoever was on the opposite side.

Mike exploded his last troop carrier and melted the tank's gun, then paused to watch Sara as she began to employ her own expanding talents. She brought an interior view to their oversized screens—one from surveillance cameras within the building. Here there was still gunfire as the Taliban rebels advanced down a long, broad corridor toward a huge set of closed doors before which defenders had stacked random pieces of furniture. Sara chose this stage to make a showy appearance.

Her avatar shimmered into existence before the hastily barricaded doors like a landing party from *Star Trek*. This was her own construct. It was recognizable as Sara, but an eerily perfect Sara dressed in gleaming, body-hugging black leather with shoulder-length hair the color of eggplant and pale skin with the sheen of pearl. She wore no mask this time, and her eyes shone like moons.

After a moment of shocked hesitation, one of the officers strode up to the offensive figure and raised a hand to strike her. He snarled something in Pashto and swung. His arm went through her head and he lost his balance, staggering almost to his knees. He regained his footing roaring with rage and pointed his rifle at Sara's midsection. She smiled, then grasped the muzzle of the gun and wrenched it from the man's hands. Then she hit him in the head with it, knocking him down. He skidded across the polished marble of the floor and fetched up against a wall.

Tim crowed. "Awesome move, Sara!"

The other soldiers reacted by firing past their fallen leader at this outrageous creature quite as if they still expected her to behave like any woman of their acquaintance. Sara crossed her arms over her breasts and regarded her would-be murderers with calm disdain. The bullets passed right through her.

"Mike," she said, quietly, "disarm them, please."

He did, exciting the atoms in first the muzzles of their guns, then the firing mechanisms. The guns grew too hot to handle, and the soldiers were forced to drop them or be horribly burned. The rifles clattered to the floor amid cries of distress, and there they warped and smoked.

The broad hallway fell into a brief, stunned silence before every man in it began to roar his outrage and fury. They advanced on Sara's avatar, which she had now clothed in a frenetic halo of static energy.

"Mike, can you make an earthquake?" she asked him.

"No, don't think so."

"No, I mean *create* an earthquake. Shake the building, jiggle some beams and bolts."

"I think that's doable . . ."

"I'll need that on my mark. Tim, do you have a translation program online somewhere?"

"Uh, yeah. Arabic, I guess?"

"No—this is Afghanistan. Pashto. Let me know when you—"

"You've got it."

"Good deal." She thrust her arms out, her avatar mirroring the movement. "Mike, make me an earthquake."

He did. He did more. He brought down bits of the ceiling in a highly localized trembler. The shouts of outrage stopped as the soldiers were forced to focus on keeping their feet.

Sara, her hands still extended, demanded, "You want this to stop?" She made the demand in English, but in the video feed, the words came out of the avatar's mouth in Pashto. "If you want this to stop, *shut up*!"

The men only shouted more loudly and shook useless fists.

"I said, *stop talking*!"

Mike punctuated the words with sharp jolts that shot dust into the air.

The shouting stopped.

Sara shot Mike a look and lowered her arms, palms down. He brought the tremors slowly to a halt. The silence was complete but for the sound of plaster crumbling to the floor and muted chaos from the forecourt.

"Your leaders were warned," Sara told the Taliban fighters. "Perhaps they didn't tell you that. Perhaps they didn't inform you that they are no longer in control of their own fate or yours. *We* are."

"Who are you?" asked the first man Sara had felled. His speech was translated into stilted English. "Are you a demon?"

"I am the *future*."

"Hell," murmured Tim, "she's their worst nightmare—a woman with power."

"Who has sent you?" the Afghani asked.

"God has sent me. He has sent me with a message for you and your leaders. Your weapons are useless and your ideology is bankrupt. God has demanded that all wars on this world cease. That all conflicts be resolved. The Afghani government and the Americans stopped fighting because they understand the consequences of not obeying these commandments. Do you now understand?"

The man sneered. "You speak for God? You—a *woman*?"

Sara flicked a glance back at Mike. He shook the room again, raining more plaster onto the men below. As if on cue, a chunk of ceiling the size of a grapefruit struck one man in the shoulder, toppling him. Every man in the room backed up a step.

"Now that I've got your attention, understand this. Your petty war with the Afghani government will cease. You will stop trying to force your interpretation of Islam and your philosophies on anyone. Moreover, you will let girls and women be educated and you will grant them such rights as they request and you will let *them* decide if they wish to veil themselves. If you do not do these things, you will not know the rewards of paradise nor will God remember your names."

"You *are* a demon!" muttered the officer Sara had struck. He looked at her as if he might try to attack her again.

"No, I'm more of an avenging angel. You want demons? I'll give you demons."

Tim chuckled. In the time it took for Mike to draw a breath, the broad entry was overrun with small, monkey-like creatures with horrific faces and many sharp teeth. They moved like smoke and made a sound that grated on the ears like nails on chalkboard.

Next, he conjured a pair of gargoyles that lumbered into the hall through the wide-open statehouse doors and took up positions on either side.

Several of the men literally cowered before them and began loudly praying for deliverance.

"Whatever I am," Sara told the soldiers, "I am not something you can understand, much less control. You will leave now and you will not return. If your leaders try to make you return, show them your ruined weapons, then flee from them, for they'll be the next to feel the wrath of God. Leave. Now. My creatures won't harm you—if you do as I say."

After a moment of hesitation, the soldiers turned and fled the Assembly building, carefully avoiding the sentinel gargoyles, who watched with hungry gazes through eyes like flaming orbs. Sara waited until they had gathered their comrades and melted away before she allowed her avatar to disappear. The screens defaulted to the video feed from an Al Jazeera camera on a neighboring rooftop.

Mike's throat closed up. The forecourt of the building and the street beyond were littered with bodies—some twisted horribly, others blackened and smoking. Blood pooled in the gutters and spattered walls. The waters of the fountain in the center of the courtyard ran red. Tim's minions still roamed among the dead and dying. They faded out one by one until the street was empty of anything that moved.

Mike made himself breathe. One deep breath, two, three. His head hurt and his ears rang.

"Good job, boys," Sara said. "We may have to repeat the lesson, but sooner or later they'll get it, I think." She came to stand in front of Mike. "How's your progress with the bots? How many can you control at once?"

Mike shrugged, trying to look casual. "I can do a dozen, maybe two if they're all doing the same thing."

She frowned. "I was hoping for more, but that's a start. I'm thinking it's time for us to assemble our own army. I'm sick of this place. I feel like a prisoner in here." She seemed to ponder something for a moment, then raised her eyes to his face. "Let me know when you can control fifty of them."

Mike nodded. "Sure thing. Matter of fact, I'll go down and work with the bots right now."

Sara smiled and laid a hand on his shoulder. "You're a good man, Micky."

No, Mike thought, as he made his way down to the bot bays. *No, I am* not *a good man. But I'm working on it.*

IN THE END, CHUCK DIDN'T know what to tell his team first: that Matt had been killed by the Alphas (presumably) or that it seemed Alexis would face no repercussions for nearly killing Joey Blossom. At least, none beyond being excluded from further work with the Zetas.

The team made his decision for him. When he stepped into the lab after his interview (interrogation) with Lorstad, Eugene took one look at him, then led the entire team into Chuck's office. Chuck came through and closed the tall glass door. He started to speak, but Lanfen forestalled him by raising her hand.

"First," she said, "I want you to know that there was a listening device in here an hour ago. I moved it to a different location. It's in the reconnaissance bay on the other side of the main hall. I have no idea how long it will take them to figure it out because I don't know how closely they monitor the feeds. We have several 'safe' areas we can use without fear of surveillance or having to take out one of their devices. We can still use the exercise room and some areas in the house."

"O-Okay," Chuck said, looking around nervously. "What's second?"

"Second," said Mini, "we saw Alexis walking around out there like nothing had happened. Isn't there . . . I mean, won't she face any kind of consequences for what she did to Joey?"

Chuck leaned his back against the door. "As Kristian pointed out, it was an accident. She didn't mean to hurt Joey. Kristian's pulled her from the program, though. She's not to work with us at all anymore. In fact, I suspect he just told her to stay away from us."

Mini's arms, which had been crossed tightly over her breasts, flew out in a gesture of outrage. "Well, I'm glad to hear *that,* at least. Come on, though, Chuck. It may have been an accident, but it was an accident she didn't seem to regret at all. She didn't care about Joey. Doesn't that warrant some response?"

"Yes," Chuck said, nodding. "And I agree with you on all of that. But it's not a response that any of us have the authority to give."

"I'm sure Lorstad does, though," Euge piped in. "Critically injuring a staff member doesn't warrant a transfer or at the very least a hiatus—something punitive?"

"I'm not a part of the Learned's leadership and neither are you. Look, Euge, like I said, I agree with all of you on this, I just don't see what we can do." Chuck kept a genteel tone despite the frustration he felt.

"Fish in a tank," said Eugene. "We're fish in a tank." He leaned back against the wall and crossed his arms.

Chuck spoke amid a breathy exhale: "I'm sorry, everyone. But at this moment it's between her and her maker. We should just avoid her."

"Like the plague," said Euge, and Dice muttered, "No problem there."

Chuck came farther into the room, framing what he'd say next carefully. "Everyone take a seat. I have a couple of things I need to share with you. One is that Lorstad is very interested in my part in Joey's recovery."

"So are we," said Dice. "What the hell did you do?"

Chuck met Lanfen's gaze briefly. "I've been practicing my zeta abilities with medical simulations—going into the sim software and manipulating it from within. When Joey went down, I reflexively responded as if I were inside a simulation." He looked around at his team's faces. Lanfen already understood what he'd done; he watched as, one after another, the rest of the team got it.

"Oh. My. God," breathed Euge. "You mean you were *inside* Joey's—in his *head*?"

"I inhabited Joey approximately the way that Lanfen inhabits a robot. A human brain and body is, after all, a biomechanism." He let that sink in for a moment, then added, "That is not the way I explained it to Lorstad, though. He grasped for that interpretation, and I did my best to put him off it—told him I was just manipulating Joey's wounds from the outside. Don't know how successful I was. I also went light on Lanfen's part in rescuing me. Bluntly put, I got lost in there. I couldn't get out. She had to come in and pull me out. No one outside this group needs to know that, except to know that it's incredibly dangerous, and we should *not* be experimenting with inhabiting other humans until we can do so safely. Is that understood?" He looked around the room and watched as everyone absorbed the information.

Finally, Dice spoke for the group and said, "Understood. What else?"

Moment of truth. "Matt . . ." Chuck took a deep breath. "Matt is dead."

There was silence except for Dice's whispered "No."

At length, Eugene asked, "What happened?"

"I don't know. Lorstad said he was apparently electrocuted while inside the mountain with the Alphas. A bot brought his body out."

"They killed him?" asked Dice. He looked like death—his skin gray, his mouth a grim line bracketed with white stress lines. It seemed like so long ago, but it hit Chuck that Dice had known

Matt the longest—they had been colleagues at MIT before Matt had pulled him into FK. Chuck's heart reached out to the brilliant engineer even as Dice said, "Sara and the guys *killed* him?"

"I honestly don't know. Maybe it was an accident. Here's what I *do* know." He glanced out through the glass walls of their cage. "We need to find a way out of this mountain. We need to get back east and see if we can reach the Alphas and . . . I don't know . . . *talk* to them, figure out what's going on with them. Stop them if we have to."

"How?" asked Mini. "How do we stop them?"

Chuck shook his head. "I don't know, Min. I guess that's something we'll have to figure out, too."

Chapter 12

REQUIEM

Dice was raw inside. Matt Streegman had never been an easy person to like. Respect, admire, rally around, work for, yes. Befriend—that was harder. But Dice had done it. He had gone from being Matt's student to being his postgrad assistant to being his colleague and his friend. That friendship had been challenged by Matt's choices, and there had been times Dice felt he was "cheating" on Matt with Chuck, intellectually speaking, but he'd known Matt for over a decade and losing him was one of the hardest things Dice had ever faced.

He lay on his bed staring at the ceiling, missing Brenda desperately. For a moment, he felt horribly alone and lost and found himself fighting self-pity. The moment was broken by a light tap on his bedroom door. It would be Lanfen, making her rounds. He sat up.

"Hey," he said.

She opened the door and poked her head around it. "You okay, Dice?"

"No. Not really. I'm . . . I miss Brenda and . . ."

"I know. We're all a bit shell-shocked by losing Matt. But the rest of us are still here. Don't forget that, okay?"

He smiled wanly. "You read my thoughts."

"I'll neither confirm nor deny. You're clear, by the way." She made a circular gesture with one index finger at the vaulted ceiling.

He glanced up. "Oh. Oh, yeah. Thanks. Not that it matters. I doubt they can read my handwriting anyway."

"Your handwriting?"

"I keep a handwritten journal. In kanji and Russian." He shrugged.

"Funny, I wouldn't have taken you for the handwriting type."

He smiled again. "I'm just full of surprises, I guess."

Lanfen sobered. "If you've got any more, keep them under your hat. We need every advantage we can get."

Dice nodded and wished Lanfen a good night. Then he reached into the top drawer of the bedside table, took out his journal, and opened it. The pages were empty. He gazed at it for a moment through hooded eyes and words faded into view on the pages—kanji characters interspersed with lines of Cyrillic script. Dice turned to the first still-empty page and began to make more characters appear.

LANFEN CONTINUED HER ROUNDS, WORRYING a bit over Dice. Matt's death had hit him hardest, and she sensed he felt lost. Still, he seemed to brighten a bit when she stopped by, and that was at least encouraging. Mini and Eugene were out on the deck enjoying the twilight desert air, so she swept their rooms next, then ended her rounds at Chuck's door. He was sitting cross-legged in the padded window seat that overlooked the rocky northern escarpment.

"Just came to say good night," she told him. She gestured at the room, then did an exaggerated parody of a series of kung fu moves that took out the two listening devices that had been inserted during the day.

"Don't," Chuck said, stopping her when she'd turned to leave. "Don't say good night, I mean. Can we . . . talk?"

No hesitation. She closed the door and went to sit across from him on the window seat, their knees touching. They sat in silence for a time, then Chuck asked, "How can he just be dead? How can Matt Streegman just . . . end?"

"Death and birth are two sides of the same coin. You know that. Imagine what it feels like to be a twin whose brother has just disappeared from the womb. You'd think his life had ended, but you'd be wrong. His life in the womb ended, that's all."

Chuck smiled. "You're right. And I've used that metaphor before, myself, but when it happens—suddenly—to someone you know, someone you've worked with . . ."

He looked out at the desert. Lanfen followed his gaze. The sands had gone silver in the moonlight and shadows stretched out from every rock, bush, and twisted tree as if reaching for freedom.

"Matt and I weren't friends," he said. "Not the way you and I are friends. I learned the hard way not to trust him and apparently he didn't trust me from the beginning—or, at least, he didn't respect me. So, he manipulated me. He manipulated all of us. But in the end I think he *was* trying to fix things. He failed, though, Lanfen. He *failed*. Which means that we *can't*."

He looked up at her then, with his eyes open to the soul. She read the anguish and the uncertainty and, beneath that, the raw determination. She leaned forward and framed his face with her hands, astounded by how much she had come to care for him.

No—that wasn't right.

How much she'd come to *love* him.

"Dr. Brenton, I do believe you intend to save the world." She smiled. "Can I help?"

"Save the world? Lanfen, I'm not even sure I can save *us,* or the Alphas. This may already have gone too far."

"I refuse to believe that. You'll figure it out. You're good at figuring things out. Solving problems. Making things work. It's one of the reasons I love you, I think." He was startled. She used the moment of surprise to lean in and kiss him. It was a deep, no-doubts-left kiss and she gave herself to it completely. He hesitated for the slightest of seconds, but then he, too, fell into the kiss. He raised his hands to cover hers and responded with a flood of passion that washed away any vestige of the quietly controlled scientist. Lanfen well understood what underlay that passion: sorrow, frustration, fear, even anger. That was all right, she told herself. If he needed comfort, she wanted to be the source of that comfort. If he was embarrassed and regretful in the light of day, so be it.

But, somehow, she knew he wouldn't be.

He pulled out of the kiss but held her hands and her gaze. "I think I've loved you since the first time you walked into the lab," he murmured. "No, I *know* I have. I just didn't think . . ." He hesitated and gave her a quizzical look. "Are you sure?"

She drew him back into another kiss and showed him just how sure she was.

OUT ON THE DECK, EUGENE and Mini stood side by side at the railing, stargazing. They leaned against each other, looking at the same sky, but each was wrapped in his or her own thoughts. Eugene had no way to know what Mini was thinking. She had never liked Matt and certainly hadn't trusted him, but having someone you know *murdered* (also by someone you know) would upset even a mind as mundane as Eugene Pozniaki's. Mini, who was all heart, was unquestionably affected.

"You know the saddest thing?" Mini asked as if they'd been engaged in conversation instead of marking twenty minutes of almost complete silence.

"Mmm. What?"

"Matt was alone in the world. His wife was dead, his family

estranged. I wonder if there was even anyone but us to worry about him. The Benefactors had to work hard to cover our tracks. I'm not sure Matt had any tracks for them to cover. He didn't even have a dog or a cat or a goldfish. *We* didn't even know where he was. He was a ghost before he even died."

Eugene shivered at the thought, but he knew what she meant.

She half-turned to face him. "Eugene, if we get separated for some reason, I want you to know I'm okay. I want you to be able to sense me the way I can sense you."

He looked down at her. "You can *sense* me? How does *that* work?"

She shrugged. "I don't know how it works. It just does. But it bothers me that you can't sense *me*."

Those last four words made Eugene unutterably sad. "I wish I could. I love you, Mini. You know that."

"Of course I know that. And you know I love you. So, I have a gift for you." She lifted her hands, cupped as if she were holding something between them. "Put out your hands."

Eugene hesitated.

"Your hands," she said firmly.

He raised his hands in an open cup so she could deposit her gift in them. He realized that there was light leaking from between her fingers—a fey golden light that pulsed in irregular beats. With her hands lifted above his, she opened them to reveal a perfect, miniature version of herself, but with tiny, translucent wings shot through with veins of gold. She let the little creature drop lightly into his hands, and he was surprised she had weight, substance. She tickled.

Euge knew his eyes must be as big as saucers. "Is that . . . a fairy? You just made me a fairy?"

"It's a mini me," she said, laughing. "A mini Mini. She'll be with you anytime you want her and she'll be your window to my heart and soul." She laid her hands over her heart. "If we're apart, you can look at her and see what I'm feeling. And I think she'll let me be able to feel you more clearly even if we're not together."

Eugene looked up over the little fairy's golden head. She was gazing up at him just the way Mini was. "Mini, I want us to always be together. I mean always. I mean if we ever get out of this luxury prison, I want to marry you. Then you'll never get rid of me."

"Our souls are already married, Eugene. The first time we made love was our wedding night."

Eugene flushed from head to toe with a hot wave of desire. "Um, about the mini you. Will she still be hanging around when we . . . you know?"

Mini laughed. He loved her laugh. It was like music and birdsong and water sparkling over rocks all at once.

"Goose. You can make her come and go with a thought. Try it."

He looked down into his hands and said, "It'd be cool if you could be invisible." The fairy Mini vanished with a tiny musical ping.

"Where'd she go?"

"Back into the world between your ears."

"Why'd she make that sound?"

Mini shrugged and slid her arms around his waist, pulling her body against his in a way that made his brain tilt and his limbic system crash. "I just thought it would be a nice touch."

Eugene grinned. "My wife, the artist," he said and lowered his head to kiss her.

AMAZING.

Kristian watched the video for the third time and was still in awe of Minerva Mause's talent. She had somehow taught herself to create, not just a projection that she could manipulate, but a form of semi-independent life—a self-sustaining elemental that would mirror her moods and that could vanish, then retake the form she had given it . . . *at the behest of another.*

What else might she be able to do with opportunity and the right motivation?

Clearly someone deeply trained via immersion could not easily learn to harness their zeta powers, but what might an established Zeta do if introduced to immersion entrainment? The physiological and neurological changes that had already taken place within Minerva excited him. He needed only to convince her that immersion could open doorways before her that were unimaginable to her now.

He shook his head. *Fairies.* Minerva Mause had no idea of her true potential. He was determined to find a way to open her eyes to it.

He powered off the monitor, preferring a black screen to their increasing intimacy. He was angered with himself for having to soothe burgeoning feelings that should not exist.

Chapter 13

COUNCILS OF WAR

In the days since Kabul, the Zetas staged equally impressive displays in the ISIS stronghold of Raqqa, in Ukraine, and among the drug cartels in Ciudad Juárez (for all the latter's melting into the trees, they couldn't help themselves, and between the continued violence and drugs, the Zetas were compelled to take action). Every demonstration of their abilities seemed to make Roman Bluth and his cohorts dig their heels in deeper and deeper. This was beyond Margaret Ellis's comprehension. What could the senator hope to accomplish given the circumstances? Did he really expect that he'd be able to make political hay out of the situation with the Zetas, win a presidential election, and then magically control them?

Her chief of staff opined that Bluth was like a Chihuahua. "You know what I mean," Curt said during a private conversation. "He believes with all the fervor of his little doggie heart that he's a Great Dane. Seeing a bigger dog doesn't faze him in the least. It only makes him bark more energetically."

The problem with that, of course, was that the Zetas had

them on a leash that seemed to be getting shorter by the day. For every demand that Congress resisted, the Zeta leader, Sara Crowell, made a new one or suggested that the price of resistance would increase. She had already insisted that they throw open the entirety of the NSA's considerable intranet and databases, with the threat of exposing what she and her crew already had access to. The larger threat that hung over every interaction like the sword of Damocles was that they might reveal publicly what was really going on up on Mount Olympus.

Margaret didn't want to contemplate what the public would make of their government being held hostage by a trio of human beings with the sort of abilities you only read about in comic books or saw on TV and movie screens. It would be like waking up one morning to find that Batman and the Joker were real and battling over Chicago instead of Gotham.

That made molding the public perception of what was happening crucial and problematic. The story they had released to the media in small chunks was that homegrown terrorists from a previously unknown organization they had dubbed the Triad had taken over a shuttered government facility within the Michaux State Preserve and was armed to the teeth and threatening unspecified terrorist acts. The military had them surrounded, but they had access to the Internet and were making threats against American civilians. The Ellis administration was working to corral them and disrupt their operations. The story had the virtue of being true in its essentials and therefore fit the real-world happenings closely, insofar as events in the United States were concerned.

This did not, of course, silence the conspiracy theorists. They worked 24/7 at spinning amazing yarns in the darkest shades of purple. Somehow those never sank to the lurid depths of what was happening in reality. When Al Jazeera had run with a terrifying video of the attempted Taliban takeover of the Afghani

National Assembly, the conspiracists had first called it an alien invasion, and then a complete hoax.

Margaret was surprised that Congress hadn't sprung a leak with regard to the superhuman abilities of these homegrown terrorists, but perhaps even opportunistic politicos understood that some things were too scary for public consumption.

Even Bluth resisted disseminating that information.

It had already been necessary to intercept repeated attempts by various parties to sneak into Michaux and contact the Triad leadership. The Pentagon had used a number of elite forces from all branches of the military to draw a tight but nearly invisible perimeter around Pine Ridge and had so far been able to keep all comers out. As a happy coincidence, not needing those forces on foreign soil made it a lot easier to deploy them here.

Margaret prayed that would continue. Having card-carrying members of the tinfoil brigade break through the perimeter was too terrifying to contemplate—not because of anything *they* might do, but because of what the Zetas might do to *them*. So far—other than Dr. Streegman and various armed mercenaries—no American civilians had been killed in the Zetas' pursuit of global justice, and Margaret didn't even want to imagine what might happen if that changed. The thought of Roman Bluth and his cadre gaining traction for a military strike on American soil conjured images of the great Wyrm Ouroboros eating its own tail. Margaret Ellis wasn't certain that wouldn't be the beginning of the end of the union.

The problem was, though, that while it had been possible for Ellis to flex her executive muscles on a lot of the Zetas' demands, Sara Crowell had essentially issued an ultimatum that was constitutionally unattainable and democratically unthinkable. Even if it could be met, Sara and her two partners would be calling the shots. A tyrannical triumvirate ruling the world from beneath a mountain, it was something out of myth. Her one concession—

that the government could continue to *seem* to be in control if they met the impossible demands—was meaningless. It wasn't Margaret Ellis's personal control that was at issue—it was the right of U.S. citizens to self-determination.

It struck her hard, then: the world had changed irrevocably and there was no prior history that could help her deal with the threat the Zetas posed. This really was terra incognita; falling back into old thought habits would ultimately be self-defeating.

On the heels of that horrific epiphany, Margaret called Joan Hand and Curt Chamberlin to the Oval Office and sat down to discuss how they could reach Charles Brenton without creating even more public chaos.

"WE CLEAR?" CHUCK ASKED, FALLING into a seat between Dice and Lanfen at the conference table in his office. It was 6 A.M. and the rest of the facility was still and dark.

Lanfen sat unmoving for a moment, her eyes closed.

"Clear."

"Fantastic. Let's go. First problem: I can't get Lorstad to give an inch on his conviction that he has to shield us from what the Alphas are doing and from the chaos they're causing outside. I've stopped pressing, because he's looking for any excuse to cut us off from the world completely again. We've gone into transactional mode. I give him something; he gives me something. I told you he asked how I healed Joey. I didn't tell him everything, and I'm certain he knows that. He's not going to let us go until we've been able to make Zetas out of his novices *and* given him a formula for predictable results I'm not even sure exists."

"Okay," said Euge. "Then what are our options?"

Chuck took a deep breath, knowing what he was about to suggest would not be popular. No one had enjoyed their terrifying and exhausting initial cross-country flight, or hiding out in Doug Boston's beachfront cottage hoping not to be found.

"We may need to pull off another great escape. Lanfen has been monitoring the new security measures and she thinks it's doable. The greatest outstanding problem we have is securing transport."

"Maybe Joey can help with that," Dice suggested.

"As much as I'd like to believe we can trust him," Chuck said, "I'm not sure we can. We need to keep Joey out of this—at least for now. That's for his own protection as well as our own. He doesn't have to conceal what he doesn't know. Make sense?"

He looked around the table at the furrowed brows and felt their anxiety as a creeping of the skin across the bridge of his nose. Weird. One by one, they nodded.

"Lanfen, can you give a rundown on what you've found?"

She pushed her iPad to the center of the table. "Okay, here's an elevation of the house and its surroundings. Yellow triangles mark cameras; red squares mark laser sensors; green lines indicate patrol routes. There are three pairs of men in the patrol. The teams are equidistant from each other and patrol at a distance of twenty yards from the house. They're in constant motion. So, if you're looking down on the desert from the deck"—she tapped the screen with a finger—"one of the patrols will go by below at intervals of eight minutes."

"Eight minutes!" repeated Eugene. "That doesn't give us a lot of time to get out of their way."

"No, it does not. *But,* we have an ace up our sleeve. We have Mini."

All eyes turned to the pert strawberry blonde. She grinned.

"Mini can make them see—or not see—whatever we want. She can also fool the cameras."

"But I can't fool the lasers," Mini admitted. "I'm not sure why, exactly, but I think it's because while I can construct 'real' things that have a sort of substance, I can't make substance go away. Invisibility is just an illusion; the lasers will still hit something solid if one of us blunders into them."

"So," Lanfen added, "I have to take care of the lasers *my* way. Which should be fine, because I think I can jam them without making it glaringly apparent they've been jammed. That means we just have to solve the transportation problem."

"What if we forget about trying to escape into the desert and just go straight for their vehicles?" Dice asked.

"For starters, I'm not even sure where they keep the vehicles," said Chuck, "which I'm sure is what they intend."

"They're housed here." Dice put a fingertip solidly on a blank area just to the north of the house. "It's underground and the entry is screened behind some boulders and a couple of piñons. It's connected to the house through the solarium on that side, and to the highest level of the underground facility through the med wing."

Chuck stared at his robotics expert. "How do you know all that?"

Dice tapped his temple. "Schematics. I've been practicing my art by tracing the electrical and data trails throughout the installation. It's amazing how much you can determine about a space by the way its circuitry is laid out. If we can get to the vehicles physically, we can manipulate any electronic or computerized systems that are involved in their storage or monitoring."

Chuck found himself nodding. "Yes. That makes a lot more sense than trying to escape across the desert."

Mini was smiling again, mischief in every dimple. "But when we finally make our move," she said, "I bet I can convince them that's exactly what we've done."

Euge gave her a wide-eyed look of awe. "Have I told you lately how amazing you are?"

"Last night?"

Eugene blushed from the base of his neck to the roots of his hair.

Even Dice laughed.

"Incoming," said Lanfen when their nervous mirth had been

spent. "Joey's in the lab. We should probably open the meeting up and welcome him back from the dead." Chuck nodded and Lanfen moved to open the door and invite the engineer in. Dice turned to Chuck and lowered his voice. "You said you were afraid Lorstad would cut us off from the outside world again."

"Yes. I know he's still blocking things he doesn't want us to see."

"Not as of this morning, he's not. And he can't. He can't block incoming content and he can't keep us from messaging out. I can keep us connected to the outside world no matter what he does—unless he's willing to cut the entire Center off from his own intranet, and I'm willing to bet he'd never do that."

"How?" Chuck asked, nearly whispering. He could hear Lanfen chatting happily with Joey at the office door.

Dice's smile was strained. "Like I said, I've been practicing."

KRISTIAN WAS NOT BLIND TO the frustration and unease among Charles Brenton's team. He warned the Learned Council that this unease and dissatisfaction could yield rebellion, but they doubted these new "talents" posed any challenge for the Learned residing at the Center. Lorstad could not convince them otherwise. Alexis was no help. She flatly told the Council that he was enamored of the Zetas and grossly overestimated their abilities.

How much he wanted to yell at them that they grossly *under*-estimated the Zetas. But he knew it wouldn't get anywhere.

Kristian left the videoconference with the same mandate he'd always had: work with the Zetas to quantify the Brenton-Streegman process for training zeta talents and explore the possibility that a Zeta exposed to their technology and immersion might be the ultimate in human enhancement. He knew, of course, that Brenton's frustration had already resulted in token resistance. He was aware of Lanfen's jamming of Center surveillance, knew how often Eugene collided with their reverse firewall, and suspected they discussed more than training programs and formulas in their private meetings in Brenton's office.

He allowed them their little subterfuges. If he'd learned one thing in his lifetime, it was to choose his battles carefully. Thus he let the Zetas believe they were advancing in some manner so they would continue their work without direct confrontation. Still, it was clear to him, if not to Alexis and the other members of the Council, that in order to ensure Brenton's continued cooperation, he was going to have to make concessions that went beyond nominal access to the Internet. If he made the right compromises, he might even be able to enlist the help of someone inside Charles Brenton's tight organization. Because it had not escaped Kristian's attention that four of them had paired off, leaving Daisuke Kobayashi as the odd man out. There might be a point of ingress there. In the meantime, Lorstad believed he might have found a means of winning Mini's trust as well.

One way or another, he *was* going to get what he needed from them. And then he could worry about what to do with Charles Brenton and their little rebellion.

MINI SENSED LORSTAD BEFORE SHE heard him call her name. She looked up from the corps of eight miniature dancers she had created and set in motion to see him approaching from the lab doorway. She smiled at him but knew the smile didn't go all the way to her eyes. She had liked this man at first, but gradually had come to feel that she was less a person to him than an interesting puzzle to solve . . . or an asset. His obvious dismay over her relationship with Eugene made her angry; his unsubtle attempts to inure her to the immersion labs made her nervous. She shook herself free of dark thoughts as he drew near.

His eyes went to the dancing figures on her worktable. "What are these? Mini, they are wonderful!" He stopped to watch them perform the intricate moves of a quadrille.

"They're a sort of drill," she explained. "I'm working at manipulating a group of figures through complex patterns. You see, I have to consider their form, the details of hair and dress, and the patterns of movement before I set them in motion."

"You've become a programmer," Lorstad enthused.

"Me? A programmer?" She laughed and knew from the light in his eyes that he was delighted. The idea smothered her mirth. She glanced across the lab at where Eugene worked at his computer, going over the data from their sessions with several new novice Learned. He didn't even try to pretend he wasn't watching. He was frightened for her, she realized, and that frightened her, too.

"I'm just an artist," she parried.

Lorstad shook his head. "As Charles and I have told you repeatedly, there is no 'just' when it comes to your spectacular talent. In fact, I think your mastery would be very helpful to me with a most delicate situation."

"Really? How so?"

He glanced back at the dancers. "Can you re-create these anywhere?"

"Of course."

"Then come. I'd like you to meet someone." He held out his hand.

"Who?"

"We have a new initiate who has just been sent to us from Estonia. She is young and a bit frightened and very shy about entering into company. I think if she met you, she might be less afraid. And if she were to see what you can do, I think she might very much want to do it herself. Will you come meet her?"

She glanced at Eugene again, then at Lorstad's hand. She folded her own hands in front of her, smiled, and said, brightly, "Lead on, Macduff."

He frowned slightly at the snub but quickly regained his composure, withdrew his hand, and turned to escort her from the room. She felt Eugene's anxious regard until they were out of his line of sight. She knew a pair of disembodied lips planting a peck on his cheek then vanishing would be a small yet effective balm for his nerves, and so she sent her message of assurance to the man she loved.

EUGENE WATCHED LORSTAD ESCORT MINI from the lab, his mind fighting turmoil. He didn't trust Lorstad and knew that Mini didn't, either. At least that was what he construed from her refusal to take the older man's hand.

He fumed for a moment, wishing he could be a fly on the wall or that he had epic zeta abilities. In the midst of berating himself for being such a schlub when it came to learning how to master his own brain waves, he suddenly realized that he had the next-best thing. He thought of a box in his mind—a beautiful golden chest—and imagined it opening. His mini Mini popped out and he pictured her sitting on the upper edge of his keyboard. She appeared there as solid and real as when Mini had first conjured her.

He focused all his attention on her face so he could read every expression.

Then he felt it, a peck on his cheek. He swore he heard a giggle. He touched his face where the phantom smooch had landed. A kiss and his mini Mini were the perfect remedy. He couldn't completely relax, but at least he wouldn't go completely nuts.

"THEY STILL DANCED," LORSTAD SAID as they approached the elevator core. "Even as we left the room, the little fairies danced. How did you accomplish that?"

Mini shrugged, her eyes on the elevator, wondering if he would take her to the med wing. "It's like you said, I guess. I programmed them. I gave them a pattern to follow and they followed it. They'll follow it until I change it or . . . put them away."

"Why fairies?"

She shrugged. "When I was a little girl I had a fairy-tale book that had a story in it about a box full of fairies that loved to come out of their box and dance. But if you let them out, it was almost impossible to get them to go back in." She paused, struck by a sudden thought. "That's like our zeta abilities, isn't it? Fairies you can't put back in the box; genies you can't get back into the bottle."

"Ah, Mini, you are an astonishment. The perfect balance of creative whimsy and wisdom. Yulia will adore you."

She glanced at him in surprise. "That's the first time you've called me 'Mini.'"

"I suppose I have learned to call you that because those closest to you call you that. I bow to their wisdom where you are concerned."

They got into the elevator and Mini tensed, dreading the elevator's descent. She relaxed when, instead, it rose. When the doors opened, she found herself in what must have been the uppermost level of the house on the side opposite her own room. They stepped out into a transverse corridor with a wall papered in raw silk of spring green and broken by several doors. Lorstad steered her to the left toward the uphill side of the house, then left again at the next intersection. He stopped at a door on the right side at the end of the hall. He knocked, but there was no answer.

"Yulia," he called. "I've brought someone to meet you. Her name is Mini and she is magical. She has taught herself to make fairies."

Mini concentrated on the room beyond the door and realized that she could sense the chaotic flux of energies there: trepidation, loneliness, stubbornness . . . curiosity. She put a hand on Lorstad's arm. "Let me try something," she said.

He gestured for her to proceed.

She stepped close to the door and called, "Yulia? Hello. I'm Mini. I have something I want to show you." She concentrated on a spot just inside the door and created one of her little dancers—a young man with dark, curly hair dressed in knee breeches with a long, flyaway coat and a tricorn hat. She saw him clearly in her mind's eye standing proudly erect, then sweeping off his hat and giving a deep, courtly bow before executing a crisp jig.

There was an audible exclamation from the other side of the door. A moment later, the door opened. The girl who peered out at Mini was no older than twelve, but fully as tall as she was. She was thin and dark with a heart-shaped face and huge brown eyes.

"You made this dancing man?" she asked, in faintly accented English, pointing at the little figure who had returned to an upright position with his hat tucked beneath one arm.

"I did," Mini said. "I'm an artist and he's sort of . . . a living statue." She sent the little dancer a thought and he turned to look at Yulia with an expression of expectation on his tiny perfect face.

"You taught yourself to do this?"

Mini nodded.

"Can . . . can I learn it, too?"

"You can," said Lorstad. "Mini and her friends will show you how. But you need to come down to their . . . to Mini's studio first. Will you do that, Yulia?"

The girl studied Mini for a moment longer, then nodded. "If she will be there." Then, shyly, "And him," she said, pointing at the dancing man.

"Oh, he'll be there," Mini said with a smile. She held out her hand and the girl took it with only slight hesitation. She came willingly, if cautiously, with them down to the lab, which she entered with her head swiveling every which way and her eyes as big as quarters.

Lorstad and Mini stood patiently by as she took in the long, high-ceilinged room with its varied work areas, then they introduced her to the assembled team. She greeted each with lowered eyes and shy demeanor until she got to Eugene. Then she did a double take, shot Mini a surprised glance, and smiled.

"Oh," she said, "you are the tiny man that Mini made dance in my room!"

"I'm the *what*?"

"I'll tell you later," Mini said. "I think Yulia would like to have her first zeta lesson. She wants to learn to make dancing men of her own."

EMBARRASSED, YET SOMEHOW GRATIFIED, EUGENE returned to his workstation to continue clandestinely monitoring happenings in the outer world. Dice, true to his promise, had given them untrammeled access to the Internet.

He'd set up a search on Chuck's name and had a list of hits to pore over. One of them, oddly, was the whitehouse.gov page. Eugene followed the link and found something that made every too-curly hair stand up on his head and quiver with excitement. He glanced down the room at the test bay where Dice, Joey, and Chuck were showing Yulia the machinery. He slid from his seat and approached the group, sidling up beside Chuck as surreptitiously as possible.

"Doc, if you've got a minute, we really need to talk."

"Can it wait?"

"Not really. I need to show you something I just found. In your office?"

Chuck turned to look at him. "You found something in my office?"

"No, I want to . . . can we just—" He gestured with his chin at the inner "fishbowl." "God—just go to your office!"

Chuck's eyes widened in surprise at the outburst, but seeing Eugene's face, he nodded and followed Eugene into the inner sanctum. "Does Lanfen need to—"

"I don't think so. I just need you to see something."

He hurried into Chuck's office and moved to his desk to wake his laptop. By the time Chuck had come to the desk, Eugene had entered the password and gone online. Chuck frowned at him. "You know my password?"

Eugene snorted. "Doc, I've known your password for years. And I'm pretty sure you know mine. Here, this—this is what I wanted to show you." He turned the computer so Chuck could read the screen.

There, on the White House website, was a personal message from President Margaret Ellis. It read:

My fellow Americans:

Our current situation requires wisdom, patience, courage, and restraint. We are seeking to contact experts who can aid us in understanding how we may best negotiate with the Triad—the terrorists holding the abandoned military outpost in Pennsylvania.

Anyone with knowledge of the whereabouts of the following individuals is encouraged to contact my administration through the office of Chief of Staff Curtis Chamberlin: Dr. Charles Brenton, Dr. Daisuke Kobayashi, Dr. Eugene Pozniaki, Ms. Chen Lanfen, and Ms. Minerva Mause.

We believe these individuals may have much to contribute to the solution of our present dilemma.

Dr. Brenton, if you should happen to see this appeal, I beg you, please make contact with the White House. This is a matter of grave urgency.

This was followed by the president's signature and a specially assigned phone number and e-mail address.

Eugene looked up at Chuck, taking in the stunned expression on his face. "What do you think we should do?"

"I think we should try to contact the president's chief of staff."

"DAMMIT, ROMAN! WHAT PART OF 'they don't care about our politics' do you not understand?" Margaret was at the end of her rope. She got up from her desk (reminding herself that it was the *Resolute* desk) and rounded it to sit across from Roman Bluth in the seating area in front of the fireplace.

"This isn't about politics, Madam President," Bluth countered smoothly.

"Really? You're not using this as a declaration of your intent to run against me? Please—I'm not a child, Bluth. But forget that for a second. If this isn't about politics, then what's it about? What do you think stonewalling these people is going to accomplish? If I could make sense of your position—if you've got some brilliant plan I don't see, that Curt doesn't see, that *Joan* doesn't see—then for God's sake *share* it. If it's reasonable, if it's workable . . ." She spread her hands.

"Well," he said, running a well-manicured hand down his tie, "these things aren't simple . . ."

Margaret read the gesture as a defensive one, and yet she still almost laughed at the ridiculousness of what he'd just said. "You're preaching to the choir, Roman. Tell me something I don't know—and I mean that quite literally: tell me what I don't know. Why are you pushing back on this, when you know we really don't have a choice? We can either play this the way the Zetas want or we can expect disaster. You saw what they did in Afghanistan, in Syria, in Ukraine, in Korea, in the Congo—hell, in *Mexico.* Do you want another Washington Monument or worse?"

"Of course not. But to be honest, Madam President, blind obedience to these terrorists is more likely to end badly for us than standing up to them . . . or negotiating from a position of strength."

"Position of strength? There *is* no position of strength. Did you not hear what I just said? You've seen the same evidence I've seen—I've been very clear in making sure Congress was fully aware of all the info I have. Why are you treating this as if it were—" She cut off, reading the answer to her aborted question in his eyes before he glanced away. "Oh . . . I see." She shook her head at the dawning realization. "You don't believe this is real. You think we're being hoaxed."

He shrugged.

"What—the attack in Kabul happened on a soundstage?"

"It's possible."

"To what end? We had verification from multiple sources—all reliable, some even antagonistic to each other. Not all of them American, meaning I'd have no power over them. Besides all that, you drive past proof every day: the Washington Monument is in ruins, Roman. That was no Hollywood stunt."

"One of our own helicopters did that."

She stared at him. "Fine. Imagine for a moment everything we've seen so far has somehow been faked—which it hasn't, but we'll play that hypothetical game for the time being. What will it take to convince you that this is real? More dead bodies?"

He smiled, and Margaret realized how much she hated that smile.

"I don't know," he said. "But I'll know it when I see it."

She almost threw her hands up in disgust at that. "I'm not sure you would," she told him, standing. "Or if you saw it and knew it, I'm not sure you'd admit it." Bluth tilted his head back ever so slightly, and Margaret knew she had hit the mark. She pressed. "So that's *actually* it. I don't think you really believe we're being hoaxed; I think you just *want* to believe it."

He stood, too, frowning, but with the smile still in place. "That's hardly fair to me, Margaret."

"Really, Roman? *Really*? And how fair is it to me for you to use this situation for political attack ads? Your behavior on the floor of the Senate has been all about how much better you and your party could handle this. It's perfect timing isn't it? You take over the media cycle just as your party is about to name a candidate—very convenient, no? Well, Senator, I'm asking you—no, I'm *begging* you—to put your money where your mouth is. If you've got ideas, I want to hear them. And you and your party can have all due credit for them.

"I'm calling your hand, Senator Bluth. What have you got?"

She stood toe-to-toe with him on opposite sides of the National Seal for a long, tense moment in which she thought he was scrambling for a clever comeback and coming up empty. A chill crept up her spine. His smirk revealed that he *did* have something, a card up his sleeve, something to be played against her. He remained silent, feigning defeat, but Margaret knew better.

"That's what I thought," she said, then turned on her heel and returned to her desk. "I'll see you on the floor of the Senate, Senator Bluth."

He had started to move toward the door, but paused to look at her, his hand going once more to his tie. "What? That's highly irregular."

She looked up at him from behind the *Resolute* desk. "That's what I've been trying to tell you, Senator. These are highly irregular times."

"Apparently so." Bluth's strangely calm demeanor did not rest well with Margaret. It could mean any number of things, but more than likely it confirmed her suspicion that he had something to be played against her.

He left, and Margaret lost herself in going over press releases, threading a zigzag path between truth and fiction. She had been asked to account for the bizarre abilities that a myriad viral videos showed the "terrorists" possessed. She described them as a combination of high-tech tools, staging, and CGI. The irony was not lost on her that, even as she was trying to convince America that the supernatural aspects of the terrorist attacks were fake, she was desperate to assure Congress that they weren't.

She looked up at the sound of a tap on the door from her chief of staff's office. "Come."

Curt Chamberlin entered the room with a look on his face

Margaret was pretty sure she'd never seen before. She couldn't read him.

"Curt? What is it? What's happened?" She started to rise, but he waved her back.

"I just got an Internet call."

"That's fascinating, Curt, but unless it's for something to wash the stink of Roman Bluth from this room—"

"A call from Dr. Charles Brenton."

Margaret sat back in her chair. "*You* just got a call . . . That means he made it through the verification process." It amazed her how many people lied just for fun.

"Yes. Yes, he did."

"You're telling me we're in contact with the real Charles Brenton." Margaret was pretty sure her facial expression now mirrored her chief's. "Well, we need to bring him in."

"That may not be as simple as it sounds."

What in this new world we live in is?

Chapter 14

BENEATH THE SURFACE

Kristian Lorstad was no longer comfortable with all the attempts Chuck's team had been making to mask their conversations. It had been expected, of course, but with progress on his requested process and formula stalling, frustration and suspicion were enough for him to stop being coy about what he knew and what he didn't. So he simply decided to confront them openly, knowing Charles did not like to tell falsehoods and often gave himself away when he tried, and Eugene was equally an open book.

The time for games was over.

After the team's morning session with Giles and Yulia, Kristian dismissed the two trainees and requested that the entire kinetics team assemble in Brenton's office around the conference table. They exchanged wary looks, which the Learned pretended to ignore, and complied. Once they were all seated, they gave him their entire attention. He made a point of meeting each person's gaze before turning to their leader.

"Charles," he said, "I must ask you something. It is obvious that you and your team feel frustrated here and wish to reach out to your fellow adepts in Pennsylvania. We are not unaware of the measures you have taken to keep your private quarters and this room free of our surveillance devices. I am disturbed by this—"

"Then we're even," said Kobayashi. "*We're* disturbed by your surveillance devices."

"Be that as it may, I must ask directly: Charles, are you planning an escape?"

Brenton looked up and met Kristian's eyes, then laughed softly. "'Escape' is an interesting choice of words, Kristian . . . but what would be the point? We've tested your security—both live and virtual. So, we know how tight it is. I'm sure your tech people have informed you of every poke and prod. I imagine we'll get out of here when you're good and ready to let us go. I just hope that's in time to do something about what's happening beyond the walls of your . . . fey kingdom. Of course, this brings up an interesting—and rather disappointing—thought."

"Oh?"

"Quite frankly I am surprised we are regarded as inmates needing to escape, as you put it."

Kristian tried to read the other man. Charles Brenton did not seem at all like someone who had just been confronted with plotting an escape. He seemed resigned to his fate. Kristian looked to Daisuke Kobayashi next. The engineer was regarding him with narrowed eyes, his jaw tight. Clenched. Dice, Kristian suspected, was most deeply affected by Matt Streegman's death. Which made him emotionally vulnerable.

"You're angry, Dr. Kobayashi," he observed.

"Yeah, I'm angry. I feel like my hands are tied. I've lost a lot in the last several months—a colleague, connections with family, my fiancée, my life. It's like standing on a riverbank watching people you know drown, and knowing you won't let me even try to save them. This rescue of yours is feeling more and more like a prison sentence every day. But all you care about is your precious evolution. You want to be masters of the universe while everyone else . . . Well, that's the whole point, Lorstad—you don't give a rat's ass about everyone else."

Kristian shook his head. "I assure you, Dr. Kobayashi, that is not true."

"No?" That was Eugene. "You expect us to trust you, to work with you—hell, to work *for* you—but you give damn little in return."

"How about the fact that we took you in and protected you from Deep Shield and the Alphas? That we continue to do so."

"Yes, but it wasn't as if you did that out of the goodness of your hearts. We're assets. Tools." Eugene's face was flushed. "*Profane* tools."

Lanfen jumped in, her dark eyes glinting with distrust. "You observe us as if we were lab specimens. You make us perform for you, show you the extent of our capacities. You want to know everything about us, but you share nothing about yourselves."

Charles had turned his head to look at her, his expression bemused. She afforded him a glance, then said, "What if we simply stop performing, Kristian? What if we decide that we want to be as big a mystery to you as you are to us?"

Kristian opened his mouth to ask what they'd like to know, then decided this was an opportunity to show rather than tell—and show something that would make his guests feel that they were well rewarded for their trust. Theoretically, that might make them more inclined to trust in return. He had been preparing for the eventuality of having to do something as bold as what he was now contemplating, though he had intended it to be more reward than incentive.

"I understand, Ms. Chen. And I am willing to share with you now one of the things that immersion has allowed me to do." He smiled briefly, stood up . . .

And *vanished*.

CHUCK ALL BUT LEAPT OUT of his chair. Eugene, who'd been sitting right next to Lorstad, let out a yip of surprise.

"Holy shit!" he gasped, thrusting his chair back from the table. "Holy freaking shit!"

Mini shook her head, an expression of wonderment on her face. "Quantum physics."

"What?" asked Eugene.

Mini fixed Chuck with her bright gaze. "You remember, don't you, Chuck? I said he told me his area of expertise was quantum physics?"

"Quantum . . ." He looked at Dice, who'd also come to his feet. "Quantum *entanglement*?"

"In English, please," said Lanfen.

"I'm not sure *quantum entanglement* translates to English," said Dice. "It's hard to—"

He was interrupted by the sudden reappearance of Kristian Lorstad in company with a wide-eyed Brenda Tansy. They simply were not there one moment and then there the next. There was only the tiniest breeze from the sudden displacement of air.

"—explain," Dice finished.

Bren released the lapel of Lorstad's suit coat and gaped at the other people in the room, her blue eyes wide. "Oh my God, you weren't kidding!" she exclaimed, then turned and threw her arms around Dice's neck.

Mini laughed and applauded. Chuck wished he could take such childlike enjoyment in the moment, but he had to wonder what Lorstad expected to gain from such a display. Did he think that by giving Dice what he most wanted in the world, he would win his loyalty? Or was he just throwing them a bone? Chuck hated the tenor of his thoughts. He'd gotten through life this far without becoming a cynic. And he was genuinely happy for Dice and Brenda—the look on their faces was one of the best things he'd seen in the last few weeks. Still, he wondered if he'd ever trust anyone again.

"That's quite an ability," he told Lorstad. "You just went to the east coast and brought Bren back here in roughly two minutes. Am I right in thinking you're practicing a form of quantum entanglement?"

Lorstad smiled, his eyes lighting. "Yes. I can induce quantum entanglement in my own body and, as you've seen, in anything or anyone touching it."

"But how?" asked Eugene. "How's that possible?"

Lorstad smiled. "Well, in the simplest terms, I project a matter/antimatter version of myself, very briefly—essentially, creating a distant receptacle for my consciousness. Then I project my consciousness—or soul, if you will—into the receptacle. I'm able to change the polarity of my two selves at will. The antimatter version fades away as my consciousness is transferred to this new self—one made of matter."

Romantic reunion or no, Lorstad seemed to have captured Dice's attention. He stared at the Benefactor over Bren's shoulder. "You re-create yourself . . . atom for atom?"

"Indeed. There is one rather significant hazard: my fading antimatter self has to remain undisturbed during the process. It would be . . . unfortunate if it were not."

"How, unfortunate?" asked Eugene.

Lorstad turned to look at him. "Unfortunate."

Eugene nodded. "Okay. Important safety tip: avoid touching Lorstad when he's . . . entangling."

"That would be best." Lorstad moved to the office door. "Now, if you don't mind, I will see to Ms. Tansy's lodging and amenities while you continue with your work—I trust Dr. Kobayashi will want some time alone with Ms. Tansy. We will speak again soon."

Chuck waited until the other man was safely out of the lab before he turned to Lanfen. "We are not going to get answers out of him. Have to hand it to him, he simply directed the conversation and used a bit of quantum sleight of hand to rework this entire situation. To avoid and misdirect away from the question at hand."

"Question*s*," Lanfen added. "Are we prisoners here and what is their endgame? He traveled across the country to avoid those pressing points."

Chuck nodded. "Did you intend to push him into that display of—of talent?"

"I thought it might be important to get some sense of what he was capable of. It seemed logical to get an understanding of who we are facing should we have to run. What if the Benefactors and Lorstad turn on us? What abilities are we facing? I thought this was an opportunity to coerce him into showing at least some of his cards. But that's not the whole deck, I'm willing to bet."

"We need to know more about what's going on out there in the world before we rush back into it. We will press him again soon after we get more info from outside."

Dice came around to their side of the table to join in the conversation, drawing Bren with him. He still had his arm tightly around her waist. "You're thinking he may have laid some groundwork for getting Bren back?"

Lanfen shrugged. "You have made a point of how important she was to you and the team for some time."

"Why does it make a difference how spontaneous he is?" Bren asked. She was worrying the tail of her waist-length braid but showed no other signs of her recent journey.

"Because, our insistence to the contrary," said Lanfen, "we *are* planning an escape. If he can just zip all over the place like that without preplanning, it's going to be very hard to outrun him. Especially given that we aren't even sure where we are."

"Actually," said Dice, looking sly, "that's something I was intending to mention at this morning's progress meeting. I managed to get a fix on this place by 'walking' back through the system to their transceiver. I know right where we are—just south of the Snake River Plain on the border between Nevada and Idaho. Now all we need is a map, and we can plot a course out of here."

"SO, THIS IS THE MAN who would be general."

Mike looked up from his screen to see what Sara was referring to. She had just come up from the gym at Tim's summons and stood looking over his shoulder at his monitor, a towel draped around her neck. Mike dimmed his own display with a thought and got up to move forward to Tim's station. He'd been practicing "waking" an increasing number of robots at one time and exploring the electrical circuitry that fed power to their stations, but he wasn't ready to reveal the extent of his work just yet.

Now he peered over Tim's shoulder at the man in the computer display. The guy looked vaguely familiar. He was staring into the monitor as if watching or reading something, his eyes scanning back and forth.

"Who is he?" Mike asked.

"That," said Tim, "is Senator Roman Bluth. He's the guy that that dweeb, Freitag, has been chatting with on a very regular basis. And I have to say, their conversations have been pretty damned interesting."

"Freitag," repeated Mike. "That was Howard's mole in the Pentagon, right?"

Sara nodded. "Documentation expert. Ironic, isn't it? We all figured Howard must have had someone high up in the military feeding him all that intel. All along it was this glorified paper pusher. Midlevel guy who just happens to have oversight of all the documentation that passes through the place."

Tim expanded. "It also puts him in a nice position to create a phony paper trail linking POTUS to Deep Shield."

"So," Mike said, "Bluth is the guy who wants to rebuild Deep Shield?"

"Yep. He wants to spawn the Son of Deep Shield, and he's already taken steps. And he doesn't want to be a general, he wants to be a president," said Tim. He tilted his head back to look at Sara. "I wonder if he's the one who arranged for that drone attack."

Sara stiffened. "No. That was Matt. It had to have been Matt."

Why? Mike thought. *Why does it* have *to be him?*

Because you have to believe he deserved what you did to him? Otherwise . . .

Yet he said nothing aloud. It wasn't exactly clear to him why he hesitated, but mostly it came down to not wanting to confront her when he'd seen what Sara did to those she believed had betrayed her. He just let her keep talking.

"But this guy," Sara was saying, "*this* guy is keeping the government from doing what needs to be done. He's manufactured enough support—and enough doubt—in Congress to hold the POTUS over a barrel. With the amount he's able to fund-raise—and as the presumptive nominee for his party—he's got a lot of clout to at least keep the wheels spinning on the Hill. I'm guessing he'll probably top it all off with some phony revelation that the president knew about Howard and Deep Shield. POTUS can't just steamroll him—he'll filibuster if he has to and his party has the House. He's been in D.C. a long time and seems to be even more influential than the Speaker. This Bluth guy thinks he is clever and that he can continue to be an obstacle to us; I think it may be time that we did something about that."

"Cool," said Tim. "What about Son of Deep Shield? Are we going to do something about that, too?"

"At some point. I'll let you plan their ultimate demise. Right now we need to jar Congress loose. There's a session in two days, and I intend to be there . . . in my fashion. I guess I should shower and change." She winked at Tim and Mike, then swung around and strode out of ops.

She was halfway to the door and Mike was halfway back to his station when Tim's speakers let out a bleat and Tim responded with "Whoa. Whoa. *Whoa!*"

Mike swung back around. "What? What is it?"

Tim looked up at him, pointing to his oversized cinema display. "Check it out. POTUS has put out a call for the Betas to come in."

"What?" Sara shouldered her way in to stare at the screen. It showed a page on the White House website.

"It's a special letter from the president. To Chuck and the guys. She's asking them to come in. Do you think they will?"

Sara smiled. Mike hadn't seen an expression like that on her face in a very long time. It seemed to be a genuine expression of happiness.

"Knowing Chuck," she said, "I'd say he'd feel it was his patriotic duty. This is great, guys. If we can get Chuck back in the game, our operations will have far more scope and power. It will change everything."

Mike imagined that was so, but he wondered if it would change in a way Sara would like. He returned to his workstation and went back to his remote drills with the robots. He was progressing swiftly in the number of units he could control. He'd laid claim to a couple dozen most recently, but the true number was about three times that many. He was still queasy when he thought of how Sara might ask him to deploy them, though, and so continued to keep all of this to himself. He hoped that being reunited with Chuck would allow him to stop growing that particular ulcer.

Chapter 15

THE LOYAL OPPOSITION

Margaret knew what she was doing wasn't in the congressional "rulebook." It was, as Roman Bluth had noted, irregular. Presidents simply did not crash the Senate without official notice. But she wanted to impress on both houses of Congress that there was no rulebook for their current situation. Her own party had a majority in the Senate; it would be easier to barge in. The House would be a different matter. Partisan posturing would likely drag out an audience with the opposition-led lower chamber—time she didn't have. She needed to do something now and this was the quickest route. The House members would be watching on closed-circuit TV anyway. She was anxious and angry as she made her way to the Senate chambers with Curt Chamberlin at her side. Anxious, because she was doing something unprecedented—angry because she *had* to do it. One-on-one meetings with the senators in the "loyal opposition" had gone nowhere because Roman Bluth had wielded the power of his position so skillfully.

So it was time to show that she was pretty skillful at this game, too.

When she saw the startled, nervous looks on the faces of the young men guarding the Senate chambers, anxiety guttered to be replaced with a calm, icy resolve. She had to bull past Roman Bluth and make the rest of his cohort understand: this wasn't a hoax, and it wasn't any sort of "normal" terrorist situation.

"M-Madam President," stammered the first guard she encountered. "The Senate is in session. I mean, right now, they're in session."

"Yes, I know . . . Mr. Tyler, is it?" She read the name from his badge. "That's why I'm here. I need to speak to the Senate while they're assembled."

He blinked, shared a startled glance with his partner, then opened the doors. She smiled, said, "Thank you," and led Curt into the chamber.

Margaret had chosen to enter from the rear of the room so that her vice president, Harvey Feinberg, would see her from his position next to Roman Bluth at the head of the room. As it happened, Harvey saw her before the minority leader did. She was halfway down the central aisle before Bluth looked up and saw her.

The expression on his face was priceless: Surprise that she'd actually done what she'd promised. Suspicion. Annoyance. Anger. She watched the emotions chase across his face one after the other.

Harvey stood, interrupting the Senate clerk in the process of distributing briefing materials. "Madam President, this is a rare honor." The occupants of the chamber rose, some slower than others.

"It's highly irregular, is what it is, President Ellis," said Bluth. "May I ask that you arrange with the Senate—"

"I need to speak to the Senate *now,*" Margaret said loudly.

Bluth shook his head. "There are protocols, President Ellis—"

Harvey stepped away from his desk and waved Margaret toward it. "Please, Madam President, you can use my microphone."

Bluth feigned anger then regained his oleaginous façade. "The dignity of the Senate will not be hijacked for partisan purposes."

"Senator Bluth," Margaret said sharply, "you are out of line. You know all too well this has nothing to do with partisanship—or at least, it doesn't as far as I'm concerned. Is it a partisan issue to you?"

He didn't answer. Of course he wouldn't, as this was all being filmed, recorded, and broadcast throughout the Capitol Building. He had his sound bite anyway, so anything else would just be seen as a petulant tantrum, and she knew he was too polished to succumb to that . . . for now.

Ellis mounted the dais to the vice president's desk, pulled the microphone stand to its fullest extension, and looked out at the assemblage of startled senators.

"Distinguished members of the Senate," she addressed them, "I beg your indulgence. As the minority leader has noted, my appearance here is highly unusual. Unprecedented. But we are faced with an unprecedented situation. As you know, the unwarranted and unapproved experimentation funded and carried out by Deep Shield—a secret paramilitary organization operating alongside our legitimate forces—has resulted in the global community being coerced into changing its ways. The people issuing these ultimatums have repeatedly proven that they have the ability to intercede in ways that I frankly found unbelievable until I witnessed their work firsthand.

"Senators, if we have ever been faced with a need to suspend business as usual and take extraordinary measures, it is now. We have been issued an ultimatum: chiefly, that if we do not withdraw our forces from disputed areas and stop selling arms to our allies, they will take whatever steps are necessary to remove those forces and stop that commerce for us. Having seen what they are capable of doing, I am disturbed by the thought of what those steps might involve. I am therefore asking you—no, *imploring* you—to authorize me to adopt whatever measures will save American lives.

"First: I am hoping to establish a direct connection with the so-called Zetas and to work with them on the diplomatic front—"

"You want carte blanche, you mean." Roman Bluth glared at her from his own podium. "I'm sorry, Madam President, to find it necessary to be so skeptical of what you're saying, but it seems to me that this whole situation is timed with amazing convenience."

There was a ragged grumble from the floor.

"What do you mean?" Margaret asked.

"Isn't it obvious? You're nearing the end of your first term as president. This situation would allow you to suspend elections, pleading that you should be the one to negotiate with these Zetas." He leaned heavily on the last word as if to show his scorn.

A number of senators loudly voiced their displeasure at Bluth's words, while others made noises of approval.

Margaret ignored the commentary. "I can negotiate with the Zetas whether I am president or not—if I am not fortunate enough to continue my role as president I shall support the will of my successor. I promise you, I have no intention of trying to extend my term in office. Not only is it not constitutionally viable without amendment—which I'm savvy enough to know wouldn't pass—but it's not something I'd seek anyway."

"So you *say,* but this manufactured threat is tailor-made to do exactly that."

She was no longer merely angry; she was furious. Yet she kept her calm, knowing it infuriated Bluth just as much. "Tailor-made by whom, Roman? Do you really think I possess the scientific acumen or resources to do what the Zetas have done?"

"Ah, but you might know the people who *do* have that acumen," Bluth noted. "I notice you've issued a call to a Dr. Charles

Brenton to bring himself and his staff out of hiding. Perhaps Dr. Brenton is your 'tailor,' Madam President. And perhaps the conveniently destroyed Deep Shield provided the resources."

Margaret stepped back from the Senate president's podium, shaking her head ruefully, before once more approaching the microphone. "I asked because *I* know my limitations, Senator. I suggested he come and meet me because the people elected me to lead during these times, and Dr. Brenton is one of the few people who might be able to help us deal with these Zetas. He created them, trained them. He may be the only one who can talk to them in a way they'll understand. I have no idea whose creation Deep Shield was—"

"Oh, please, Madam President, I find that hard to believe."

"Because you *choose*—"

Bluth shouted over her. "I motion that a special inquiry be launched to ascertain Madam President's foreknowledge of this matter."

No doubt that investigation would discover utterly fabricated communications between President Ellis and Deep Shield. Redacted and doctored just enough to reveal criminality and appear authentic.

Bluth plowed on. "Once we can assure ourselves that we are being dealt with fairly and honestly by the White House, then and only then can we proceed with any dialogue."

Before Ellis could respond to this ludicrous call—essentially a vote of no confidence that the Constitution didn't actually allow for—the shouting from the floor of the Senate swelled suddenly with outcries of anger and distrust winging between the distinguished members. In one corner, a couple of male Senate aides got into a shoving match and seemed ready to come to blows. In another, a quartet of senators faced off against each other. As the chaos reached a peak, there was a searing flash of light near the domed ceiling of the chamber and a beam of sheer golden radiance fell from there to the Senate floor as if a door had opened in the dome. A woman appeared at the top of the beam and rode it downward as if it were an escalator. She was clad in gleaming black leather or vinyl and her dark hair fell, sleek and straight, to her shoulders.

Margaret had seen her before. This was a new version of the woman she'd watched destroy the insurgents in Kabul, and looked much more like the photographs she'd seen of Sara Crowell in the Forward Kinetics materials she'd pored over.

"Do you find *me* hard to believe, Senator Bluth?" Sara Crowell's avatar asked as she reached the floor of the Senate on her luminous escalator. Her voice—a rich contralto—carried unnaturally over the sounds of surprise, shock, fear, and anger rising from the floor. "I know that's my reaction to *you*."

Between the dais that supported the Senate leadership and the curved rows of desks that housed the general assembly, Sara Crowell's avatar stood, showered in light from an unseen source. It took all of Margaret's focus to remember that this seemingly solid, three-dimensional construct was just that—a construct—and that the real, living, breathing woman was miles away under a mountain in Pennsylvania.

The sergeant at arms, whose florid face betrayed his agitation, proved the effectiveness of the Zeta's illusion. He shouted a team of guards to his side and plunged down the central aisle past stupefied senators, pages, and guests. The Senate guards reached their uninvited guest and surrounded her, Tasers drawn. They were quickly joined by more than one Secret Service detail, only they had P90s. It was only then that she deigned to notice them. She pivoted slowly, smiling at them each in turn.

"Are you going to shoot me, gentlemen? I'd advise against it. I doubt you'd appreciate the results. I need to talk to your leadership now, okay? Why don't you all just run along?" She crooked a thumb at the exit.

The sergeant at arms gestured at two of his men and they stepped smartly forward and grabbed Sara's arms—or tried to.

Their hands passed through her suddenly translucent body as if through empty air. One reacted by raising his Taser. Sara wheeled smartly and slapped it out of his hand. His partner shouted and fired his own weapon at Sara's torso. She laughed as the electrified pins passed through her and connected with the sergeant at arms's beefy shoulder. He went down like a felled tree.

Margaret was stunned herself. She'd seen this before—this bizarre ability of the Zetas to make their doppelgängers seem solid or vaporous at will. She hoped Charles Brenton had some idea how that was possible and could help them counteract it when he came out of hiding—*if* he came out of hiding.

There was a moment of chaos in the chamber as the senators raged and the Zeta simply stood with her hands on her hips, smiling and looking like something out of a superhero movie. It was not hard to believe that she saw herself and her companions that way—as valiant superheroes besieged by terrified mundanes. Was that what they were?

A group of men rushed the chamber doors but Sara raised a fist and the doors refused to be opened. Her frightened, angry prisoners rattled them futilely. Several more of their fellow legislators, watching this display, seated themselves and gave Sara their entire attention.

The Secret Service was another matter. Agents were feverishly working to secure an exit for the president. They opened fire on one of Sara's sealed doors only to see the splintered remains float back up and press against the door like a shattered coffee mug clumsily glued back together. Pieces of chairs were torn from their frames and used to buttress the barriers further.

"Madam President, no one is leaving just yet."

How many times had Margaret wished she could simply exert mind powers to stop a disaster, an injustice, a political trend she felt was destructive or ill-advised? How often had she wanted to psychically send Roman Bluth a sudden case of laryngitis? These people actually had something approaching that ability. Did that make them villains or heroes or a bit of both?

Even as she mused, the scrambles continued. The chaos only ended as Harvey Feinberg stepped back to the podium and wielded the gavel with deafening effectiveness. The chamber stilled. The Sara avatar turned to the vice president with a smile and an airy salute.

"Thank you, Mr. Vice President. As I was saying, I'd like to talk to the Senate about you, Senator Bluth. Specifically your relationship with a Mr. Ted Freitag."

The effect of that name on Roman Bluth was electrifying, although Margaret had no idea why. This Freitag must be someone particularly damaging, though, because Bluth took a step backward, his hands coming up to his tie in the defensive gesture the president knew only too well.

"I don't know anyone—"

"Stuff it, Senator," snarled Crowell, anger flashing quite literally in her avatar's eyes. "You forget who you're dealing with here. My friends and I have been monitoring Mr. Freitag's online activities since we were reconnected to the outside world. Mr. Freitag, you should all know, works at the Pentagon as a documentation specialist. He is a former associate of one General Leighton Howard, functional head of Deep Shield." She paused and turned to the vice president. "I assume Congress has been briefed about Deep Shield."

Harvey offered a bemused nod. Margaret noticed that several senators returned to their seats, interest piqued by what they were hearing.

"Mr. Freitag was in contact with Senator Bluth within days of our destruction of Deep Shield. Their conversations have centered around—"

"I don't need to stand here and listen to this!" Bluth snapped. He turned and started to descend from the podium.

The Zeta seemed to blur as she leapt to intercept him. Eyes glittering, she thrust one hand toward him, palm out. He froze in place as if the air around him had suddenly congealed. His eyes went wide and his mouth worked silently.

"Yes, Senator, you *do* have to stand here and listen to this," Sara said, then scanned the large chamber with her laser-bright gaze. "You *all* have to listen."

"No!" someone shouted, followed by a chorus of negatives in strident male voices.

"I know, it's a bitch, isn't it?" Sara asked tartly. "Some woman comes into *your* house and tells you what you can and cannot do. Must offend the hell out of your exalted sensibilities. *Who the hell does she think she is?* That's what you're all thinking, isn't it? *Isn't it?*"

She roared those last words, her voice like the ringing of a great bell. The chamber fell silent.

Sara glanced at Margaret, shaking her head. "How the hell do you tolerate them? Guys, I'd say I'm your worst nightmare, but that would be horribly cliché. What I am, you can't even imagine. *I'm* not even sure of what I am, but I'm having a hell of a time finding out. Some of you think I'm a hoax. I'm not. Sara Crowell—the real Sara Crowell—isn't even here. She's in a bunker underneath a mountain that, as you've already seen, is unbreachable. I'm not a Hollywood special effect. I'm not a hologram. You've all seen it and now Senator Bluth has *felt* it. He *knows* it. Don't you, Senator?"

Still frozen, he stared at her, sweating, his face bloodless, his lips quivering. In that moment, Margaret felt genuine sympathy for him. Whatever his motives had been in stalling her, no one deserved to be toyed with like that. And seeing their power wielded so unabashedly, she even started to wonder if he wasn't wrong about not giving in to the Zetas.

"As I was saying, all the while Senator Bluth has been stalling Congress, he and Ted Freitag have spent a considerable amount of time planning the reanimation of Deep Shield and the good senator's accession to the executive office. The senator has expressed a great desire to have an ace in the hole that would serve him well whether or not he is elected president. Something in the nature of a personal special forces unit. Some of you think President Ellis has been lying to you about the Zeta program. She hasn't. Any documentation that may point to the president's knowledge of Deep Shield and the Zeta program was fabricated by the intrepid Mr. Freitag at the behest of Senator Bluth. Madam President was completely in the dark on all of this. Some of you think we've been lying to her. We haven't. Some of you think the footage you've seen from Kabul and other locations is Hollywood-style special effects, even though you've checked with every independent source available to verify that it's not. Get your heads out of your butts, ladies and gentlemen. This is not Hollywood. This is real. *I'm real.*"

She cocked her head to one side and grinned. "Well, after a manner of speaking. Now get off your collective asses and meet our demands. We're not making them because we're narcissistic dictators. We're making them for the good of the whole world—a world you and your greed and your political ambitions have sacrificed for far too long. You need to start thinking of *that* instead of calculating how to win elections or sucking up to your constituents. Put something besides your own fragile egos first, and do it now. And if you're tempted to rattle your sabers and tout your alleged exceptionalism, just think of what we did in Kabul. What we've done since. That, my friends, was just a proof of concept. I can assure you that, with every day that passes, we grow in strength and ability."

She turned to Margaret, inclining her head in a mild show of respect. "President Ellis has a complete list of our demands. She knows what we want and she's been trying to work with you to see that we get it. All our communications will come through her unless another little meeting like this one is necessary to remind you of why you're setting aside your partisan ass-hattery and working together. I mean, after all, you're all on Team USA, right?"

She wheeled then and, with one fist raised, began to ascend her beam of light chanting "USA! USA!"

She was perhaps two-thirds of the way up when two things happened in quick succession: Roman Bluth toppled out of his invisible prison and every door in the Senate chamber flew open, admitting teams of heavily armed soldiers. As one, they aimed their guns at the rising figure in the center of the room and opened fire.

Margaret screamed, her voice joining the cacophony of shouts and shrieks and the rattle and roar of gunfire. In the upper gallery, lights exploded; wall paneling and gallery rails splintered and rained down on the chamber floor. Caught in the downpour, senators and their aides dove beneath their desks or simply huddled and tried to cover their heads.

In the midst of it all, the Sara avatar dissolved in a shimmer of motes only to re-form in midair, her feet planted solidly on nothing. She was laughing. Several of the security guards below tracked her and resumed firing. Sara exploded like an Independence Day firework, sending streamers of light and fire into every corner of the huge room.

When the last streamer fell to the carpet and dissolved, the Senate chamber fell into an eerie silence. Margaret's ears were ringing from the gunfire, her eyes half-blinded by the explosions of light followed by semidarkness, her nose full of the pungent odor of cordite. She sucked in an enormous breath, laden with gun smoke and fear, and wondered what she should do next.

She was saved from that decision by gales of dark feminine laughter that cascaded from the vault of the ceiling. She looked up to see Sara Crowell's avatar floating there in a blaze of light. One of the marksmen raised his rifle. Sara pointed an elegant finger at him and the muzzle of his gun rippled and pinched in on itself.

"What is *wrong* with you people?" the apparition asked. "You've proved that you can't shoot me. You're failing to adjust to reality, gentlemen. Get with the program and remember Kabul . . . and Raqqa . . . and Ciudad Juárez. Or the day all those military bases went dark.

"Did I mention Kabul?"

She simply winked out of existence then, the air ringing with the echoes of her laughter. Margaret felt behind her, found a chair, and sank into it.

THEY ARE PLOTTING, KRISTIAN. I can feel it, if you can't. Alexis stood by the long window in Kristian's inner sanctum, looking down into the Center's cavernous main room. She could not see into Brenton's lab from where she stood, but she stared at the glass wall as if her thoughts could penetrate it.

"You can *feel* it?" he repeated, aloud. "What does it feel like, this plotting?"

She turned to regard him coolly, her arms crossed in front of her—guarded and annoyed. "You are no fool, Kristian. You know what I'm talking about. That's why you brought their robotics expert his lady love." She said the last word with a mocking drawl and an inner disdain. In his head he heard her saying, *You think you can placate them, but you can't. And you seem to be oblivious to the energies they broadcast when they're being secretive. They are planning something. I wake in the night with their scheming tickling my mind. You,* she added, *have the ability to confirm what I sense. I wonder why you haven't yet done it. I wonder, because I can get no sense of your reasoning.*

She was right, of course, and Kristian had wondered at his own reluctance. Just as he wondered at his increasing misgivings about allowing her to access more than a fraction of what was going on in his mind.

"Is it the little artist?" she asked aloud. "I know she intrigues you. Are you afraid of losing her trust?"

He met her eyes and failed to read them. Tried to read her emotions and found them confusing. He was not the only one doing a mental dance of veils. He laughed. "Alexis, my interest in Minerva Mause is not romantic, as you ought to know by now." Even as he said this aloud, though, the words felt false to him. *Were they?* He was stung with a touch of shame that he was not entirely sure.

"And I *would* be a fool if I believed she trusted me. She doesn't. I haven't done anything about their plotting because letting them scheme causes them to double their efforts in teaching our young learners the use of their zeta powers. Charles is not only a victim of guilt, he is uncomfortable with dishonesty. He told me outright of their efforts to find a means of reaching the outside world."

"And you chose to believe him? Why, because you think he cannot lie to you? Even an inherently honest man will lie if the stakes are high enough. A man like Charles Brenton, who is inclined to altruism, will sacrifice his personal standards if he thinks it may benefit others."

She was right, of course.

"Yes," Kristian said at length. "Yes, I think you may be right. I'll take care of it. Tonight."

Alexis relaxed her arms to her sides and smiled crookedly. *I'm pleased to see that my opinion still counts for something with you.*

He felt the irony in her thoughts but kept himself cloaked. "Jealousy does not become you, Alexis. Nor is it necessary."

She came around the side of his desk and perched within arm's length, reaching out a hand to touch his cheek. *I know that. After all, you and I have shared a deep connection from childhood. If I were to be jealous of any of them, it would be Dr. Brenton—his is the mind behind all that the others can do. The mind that can switch off your natural suspicion. In ways that I cannot.*

Nettled, Kristian grasped the stroking hand and held it, letting her feel his irritation. *He has not done that. I assure you, Alexis. My suspicious nature is entirely intact.*

Yes, but now you seem suspicious of me. *I wonder why.*

LATER THAT NIGHT, WHEN THE Center neared dormancy and its inhabitants left their workstations, Kristian entered the kinetics lab to find the team wrapping up their work with Yulia and Giles. The pair of youngsters showed off their new strides, moving Roboticus through a series of complicated moves at varied speeds, then showing their baby steps in chosen disciplines. Giles, who had a keen interest in meteorology, was working with atmospheric modeling. He showed his nascent ability to run his models using his zeta powers. Yulia was, like Mini, an artist. She wanted to sculpt without the aid of her fingers. Her first steps in that direction were tentative, but Kristian could see her potential. He had no doubt that, someday, Giles would move more than ersatz clouds in a holographic display and that Yulia would move mountains and remodel landscapes as easily as she molded clay.

He praised the pair for their progress, then announced his intention to adjourn to his immersion chamber to "recharge." "I will probably not see any of you before tomorrow morning," he told them. "So, until then . . ."

He did not miss the looks that passed between Charles Brenton and his staff. The "cat" would be asleep—what more could a scheming pack of mice want?

Two hours later, Kristian Lorstad looked down into Dr. Brenton's office from a vantage point above the conference table. He was not an electronic signal that they could jam, or a surveillance camera that they could point in the wrong direction. He was something they had no idea existed—a disembodied intellect that could perceive in ways physical senses could not. A heretofore unused ace up Lorstad's sleeve.

So it was that he got a shock that ran to his very soul. Not that his guests had hatched an ambitious escape plan and disguised it with blundering feints at the Center's integrated security and information systems—he had already suspected that was the case. No, it was that they had been using the known talents of the two women on the team to distract from Brenton's and Kobayashi's burgeoning abilities. More disturbing, still, was the fact that they had brought Joey Blossom into their confidence and that he, too, was growing quietly in his ability to manipulate his environment.

Perhaps the most disquieting revelation was that the exact nature of the plan was veiled by the team's communication style. In the privacy of Brenton's office, they occasionally spoke a patois of half-expressed ideas that Kristian knew were the tip of a much larger iceberg. He was almost certain that Team Chuck, as they thought of themselves, had learned to communicate subverbally in some way. He hadn't seen it before, nor was it appreciable on the surveillance footage. All of the original team, with the exception of the profane neurologist, seemed to share a form of thought transference, or at least empathy.

He didn't stop to indulge his excitement at the discovery that what they shared as a group had taken him years to develop with just one other person. Whatever this gestalt was, it was dangerous. He needed to do something about this and do it soon.

TO SAY CHUCK WAS STARTLED when Lorstad popped into existence next to him on the balcony outside his room would have been an understatement. The light of dawn had just broken the horizon and Chuck had been sipping his first cup of coffee and watching the sun paint the tops of the mountains rose-gold. He was clad only in flannel pajama bottoms and a "Failure is not an option" hoodie and very nearly dropped the coffee on his cold, bare feet. The expression on Lorstad's face was one Chuck hadn't seen before—anger. He was surprised at his strong conviction that the anger was false and that what lay beneath it was truer. The problem was, he couldn't read what was beneath it with any clarity.

"Um," Chuck said. "Good morning?"

"Hardly that. I know what you're planning, Charles—you and your co-conspirators. I know that you're actively seeking to go back to the east coast."

Damn. He wasn't bluffing. He *knew.* "I suppose I'm not surprised, but how did you—"

"How I know is unimportant. What is important is that you stop trying to escape and honor our agreement—discovering a formula that will allow your zeta training to apply to even the most adept among the Learned, and deriving from that a training regimen. I have given you and your team sanctuary, yet you are not fulfilling your promises to me, Charles, and that angers me."

Like hell it does. Chuck studied the other man for a long moment, employing every sense he possessed. Then he set his coffee mug carefully on the deck railing and shoved his hands into the pockets of his hoodie.

"When we agreed to come here," he said quietly, "you promised me that you'd help defeat men like Leighton Howard. You said, in effect, that it was as much your goal as it was ours."

"Yes. And Howard is more than defeated. He is dead. What is left of his organization is scattered to the four winds."

"Howard was, in all likelihood, the tip of the iceberg. He wasn't the head of Deep Shield. He was merely in upper management. Whoever was pulling his strings is still out there. Then there are the Alphas. They are more dangerous to this country—to this world—than Howard ever was, and they are growing in power with every passing day. I need to get to them, Kristian. I need to try to reason with them before they go beyond reason. If they haven't already," he added, thinking of Matt.

"Dr. Brenton, what you're doing here—"

"Is *nothing* compared to what I could potentially do *there*." Chuck was beginning to be royally pissed at Lorstad's patronizing calm and his feigned outrage. "I helped these people discover and use the abilities they're wielding. They may think they're doing God's business now, but I know how power works. They will ultimately use their abilities against anyone who gets in their way. *Anyone*. That includes me and it includes you. You may have noticed that they haven't stopped at the U.S. border. They're reaching out far beyond their base. Reaching out to the world through every electronic avenue in existence. They're putting the entire world at risk, Kristian. Their power could potentially grow to the point that a stray thought, a moment of rage, could result in calamities we can't even imagine."

Lorstad opened his mouth to retort, but Chuck didn't let him get a word in. "Yes, I know you're not part of the world. You and your—your *Learned* exist in some rarefied ether above everybody else. But I suspect you'd like the Benefactors' community—or whatever you call it—to evolve. I know you'd be thrilled to find more Learned that can be zeta trained. But if the Alphas can't be stopped before what Howard did to them and the power they're wielding drives them mad, then they may very well be competing with you for prodigies. Or worse, they may destroy them before you can find them. I assure you, after their experience with Deep Shield, they will destroy anyone that looks or acts or smells like the enemy. *They killed Matt Streegman*. Don't forget that. I know I can't."

Lorstad's face went completely blank, and Chuck knew he'd gained some ground. He pressed on.

"You've seen what they can do. So have we. So, no, Kristian. We will not stop trying to escape your lovely safe house. And while I will continue to raise up more Zetas, I'm no longer committed to your stupid formula, mostly because I don't think there is such a thing. There are some things you can't quantify and there are some things you can't have unless you're willing to sacrifice something else."

Lorstad fixed him with a chill look. "You mean you won't tell me what you've learned about zeta abilities unless I let you all go. Is that it?"

"Not at all. God, Kristian—you're not listening to me! I keep telling you that what I've learned can't be put into a neat little package. Any insights I have on the elements you're missing are in nascent form. It's not as simple as applying a measurable amount of element Z and ta-da—you've got Zetas. And, no, I'm not holding out on you so you'll let us go."

"Then what are you saying?"

"What I'm saying, ultimately, is that you may have to give up part of what you are to become what *we* are. If anything, *that's* the formula."

The expression on Lorstad's face was indecipherable, but the emotions behind it were forceful and vivid.

Chuck smiled. "Scary thought, isn't it? But here's the deal—and it's something you already know—your means of gaining your abilities is limited and has to be maintained. Ours . . . well, let's just say the potential is infinite. We literally don't know what we can rise to . . . or sink to. Your choice, Kristian. Throw in with us or throw us out. Now—I have work to do. Let me know what you decide."

He retrieved his coffee and went back inside, leaving Lorstad standing statue still in the desert sunrise.

Chapter 16

EMERGENCE

Mike had gone past any sort of nerves into a sort of eerie, watchful calm by the time he and his companions finally emerged from their mountain bunker. They had the assurances of the president herself that no attempt would be made to harm them. The armed forces there would be for the purpose of protecting the president's delegation from harm and to keep any third party from attempting to sabotage the proceedings.

Of course, that might not keep Senator Bluth from trying something using whatever tools he still had at his disposal. Because even though Bluth vehemently denied any association with Freitag, suspicion had fallen rather heavily on him. Scalded as he'd been by Sara's grandstanding in the Senate, Mike thought Bluth aimed to humiliate the president, not kill her. He was under house arrest, according to President Ellis, and allowed to speak only with his legal team. Freitag had been taken into custody by the FBI, but God only knew how far they had gotten with their plans to resuscitate Deep Shield.

Mike comforted himself that if he knew it would be stupid to stage an attack that risked the lives of the president's negotiating team, anybody with even a trace amount of strategic savvy would come to the same conclusion.

Although that didn't stop them from making an attempt when Matt was here.

Mike found he didn't much care who was plotting what. He was almost as sanguine about being blown off the face of the earth as he was about making it out of the mountain to the parley with the POTUS. Oddly, he found he trusted Margaret Ellis. He hadn't voted for her. He hoped that wouldn't come up . . . then laughed at himself for even having the thought. As if she'd care, at this point.

Sara, naturally, was stoked at having finally gotten through to the recalcitrant U.S. Congress. What had happened in the Senate had had the immediate effect of reducing the passive-aggressive behavior that possessed the members of both houses. Now the number of senators and representatives who considered the Zetas merely high-tech terrorists—or worse, a hoax—was in the single digits. Sara had refused to meet with the entirety of Congress but had insisted that a negotiating party be put together that included the president, the secretary of state, the head of the Joint Chiefs, and the majority and minority leadership of the lower and upper houses of the legislature.

Tim was exultant, crowing, swaggering, and hyped. He had insisted—and Sara had done little to dissuade him—that a handful of his zeta-made creatures be part of their escort, along with half a dozen of the robots, controlled by Mike.

So it was that the trio, with their bizarre troop of bodyguards, made their way out of the mountain via the main egress. Sara had insisted they use that access because it would provide the best opportunity for a spectacular emergence into the outside world, and because she did not want outsiders to know about any of their back doors. The journey took half an hour and required bulling their way through the debris and wreckage of past battles. All of this was duly recorded by Tim in a sort of rolling selfie.

It was this process that made Mike realize he wasn't the only one who had been secretive about personal progress with zeta manipulation. At the first major obstacle they came to—a slagged howitzer that had formed a Daliesque installation in the middle of the main egress—Mike had expected Sara to defer to his prowess with gross physical objects. She didn't. She made an almost lazy downward gesture and caused the misshapen mass of metal to grind itself back down into the turret from which it had risen. Then she levitated herself over the resulting chasm, alighting agilely on the opposite side.

Tim whooped and tried to get one of his gargoyles to carry him across. He ran into trouble almost immediately. His creations could become semisolid, but he had not yet mastered giving them mass and real density. Mike interceded to make sure he didn't fall down the dark hole beneath the destroyed weapon, then rode across the gaping hole, himself, in the arms of the Thorin dwarf-bot.

Mike wondered at himself: why had he decided to bring that particular robot along? It had been Brian Reynolds's remote unit and it reminded him, forcefully, of how Lieutenant Reynolds had died—how his entire team had died. It reminded him of his own part in those deaths. He supposed that made him a masochist. Or maybe it just made him more self-aware.

Sara decided that the three of them should take turns dealing with the wreckage in the mountain egress, every action calculated to impress and even terrify the people watching Tim's streaming video. When they reached the final barrier—a twisted and malformed blast door fifteen feet high and twice as wide—Sara simply blew it apart. The huge halves flew through the clear mountain air, one to the left, one to the right. When they started to tumble, Mike made sure they landed safely away from anyone awaiting their appearance outside. It caused him to wonder about the limits of Sara's ability to manipulate atomic structures. Had she been unable to manage objects going in opposite directions, or had she simply lost interest once her explosive maneuver had had the desired effect?

Mike felt the sun on his face for the first time in months and took a deep breath of the chill air. He smelled pine and cedar and earth. He blinked back tears, startled at how badly he wanted to never go back into that mountain again. It stank of machinery and antiseptic and death.

Arrayed in a rough arc around the entrance to the mountain was a contingent of troops, all armed, but none at combat ready. Every muzzle of every gun was pointed at the ground. Mike could feel the soldiers' fear, see it in the wary glances they exchanged.

Sara stepped front and center and waited for a leader to emerge from among the troops. A tall, strongly built woman with red-brown skin and midnight black hair, wearing a uniform with an admiral's stars and bars, stepped from between a pair of wary-looking officers and came to face Sara. Mike guessed she was in her sixties and that she had a fair amount of Native American blood running in her veins. She met Sara's eyes dead on.

"Sara Crowell, I presume?"

Sara nodded. Mike read the expression on her face and realized that she was impressed with the other woman.

"I'm Admiral Joan Hand, chairman of the Joint Chiefs."

Tim giggled. "Cool. You're Native American, aren't you? What tribe?"

Sara rolled her eyes, but Joan Hand gave Tim her full attention. "Osage."

"Cool," he said again. "Take us to your chief, Chief."

Mike winced, but thought the admiral almost smiled.

ALEXIS HAD NOT UNDERSTOOD HIS decision. Kristian was surprised by that. He had somehow expected that she would see the logic of helping the Zetas deal with their more volatile comrades back east. Once that had been handled, he'd tried to convince her, their own Zetas would be able and willing to put their utmost efforts into raising up a generation of Learned who would be free of immersion. Ironically, she had found that even more unsettling an idea than Kristian had when he had first confronted it.

He had always considered Alexis the more rational of the two of them. She had always been so cool, so poised. Charles Brenton's Zetas seemed to challenge that poise in ways he had never seen before. He had striven, during their last conversation, to get at the rationale for that—even though he understood it, having studied his own unease. Certainly, immersion had become part of his identity—the talents he'd gained formed the core of that identity—but he was able to divorce himself from it and recognize the benefits of not having to immerse in order to keep his skills. The thought of actually expanding and extending his skills intrigued and excited him.

It was during their last conversation—one in which he'd been able only to get Alexis's grudging acquiescence to his plan—that he'd realized the depth of her distrust of the Zetas and begun to understand the real shape of her fear of them. Alexis loathed the idea that literally *anyone* of any bloodline or class or ethnicity might master the mind's latent capacities and join the so-far elite ranks of the Learned. With the class-conscious Alexis, it was all about bloodlines. She and Kristian were from founding families of the Learned. She was a matrilineal descendant of the Vandias; his lineage went back further still, to the founder of the organization—Lord Julian Sorel, who had discovered his talents while orchestrating his own recovery from the Black Death.

Perhaps Kristian's descent from Julian Sorel—who had focused his mind's healing abilities by submerging himself in a tub of warm water—was what caused Kristian Lorstad to view things differently than his associate. What he found gratifying, ultimately, Alexis found terrifying. She attempted to conceal that, though, blocking her emotions by forming audible words. It was a dance they did more and more, day by day.

"Don't you see?" she had all but pleaded with him when he went to her with his recommendation that they aid the Zetas in trying to control their fractious kindred.

"Don't you see how wrongheaded this is? Yes, you might win their loyalty, but at what cost?"

"I guess I don't, Alexis," he had admitted in frustration. "What is it you see?"

"More than you do. Every day you work with them—treating them as equals, even mentors, granting importance to their concerns—you build a future in which the Learned are subsumed into *their* world rather than using them to benefit and enhance our own. Their philosophy dictates that everyone be offered a chance to build zeta capacities. Has not their experience with their Alpha cohort schooled you on how dangerous that would be? Imagine it, Kristian. Imagine a world in which anyone of any intelligence level, of any educational background, of any temperament, of any heritage, is encouraged to build the same sort of capabilities we possess. We've both seen the carnage that resulted from the Alphas' taking of their mountain stronghold. Can you imagine what it would be to have that level of destruction become de rigueur? To have our evolution disrupted by powerful individuals too ignorant and benighted to use their abilities with wisdom?"

He could well imagine it, but—

Alexis, that is precisely why I feel Charles is right. We must deal with these three rogue Zetas now, before confronting them will exact a devastating toll on our own resources. I have been blinded to that threat, but no longer.

He had spoken directly to her soul, then—hit her with the full force of his conviction that he was right.

She had acquiesced. "Will you try to placate them—these Alphas? Will you attempt to bring them in?"

"That is my intention. Or, rather, it is my hope."

"Yours or Dr. Brenton's?"

"Does it matter?"

I suppose not. And if your hope is futile?

He had gone away from their encounter unable to answer that question. He knew, if Charles Brenton did not, that it might already be too late for the Alphas. They had come to think of themselves as Olympians, judging by their communications with the world's governments, and when one came to think of himself as a god, there was little chance of convincing him that there was honor in being merely human. He knew this firsthand—he'd witnessed it when Alexis threw a small robot into Joey Blossom's ribs.

Alexis's fears and prejudices aside, Kristian presented himself to Charles's team as the sun began its descent into the western hills and threw in with them. They would go to Pennsylvania and try to talk the gods out of Olympus.

"THE FIRST THING WE NEED to do, I think," Chuck said to the assembled team, which now included Kristian Lorstad as well as Joey Blossom, "is to make contact with the White House once again. They can facilitate contact with the Alphas."

"To what end?" Dice asked. "They've killed people, Chuck. How do they walk that back?"

"They were defending themselves against an implacable foe, Dice. A foe that imprisoned them, tried to use them like a weapon, dehumanized them. We need to let them know that we get that—that we see what's been done to them. What they did to Deep Shield they did in self-defense."

"And Matt?" Dice asked, his voice incredulous. "What about what they did to Matt?"

"We really don't know what happened with Matt. We don't

know if that was . . . I'm hoping that was an accident. I have to believe it was an accident."

Lanfen put a hand on his arm. "Chuck, think about that. They might have neutralized Deep Shield's power without killing them all, but they chose not to."

Chuck closed his eyes, shook his head. "I have to believe they felt they had no choice. Until proven otherwise, I'm going to continue to believe that they're just three human beings who got backed into a corner they saw no way to escape."

All eyes were upon him, and not a single pair showed concord.

"Fine—that's a noble sentiment," Lorstad said quietly. "But what if they have become more than that, Charles? What if they believe they have become avenging angels? Or *gods*? Then what?"

Chuck fought the sudden image in his mind of Pine Ridge splitting asunder to reveal three godlike creatures emerging from it like deadly butterflies from a high-tech cocoon. "Then, I suppose we need a plan B. We need some way to neutralize their power and subdue them."

"Then what?" asked Mini. Her voice trembled as if she were afraid of the answer.

"I don't know," Chuck admitted. "I don't know how to undo or control their zeta abilities."

"But I might," Lorstad admitted. "If we can tranquilize them and get them into isolation units, we can keep them in a sleep state for some time and use beat therapy and immersion to alter their brain waves. It should enable us to subdue them. Hopefully long enough for you to find some way to . . . short-circuit their zeta powers. The brain, after all, does carry out the mind's instructions via electromagnetic impulses. If those impulses can be altered in some way . . ."

Chuck felt himself slipping into what Lanfen called his fugue state. "Yes," he said, barely aware of forming words. "Yes, that . . . ought to be . . . possible. If we can . . ." He snapped suddenly back to the gathering, his eyes focusing on Lorstad's serene face. "If they won't come out, if it becomes necessary to take them by guile, then we would have our best chance of subduing them if we can separate them—deal with them one at a time."

"A kingdom divided?" suggested Lorstad.

Chuck smiled grimly. "A time-honored way of evening the odds. Plus we have a hidden card up our sleeve." His lip curled slightly, accompanied by a half nod in Lorstad's direction.

"How do you wish to proceed?" Lorstad asked.

Chuck looked him in the eye. "Like I said, we need to talk to the White House, and this time I want to talk to the president directly.

"I expect you can make that happen."

Chapter 17

A KINGDOM DIVIDED

One moment, Chuck was standing in his office at the Center; the next he was quivering in the middle of the National Seal worked into the carpet of the Oval Office. The tiny airless gasp he heard from his left turned out to be a stunned President Ellis, who was staring at him and Lorstad as if they had just materialized out of the ether exactly as they had done.

Chuck stared back, unsure whether he was more awed at being in the Oval Office with the president of the United States or at having been transported more than two thousand miles across the continental United States by a man who could induce quantum entanglement pretty much at will.

It's pretty much a wash, he thought with a smile.

Lorstad was the first to speak. "Madam President, may I present to you Dr. Charles Brenton of Forward Kinetics. I believe you have been wanting to meet—"

"Freeze!"

A centipede of government-issue black suits filed into the office, guns up and at the ready.

"On your knees!"

Chuck inhaled deeply and complied. Hands rifled through his pockets and brushed up and down his limbs. Lorstad looked almost serene as he submitted to the same treatment.

The lead Secret Service agent produced a zip tie and forcefully tugged Chuck's arms behind him.

"No."

"Madam President?"

"Let them up, Pete."

The president glanced at Lorstad, then returned her gaze to Chuck. "I have very much wanted to meet him, but who—"

"This is Kristian Lorstad," Chuck managed to say. "He and his people more or less rescued my team from Deep Shield and kept us hidden until now. He's . . . got a few talents of his own, as you can see."

"I . . . yes, I see. I'm . . ."

Chuck saw her eyes snap into focus as she forced herself past the shock of this surreal situation. She stood, straightened her jacket, and came around her desk, extending her hand to him.

"Thank you for coming in, Dr. Brenton. Please, have a seat." She gestured at the sofas and chairs in the center of the room. "Pete, have your detail monitor from outside." In mere moments the president, Chuck, and Lorstad had the room.

Chuck took a seat on the edge of one of the two sofas. Lorstad perched on one arm, affording himself a higher vantage point. President Ellis gave him a speculative glance, then lowered herself into a wingback chair directly across from Chuck.

"Talk to me, Dr. Brenton. Tell me there's something we can do to retrieve this situation from the edge of oblivion. Let me be clear. I'm not completely averse to what the Zetas are trying to accomplish. I just mistrust their methods . . . and them, to be honest. They have shown little reluctance to kill. Granted, the people they've killed have been violent themselves—and have less provocation to be that way—but I'm disturbed by that trend in combination with the growth of their capacities."

Chuck's heart clenched in his chest. He had not wanted to face that reality. He nodded. "I'm afraid you may be right. There's no way for you to negotiate your way into a position of power or even equity with them."

"I realize that more than you know. We—I and a number of members of my administration and congressional leaders—had a meeting with them yesterday."

"They came out?"

"Briefly. Just long enough to impress us with their presence and make their intentions clear. Then they returned to their castle and pulled up the drawbridge. There is, as you say, no way to negotiate with a power that sees itself as absolute." The president leaned forward, elbows on her knees. "Tell me you have some way of dealing with them."

"We think we do. We propose that I go in and meet with them first. Get my own sense of where their weak points are."

The president was shaking her head. "Doctor, that could be lethal. Your partner went in and—"

"My partner wasn't one of them. He wasn't a Zeta, himself."

"Yes—and?"

"Well you just saw us appear in the Oval Office out of nowhere, so . . ."

Her eyes widened. "You . . . you can—" She made an abracadabra gesture with one hand. "May I ask what you do, exactly?"

"I'm a neuroscientist. My . . . *talents* lie in the area of medical diagnoses." He stopped there, not mentioning that he could do more than diagnose. President Ellis was concerned about the weaponization of zeta abilities; the last thing they needed was for her to know what he could potentially do.

"And the rest of your team?" she asked. "No offense, Doctor, but I am hoping they have more, shall we say, martial powers to bring to bear."

"We ran from Deep Shield, President Ellis. We didn't go through what the Alphas went through. We have had no reason to even consider weaponizing our talents." *Until now,* whispered a dark little voice in the back of Chuck's head.

She gave him a disconcertingly direct look. "Yet, that may be what we're asking you to do, Charles. May I call you Charles?"

"Chuck," he said reflexively, adding, "Please."

She smiled briefly. "Chuck. Suppose you and your team have the ability to challenge Ms. Crowell and her accomplices. Are you going to be able to use your own abilities against your friends?"

"Not to harm them. I mean, I hope we won't have to harm them. What we hope to do is talk them out. Barring that, we plan to separate them, get them to leave the mountain independently, tranquilize them—rendering their zeta abilities moot—then move them quickly into sensory deprivation chambers where their brain waves can be monitored and controlled."

"And modified," added Lorstad, entering the conversation at last. "We will do everything in our power to save their lives, but they can't be allowed to make themselves powerful dictators."

"What if it's impossible to modify them sufficiently?" the president asked.

Chuck closed his eyes tightly and swallowed the sudden tightness in his throat. "I can't let myself believe it's impossible, Madam President."

"It sounds like you and I are on the same team now. How soon can you put your plan into action?"

Lorstad stood. "We have some assets we need to put into place and, obviously, some of them will need to be installed without drawing notice. I think that we can have Charles and his team in place within the next two days. The other assets will take a few days longer. Four days, and we should be ready to draw the Alphas out of their mountain."

Margaret Ellis nodded. "What do you need me to do?"

Chuck spoke before Lorstad could. "Let the Alphas know that you've been in touch with me and that I'll be in contact with them within the week. Tell them . . . tell them I'm looking forward to reuniting with them. I've missed them." That was true.

"We should go," Lorstad said.

Chuck rose and moved to stand next to the Learned. He gave Margaret Ellis a last, anguished look. "I wish I could have saved them from Deep Shield. What Howard did to them . . . changed them. I pray it was not too much." He put his hand on Lorstad's sleeve, closed his eyes in the Oval Office, and opened them in his own.

"Prayer, Charles?" asked Lorstad as he separated from Chuck. "Do you really believe prayer has any effect on the situation?"

Chuck didn't have the bandwidth to debate the logic of faith and God. He said simply, "Even if the only thing it has an effect on is me or my psyche, then yes, I believe it always has an effect."

Lorstad studied him for a moment, then smiled and turned to leave the room. "I'm going to put things in motion, Charles. You need to assemble your team. Lead them in prayer if you wish. I suppose it couldn't hurt."

"Don't," said Chuck, surprising himself with the force with which the word came out of his mouth.

Lorstad stopped unsteadily just short of the door and turned back with a puzzled frown.

"Don't patronize me. Don't condescend to me. Don't let yourself believe I'm enfeebled by my faith in God or in my fellow human beings. Consider what you place your faith in, then tell me I am wrong in where I place mine."

Lorstad's smile slipped a bit as he let himself out of the office. Chuck shook away his momentary irritation and went to gather his team.

"CHUCK IS COMING TO OLYMPUS."

Sara made the announcement from the doorway of the break room they had turned into their main kitchen because of its proximity to their quarters. There were plenty of food stores in the mountain—enough for a small army, appropriately enough. Plus they'd been tinkering with hydroponics. They transferred the food out of cold storage as needed and used the microwaves in the break room to cook. Mike had been eating a prefab burrito and pondering the possibility of cooking via zeta waves (he understood the basic physics of generating heat, after all), but his thoughts scattered to the four winds as what Sara had said registered.

He swallowed a half-chewed mouthful of carnitas and said, "That's great." He meant it, too. Somehow the thought of Chuck coming here gave him an absurd sense of hope. Though, given what Sara had done to Matt Streegman, he wasn't sure it should. The burrito was suddenly completely unappetizing. That seemed to happen a lot these days. He set it down on the plate.

"Listen, Sara . . . you're not planning on . . . I mean, what happened with Matt . . ."

Her facial expression warped through several twisted moments of pain and anger before she shook her head emphatically, her dark hair swinging freely around her face. "No, Mike. Chuck isn't like Matt. Matt was a greedy, soulless bastard. He sold us to that black ops jackass for profit. Chuck tried to keep it from happening. He just didn't have enough time. He's going to help get us out of here for good. He's going to find a way to . . ." She paused, licked her lips, shook her head again. "He'll bring us into the outside world. You'll see. It'll be our triumph."

There was something plaintive about her words and tone. She sounded like a kid who was certain that her daddy could do anything. Mike had the impression she'd almost said that Chuck would find a way to *save* them.

God, I wish.

"So, how comes the robot army?" she asked next.

"It's coming good," Mike said, truthfully. "I can handle about three dozen of them at once and I've been experimenting with controlling other systems in the base. You know, just in case they try to penetrate our defenses again." Truthfully, he could handle more than one hundred bots at this juncture and had the entire electrical grid in his head. If there was a schematic for a system that was anywhere close to reality, he found he could control the system.

She smiled. "Good man. Though I was hoping you'd be able to manage more than that by now."

He raised his hands in a gesture of surrender. "Hey, Sara, I'm just a blue-collar guy. I don't have the sophisticated chops you and Timmy have. It's just brute force with me. I think Tim might have an easier time at this than—"

"It's because Tim and I are able to do the more sophisticated maneuvers that we need you to keep after the 'brute force' items on the agenda. I know you can do this, Micky. I *know* you can. You may be uneducated, but you're damned smart."

He shook his head in denial and looked down at the discarded burrito.

Sara tilted her head to one side appraisingly. "Something's eating at you. I can tell."

He looked up. "What?"

She came slowly into the kitchen and sat down across from him at the table. He held his breath. Could she read him? Had she figured out how he really felt about being an Olympian?

"It's your family, isn't it? I know you miss them."

Relief washed over him, leaving him weak and shaking. "Yeah," he said, his voice barely above a whisper. "Yeah, it's . . . I've never been away from Helen or the kids this long, ever. It's killing me, Sara. I mean it." It *was* killing him. Sometimes he wished it just *would* kill him and get it over with.

Sara put her hand over his. "I'm sorry, Micky. Look, we've got a direct line to the president now. Maybe she can have the CIA pick them up and bring them here. Wouldn't you just love to have your kids see this place? Have your wife see what sort of things you can do?"

He blinked at her, horror pumping adrenaline through his veins. The thought of his family here in this sanitized hell made his skin crawl. The thought of them knowing what he could do—what he had done—filled him with screaming terror.

Maintain. Maintain, Yenotov.

"No thanks. At least, not until we've gotten good and comfortable with our new role in the world. If we have the CIA bring them here now, they could be used as leverage. And besides, with all we've got to do, as much as I love 'em, they'd be a distraction. You know? Complicate things."

Sara smiled. "You *are* a good man, Mike Yenotov. I wish Tim could focus half as well as you can. Little Troll still hasn't gotten the hang of making his wraiths consistently more solid. Relies on you a little too much for help."

Mike didn't say that she relied on him an awful lot, too, for "brute force" stuff. "Yeah. It'd be good if he could carry his own weight in that department. But hey, I haven't given you the army you want yet, either. You're better at this than either of us, Sara." He looked into her eyes when he said it, willed her to believe it, though he knew he lacked that particular talent.

Her smile became a grin. "Flattery will get you everywhere, good sir. But I'm sure you'll both catch up. Especially you. You're smarter than you think you are." She squeezed his hand, rose, and strode out of the room, confidence unfurling in her wake like a superhero's cape.

Smarter than he thought he was? God, how he wished that were true.

He got up and threw the remnants of the burrito into a compost receptacle. It was part of a network of such depositories that carried waste away to a central sorting area on the lowest level of the mountain—recyclables to the north, garbage to the south, compost in the solid waste tank in between. Sometimes Mike wished he could just throw himself into the compost bin and dissolve along with the rest of the organic garbage—become part of the methane exhalation that powered parts of the facility.

Ironic, Mike thought, Olympus was powered in part by a noxious miasma of gases given off by decay. Or maybe it was just appropriate. Depressing thoughts notwithstanding, Mike was surprised to find that his heart still harbored hope. Maybe, like Sara, he had come to think of Chuck as their savior.

TEAM CHUCK'S ASSETS TOOK THREE days to put in place. Those assets consisted of a rather spartan base camp with two modular buildings and a wood-framed winterized tent, set up in a cleared semicircle roughly forty feet in diameter. Two nondescript SUVs were parked beneath a venerable cedar.

The camp was populated only by the Zetas, Lorstad, and Joey Blossom, and they made no effort to disguise it. The Alphas were expecting them; it made no sense to attempt to hide the existence of the camp. What they were concealing was the equipment in one of the modules—a trio of isolation chambers and the equipment that fed them binaural audio and subliminal programming. There were no computers here save the nonnetworked ones that ran the immersion chambers and interpreted brain waves—no electronic pathways that Tim or Sara could exploit from a distance.

The Betas were hopeful that this would tip the balance in their favor. Mike Yenotov was the key—or perhaps wild card was a more apt metaphor. Mike, Chuck knew, would be the biggest threat if he saw them as enemies—his ability to manipulate physical objects. But, with his family, he also had the most to gain by resolving this quickly.

The Beta base camp was just under a quarter of a mile from the military communications camp (or Spiderweb, as Admiral Hand had dubbed it) through which the Alphas had connected with the outside world and through which they had been communicating with the U.S. government . . . and beyond. Any and all weaponry was there. Team Chuck was entirely unarmed except for their zeta talents and their wits.

Chuck watched Lorstad make a final check of the immersion chambers before they made contact with the Alphas. The Learned intended to remain in hiding; Chuck feared what effect a stranger's presence might have on the no-doubt-paranoid Alphas. Lorstad, he knew, had other concerns.

"Are you certain you will not reconsider sending Mini and Eugene back to the Center?" Kristian asked. "Eugene will certainly not be of any use to you without his computers, and Mini is an artist—I can't imagine what tactical advantage she would give you."

"That," Chuck said mildly, "is one of the most disingenuous things you've ever said to me—and you've said a fair number of disingenuous things. I'm pretty sure you have a keen appreciation that Mini's art is neither passive nor static. I expect it will give us both a strategic and tactical advantage. They both stay."

Lorstad gave him a sharp look that made Chuck smile.

"Yes, I know—the mouse that roared. You're not used to getting toothy comebacks from me. Get used to it. I'm not the same man I was when we came to you."

Lorstad straightened from his inspection of a vital signs monitor, a half smile on his lips. "That much is certain. The equipment is functional. You may make contact with the Alphas as soon as you're ready. I would like you to consider something, though. I'd like you to consider that, at least with Mikhail Yenotov, we have a potential for leverage."

Chuck frowned. "Leverage? I don't follow."

"His family. Especially his children. If he chooses to be unco-operative, the presence of his son or daughter—"

While Chuck had considered Mike's family as a way in, he never thought of them as leverage. The swell of anger in Chuck's breast was swift and sudden. "Absolutely not. We can't do that to them. That's exactly what Howard did—he treated them like hostages. He tried to enslave them. We can't do that to them," he repeated. "Not just because it would be cruel, but because it would be counterproductive. In order for our plan to work, we need to actually gain their trust. Otherwise, we're going to be flying by the seat of our pants."

"I understand your reservations, Charles, but you've said yourself that Yenotov's primary concern all along has been his family. He's been separated from them for some time. It's possible that he would respond to a plea from one of them that he wouldn't listen to if it came from you. It may take a member of his family to reason with him."

Chuck couldn't argue the logic of that, but it still didn't sit right with him. He shook his head. It was ironic: he was about to go tell his team to use their instincts; he was telling Lorstad *not* to use his.

The thing was, he trusted his team's instincts.

"Let me try to get a sense of what's going on up there before you set things in motion that can't be undone."

Lorstad inclined his head. "But I must monitor your situation. If things get out of control up on that mountain, I will act as I feel I must."

Chuck took a deep breath and nodded, then slipped out of the building to meet with his team. They convened in the winter tent from which they could see the peak of "Olympus." They went over their various roles, but mostly Chuck stressed the need to be intuitive and flexible.

"Trust your instincts," he told them. "Sara and the guys are expecting us to befriend them, maybe even give them direction. I'll know more after I've met with them, of course, but we all need to be tuned in to their emotions, ready to . . ." He hesitated.

"If it's necessary," Lanfen said, "I can take Tim on if he gets wild. I've watched every bit of footage of the Alphas. I think I have a pretty good grasp of his abilities and where they overlap with Sara's and Mike's. I've observed something about the way they work. Their talents mesh, but they don't coordinate naturally. There are seams."

Eugene had been watching the mountain through a set of military-grade field glasses. He glanced aside, his brow furrowed. "What's that mean?"

"Well, watching the episodes in Kabul and Ciudad Juárez and the footage from the congressional meeting, it seems as if Sara has to cue the others to perform their parts in a scenario."

"Visually," said Mini, nodding. "I noticed that, too."

"Yes," Lanfen went on. "And in Kabul, Sara actually gave verbal cues. I think—"

"We'll be quicker on the uptake," said Mini.

"Right." Lanfen turned to Chuck. "Are you sure you don't want to take me with you when you go?" She nodded toward the mountain peak centered in the tent's large window.

"No. I *want* to. But I'm not going to. Lorstad says he'll be monitoring—whatever that means."

"Check it out." Eugene handed the field glasses to Chuck. "They've got some sort of observation deck up there."

Chuck moved to the window and put the glasses up to his eyes. There was, indeed, an observation deck jutting out from the summit of Pine Ridge; Sara and Tim stood on it, side by side. They were both dressed in midnight blue coveralls with some sort of insignia on the breast. They looked like the Sara and Tim he had known back before the world went mad, yet somehow subtly different. Though the winds at the elevation of the deck bent the tops of the pine trees, Sara's hair wasn't windblown; it floated gently on a slow-motion Hollywood breeze. Her eyes and skin seemed to glow as she looked out over the slope, her face turned toward the Betas' camp. Tim, meanwhile, looked as if he'd stuck his finger in a light socket. His curly hair stood on end and a bristling halo of energy danced among the strands and around his body.

Chuck frowned, handing the binoculars to Lanfen. Was that what they really looked like, he wondered, or was that the way they saw themselves? Did it require energy and even mental attention to keep up the projection, or were they, like Mini, capable of creating self-sustaining phenomena? He supposed there was no way to find out but to go up the mountain and ask.

"I'm going over to the Spiderweb," Chuck said. "Let them know I'm ready to visit Olympus. Wish me luck."

He started for the door of the tent, but Lanfen grasped his hand and pulled him back. She planted a quick, urgent kiss on his lips, then let him go. They exchanged a telling glance, then he left before he could change his mind about taking her with him.

Chapter 18

BEST-LAID PLANS

Sara's reaction to Chuck's hail was immediate and cordial. "Doc! It's good to hear your voice. Can I get you to show yourself?"

Chuck looked at Admiral Hand; she was standing opposite him on the left side of the communications technician who had initiated the call and was recording it. "Can I?"

Hand signaled the tech to mute their end of the conversation, then asked, "Are you sure you want to? I know whenever I've chatted with them via video uplink it's made me feel freakishly vulnerable. I've seen them literally reach out of a video display into the room."

Chuck considered that. "I have to trust them, Admiral, if I'm going to get them to trust me."

She studied him for a moment, then nodded at the tech. The large, flat cinema display that dominated the communications station came online. All three of the Alphas were there—Sara stood at the center; Tim leaned casually against a console next to her; Mike was seated in a swivel chair just behind and to her left. Chuck tried to read their faces: Sara smiled when she saw him—the expression reaching all the way to her eyes. Tim was grinning lopsidedly. Mike . . . Mike looked queasy or unhappy or maybe just plain scared.

Chuck maintained eye contact with him until Sara spoke.

"Chuck, you have no idea how good it is to see you. When I heard the president had asked you to come in, I was thrilled. You're the only person I have any faith can help expedite this process."

"The disarming of the world, you mean?" Chuck asked. "And it's good to see you, too."

"Beating swords into plowshares," Sara said, smiling. "I know that's something you'd like to see, too."

"I would. I'd love to see it. It looks as if you've had a pretty powerful impact on the world scene. You've stopped half a dozen wars dead in their tracks. That's an amazing feat."

Sara's smile deepened. "Why thank you, kind sir. I wish I could say that was enough, but it's not. We still have holdouts—the U.S. government among them, until now. I understand you've talked the president into taking us seriously."

"Oh, she's always taken you seriously, Sara. She's done everything in her power to"—he stopped himself from saying *meet your demands* and substituted—"honor your requests. She's a good woman. A straight shooter. You can trust her."

A fleeting spark of something like relief flickered in Sara's eyes, then she asked, "Is she being straight about not being able to decommission the nuclear silos? She said it would be dangerous to abandon them."

Chuck hadn't spoken to President Ellis about nuclear missiles specifically, but he had discussed the various demands the Alphas were making with the Joint Chiefs and DHS. "Well, think about it, Sara. If the military pulls all of their staff out of those facilities, what's to keep some other players from getting in and doing God knows what with the raw materials? Even if they shut down the facilities and take them off the grid entirely, the raw materials are still there to be abused." He glanced at Admiral Hand, who nodded an affirmation.

Sara was nodding, too, her brow knit. Her need for reassurance reminded Chuck that, though she was powerful and knew how to manipulate reality, she hadn't gained any godlike knowledge to go with her godlike abilities. That for all her understanding of global politics and military strategy, she was still just an architect playing this all by ear.

That was both comforting and daunting.

"That makes sense," Sara said. "I suppose we'll have to figure out some way of adequately protecting them until we can figure out a way to destroy the dangerous components. You need to make us a Zeta physicist, Doc. Someone who can turn their talents to unweaponizing the nuclear stuff."

"That's a great idea," Chuck said in all sincerity. "We've been working with several new Zetas. None of them are physicists, exactly, but there is a—a potential adept who has a background in physics. He might be able to come up with some way of neutralizing the radioactive materials."

Can *Lorstad do something like that,* he wondered, *or is his ability specialized to quantum entanglement and some token atomic manipulation?*

It was certainly an interesting avenue to explore—later.

"New Zetas?" Sara repeated, her eyes widening. "How many? What are their skill sets? Does this mean you were able to salvage some of the equipment? That you found a place to continue your work?"

"Yeah. Where did you go, Doc?" Mike asked before Chuck could even begin to answer Sara's question. He leaned forward in his chair. "You just disappeared. What happened?"

Chuck took a deep breath. Here was an opportunity to present himself and his team as allies. "You probably know that Deep Shield was after us."

Sara and Mike exchanged a glance. "Yeah," said Mike. "Matt . . .

Matt told us about that. He said they thought they had you and you just disappeared. Where've you been?"

"Out in the middle of nowhere," Chuck answered, hyperconscious of Admiral Hand's solid presence to his left. "We were taken to a facility on the Nevada-Idaho border that wasn't much less secret than Deep Shield, if a lot less frightening."

"By whom?" asked Sara, frowning. "The government?"

"No, not the government. By well-connected allies. People who realized what might happen to us if we fell into the wrong hands."

"*We* fell into the wrong hands," Sara said, her voice harsh.

"Yes, and that was my fault. I moved too slowly. I dithered. I wasn't sure who to trust. I wanted to trust Matt, but he seemed to be in Howard's pocket—"

Sara was shaking her head. "Don't beat yourself up, Doc. We waited too late to move, too. We let them split the teams up. That was a mistake. Trusting Matt was a mistake."

"A mistake we didn't make twice," added Tim.

The expression on his face—equal parts glee and remembered rage—turned Chuck's blood to ice. "Sara, I have to ask: What happened with Matt? How did . . . why did he die?"

Mike, looking sicker than ever, turned his face away from the camera. Tim's expression was all rage, and Sara's matched it.

"You have to ask?" she snarled. "The bastard betrayed us *again*. He came in here promising he was trying to help. Telling us he was going to put us in solid contact with the government—with the president. He was wearing a wire. *And* he was a damned decoy. His handlers, whoever they were, tried to take us out with some sort of poison. He got what he deserved—nothing more and nothing less. I couldn't see letting him betray us any further."

Again, Chuck met Joan Hand's dark gaze. They both knew that Matt had gone into the mountain in complete sympathy with the Alphas. "Sara," he said as gently as he knew how, "that attack wasn't Matt and it wasn't the government—at least it wasn't the

Ellis administration. You know there are people trying to resurrect Deep Shield . . ."

She was shaking her head in denial. "They wouldn't have tried to kill us. We were an asset—a weapon in their fantasy arsenal. Without us, those robots are just geeky hat racks."

Hand shifted so that she would also appear in the Alphas' video feed. "Ms. Crowell, we analyzed the canisters that were dropped on the mountain by those drones—which, by the way, were as big a surprise to us as they were to you. They didn't contain poison. They contained a sedative. You would have been rendered unconscious and awakened with a horrific headache, but you wouldn't have died. We have every reason to believe those drones were arranged for by the people behind the Deep Shield initiative. Specifically, Senator Roman Bluth."

"That just means Matt was working with them—"

"No, ma'am, he was working with *us*. His goal was to extricate you from this . . . situation you're in. He really was trying to help—same as Dr. Brenton here."

Tim looked confused and Mike rose unsteadily and strode out of range of the camera. Sara was still shaking her head. "No. You've got it wrong. The timing was too perfect to be coincidental. Matt comes in here wearing a wire and someone tries to take us out—"

"Sara," said Chuck, "why would they attack while Matt was in the mountain with you? That doesn't make sense. He'd have been affected by the gas, too."

"Sacrificial lamb. Either way, say you're right about that part of it. That they didn't want to kill us. It still means they wanted to incapacitate us so they could come in and extract us. They needed him in here with his wire and probably a positioning beacon so they knew where to drop the stuff and where to find us once they got inside. We are going to be no one's slave labor again, dammit. Not ever again. In the big scheme of things, Matt was expendable—to his handlers and to us."

Chuck realized, with a sick jolt, that he was foolish to think he'd be safe inside that mountain with Sara and Tim. Mike seemed to have deep regrets about what they'd done to Matt Streegman, but Sara and Tim had not an atom of remorse between the two of them.

"What about me, Sara?" Chuck asked quietly. "Am I expendable, too? Just a pawn in your chess game?"

"No!" Her face went white and her eyes glistened with sudden emotion. Chuck only wished he knew what that emotion was. "No! You're not one of them, you're one of us. You *made* us. I know you, Chuck. You wouldn't do anything to harm us. It would be like . . . like harming your own child."

She was dead right. It would be like harming his own child. But what if that child had become a cold-blooded serial killer? What then?

I made them.

"Matt made you, too, Sara. If I'm like a parent to your abilities, so was Matt."

"Matt," she said deliberately, "was a crass materialist. He was a lying, double-dealing, opportunistic snake, and it got him killed. His entire contribution to our making was a mathematical formula—a catalyst. A sperm cell, nothing more. You're the real mother of invention, Chuck. The real wizard."

"If he was a crass materialist," argued Chuck, "he wouldn't have bankrolled the venture. He put everything material and spiritual he had into Forward Kinetics—into you."

She laughed. "He didn't believe in the spiritual, Chuck. He was an atheist who didn't even understand that to acknowledge the human intellect is to acknowledge the divine in all of us."

"So, he had blind spots. We all do have blind spots." *Even me.* Especially *me.* "So, what's next, Sara? Where do we go from here?"

"You come visit Olympus," said Tim brightly. "You'll be abso-freakin'-lutely amazed at what we've done here. We could survive in here indefinitely. Did you know they even had an experimental hydroponics garden down here? It's not experimental anymore. Mike got the filtration system working and figured out how they were bringing sunlight in from the surface, and I've got the whole shebang synced to a computer that regulates everything from water temp to aeration to positioning the sun-catchers. It's ultracool. We could even tan—"

Sara cut him off. "Tim's right. You need to see what we've done. Do you have Dice with you? And Lanfen? You should bring them. We'll send down an escort. Mike can handle those robots as easily as if they were that stupid John Deere he loved so much. We'll have him send—"

"No. No, Sara, I think I'll pass on the tour of Olympus. I'm . . . claustrophobic, as it turns out. Underground spaces make me break out in a cold sweat and have panic attacks. But Dice and I do want to map your abilities and contrast and compare them to those of the other Zetas. What you've accomplished is remarkable. Can you give me a thumbnail sketch of what you're able to do? The Kabul event—how did you pull that off?" He knew in a broad sense what had transpired during their virtual forays into the outside world, but he hoped for more details.

Sara and Tim both smiled, then Tim said, "It was pretty cool. I handled the forces outside the parliament building—providing them with awesome targets so they weren't shooting real people—while Sara handled the inside. She totally saved the asses of the guys holed up in that conference room."

"What about Mike?" Chuck asked. "What did Mike do?"

Tim laughed. "Mike made us look good. He's sort of our stunt double and explosives guy. He can move stuff with pure kinetic force without half-thinking about it. Very handy. I provide the style, he provides the substance—well, or most of it."

That confirmed Chuck's suspicions about the division of labor in the group, but he'd watched the video of their emergence from the mountain and had seen Sara blow blast doors weighing several tons apiece completely apart.

"Then you and Sara can't directly affect physical objects . . . like Mike can?" he added.

Sara's eyes kindled. "Of course we can. But Tim and I specialize in working with electronic signals and digital data. Mike doesn't have an aptitude for that." She turned to look back at the chair Mike had been sitting in, saw that it was empty, and shrugged. "Mike's sort of a blue-collar Zeta."

"Yeah," Tim agreed. "Besides, that sort of brute manipulation takes a lot out of you. I mean, it takes a lot out of *us*. You wouldn't know, I guess."

Chuck was not about to admit to being a Zeta himself and give up the advantage of surprise. "Huh. That's interesting. I haven't noticed that sort of sapping effect on Lanfen or Mini or the other Zetas."

Sara took a quick step toward the camera. "Other Zetas? You mentioned them before. Who are they? What can they do?"

Chuck considered how to play this—how to draw them out. "They're young. They're incredibly bright, and two of them have had some special training that none of you got exposed to. One of them is learning to manipulate the local atmosphere, another is learning to create self-sustaining constructs, and another is a software guy—sort of a combination of you and Tim. He's amazing. Lanfen, by the way, is developing all sorts of new talents. I'd love to do a side-by-side study of her and Tim since they seem to be progressing at an equal rate."

As Chuck had hoped, Tim took the bait. He straightened, faced the camera dead-on, and crossed his arms over his chest. "A study, huh? Name the time and place. I'll be there. And I'm gonna bet right now that you're wrong. I got a head start on Ninja Girl. I doubt she's as good at pushing electrons and photons around as I am."

Chuck nodded, smiling. "Okay. Great. I'll go set some experiments up over in our camp. In the meantime, is there anything you'd like me to tell the president?"

"Yeah," said Sara. "You tell her she's done a halfway decent job of getting her trained monkeys under control and because of that, she's gained my respect. Let her know our thoughts on the nuclear facilities and see if your physics guy has any ideas about how we can put them out of business."

"She's going to ask about other nations' nuclear stockpiles."

Sara's smile tilted. "Tell her not to worry. Tim's monitoring every last one of them—even ones she doesn't know about."

"No shit," agreed Tim. "If they so much as let off a nuclear fart, well, we might not have a good way to destroy the nukes directly, but I'll turn anything that makes them deployable or launchable to slag."

"Good God, Tim." Sara sounded exasperated. "Do you honestly think that she'd nuke Pennsylvania? Do you have any concept of how a nuclear missile works?"

Tim scowled. "I—yeah. Of course, I know how nukes work."

Sara turned back to the screen. "No threats right now. Margaret Ellis has been a solid ally so far. If you trust her, so will I. Just tell her that other people's nukes—the ones that are left, anyway—aren't a problem."

"I'll tell her. Anything else?"

"Universal health care," Sara said. "She needs to get experts to research other international systems and design one for the U.S. I'd like that to be taken up by the next session of Congress."

The change of subject made Chuck's head spin, until he recalled that Sara's mother had died of cancer that had gone undetected because she couldn't afford health insurance or out-of-pocket payments to doctors. What he was getting ready to do gave him a wriggle of guilt. Sara wasn't evil. She was merely so powerful she felt her power was all it took to bring about a change in human civilization.

"And," Sara added, taking another step toward the camera so that her face was all Chuck could see, "you need to vouch for us. Tell them we are not the enemy. We're trying to save them. They need to get that through their thick little hominid skulls. Everything we've done—everything we're doing and going to do—is in their best interests. Make them understand that, Doc. We're counting on you."

Chuck felt a bead of sweat run down his back, chased by a trickle of dread that made his skin crawl. When was the last time he'd heard someone proclaim that they knew what was best for everyone else and would therefore simply make it happen? Hadn't that been Leighton Howard's motto?

If he spoke, she'd surely hear the lie in his voice, so he simply nodded. The truth was, he couldn't vouch for them—at least, not for Sara and Tim. Mike—well, there was still a chance for Mike, he thought, but Sara and Tim were too dazzled by their own press. He reached over to sign off. In the few seconds the connection was still open, though, Chuck heard Tim announce he was going to build himself a "cyber-throne" for when the world leaders came to the mountain to pay homage. The feed cut off.

He felt sick.

The admiral laid a firm hand on his shoulder. "I know this is damn hard, Dr. Brenton. But I think we both know what has to be done."

"Yes. Yes we do. I'll let you know as soon as we have something in place."

A few minutes later, Chuck approached Beta Camp with a thousand thoughts racing through his head. He was brought up short just north of the clearing by a static charge of uneasiness that blew those thoughts to flinders. Heart pounding, mouth going dry, he picked up his pace and broke into the clearing at a run.

Lanfen appeared as if out of nowhere, her face eloquent with the dread Chuck was feeling. Had it been her emotions that had given him that static charge?

He grasped her shoulders. "Lanfen, what is it? What's happened?"

"Nothing's *happened* exactly. I just—I can't find Lorstad."

"He was in the isolation cabin." Chuck's gaze darted in that direction.

"He isn't now. And he didn't leave by the front door or we would have seen him. I went in to discuss how we were going to handle Tim and he was gone."

"You think he . . ." *What did you call what Lorstad did?* "He leapt?"

"Only thing I can think of. Do you have any idea why he might do that or where he'd go if he did?"

Chuck strode toward the immersion cabin not sure what he'd do if he got there and Lorstad had returned. "I have my suspicions. I hope I'm wrong."

The cabin was empty—the three immersion tanks and their control console were the only contents of the room. Chuck eddied for a moment, uncertain of what to do. If they were going to lure Tim down to their camp, they needed to have someone minding the isolation units. Ideally that was Lorstad, although Joey could act as a far less experienced stand-in.

Chuck went into fugue mode, his eyes out of focus, barely noticing the green and red lights on the control console.

Green and red lights?

Chuck's eyes snapped back into focus. Three lights: one green, two red. He swiveled his head to stare at the rightmost tank. A green light blinked on its control panel, as well.

"What is it?" Lanfen asked, following his gaze. "Oh. Oh my God."

Chuck went to the control console and slid into the seat. The press of a button brought the internal monitor of the active unit online. Kristian Lorstad floated in the tank in a black dry suit, eyes and ears covered by a half helm, limbs relaxed at his sides.

"What is he doing?" Lanfen murmured.

Chuck shook his head. "I don't know. Get Joey. Maybe he'll know if there's any way to find out."

KRISTIAN ENTERED SPIDERWEB AT THE southern checkpoint set up specifically for the denizens of Beta Camp. He began talking almost the moment he saw the armed guards there, hoping they would not notice that his feet left no imprints upon the ground and made no sound as he walked.

"I beg your pardon, gentlemen," he said smoothly. "I'm Kristian Lorstad and I have a message from Dr. Brenton for Lieutenant Epstein."

The guards at the checkpoint knew him, of course. They'd been introduced all around their first day here so that everyone at Spiderweb knew them on sight. One of them greeted him politely and offered to take him to the lieutenant's office. He accepted the offer; he had no way of opening the door himself. The younger of the two men led him smartly into the camp and up to the front of one of the glorified trailers they used as offices. He tapped on the door, then opened it, announcing Kristian with all due formality, then he held it open.

Kristian nodded, smiling, and carefully mounted the step to enter. Steps were sometimes difficult under these circumstances—regimented changes in the spatial plane required tight concentration or you could appear to be floating above the ground. If the MP noticed that the visitor's feet made no sound on the composite surface of the step, he said nothing of it. He turned on his heel and returned to his post.

Inside the trailer, Kristian found himself facing a thirty-something woman with blond hair pulled back in a ponytail and lieutenant's bars on her uniform jacket. "Lieutenant Epstein, thank you for seeing me."

"Is there a problem, Mr. Lorstad?"

"Not precisely. More a concern. Dr. Brenton wished me to inquire about Mikhail Yenotov's family. It seems he hasn't heard from them in some time and there is concern that Deep Shield might have—well, that they might have come to harm."

Epstein met Kristian's eyes. "Tell Dr. Brenton that at last report Yenotov's family was fine. Deep Shield was not inclined to cross international boundaries to get to them and we appropriated any surveillance equipment they put in place."

"Ah, so you're watching them, then. They're still in Canada, I presume. Winnipeg, was it, or Toronto? Dr. Brenton wasn't sure."

"I'm sorry, sir, but I can't divulge that information. It's classified."

"I see. Well, if you'd kindly check on them, it would greatly help us in our efforts to reach out to the people inside the mountain. Mr. Yenotov has some immediate concerns that things are not as they should be. It seems he's developed an ability to sense the emotions of individual members of his family and has lost touch with his son, Anton."

The woman's expression softened. "I can certainly empathize with that. I have a son of my own. I'll tell you what. I'll check on the Yenotovs' status and relay the information to Mr. Yenotov and to your camp. Will that be sufficient?"

"Oh, yes. Thank you."

Kristian left the office, giving the door a kinetic push, and hurried out of the camp and into the woods. The moment he was out of sight of the checkpoint, he faded to nothingness. A far more discreet presence then entered the camp from the south and moved to the rear of Lieutenant Epstein's trailer office. He passed through the wall directly behind her desk and was able to see exactly what she saw as she checked the surveillance feeds from her laptop—surveillance feeds from the security cameras posted around the current residence of Helen Yenotov and her two children.

Moments later, his objective obtained, Kristian Lorstad returned to his immersed body as swiftly as thought, then moved on to his next destination.

"I DON'T KNOW HOW TO wake them up safely," Joey said, staring at the image of Lorstad's still form floating in the center of the isolation unit. "I programmed some of the software, sure, but *they* always decide when they're ready to come out. Or one of their mentors does." He chewed his lower lip and played with the end of his braid. "Maybe I can see if there's a timing sequence in the routine he's running."

"Okay, yes," said Chuck. "Try that. Try anything."

He watched as Joey sat at the console's controls and called up a programming module that allowed him to go behind the user interface to look at the code being run. Joey was kind enough to give a blow-by-blow of his machinations. He searched for a timing subroutine and found nothing. He tried looking for an elapsed time setting. More nothing.

"What was he thinking?" asked Lanfen. "Why would he tank when we were about to make a move? Do you think he—I don't know—ran out of energy or something? I thought he tanked just before we left."

"He did," Joey replied, his eyes still on the scrolling lines of computer code. "He shouldn't be needing to do this. I don't get it."

Chuck, feeling sick to the pit of his stomach, glanced back up at the immersion unit's monitor and froze. Where the recumbent form of the Learned had been not two seconds before, there was a whole lot of nothing. Lorstad was gone, riding the quantum tangles.

Chapter 19

OF GODS AND MEN

It was a grim group that gathered in the habitat unit of their makeshift camp. Lorstad had yet to return, and the Beta team was faced with the possibility that they would have to put their plans in motion without him.

They all wanted to subdue the Alphas without harming them. That made distraction their best weapon. Lanfen had volunteered for that duty. She and Tim would uplink to the Brewster-Brenton monitor to do a baseline of their brain waves. That was supposed to allow Dice and Brenda to treat him to enough of an electrical shock to incapacitate him, after which someone else would administer a special sedative.

That someone else was supposed to have been Lorstad. His sudden disappearance meant they had to reassign tasks. It now fell to Brenda to tranq Tim and to Joey to install him in the isolation chamber—which he'd now be running solo instead of acting as Lorstad's assistant.

"If we can bring him down," said Chuck, "we can get him into the tank. If we can get him into the tank, Joey can run the program the Benefactors use to condition new trainees."

"And if we can't bring him down?" Euge asked the question that loomed like the invisible monster in the room. "I mean, if the shock and the tranq don't work, what then?"

"Then maybe I have to help Lanfen keep him occupied while we try again," offered Mini. She sat next to Eugene on his bed. "My gosh, we've got enough sedative to march an army to dreamland."

"You're assuming," said Euge pessimistically, "that the damn stuff even works on these guys. Or that he's going to let us try a second time."

There was a long moment of silence in which everyone looked uncomfortably at anything but each other. Lanfen finally ended it—saying what no one wanted to even think.

"I know what Lorstad would say—what he's suggested several times already. We have to be prepared for the worst-case scenario. We have to be prepared to take Tim on—those of us who can."

Chuck told himself he was not one of those who could take Tim on. He said it aloud, too, as if that would somehow make it true. Deep inside, he knew it *wasn't* true. Deep inside, he knew that he—possibly more than anyone—was capable of getting to Tim in ways the Alpha would be incapable of defending himself against. But that's not who he was; that was a person he was determined never to become. He would do no harm.

Do no harm. He let that Hippocratic clause run through his mind, a binding mantra. Binding until the inevitable fine print pushed its way in.

Until you have no choice.

Chuck stood. "While you're getting set up for Tim, I think I'm going to have to take Sara up on her invitation to visit Olympus."

There was a general outburst of disagreement at that announcement; even Mini loudly questioned his sanity.

Lanfen stared up at him from the arm of the chair he'd been sitting in. "Why? You declined the invitation before, so why accept it now?"

"Because we can't let Sara get an inkling of what's going on down here. And because I need to try to make direct and private contact with Mike. He's clearly not completely on board with what they're doing, and he's a large part of their offense—Tim admitted as much when I spoke to them earlier. A lot of the flashbang we've seen on those videos is, as we suspected, Mike muscling things around while Sara and Tim call the shots. Once Tim is subdued, we can go after Sara. And maybe, just maybe, Mike will help us."

"Best-case scenario, yes," said Lanfen. "But there's no guarantee that's what we're going to get. Even if we do get them all into tanks, what if that's not the end of it? What if Lorstad and his Learned can't reprogram them? What if they're proof to the immersion tech? What if we can't put the spirits back into Pandora's box, Chuck?"

"Then this won't be over until they're dead," murmured Chuck. "I'm beginning to wish I'd never pursued this line of research."

"Don't say that," said Lanfen, reaching up to grasp his wrist. "It wasn't your fault that Matt sold us out to Deep Shield. It wasn't even really his fault. He didn't know who they were—what they were. If things had developed the way you'd hoped, none of us would be here getting ready to maybe fight people who should be our friends. We'd still be back at Forward Kinetics, giving quadriplegics a new lease on life. If we manage to pull this off, maybe we can still do that."

Chuck nodded. He wanted to believe what she was saying. He *did* believe it on some level, but he suspected that, after this scare, even the benign abilities of the Betas would seem frightening to—to *normal* human beings. He stumbled over the thought.

Evolution, he thought wryly, *is not for the weak of heart.*

"Okay," he said. "Here's what we'll do. Mini, Euge, and I will go over to Spiderweb. I'll ping the mountain and let them know you're ready for Tim and that I'm up for a visit. Once I'm inside, I'll let Spiderweb know I'm okay. Euge, Mini—that will be your cue to come back here, which will be *your* cue," he added, nodding at Dice—

"To deliver the one-two punch," the robotics engineer finished. "Yeah. That'll work. But you—"

He stood. "I'll be fine. Euge, Mini, you ready to go?"

Euge nodded and Mini said, "Ready as we'll ever be. I feel sort of useless just acting as a courier. I wish I could be here in case something goes wrong early on. I'm pretty good at providing distraction." She shot Eugene a sidewise grin, which caused him to blush profusely.

He cleared his throat. "I, on the other hand, am just useless. I'm lucky I qualify for courier."

Mini punched his shoulder. "Shut up and let's go take a walk in the woods."

Chuck walked several paces behind Eugene and Mini on the short hike through the forest. They held hands and walked with their heads tilted toward each other just like any young lovers. It made Chuck simultaneously happy and sorrowful. Happy because they were capable of shutting out the dire nature of their situation momentarily, and sorrowful because they were not like any young lovers and possibly never could be.

At the government camp, Chuck went directly to the communications center and contacted Sara. She was surprised by his change of mind.

"I don't get it. I thought you had claustrophobia." She peered at him out of the flat display, trying to read his expression.

He chuckled ruefully and scratched behind one ear. "Yeah. Something I developed after months of being cooped up in an underground lab. But after being out in nature for a while, the thought of going back underground isn't quite so terrifying. Besides, I'd really like to see what you've done with the place.

I couldn't help but notice the observation deck you built at the summit."

She brightened; she seemed pleased. "You know it's always boggled my mind that you and Streegman would end up partners in anything. You were like the odd couple of science. You're so unlike him. He was always quick to criticize and had no appreciation for the subtleties of the human spirit. You're not like that, which is why you're welcome here. I'll have Mike send down an escort."

"Great. And if Tim's ready for his checkup, you can send him down to our base camp. We've got all the equipment set up over there and Dice is ready to take some baseline measures. I'm willing to bet you guys are off the charts when it comes to sheer output. I can hardly wait to see the zeta plots."

"Oh, we're off the charts all right. You said you thought Tim and Lanfen were equivalent. Did you really mean that?"

She glanced to one side; Chuck suspected that meant Tim was in the room with her—had maybe prompted her to ask that question. Good. Tim's hypercompetitive nature was something they were banking on.

"Their talents lie in different areas, though they overlap. Frankly, in some ways Lanfen is a better match for Mike in terms of how she uses her abilities. What I mainly want to see is if they're working in the same wave range. Eventually, I hope to get benchmarks on everyone so we can see just how far we can go with this."

Tim stuck his head into the frame, grinning. "Oh, sky's the limit, Doc. Sky's the limit."

Chuck smiled in return, but there was no joy in it. He went out to the western perimeter of the camp to wait for his escort.

TIM ARRIVED AT BETA CAMP in the company of two of his gargoyle constructs. Brenda, who hadn't seen them before, let out a yip of fear, but Dice and Lanfen had some idea of what to expect and tried to calm her down.

"They're just illusions," Lanfen told Bren quietly as Dice strode out to meet Tim. "Remember? They aren't quite as solid as they look. If you tossed a Ping-Pong ball it might bounce off, but it can't hurt you."

"Easy for you to say," Bren growled.

Lanfen bit her lip and watched Dice pump Tim's hand and admire the gargoyles. It wasn't as easy for either of them as Bren supposed.

"Hey, Tim! I like your sidekicks, dude. Very effective. Their drool sort of disappears before it hits the ground, though."

"Yeah, well, I bet it's more than anyone else can do." Glancing at Lanfen. "Am I right? Hey, Bren. Hey, Lanfen," he added, waving.

The gargoyles waved with him. *Interesting.*

"Yeah," Dice said. "It takes me weeks to perfect my bots; you've got instant minions. Must be nice to be a Zeta I guess." He glanced back at the women, who both gave him raised eyebrows. He'd already showed off enough to suitably impress Brenda with exactly what he could do with anything that generated energy pulses. Lanfen knew he wasn't about to let Tim in on his secret talents.

Tim did a lazy 360, taking in the spartan, woodsy environs in which they'd set up their two modular metal cabins and their wood-framed winter tent and the two SUVs parked in the shade of a colossal red cedar.

"I gotta say, this place is a dump. I mean, compared to our digs. You live like hermits. We live like kings. Like gods. Join up with us and you could live like gods, too."

Dice snorted. "Yeah, you know, I've been to Deepshieldia. I didn't think it was all that great."

"That was *before* we redesigned it. Or at least the parts we use. We've got a construction engineer on our team, remember? An engineer who can build things with his *mind.*" He made a magicky finger waggle at his head. "It's awesome. You've got glorified toolsheds; we've got a *domain.*"

"Denizens of the underworld, huh?" said Bren, digging her hands into the pockets of her jacket. Lanfen could tell they were clenched. "So which one of you is Hades? And does that make Sara Persephone?"

Tim looked at her quizzically. "Huh. I never thought of that. I prefer to think of it as Moria. Peopled by dwarves and hobbitses and . . ."

"And Gollum?" asked Bren, drawing a startled glance from both Dice and Lanfen.

"I was going to say, and greater beings such as Maiar and Valar."

"So that makes you, what, the Balrog?"

Lanfen was surprised when, instead of taking umbrage, Tim laughed with delight. "Yeah, that's me—the Balrog." He shook his head and, in the blink of an eye, where he'd been standing was a ten-foot-tall, flaming demon with horns and glowing red eyes.

"Holy shit!" Dice yelped and leapt back several feet, nearly colliding with Lanfen, who steadied him, her eyes never leaving Tim.

The programmer dropped the illusion, doubled over with laughter. "You totally should have seen the look on your face, man. It was priceless."

"Har, har," Dice said wryly. "You ready to take some tests, bad boy?"

"Sure." He made a flipping gesture with his hands and his two slobbering gargoyle bodyguards vanished.

Lanfen noticed with interest that their passage hadn't even disturbed the pine needles that littered the clearing. Dice beckoned for Tim to follow him to the tent where they'd set up the Brewster-Brenton. Tim followed, still grinning, and Lanfen fell into step with him.

"Hey, Tim, can I ask you something?"

"Sure."

"If your gargoyles don't have real drool, how did you do that amazing thing with the dragons when you guys fought off the Deeps? That was real ordnance they were firing."

Tim seemed to grow in stature and the electricity they'd seen haloing him earlier reappeared. "Oh, you saw that, did you?"

"Of course. We were suitably impressed."

"It was dead simple. The howitzers were wearing dragon suits. I had to split my attention, but the gun turrets were computerized, right? So I triggered, aimed, and fired those electronically, and then just applied my own special brand of, uh, costuming."

"Pretty spectacular."

"Hey, that was a while back, too. I've got quite a few more tricks up my sleeve, believe me."

"I believe you." Lanfen caught Dice's eye as he turned to usher Tim into the lab tent. They were going to have to tread carefully if they didn't want to find out the extent of Timmy's new tricks the dangerous way.

"I can hardly wait to see what sort of measurements we get once we've got you hooked up to the system," Dice enthused. "This is going to be awesome."

"Well, sure. 'Cause *I'm* awesome."

Lanfen glanced at Brenda, who rolled her eyes but didn't make any further acidic comments.

They gathered in the tent where the kinetic rig was set up. Having watched what Mike could do to metal walls and how easily a steel door could become warped and unusable, the Beta team had decided that a structure of thick fabric offered far fewer opportunities for serious mayhem. They'd minimized the potential for turning their lab equipment into deadly projectiles by removing the components—now far smaller than their parent devices anyway—from their metal racks and having them laid out on a table, which would theoretically keep them from being manipulated as a unit. Lanfen was still concerned about the wood in the tent's frame. Her job was to keep a close eye—and her "spidey senses," as Eugene called them—on Tim, and be prepared to go "full ninja" (also a Euge-ism) at the first sign of trouble.

She was hoping—they were all hoping—that it wouldn't be necessary for her to go that far. She spared a thought for Joey Blossom, who was waiting for them in the isolation cabin, and ran through the drill again in her head: they'd take real measurements of Tim's zeta capacity, and compare and contrast it with her own. What they'd really be doing, though, was keeping him occupied until Mini and Euge appeared, then administering a jolt of electricity and a tranq.

Then, into the tank.

Of course, there was always a chance Eugene and Mini wouldn't show before Tim felt he'd overstayed his welcome . . . or they felt he had. In that case, they'd have to tranq him anyway and trust that Chuck had made it safely into the mountain.

It would work, she told herself, as Dice explained to Tim what sort of measures they were hoping to get and how they would quantify them. It had to work. She met Dice's gaze as he placed the neural net on Tim's head. He nodded and she had the eerie sense that he knew what she'd been feeling. More than that, she knew what he was feeling, as well. He was scared—something she prayed Tim wouldn't pick up on.

"Hey," Tim said, looking puzzled. He lifted the thin plait of wires that ran from the transceiver cap to the BPM. "Why are we hardwired? You going all Luddite on me? We scrapped hard connections ages ago."

Dice shrugged. "No Wi-Fi here, Tim. We're running the barebones minimum of tech. Had to set this up in kind of a hurry. So, if I want readings from your brainpan . . ."

"Yeah, I can see that would be a little restrictive. Gotta be hard for you and Euge, being offline like this."

"You have no idea." Dice put a second net on Lanfen's head, then set the brain pattern monitor to read zeta waves. "Okay, ladies and gent, we are ready to begin. Lanfen, why don't you start? Do something basic."

"Mind if I get up and move around?" She pointed to the wide-open double-wide tent door and the grassy clearing beyond.

"Within reason," Dice said. "You've got about twelve feet of cable. Use it wisely."

She caught the grin in his words before she saw it on his face. They'd discussed at some length what sort of "tricks" she should perform. They wanted to impress, but without tipping their hand. Mostly, they wanted to play for time—give Chuck a good window of opportunity to get into the mountain and establish relations with Mike and Sara. It made Lanfen's skin crawl, thinking of Chuck trapped in there with two potentially deadly people. Then she reminded herself that he wasn't trapped. He had talents at his disposal that she wasn't sure even he fully fathomed.

Still . . . she was going to worry a little.

She looked out at the shade-speckled glade and concentrated on the pine needles. She began to make a circling motion with one hand as if she were stirring something with the tips of her fingers. In the center of the glade, pine needles rippled and rose. In moments, she had a fifteen-foot-tall tornado of dried forest debris dancing in the sunlight, juggling pinecones and making a sound like white-water rapids. She let it perform for a minute or two, then bent the top down so it looked like a whirlwind Slinky.

She heard Tim's laughter, and smiled before whipping what had been the bottom of the tornado over the top. She then repeated the flip-flop until the weird little cyclone had made a circuit of the entire glade, setting every tree branch and bough along the perimeter tossing wildly. She brought the thing to a stop right before the tent and, with her hair flying in its winds, made it bow before her. Then, she just let go of it.

The silence was sudden; the pinecones dropped to the ground, followed by the slowly wafting needles. In seconds, the glade was quiet and peaceful once more.

She turned to look at Dice. "Got what you need?"

"Yeah. That was great. Tim, if you would do basically the same thing Lanfen just did, it will give me a baseline for the amount of energy you're generating and what effect it's having on you."

Tim made a face. "Really? You want me to just do a little parlor trick? I mean, I can do—you know—*way* more impressive things than that."

"I'm sure you can," said Dice. "And that time will come, believe me. You know how this works, Tim. I need a baseline—a benchmark."

"Sure. Okay. I get it." Tim moved to the door of the tent, then glanced over at Lanfen. "Notice that I don't have to use those cute little hand gestures to get it going like you do. I mean, it's very martial-artsy and all, Fen, but you look like you're doing interpretive dance. Besides, I can tell what you're going to do when you give it away like that. In a battle," he added, darkness creeping into his eyes, "you don't want to give *anything* away."

He gave his attention back to the center of the clearing. After a moment, the little pile of needles Lanfen had left there stirred. They eddied, they started to rise . . . they subsided again. Tim's brow knit and his mouth puckered in concentration. Clearly this was not something he was used to doing. It took him a moment, but at last he got the pine needles moving in a spiral and rising up from the grassy ground. The form of the tornado was noticeably less coherent and robust than Lanfen's. It was still loose and unstable as it made its rounds; every Slinky move threatened to cause the whole thing to collapse.

Lanfen watched Tim's face closely. He was twitchy and visibly annoyed that he was finding this "parlor trick" harder than he'd expected. As she watched, a sly smile tugged at the corner of his mouth. There was a flutter in the little cyclone, causing it to shed some of its needles, and it suddenly stabilized and appeared as solid and controlled as Lanfen's—maybe even more so.

She turned to look at it, wondering what had caused the change. Had Tim just stepped through a learning threshold? The tornado was as coherent as hers, but it didn't *look* like hers; it was smooth and shiny . . . like one of Tim's constructs. And then she got it: *Tim was cheating.* He was using his ability to project a photonic construct. His pine needle tornado was a fake.

Lanfen glanced at Dice, who was watching from just behind her. He nodded, once. He knew.

The ersatz tornado flip-flopped, Slinky-style, around the camp, then came to a stop in front of the tent and bowed, just as Lanfen's had. But Tim couldn't resist putting a flourish on the gesture; a pair of red glowing eyes leered at them from within the vortex.

A BOT MIKE HAD NAMED "Bradley" came for Chuck at the edge of the military camp. It was less a name than a description. The robot had a lot in common with a Bradley tank—treads, for one thing—and was outfitted with a seat that would accommodate a passenger or two.

Eugene was terrified of the damn thing until Mike's voice issued from its speakers, which were mounted in the peculiar, turret-shaped head. It still weirded him out to watch Chuck climb into the passenger seat behind the squat, forward-leaning torso.

As if he sensed Eugene's trepidation, Mike said, "Don't worry, Euge. I'll take care of Chuck. He'll be okay. Promise."

Then he turned the bot and sent it rolling back up the mountain at a clip that Eugene found nauseating to even watch. "Do you think he meant that?" he asked Mini, when she slipped up beside him and took his hand. "About taking care of Chuck, I mean?"

"I'm sure he did. They think Chuck is an ally. And, in a way, he is. We are. We need to remind ourselves of that. If we start thinking of them as enemies, it will change how we react to them. We're doing this for them, too."

Euge looked down at her and realized that as long as he was in her company, he'd believe anything. He tried to keep what she'd said in mind as they returned to the communications trailer and waited for Chuck's go-ahead.

BRADLEY-MIKE BROUGHT CHUCK THROUGH THE broad front entry of the mountain, which both surprised and unsettled him. The horrific evidence of the battle waged there was everywhere, and his passage through the scorched and devastated tunnel seemed glacial. At one point, they traversed a steel bridge over a dark well in which Chuck, looking down, could just make out what was left of a howitzer—or at least, that's what he thought it was.

"This can't be the only way into the Deep," he said, his voice sounding tiny and pale in the cavernous passage.

"No, definitely not," Mike replied. "We've got all sorts of ins and outs, but nothing we want to give away just now." He lowered his voice and added, "Besides, Sara wants you to know what we're capable of. She figures if you're going to carry tales back to the POTUS and all, they ought to be really scary ones."

"Is that what you want, too, Mike? For me to know what you're capable of?" Chuck asked, cringing at the cold, oily, earthy touch of the cavern air on his skin.

There was a moment of silence, then Mike said quickly, "Yeah. But not the same way Sara does. I don't want you to be afraid of me, Doc. Don't be afraid of me."

That sounded like a plea. "I don't want to be afraid of you, either, Mike."

The bot came to the end of its trek and rolled through a set of thick steel doors and down a concrete ramp lit by strip LEDs. The bot had gone perhaps ten feet into the corridor when the doors ground shut behind it. Chuck tried to ignore the frisson of dread that ran up the back of his neck and focused his senses ahead.

In a minute or so, they came to another set of steel doors and Bradley-Mike said wryly, "You have arrived at your destination."

The doors slid back. Mike was framed in the aperture. For a relieved moment, Chuck thought he might have an opportunity to speak to Mike alone. A second later, though, Sara appeared from around a corner in the corridor behind Mike and strode forward to meet him.

"Welcome to Olympus, Chuck," she said. "You'll have to leave your chariot without. The treads sort of tear up the floors."

"Ah. Of course."

Chuck climbed out of Bradley's passenger seat and entered the Deep once more. He felt the weight of the mountain pressing down on him. He was surprised out of the depressing funk when Sara threw her arms around him in a bear hug.

"It's good to see you face-to-face, Doc. Really good."

She stepped back so he could shake hands with Mike. Her eyes were bright, her cheeks flushed. She looked healthy—radiant even—and she generated a field of what seemed like electrostatic energy that Chuck felt as tiny prickles on his skin. Mike . . . Mike was a different story altogether. He'd lost weight and while he'd clearly been working out, he didn't seem to be in good health. His color wasn't encouraging and the exhaustion Chuck saw in his eyes was underscored with dark circles. His mouth was stretched at the corners, his smile strained.

"Ready for the grand tour?" Sara asked.

"As soon as I let the admiral know I'm safely inside," Chuck said. "She doesn't seem to trust your robots to get me from point A to point B without incident."

"As you wish," Sara said, smiling, and turned to lead the way farther into her domain.

Chuck fell into step between the two Alphas. He heard the doors swish shut behind them and pretended he had not.

"WHAT AM I LOOKING AT?" Tim asked, peering at the side-by-side display of brain wave patterns. "I mean, I know those are my readings and these are Lanfen's, but what do they tell you about me?"

"That you've been growing, young man," Dice said. "And that you're outputting a lot of kinetic energy." He swept a finger along the jagged peaks that represented Tim's attempts to herd pine needles.

"What does it mean that it smooths out like that?" Tim pointed to a decidedly lower-output segment of his pattern.

"It means that you mastered the task," Dice lied. What it actually meant was that he'd switched to a modality that he was familiar with—that is, he'd cheated, and swapped learning to manhandle real objects for tailoring one of his projections to the task at hand. He had managed to keep some of the needles airborne, but sloppily.

"So, Lanfen didn't do as well on the test, did she?" Tim concluded, glancing at the martial arts master's clean, smooth, regular pattern. "I put out more raw energy, didn't I?"

"You did," admitted Dice, but did not say that all his raw power had failed to accomplish what Lanfen's controlled expenditure of zeta energy had. His exaggerated, vivid mountain range of output had been like a weight lifter straining to raise a barbell that was simply too heavy. That was the good news. The bad news was that his demonstration of raw power showed that Tim Desmond had huge untapped reserves. If he had been able to channel them properly toward manipulating solid objects, he'd be a formidable adversary.

"So, since that was clearly a piece of cake," Dice said, "are you game to try something more challenging?"

"You have to ask?" Tim's enjoyment was obvious.

"Okay," said Lanfen. "You choose something. Something spectacular. I'll try to emulate it."

Tim grinned from ear to ear and rubbed his hands together. His spiky aura of blue-white static brightened perceptibly. "All righty, then. What shall I do?" He looked around, then peered through the door of the tent. "Oh, I know. Hey, Lanfen, can you do this?"

His gaze fixed on something across the glade and a second later, the engine of one of the SUVs roared to life. The vehicle backed out from under its sheltering tree and into the center of the clearing.

Dice laughed nervously. "Dude, don't go wrecking our cars, okay?"

"Wouldn't think of it, Dice. Watch this." Tim spun the SUV around in reverse, spewing fallen leaves and pine needles everywhere.

Dice glanced at the brain pattern monitor; the waves were smooth, but elevated. Tim was in his wheelhouse—manipulating the car's computer systems. A moment later, he was spiking way up into the 9 mHz range and the front end of the SUV tilted toward the sky as it danced and pivoted on its rear wheels. Dice looked at Tim. The veil of blue-white iridescence around him had intensified with his effort to physically manipulate the vehicle.

"This is child's play, you know," Tim said, watching the results of his work.

Dice's eyes were drawn past the capering car to the verge of the wood. Eugene and Mini had appeared there, hand in hand, their eyes on the SUV's performance. Dice gave Bren a glance; she showed him the infuser she'd palmed. He caught Lanfen's eye and knew she'd seen the couple, too.

Lanfen pointed. "Hey, look who's here."

Bren crossed the tent to stand on Tim's opposite side. "Hey, it's Mini and Euge!" She waved.

Tim, distracted, let the SUV drop back to four wheels, though it still cut a tight circle in the clearing. Dice hit a switch on the Brewster-Brenton and flooded the neural net on the programmer's head with an electrical charge. Tim's body jerked, his aura faltered, and his eyes rolled back in his head. Bren chose that moment to jab his neck with the infuser.

Tim's halo of energy proved to be more than just a keen special effect. A second after dimming, it was back full force. Brenda cried out and wrenched her hand back. Tim sent a wild charge of energy back down the line to the brain pattern monitor. The machine overloaded, sending sparks everywhere. Dice leapt out of their way, watching Tim writhe and try to pull the neural net from his head. He succeeded only in getting his fingers tangled in it. As he staggered, on the verge of falling, Lanfen stepped in and administered a karate chop to Tim's neck.

The nimbus of static energy went white, Tim lurched forward, and Lanfen went flying. She tumbled through the door of the tent and out into the clearing, where she hit the ground and rolled—directly into the path of the spinning SUV.

For a frozen moment, Dice was certain she'd be crushed. The upward cut she made with one hand could not be quick enough . . .

But it was.

The vehicle flipped over, landing on one side, its wheels spinning futilely. They stopped when the engine went silent. Lanfen leapt to her feet and gave a quick glance over her shoulder at Mini and Eugene before racing back to the tent.

Dice moved at the same time to where Tim now lay—half-in and half-out of the tent. He was clearly unconscious, but the veil of energy sizzled fitfully around him. Dice reached down and tried to touch him, only to receive an unpleasant jolt when his hand was more than three inches away.

"Wow," said Euge, peering around Lanfen. "That's quite a security system he's got there."

"Yeah. How are we supposed to get him into a tank?" Bren asked, still massaging her wounded hand.

Lanfen and Mini exchanged glances. "I think Mini and I can work that out," Lanfen said. "And thanks, Min. I appreciated the help out there. I'm pretty sure I didn't flip that car on my own."

The other woman tilted her head and smiled. "What are friends for?"

"Right now," said Dice, "they're for getting this guy on ice. Ladies, you said you have a plan?"

They did. Without using their hands, they lifted the programmer's body and floated it toward the immersion cabin. Dice hurried ahead of them and opened the door. Joey popped the closest tank open the moment he saw Dice and, together, the two women hoisted Tim into the unit and lowered him until his head and shoulders were just above the gelatinous contents of the tank.

"Why's he all lit up like that?" Joey asked in hushed tones.

"He's projecting some sort of energy field," Dice explained. "A very potent one, at the moment. Which raises the question of how we're going to get the entraining helm on his head."

"No worries," said Lanfen. "Mini, can you just hold him there?"

"You got it."

The artist's face took on an expression of intense concentration as she stepped up onto the isolation unit's surrounding platform and peered down into the tank. Dice, watching through one of the unit's ports, thought he saw the barest suggestion of a translucent figure standing in the tank holding Tim's head and upper torso out of the gel. Standing beside Mini on the platform, Lanfen set her gaze firmly on the unit's half helm. She moved it deftly into position on Tim's head with the concentration of a major-league pitcher threading a slider through a narrow strike zone.

"Can you teach me to do that?" Joey asked as he took a seat at the control console. "That is a very cool talent." His hands moved on the control keyboard and the lid of the SDU glided shut, sealing Tim Desmond within.

"Maybe some other time," Lanfen said through gritted teeth.

"Oh . . . right."

A moment later, a light on the half helm began to pulse as the system fed binaural beats into Tim's unconscious brain. The static halo began to fade. In moments, it was gone.

"Okay, Eugene," she said, "time for you to go ping Chuck. Let him know the trap's been sprung."

"Yeah," Eugene murmured. "I'll just do that." He turned in the doorway, and left the cabin at a run.

Dice raised his eyes to the isolation unit's interior monitor and wondered again what was possible to a zeta adept. He laid a hand on Joey's shoulder. "Whatever you do, don't let him dream."

Chapter 20

ADEPTS

Sara and Mike gave Chuck a tour of their mountain. They had made the portions they used more than livable. Mike's talent for construction, coupled with Sara's sense of design, had resulted in an environment that was both beautiful and functional. The living quarters were comfortable without being opulent; the kitchen/dining room was a study in convenience and functionality; the ops center looked like something out of *Star Trek*. But the robotics bays were a revelation. Chuck had seen them through Thorin's optics when Lanfen had gone on her espionage mission within Deep Shield. Then they had been a series of long, narrow rooms arranged around a hub. Now the dividing walls were gone (he guessed Mike had done that) and long lines of robots seemed to march off into infinity on both sides of the labs.

The lab tables and equipment that had once stood in the center of the rooms were also gone, which gave the place the atmosphere of a futuristic warehouse full of larger-than-life toys. The knowledge that they weren't toys made Chuck shiver.

"Impressive," he said, forcing his voice to sound enthusiastic instead of terrified. "You've done an amazing job of making this place less . . . spartan and military. If we could train a generation of architects and construction engineers in zeta tech, it would revolutionize the construction industry and allow people with disabilities to stay productive."

Sara laughed. "Doc, that is so *you*. That sort of thinking is why we need you here in Olympus. Here you could be the architect of a new world. With the whole team here, there's nothing we couldn't accomplish."

"I was hoping to take you out into the real world, Sara. To get all of us out of the shadows—out from underground."

She looked away from him down the length of the robot bays. "Yeah, I was hoping that, too, but there's hope and then there's reality. Reality, Doc, is what you saw on the way in. We did that. I don't know how many soldiers died when we repelled that invasion, but I do know that the fact of their death makes us coming out into polite company . . . well, a bit problematic."

"They were black ops, Sara," Chuck said. "No—more than that. They were enemies of the United States and every citizen in it. Enemies of its government. You blew their cover sky-high. More than that, you uncovered the men behind them. I know the president is grateful for that."

Sara gave him a look that was almost pitying. "Watch this, Doc," she said, then launched herself into the air.

It was not like one of Lanfen's gymnastic vaults; it was a slow-motion lift, like a heron taking flight or a circus acrobat riding her tether into the big top. She flew down the length of the robot bays, her back arched, then turned a series of lazy loops in the air.

Chuck glanced at Mike. He was watching Sara, too, his expression unreadable. "How long has she been able to do that?" Chuck asked.

Mike shrugged. "Not that long. I first saw her do something like this about a week ago, I guess. She and Tim both mostly work with electronics. Me, I'm more of a Luddite."

"Nonsense," Sara said, touching down between the two men. "You're amazing, Mike. Show Chuck what you can do with the robots."

Mike acquiesced in a way that sent chills through the very marrow of Chuck's bones. Could he really wrest Mike from Sara's grasp? Mike merely turned to look down the long gallery and every single unit visible from Chuck's vantage point came to life and stepped down from its charging station in unison so perfect, he couldn't make out the sounds of individual footfalls, but only heard one single, titanic step.

"Are they . . . that is, do they have to move in lockstep? Or can you—"

With a glance at Sara, Mike had the first ten bots face left and march in place while the ten beyond them took two perfectly timed steps out, turned, and marched up beside them. A third decade marched up beside those. Chuck had expected the sound to be deafening, but the soft soles of the robots' feet made them sound more like a squadron of sneakered cheerleaders than a pack of metal men.

All thirty bots continued to march until Mike interrupted them with a drill sergeant's shout, "Halt!" The robots went completely still.

Chuck was about to ask another question when Mike put his metal minions through a series of exercises that reminded him alternately of the Rockettes, a martial arts class, and a bunch of kids doing the hokey-pokey. The effect was so absurd, he wanted to laugh, but found he couldn't.

"That's truly impressive," he said—and meant it. "Both of you. Sara, I'm curious—how high an elevation can you manage with your levitation?"

"I've touched the ceiling in ops," she told him with obvious pride. "That's a good twenty or thirty feet. Didn't feel like too much of a strain. It's just a matter of packing sufficient molecules together."

He nodded. *Just*. "Mike, I get the feeling that you're pretty agnostic about what kind of machinery you operate. I mean, it doesn't matter to you what sort of machinery it is, right?"

Mike's smile seemed grim. "If it's got moving parts, I can make them move. If it doesn't . . ." He shrugged eloquently. "I can *make* it have moving parts."

Chuck wondered if Mike had tumbled to the idea that human beings were just different kinds of machines . . . at least on the outside. He hoped not, or that if he had, the thought terrified him as much as it did Chuck.

Chuck shook off the cold, dark niggle of fear that jittered down his spine and went to another of his time-wasting tactics. "You know, I'd love to get some baseline measurements on amplitude from both of you while I'm here. Do you have an EEG machine?"

"Yeah, we do," Mike said. "In the infirmary. Do you wanna—"

Sara cut him off. "That can wait. Besides, I figured you'd want us to come down the mountain so you could use your state-of-the-art tools to take measurements."

"True enough. I'm just intensely curious about what levels of amplitude you're pushing. I mean, being able to affect enough molecular material to levitate or blow down a wall must take significant output."

Sara grinned. "Same old Chuck. Okay, Dad, we'll let you measure our growth before we talk about strategy. But first, I want to show you something." She started for the laboratory doors.

Chuck had no recourse but to fall into step. "Oh? What's that?"

She glanced back over her shoulder at him. "A God's-eye view of Pine Flat."

Chuck swore that, for a split second, he forgot how to walk. The last thing he needed was for Sara and Mike to get a God's-eye view of the area below their mountain—specifically of the Betas' base camp. He could only pray that Tim had already been incapacitated and hustled into an isolation tank. He stopped walking, causing Sara and Mike to stop, too.

"How, uh, how high up is that, exactly?"

Mike shot him a glance. "You afraid of heights, Doc?"

"Oh, well, uh, *afraid* is maybe not quite the right word. Let's just say my visits to New York have never included the Empire State Building tour." Feigning a fear of heights was the only gambit Chuck's panicked mind could conjure.

"It's perfectly safe," said Sara. "After all, there's an entire mountain holding you up. And the deck is solid as the rock it's sitting on. Mike built it. Come on, Chuck, live a little. You can't be afraid to be *in* a mountain and afraid to be *on* one, too."

I sure as hell can, he thought. But Chuck looked at the construction engineer and smiled, hoping he looked as if he were attempting to hide panic. "Well, that's a ringing endorsement. I guess I can close my eyes. How do you get up there?"

"I built an elevator," Mike told him. "You're not afraid of elevators, are you?"

"Only mildly concerned. How many stories do you think it is?"

"Don't worry about it, Doc," Mike said, patting his shoulder. "I promise, you'll be okay."

Chuck nodded and they began to move again, down the long axis of the installation, to the operations center. Mike's elevator had been installed in a large empty room some yards to the northeast of ops.

The room wasn't quite empty, Chuck realized, as overhead lights snapped on following their progress across the concrete floor. There were large tables or workbenches, several of which were damaged, and beyond them was a mound of wreckage. As they drew near, their footfalls echoing eerily on the hard, polished cement, he realized that it was a huge robot of a type he'd never seen before. The torso was immense and the head had a clear, bubble face mask that was pitted and shot through with crazing. It took him a breathless moment to realize that the robot had been intended to hold a human pilot and that the rust-colored stains on the bot and the walls and floor around it were dried blood.

"Dear God, what is that?" The words sprang from his lips before he could think better of saying them.

"That," said Sara, "was a little top secret number that General Coward"—she emphasized the *C*—"had hidden deep in the bowels of Olympus. He threw it at us in a sort of last-ditch kamikaze attack."

"The—the pilot . . ."

"The pilot didn't survive," said Sara coldly. "Like I said, it was a suicide mission. He wasn't supposed to survive, and Coward didn't care."

"It was Lieutenant Reynolds," Mike murmured.

Chuck felt suddenly queasy. "How did—"

"You'd have to ask Tim," Mike said. His voice sounded flat and dead.

"Our chariot awaits," Sara said brightly. She stopped to wave at a structure that was both minimalistic and elegant.

In the rear of the room, in a pool of bright light, was a clear Plexiglas tube with a gleaming cylindrical car that seemed to have no mechanical means of locomotion. Three ribbons of anodized steel ran up the length of the tube as far as Chuck could see—which was the point at which it disappeared into the rocky ceiling.

"Zeta powered?" Chuck asked, pushing the words out with an effort.

Sara nodded. "Wave of the future. Zeta-vators. No mechanical parts to go wrong. You just hire a Zeta to ride folks up and down as necessary. See, you've become a job creator. Hop in." Sara waved at the car and its clear door opened, sliding back along a nearly invisible track.

Under normal circumstances, Chuck would have been impressed beyond measure. Mike's talent was phenomenal. Chuck hadn't even considered how zeta abilities could adapt to improve such mundane technologies. He entered the car with deliberate hesitation. The way it disappeared into the solid rock of the mountain really did make him sweat, but far more sweat-inducing was the idea that Sara and Mike might see something they shouldn't from their observation deck. He was stuck, and could only hope the tour of the observation deck wouldn't be too revealing or too long.

DOWN AT BETA BASE CAMP, Team Chuck was in recovery mode. The blown BPM machine had burned a hole through the white canvas roof of their lab tent and filled it with acrid smoke. The SUV was still sitting where it had come to an unceremonious and violent stop, its windshield a mess of spiderweb fissures. Lanfen had rolled it back onto its tires. While she examined the vehicle to see if it was still roadworthy, Dice, Brenda, and Mini cleaned up the lab and hauled ruined equipment out into the clearing; Joey babysat Tim.

Lanfen was no auto mechanic, but she worked on her motorcycle regularly and figured that qualified her to at least spot any major damage. She had just determined that the SUV's injuries were not fatal when she felt a tug of angst from Chuck. Startled by how crystalline his distress was, she straightened and peered up over the treetops at the mountain. She felt a swift charge of concern from close by and glanced across the clearing to see Mini staring up at the peak, as well.

"You felt that, too?" Lanfen asked.

Mini turned to look at her, nodding. "What should we do?"

"Hurry."

CHUCK STEPPED OUT OF THE elevator onto the observation deck and went immediately to the northernmost corner of the structure, peering out toward where the Deep Shield camp had once sat.

"Wow," he said, making his voice as cheerful as possible.

"You've got an awesome view of the park from up here. Is that where the Deep Shield camp was—that burned area?"

Mike crossed to where Chuck was standing and followed his gaze. "Yeah. That was . . . it was scary."

Chuck nodded. "I saw the video. Tim's constructs look realistically solid. The soldiers had no idea they were shooting at each other."

Sara, lounging along the perimeter of the clear Plexiglas railing, laughed. "It was brilliant. Tim didn't have to lift a finger against anyone. He just let them . . ." Her voice trailed off, then she said, "What the hell?"

Chuck felt as if his heart had morphed into stone. He turned to look at Sara. She was standing at the rail about twelve feet to his right, her gaze directed down the slope below. Hoping that he might explain away whatever she was seeing, Chuck moved toward her until he could see what she was looking at—and knew there was no way. The Beta Camp was a mess. The tent had a large, charred hole in the top of it, and smoke was seeping out of the screened windows and open door. Mini—recognizable even from this distance—was stacking apparently ruined equipment in the middle of the glade while Lanfen crawled over one of their SUVs. Dice and Brenda were in the tent; he could see them in brief glimpses through the door and the hole in the roof. Eugene, Joey, and Tim were nowhere in sight. All in all, it was a pretty incriminating scene. It looked as if a battle had been waged and if these were the victors . . .

Chuck tried to think of something to say. Anything that might make the obviously chaotic situation seem mundane.

"Hey," said Mike, casually, "it looks like Timmy blew out all the stops. I'd say he owes you some equipment."

"Where's Tim?" said Sara through her teeth.

"Probably trying to help clean up the mess," suggested Mike.

"I don't see Tim helping to do anything," Sara said. "Chuck, what's in those modulars?"

"They're living quarters."

"There are six of you. One of those is big enough for that. What's in the second modular?"

"Equipment," Chuck said. "You know me, I never go anywhere without all my toys."

"Where's Tim?" she repeated. "What have you done with Tim?"

"How would I know?" Chuck said truthfully. "I'm sure he's fine. Why wouldn't he be?"

Sara advanced toward him. "You tell me, Doc. What did you do, throw in with the enemy?"

"The *enemy*? What are you talking about? What enemy, Sara? Who do you think is your enemy? The U.S. government? Its people? Anyone who's not a Zeta?"

Chuck glanced down at the camp. Lanfen and Mini had both stopped in their tracks and were staring up at the mountain. Sara followed his gaze. So, she saw the same thing he did—the two women unfroze to exchange a glance before they launched back into fevered activity. Mini disappeared into the western modular and Lanfen parked the SUV back under its cedar tree—without bothering to get in and start the engine. Then she headed for the westernmost building.

"Mike," said Sara, not taking her eyes from the camp, "keep Chuck here. Don't let him out of your sight. I'll deal with him later."

"Where are you going, Sara?" Mike asked quietly. "You can't think they'd hurt Tim . . ."

She turned to look at him, her eyes glowing and a gleaming aura beginning to pulse around her. "I think they're trying to pick us off one by one—that's what I think. But they've bitten off a bit more than they can chew. Keep the traitor here."

"I'm *not* a traitor, Sara," said Chuck. "I'm your friend. The Beta team are your friends. Possibly the only ones you've got in the world. You need to let us get you out of this mountain. There's a facility we can take you to where we can—"

"Where you can what, Chuck? Reprogram us? Manipulate us the way Deep Shield did?"

"No, Sara. Listen to me, for God's sake! Making people afraid of you isn't going to achieve your goals."

"I'm doing this for God's sake, Chuck. And right now, from where I sit, making people afraid of me is the only way to achieve my goals. These assholes aren't going to change out of the goodness of their hearts. I'm going to ask you one more time: what have you done to Tim?"

"I hope we've saved him."

Eyes blazing, Sara thrust one hand at him. He felt as if she'd hit him in the chest with a bowling ball. He flew backward through the air toward the transparent railing of the observation deck—and a very steep drop. A second blow forced him downward. He hit the deck and tumbled, head over heels, to fetch up hard against the railing.

Dizzy, hurting, and breathless, Chuck watched as Sara leapt lightly to the top of the railing, then launched herself into the air and down the mountainside, soaring over the treetops, heading directly for the Betas' base camp.

Lanfen . . . Mini . . . I'm sorry.

Chapter 21

RAGE

Sara's rage consumed her, drove her, lifted her over the trees and toward the Betas' camp. The clearing was empty now, and her eyes scanned for a target. When Eugene emerged from the woods on the southern edge of the camp, she did not closely examine the relief she felt that Chen Lanfen was not the first person she saw. She did not want to face the martial arts master one-on-one. The most logical target was the one she was looking at now: Eugene Pozniaki, who, as far as she knew, had never shown any zeta potential.

She aimed herself at him, letting her fury take her. Eugene was the weakest member of the team. She'd take care of him first, then figure out what they'd done with Tim. Eugene saw her when he was less than halfway across the clearing. He stopped and stared upward, then raised the alarm in an inarticulate squawk.

Sara laughed and zeroed in on her target.

AT THE SOUND OF EUGENE'S voice, Mini ran to the door of the habitat cabin and followed his gaze upward. Sara! Sara was airborne, soaring toward them, making the treetops toss in her wake.

Mini stepped out onto the frame porch and faced the incoming threat. She had opened her mouth to call Lanfen out of the immersion cabin when she realized that Sara wasn't aiming for her; she was targeting Eugene, who was still frozen halfway across the clearing.

That was not going to happen. Mini leapt from the porch and sprinted toward the middle of the camp determined not to let Sara reach Eugene. By the time Sara had made it to the perimeter of the camp, Mini had put herself between the Alpha and Eugene.

Sara pulled up just over the roof of the immersion cabin, hovering as if on invisible wings.

"What have you done with Tim?" she demanded, her eyes literally shooting sparks. The sparks disappeared when they were less than three feet from her. Mini suspected they were projections, not creations.

"Tim is fine, Sara. He's just resting. Dice's tests took a lot out of him."

"Liar. Let him go, or your boyfriend is going to pay for it."

"Eugene," Mini said quietly, "go into the tent."

He hesitated, then sprinted into the lab tent. Sara snarled and darted after him.

Mini moved as well, her hands sweeping forward to loose a barrage of tiny, fiery sprites at the other woman.

SARA NEARLY LAUGHED ALOUD. WAS Mini really stupid enough to think she'd be deterred by a bunch of glowing pixies? She plowed into the midst of the swarm in disgust when she felt the first burns. It was like diving into a nest of fire ants.

She let out an inarticulate roar of pain and rage and backflipped away from Mini's tiny warriors, landing with both feet on the roof of the westernmost cabin. Sara suspected that was where Lanfen was hiding, but she was even less inclined to face her than before. Since becoming a Zeta she was accustomed to being in a position of strength. Her rage could not quell the fear she had for Lanfen. She would need Tim's help to face her.

First things first, though. The weakest members of Chuck's team of elites were in that tent, so that was where she turned her fury.

CHUCK TOOK THE HAND MIKE extended to him and let the Alpha pull him up from the deck.

"You okay, Doc?"

"Nothing broken. A few bruises, that's all. I'll live." He glanced up into Mike's face. "If you let me."

He did not imagine the expression of pain that flitted across Mike's face.

"It's not like that, Doc. I'm not gonna hurt you. I'm not gonna let Sara hurt you, either."

Chuck nodded. "I guess I owe you a big thank-you, then. You're the one who knocked me out of the air, aren't you? You saved my life. I'm pretty sure Sara intended for me to go over the edge."

Mike looked away toward the deck railing. "Yeah, I'm pretty sure she did."

"Mike, are you really doing this? Lording over people, flaunting your power like a demigod? I say this honestly, this isn't you. This is not the Mike I know."

"You know I don't. I just . . . I just want to stop men like Howard from hurting me or anyone else."

"Do you think Sara's way is the right way to do that?"

Mike shook his head. "Probably not. No. No, I don't think her way is the right way. In fact, I think . . . I'm afraid that she . . ."

"That she's becoming like Howard?" When Mike didn't answer, he pressed on.

"Do you think she knows how you feel?"

Mike glanced up at him. "If she did, I'd probably be dead. Or exiled."

"Would you mind being exiled, really?"

"Maybe. Maybe not. But hell, Doc, what is there for me outside this mountain, huh?"

"Your family?"

Mike's laughter was forced and grim. "What sort of future do I have with my family, Doc? I *killed* people."

"People who were trying to kill you."

"I could've sent them packing. I could've maybe knocked them out and—and put them someplace where they couldn't cause any more trouble. I could've done . . . something else."

"The way Sara could have done something else besides kill Matt?"

The look on Mike's face was one of sheer desolation. "She didn't need to do that, Doc."

"No, because Matt didn't stage the attack."

"She can't let herself believe that. You understand why."

"But *you* believe it. Don't you, Mike?" Feeling a tug of emotion from Lanfen, knowing that Sara was hell-bent for destruction, Chuck moved a step closer to the Alpha. "You know this isn't right, what Sara and Tim are doing. Yes, the world needs changing, and yes, we need to be in the vanguard of those changes—but not like this. By now, Dice has gotten Tim tranquilized. Come out of here with me, Mike. Help us get Sara under control."

"You won't kill her?"

"I don't know how you can even ask me that. I have no intention to kill anyone, *ever*. And I will do everything in my power to make sure that's never even an option, Mike. Everything. Help us. With your help, there's no question that we can get all three of you to safety."

Mike's eyes were eloquent with despair. "What's the point? There is no safety out there. Not for me."

"There can be, if you—"

"Can you un-zeta me, Doc? Can you take away all this crazy shit? Can you put me back the way I was—make me *me* again?"

Chuck shook his head. "I'm sorry, Mike. I don't know any way to do that—not for any of us. We're who we are now. We will be who we become."

"Then I can't go back out there. I can't. I don't want my family to see me like this."

"But you're still—"

Chuck wasn't able to finish, as a strange exhalation came from the shadows in front of the elevator. He realized it was a child's voice crying, "Daddy! Daddy!" And then Mike's son, Anton, appeared out of nowhere and ran into his father's arms. Mike gave the child his entire attention—everyone else was forgotten.

Chuck wasn't sure whether to rejoice or gnash his teeth. "Lorstad," he said quietly, and the other man stepped out of the shadows and into the sunlight. "You couldn't keep out of this, could you?"

"Are you sure you really wanted me to? I suspect that young Anton will be able to accomplish what even you could not." Lorstad gestured at the father-and-son reunion.

Mike looked up at the two other men over his son's head. Tears filled his eyes and they blazed with anger. "Why? Why did you do this? Why did you have to bring him into this?"

"Because," Chuck answered, wishing to God that he didn't have to, but knowing Lorstad would never know how to, "we need to bring you out. I can't un-zeta you. I can't do it for any of us—not even myself. But you are a good man, a father, a husband. You are not the loathsome idea you have projected onto yourself."

The Alpha was shaking his head and mouthing *no, no, no.* He tightened his embrace on Anton, and Mike the devoted father returned. Mike the Zeta, the crusader for a new world, the dread knight of the new dark goddess, all melted away. His perspective shifted back to its original view. He loved his family and wanted to provide for them; what's more he didn't want to be apart from them. In a strange way he felt gratitude toward Lorstad for bringing his boy to him.

Chuck drew closer to him and looked him right in the eye. "Mike, you don't have to be Sara or Tim. You're *not* them. You're nothing like them. They don't want to go back. Neither of them is ready to sacrifice this power. You are. In my estimation that makes you the only one worthy of having it in the first place."

Mike swallowed. "What do I do?"

"Come down off this mountain with me, Mike. Do it for Anton. For your family. For the rest of humanity. Help us find a way to fix the world without hurting people." He held his breath, unsure how the engineer would respond. Mike wasn't even looking at Chuck—instead his eyes were lost even as his son clung tightly to his neck. Slowly, Mike began nodding, his jaw set. Chuck knew that look.

"Yeah. Okay. Yeah." He rose, gently taking Anton's arms from around his neck, but pulling the boy tightly to his side. "Let's go."

Lorstad, who had been watching the scene with his characteristic aloof interest, stirred slightly. "I will leave you to your work, gentlemen. I have something I must attend to." Then he simply disappeared.

"He do that a lot?" Mike asked.

Chuck said plainly, "Yes. And no, you don't get used to it. Now, I need to contact our people in the communications camp. You asked what you need to do. You need to destroy this." He waved a hand at the mountain. "Or at least make it inaccessible. Is that something you can do?"

A spark of zeal fired in Mike's eyes. "Oh yeah, Doc. I can do that."

SARA MOVED WITH BLINDING SPEED toward the tent, her hands outstretched. A massive bow wave of pressure moved before her.

Mini, out of its direct path, felt it as a pillow-fight blow that still sent her staggering back several steps. The tent bore the brunt of the attack, and Mini saw what was left of its canvas roof tear free and the walls sag inward like sails in the teeth of a gale. The tent collapsed, but not before Eugene escaped from the misshapen doorway.

"The car!" Mini shouted at him. "Get to the car!"

He hesitated, but only for a split second. Mini suspected that the look on her face was enough to dissuade him from debating the demand. He was helpless here; she wasn't. She turned her attention back to the tent, which now sagged atop the lab tables. She saw a flutter near the tallest peak that she took to be Dice and Bren moving about beneath the canvas.

Apparently, Sara saw it, too, for she launched herself at the movement. A second later the canvas tore, the sheared sides flying outward to reveal Dice and Bren huddled in the lee of the longest lab table.

Sara's lips drew back in a snarl. "Where's Tim? What have you done with Tim?"

"He's fine," Dice told her. "He's just where he can't do any harm."

"Harm? Damn you, Dice, *I'll* show you harm!"

She swept her arms forward, but Dice saw the attack coming. He flung his right arm out from behind his back. A lash of cabling unfurled, electricity sparking at the tip of each wire. It struck Sara's feet and for a moment, a wild jitter of blue-white static danced around her body like an electric wet suit.

Mini took the opportunity to hit her with another volley of fire pixies. Sara skipped backward in the air, shrieking in frustration. She wasted no time flailing at the pixies; instead she siphoned the electricity from the veil of energy she wore and directed it at Dice and Brenda. Dice managed to block it with his own charged field, but he lacked Sara's experience and strength.

Her attack bowled Dice and Bren over and knocked them clear of their cover. They sprawled, obviously shaken, amid the ruins of the tent.

"Leave them alone!" Mini cried, advancing toward Sara. She forced herself to breathe, to keep her thoughts and emotions under control. She mustn't let Sara get the better of her.

"Where's Tim?" Sara demanded again. "Is he there?" She directed her attention at the habitat cabin.

"Maybe," Mini said. "Are you going to find out by tearing the building apart?"

"Maybe I'll just invite myself in." Sara feinted toward the cabin and Mini moved to block her. If she could make Sara waste time and energy going after the wrong target . . .

"You're being an idiot, Mini," Sara told her. "You could save us all a lot of trouble and agony if you'd just get him and bring him to me."

"He's . . . not here. We sent him away."

Sara threw back her head and laughed. "Mini-mouse, you are the world's worst liar. Let's cut to the chase, shall we? You tell me which of these boxes my little Troll is in, okay? You do that, and I won't do something like this." She swung toward where the SUVs were parked.

Were *still* parked. Because Eugene had gotten to the undamaged car and stalled. He had not driven away, nor had he escaped through the woods to Spiderweb. He stood by the driver's-side door, watching approaching doom.

Mini screamed at him to move, and he did, abandoning the SUV and turning to flee into the trees. She put herself in motion as well, but Sara was faster. The Alpha dropped from the air and hit the ground at a dead run. The slashing gesture she made with one arm at first seemed to do nothing, then a tall cedar in Eugene's flight path groaned as if in agony and fell with a shriek of stressed wood and a tumble of limbs.

"Eugene!" Mini shrieked, but he had already disappeared beneath the wildly tossing branches. Any cry he might have uttered was drowned by the thunder of the tree's impact with the ground.

Sara turned back to gloat, a triumphant look on her face—which quickly vanished with one glance at Mini. The young woman's hard-won control exploded in a flash of white-hot fear and rage. In a heartbeat, she had clothed herself in a shimmering cloak of energy that all but blinded her. She thought thousands of tiny sprites into being, filling the air with burning darts that mobbed Sara as a swarm of sparrows might mob a crow.

Sara howled in rage and pain and thrust herself back into the air, trying to escape the swarm. Distracted from her original target, she turned to face Mini. She was so intent on battling her way to the other Zeta, she didn't seem to see Lanfen slip from the immersion cabin.

Mini knew without a doubt that the martial arts master was coiling to spring. *Stop!* she thought. *No!*

Somehow, Lanfen felt the tug of Mini's thoughts and turned to look at her. Mini darted a glance toward the fallen tree. Lanfen didn't hesitate. She ran straight for where Eugene had disappeared, leaving Mini to face Sara.

The Alpha was charging at her physically now, trying to bull her way through the never-ending horde of stinging sprites. Mini upped the ante—the sprites became butterflies with wings like fiery razors—but still Sara came.

Well, Mini thought. *I guess I need a new trick.*

INSIDE THE IMMERSION CABIN, JOEY tried to ignore the sounds of conflict from outside, and watched Tim's brain patterns on the EEG monitor for any sign that he was dreaming—or worse, shrugging off the effects of the entraining program. As far as Joey knew, every one of the Learned's recruits had been willing, even eager, to go into the tanks. They'd never had to entrain someone as decidedly unwilling as Tim Desmond, and he was worried that such resistance would be enough for Tim to break free.

He glanced over his shoulder at the door Lanfen had just exited. He knew she'd been trying to gauge when Sara was distracted enough that her entry onto the scene would be unnoticed until it was too late. He told himself she'd chosen the right moment. Everything he'd seen and heard of Doc Brenton's ninja had convinced him that she was one of the most competent human beings he'd ever met or was likely to meet.

A soft ping from the SDU instrument panel pulled his focus back to it. Something was happening in Tim's brain. He was generating some random beta events, indicating anxious thought or attempts to move. There was no regular beta rhythm yet, but . . .

Joey had one emergency option and that was to flood the Alpha's oxygen feed with an atomized sedative. The problem was, Tim had already been hit with a maximum dosage of tranquilizer. Putting him further under with a different chemical could prove harmful—might even kill him. There was no way to know, and Joey definitely wasn't a medical doctor.

Joey wiped sweat from his upper lip and focused his attention on Tim's brain waves, remembering Dice's parting words, "Whatever you do, don't let him dream."

Tim wasn't dreaming, but he might be trying to do something just as dangerous.

BUTTERFLIES. DAMNED PIXIES AND BUTTERFLIES. Sara's silent contempt was tempered with a great deal of respect. The damned things *hurt*. They drew blood. What would Mini gin up next—unicorns with steel horns? Bunnies with tusks? Whatever she came up with, she could be no match for Sara Crowell.

You can only do so much with a butterfly.

Sara forced more power into her own energy aura but was dismayed to realize it didn't keep the burning flyers out. She skimmed just above the ground, batting them away with her arms, feeling the burn and bite of their sharp wings. She wiped at her face; the back of her hand came back stained red. The sight of her own blood threw her into an even greater rage. She went at Mini with a scream of pain and anger, her hands raised to pummel the stupid child with every bit of force at her disposal. She fed the power of her fury through her fingertips, unleashing it at point-blank range.

Mini dissolved like mist in the sun.

Sara came up short, her feet on terra firma. *Well, that was something.* For a moment, she was exultant. Then a feral growl behind her made her turn. Mini stood between Sara and the second metal prefab, panting, her face red, her eyes wild.

Well, damn. Not dead, after all, but at least she was tiring. Sara approached with caution anyway, deciding that it would be best to use a little psychology.

"Nice trick, Mini-mouse. Fortunately, I know you're all art and no substance. Now, I'm willing to bet that Timmy is in that building you're blocking. I figure that's why Lanfen was holed up in there, guarding the crown jewels." She didn't miss the way Mini's eyes widened slightly. "You didn't think I noticed her, did you? I did, but I opted to let her go tend to your boyfriend. I'll deal with her later. Right now, I need to get into that building."

She attacked without any further warning, directing her force not at Mini, but at the building behind her. The force was enough to bow the front wall violently inward and rock the cabin on its steel foundation. There was a shower of sparks from the north rear corner of the building and the clearing became suddenly quieter. A murmur of sound Sara had barely noticed was now gone: the generator that had been feeding power to the cabin fell silent.

"Sorry," she said, "but I think I just pulled your plug."

JOEY PICKED HIMSELF UP OFF the floor of the immersion cabin, nursing bruised ribs and a sore hip from where he'd fallen. He'd been in an earthquake once as a kid. This was way worse. Earthquakes weren't malevolent.

It took him a moment to realize that the generator had cut out—all the control panels had gone dark and the battery-powered LED emergency lights had popped on. He scrambled to his feet, ignoring the pain in his side. The power to the tank was off; that meant neither binaural beats nor Lorstad's entraining program was feeding into the Alpha's brain. If Tim regained consciousness . . .

Joey was hit with a cold, clammy impulse to bail. He obeyed it, sprinting for a window at the rear of the cabin. He had hauled it open and grabbed the frame with both hands when he realized that without power, Tim's oxygen would be cut off and he would suffocate.

He hesitated for only a fraction of a second before he let go of the window frame and ran back to the tank. He had one foot on the platform when the top of the tank blew open in an explosion of gel and sparks.

SARA WAS ADVANCING ON MINI, wondering why she was refusing to move out of the way, when the cabin rocked a second time. This time the explosion came from inside and caused a sudden deformation of the cabin's steel roof. Sara smiled.

"Well, what now, Mini? Are you ready to surrender? Or do we have to fight over this? That little kaboom was almost certainly Tim escaping from whatever prison you put him in. Are you prepared to face both of us?"

Mini glanced over her shoulder at the cabin. Perfect timing; the door opened to reveal Tim, dripping wet and wearing some sort of scuba suit. His face was set in a rictus of unmitigated fury until he saw Sara. Then he smiled. Sara imagined that smile must have turned Mini's blood to ice—she was trapped between them.

"What's it going to be, Min? Surrender or a stupid fight you can't win?"

"No surrender," Mini said.

Sara shook her head. "I'm sorry. I'm really sorry it has to be like this, Mini. I liked you. Now, Tim."

In the flick of an eyelash, a tornado of forest floor debris rose up around the girl's slight figure, completely blocking her from view. Sara charged into the miniature storm, reaching in with her kinetic "hands." They closed on turbulent air. The artist had disappeared yet again.

Infuriating. Had Mini learned to teleport or was this just another of her illusions?

The answer came as a scream in Sara's head. She knew, somehow, that it made no sound in the material world, just as she knew that Tim was also "hearing" it. His face twisted in pain and his eyes narrowed. Sara turned, scanning the camp, seeking the source of the scream. At the center of the clearing, another Mini faced them, red rage flowing from her in waves that Sara felt as pulses of heat beating against her body and soul.

Sara leaned into the heat, shaking her head. "Come on, Mini. How long do you think smoke and mirrors is going to postpone the inevitable? What are you doing, stalling? You think Lanfen is going to abandon Eugene and come rescue you? Or Chuck? You think Chuck is going to come and talk his way out of this? He's not. Mike's holding him up on the mountain. He's not going anywhere, and I'm done listening to any more lies anyway. And your military friends—even if they could challenge us—don't know you're in trouble over here. It's over, Mini. Give it up."

"I don't give up," Mini said softly. She made a graceful, dance-like move that involved her entire body—her arms swept upward like wings, and she leapt lightly into the air. When her feet touched the ground again, she was surrounded by a flock of grotesque, batlike gargoyles the size of German shepherds that looked as if they were made of living stone. Their eyes glowed red and silvery spittle drooled from their colorless lips and gleamed on obsidian black teeth.

"I have never hated anyone in my life until now," Mini said. Her voice was pitched low and Sara had to strain to hear it. "But you—you've changed. You've *let* yourself change—both of you. You killed Matt when all he was trying to do was help you. You've tried to kill us—may have k-killed Eugene." She hiccupped, then gasped in a breath. "Because you *enjoy* killing. You're bullies. Powerful, conscienceless bullies. And that," she added, her voice rising, "is why I hate you. *I hate you!*"

Suddenly, the entire flock of gargoyles was airborne and attacking. Sara rose to meet them, wondering why the silly child was continuing with this nonsensical display. She considered simply returning to the mountain—she'd gotten Tim back, after all. Behind her, she could hear Tim laughing as he deployed his own squadron of guardians. His looked like the flying monkeys from *The Wizard of Oz*. Sara watched as they collided with Mini's gargoyles . . . or rather, she watched as Mini's gargoyles plowed through them as if they were made of mist.

Sara threw up an energy screen, but the gargoyles ripped through that as well and reached her—and Tim. She heard him scream shrilly somewhere behind her, but his cries were lost in her own. The obsidian teeth were razor sharp, so she barely felt the bite that punctured her carotid artery. The last image in her eyes was Mini bathed in red light, looking like an avenging angel.

Her last thought was the shocked realization that Mini was twice the goddess she was.

MINI WATCHED AS HER GARGOYLES winked out of existence, one by one. When the last one disappeared, she knew that Sara and Tim were dead. She had created her defenders to exist only as long as those two hearts were still beating. She didn't look at the bodies or the blood. She turned dizzily toward where the huge cedar lay across the trail to the Spiderweb.

Eugene, she thought, and may have cried his name. Then she was falling—falling into darkness.

Chapter 22

OLYMPUS FALLEN

They took one of the back doors out of the mountain, Mike leading the strange train. Chuck didn't ask, but he suspected the Alpha had no desire to have his son venture down that path of death and destruction in the main entrance. The boy was bright and curious and would certainly ask questions about the ruin he saw.

Chuck sat in one of the treaded transport robots—possibly even the one he'd used on the way in. Anton rode happily in the arms of one of Lanfen's original Hob-bots—Bilbo—while Mike was carried by his favorite, Sacha. Anatoly, Boris, and Zhenya followed, loaded with all of the Alphas' personal belongings, as Mike thought might be appreciated. Thorin was in the vanguard, carrying a white flag . . . just in case, Mike said, because he didn't want any trigger-happy soldiers taking potshots at them.

"You didn't tell me what you planned to do about the Deep," Chuck observed as they reached the bottom of the slope and came out in a meadow above and just west of the Betas' base camp. "You didn't seem to need to do any prep work for it before we left."

"Doc, I've been prepping for this for a while now. One of the first things I did was find the schematics for the power grid in there. I surfed it until I knew where everything connected, where there were vulnerable points or points where the power flow came in contact with other stuff—the garbage disposal system, for example. You'd be surprised how much methane builds up in a system like that. Then there's the armory and ordnance storage, the fuel tanks. And it's all connected by an electrical network."

Chuck swallowed and glanced back over his shoulder at the peak. "Do you think we're far enough away now?"

"Yeah. Yeah, I expect so."

"What do you need to do?"

Mike stopped Sacha and the other bots and turned to look at the mountain. "Just this."

"This" was no more than a deep breath. Whatever thoughts Mike Yenotov sent to the mountain, the results were immediate and spectacular. There was a deep, rolling, sonorous rumble that shook the ground beneath and the air above, then the mountain seemed to settle in on itself like a deflating soufflé. The rumble went on for nearly a minute, punctuated by sharper concussions. Then a cloud of dust and debris billowed out of the gaping maw that marked the main entry to the dying base. The shock wave was a primal sigh that rushed by them and was gone.

In the aftermath, the normal sounds of the forest returned—birds, insects, trees creaking in the chill breeze.

"Daddy," said Anton, obviously impressed, "you blew up a whole mountain!"

"Yeah, I did. Who knew I could do that?"

"I did," said Chuck. "I think you can do anything you put your mind to. *Anything.*"

The other man turned to look at him, a question in his dark eyes. Their gazes met and held, then Mike chuckled.

"I gotta say, Doc, I think you got more faith in me than I got."

Chuck quoted softly: "'For verily I say unto you, if ye have faith as a grain of mustard seed, ye shall say unto this mountain, Remove hence to yonder place; and it shall remove; and nothing shall be impossible unto you.'"

"Jesus said that," said Anton. "I learned that in Sunday school."

Chuck nodded. "Book of Matthew, chapter seventeen, I think."

Chuck fell silent as they moved forward again, finding himself in a moment of crystalline clarity. *Faith—belief;* that was the essential element in the formula Lorstad had demanded of him. Lanfen had put it into words some time ago, but he was now seeing the ramifications of that and realizing how faith undergirded every endeavor—even scientific ones. Faith was the way every human being organized their thoughts and feelings based on their assumptions about the universe, themselves—everything. It was not some elixir available only to the mystic; it was the basis of science, itself: in order to understand the workings of the human brain or the universe within and without, one had first to have faith that those things could be understood.

Every scientific step forward depended on someone's faith that a theory could be proven, or that a premise was sound, or that an experiment would yield logical results. Hell, it depended on faith that the entity seeking the proof or establishing the premise or performing the experiment had the capacity to do all of those things and understand the results.

How did that translate to Lorstad's quest for an evolutionary shortcut? Chuck wasn't sure. The only thing he knew was that faith was unquantifiable. How much was enough to bridge the gap between current and potential abilities? He didn't know. What he did know was that there was no formula, there was only the scientific process: hypothesize, experiment, assess results, adjust the hypothesis, rinse, and repeat—all with faith that the process would yield useful results.

It was a wonderful—and daunting—revelation.

The sound of an engine brought Chuck out of his reverie.

"Hey, Doc," Mike said. "Were you expecting a welcoming committee?"

Chuck looked up to see a military Humvee break through the brush into the meadow. It was populated by three grim-faced soldiers. They were armed, of course, but held their weapons at rest. The ranking officer, who was riding shotgun, was a lieutenant Chuck recognized from Spiderweb. His name was Decker. He seemed composed enough, though his gaze roved uneasily over the robot entourage.

The Humvee pulled to a stop eight or ten feet from Chuck and company and the officer gestured at the back seat. "Dr. Brenton, Admiral Hand sent us out to bring you in. Something's happened over at Beta Camp, but no one's reported in yet. You need to come with us."

Chuck glanced at Mike. "What about the bots?"

"I'll bring 'em in. You want them at Spiderweb or your base camp?"

"Spiderweb makes the most sense, right?" Chuck looked to the officer, who nodded.

"Lacey," Decker said to the young private in the rear seat, "you will accompany Mr. Yenotov and the boy back to the unit."

"Sir." The soldier bailed out of the Humvee and approached the robots cautiously.

Mike gave him a wry smile. "You can trade places with Doc Brenton. Lem, there, is as safe as that Humvee."

Chuck was already out of the transport bot, Lem, and halfway to the army vehicle when he thought of Lanfen. He wanted to reach out to her, but he was afraid to—what if she didn't respond? The thought was almost enough to bring him to his knees. He climbed into the Humvee. The driver—his name patch read "Wood"—turned it and headed back into the woods, cutting southeast toward Beta Camp.

They had just slipped beneath the tree canopy when Chuck heard a strange, rhythmic whisper of sound overhead. Chuck looked up to see a helicopter coming in from the west, sweeping low over the treetops. He saw that Lieutenant Decker was watching the craft as well, a frown between his brows. The copter was long, lean, sleek, and a dull, light-sucking black. Stealth. It had four small rotors in a rectangular brace above the fuselage.

"Is that one of yours?" Chuck asked.

"Sir, I was just about to ask you the same thing."

"We don't have any helicopters, Lieutenant. We have two SUVs and whatever Admiral Hand has brought to Spiderweb."

Decker turned to his driver. "Pick up the pace, Corporal. Do your best."

"Yessir."

The Humvee leapt forward and burrowed deeper beneath the trees.

AT FIRST, LANFEN COULD NOT even see Eugene amid the thick blanket of tree boughs and the profusion of shattered branches. The air was thick with the perfume of crushed cedar, a scent that she'd always associated with pleasant hikes and balmy autumn days. Lanfen was certain that, after today, it would forever remind her of quaking terror. She was scared to death that she'd find Eugene crushed and lifeless beneath the broad tree trunk. She had waded through at least eight feet of detritus—pushing at it with hands and mind—when she saw the bright turquoise of his jacket on the opposite side of the trunk.

Breathing a sigh of relief, she levitated herself over that obstacle and alit gently, hip-deep in the foliage as close to Eugene as she could get. She called his name as she shifted branches and boughs out of the way or severed them from the tree. Even with her zeta abilities, it took several minutes of digging, during which she could hear bits and pieces of the battle taking place in the camp behind her. When the clearing fell silent, she almost panicked—torn between knowing what had happened to the others and getting to Eugene.

She pulled her head back into her work. Euge needed her.

She reached him at last and was beyond relieved to find that he was breathing and that his pulse was regular, if weak. He lay facedown, his head turned to one side, which gave her a clear view of the gash on his left temple. It was bleeding freely. She wondered if "thick" atoms could serve as a compression bandage. There was only one way to find out. She gathered atoms from the air, compacted them, and imagined them pressing down on Eugene's wound.

In a second or two, the bleeding slowed. She willed the pressure to remain in place—and told herself it would—then checked his arms and legs. Relief. Nothing was broken. When she gently turned him over—a maneuver that required both physical and zeta touch—she was dismayed to find that his ribs had not fared so well. He had landed on a three-inch-thick branch that had lacerated his rib cage and fractured at least two of his ribs.

She needed to get him out of here. She was contemplating the best way of accomplishing that when she heard Dice shout her name.

She looked up, trying to see past or through the cedar barrier. That was a fruitless task. "Here!" she called. "Euge is alive! Is it safe to bring him out that way?"

"Yeah, I think so. Sara and Tim . . ." He trailed off and finished, "It's clear."

Lanfen licked her lips. The last time she'd lifted someone using her zeta fu, she'd had Mini's help. *Silly.* Of course she could do it. She just needed to pack atoms more densely beneath him, manipulate local gravity a shade. She lifted him free of the tree branches and levitated him carefully over the trunk and clear of the debris, feeling the textures and height of the surfaces over which he traveled and reacting with the same concentration she brought to kung fu. Brenda and Dice reached them just as she was lowering Eugene gently to the grassy ground.

Dice knelt next to his friend's still body and put fingers to his neck. He shook his head. "We need Chuck."

"We don't have Chuck at the moment," said Lanfen, refusing to think about why that was, "and I'm not sure what to do."

"I think we should put Euge and Mini in a car," Brenda said, gesturing toward the SUVs, "and get them over to Spiderweb. There's a doctor there."

Lanfen followed the gesture and saw Mini lying in the open several yards beyond the vehicles.

"Oh God. Is she all right?"

"I think so," Bren said. "Her pulse is strong. I think she just fainted from the effort of . . . that." She glanced back over her opposite shoulder.

Lanfen followed that movement as well, and immediately regretted it. Two misshapen forms lay on the ground near the door of the immersion cabin, looking more like bloody piles of discarded clothing than human beings.

"M-Mini did that?"

"Mini's . . . golems did it," said Dice, looking up from an examination of Eugene's head wound. "Gargoyles, I guess you'd call them. We only caught the tail end of it. Saw them a spilt second before they disappeared and Mini passed out."

Lanfen couldn't wrap any words around that, but only shook her head. "Where's Joey? He was still in the immersion cabin when I left him."

"Oh, damn," said Bren, who took off running for the modular, calling Joey's name.

Dice looked after her, then asked, "You need help getting Euge into the SUV?"

"Open the rear hatch for me?"

"You got it."

Dice rose and headed for the passenger side of the car. Lanfen lifted Eugene again and began "floating" him toward the SUV. She'd maneuvered him around to the tail of the vehicle and into the cargo area when she heard the strange, rhythmic rush of sound trembling the air and saw a shadow fall across the clearing. A sleek, black helicopter with a quartet of small rotors overflew the clearing, dropped to mere feet above the ground, and pivoted over the far end of the camp.

"What the hell . . ." said Dice.

Lanfen lowered Eugene carefully into the cargo bay, then turned to peer out from under the tree boughs toward the strange copter.

"Is that military?" Dice asked. "Why aren't they landing?"

The bad feeling that Lanfen had been fighting since the moment she first saw the copter blossomed in her chest. "Let's get Mini and Joey and get out of here."

Mini was beginning to stir now, rolling her head from side to side. Lanfen had started toward her when Lorstad winked into existence over her prone form. With a glance at Lanfen and Dice, he scooped Mini up in his arms and vanished.

The copter began to lift.

Lanfen's instincts took complete control. She knew immediately where Mini had gone and whose stealth aircraft that was. She turned and sprinted directly at the copter, rushing like the wind. She thought of flinging herself into the air as Sara had done, but was sure of her own abilities only up to about thirty feet. The copter was already that high. So she stopped beneath the craft and extended her thoughts toward it, imagining two invisible, giant hands grasping it, fore and aft. The machine wobbled and bucked, but Lanfen simply had not developed the skills to perform what Mike might have done with ease. So she did the next-best thing: Lanfen knew engines. She reached into the workings of the copter's motor and felt for a way to bring it down safely.

Air.

She thought a kink into a hose and the helicopter stuttered. It dropped half a dozen feet. So far so good. She kept the air supply sporadic and brought the copter closer and closer to the ground. When it was low enough, she'd jump.

KRISTIAN GRASPED A HANDHOLD AS the helicopter dropped out from under his feet. It had barely stabilized when Mini moaned, pulling against the restraints he'd fastened to keep her safely secured to the fold-down cot. He grappled an infuser of sedative out of the med kit and applied it to her neck, then flung the empty infuser aside and headed forward. He was almost to the tiny cockpit when the aircraft lost altitude again and shivered like a wet dog.

Alexis sat in the pilot's seat, her hands in a white-knuckle death grip on the steering yoke.

What's happening? he asked her.

She glanced up at him briefly. *Take a look.*

He grabbed the back of her seat and peered out through the large slanted window. Lanfen stood in the clearing below, the wind of the copter's rotors whipping around her, her gaze riveted to the craft and her fists clenched at her sides.

What's she doing?

Alexis shook her head. *I don't know. But she'll bring this damn thing down if we don't do something and do it fast. Take the controls.*

She slid sidewise out of the seat, her fist still closed on the steering yoke. He had no choice but to slide in from the opposite side.

Don't kill her, Alexis.

I may not have a choice.

You always have a choice.

Alexis gave him an unreadable look, then crouched by the pilot's seat, peering from the window at the woman below. Lorstad knew what she could do—she could reverse the polarity of synaptic potentials in the motor strip of the other woman's neocortex. She could shut down voluntary processes in a subject's brain. Depending on what she did, the effect could be merely incapacitating or dangerous.

He wasn't sure what she did now, but with the copter mere feet from the ground, Chen Lanfen went completely limp and tumbled like a marionette whose strings had been cut. The copter bobbed upward and Lorstad pivoted it up and away from the Beta Camp.

There, Alexis thought at him. *I didn't kill her. Happy? She's watching us fly away wondering why she can't move. She'll wonder that for approximately five minutes, then she'll be fine.* She made a gesture that meant "move" and he relinquished the controls back into her capable hands. *I just hope your little artist is as great a creator as you think she is and that what she can do can be controlled and taught. I'd hate to think we've exposed ourselves to this degree for nothing.*

Kristian muzzled his own thoughts. He hoped for the same thing but wasn't prepared to have Alexis know how uncertain he was about the possibility. He was certain only that Minerva Mause represented—more than any other zeta talent—the next step in human evolution. The others might stretch physical and mental abilities to previously impossible lengths, manipulate atoms, or create clever projections, but only Mini could create what might be an emergent form of life. With more focus and the addition of immersion entrainment, he hoped that capacity might be brought to flower.

There was more to it than that, of course. A human capacity could not be deemed truly evolutionary until it could be encoded into the DNA. That was beyond Kristian Lorstad's abilities. That was a task for the Learned geneticists.

He gazed down into Mini's face. He stymied a reflex to stroke her cheek. He bit his tongue rather than whisper *don't worry.* He did not envy her the next several months of her life, but he was hopeful that in the end, she would realize what a great gift she had been given and what a great destiny might await her.

And, perhaps, appreciate who had given it to her.

THE MILITARY HUMVEE BROKE THROUGH the perimeter woods into the Beta base camp just as the stealth copter bobbed skyward and pivoted in the air high above the camp. Corporal Wood brought the vehicle to a sliding halt next to the immersion modular. Lieutenant Decker had already raised his assault rifle and was taking aim.

A piercing dart of thought that felt like Dice caused Chuck to reach out reflexively to keep Decker from firing. The lieutenant grunted in surprise at his sudden inability to fire his rifle.

"No more deaths," Chuck said, and released his zeta hold on the man's reflexes.

He leapt from the vehicle and gazed up at the aircraft. He could do nothing to the mechanics of the thing, but he might be able to reach its human crew. He reached out with every ounce of zeta capacity he had and felt the three life signatures aboard the copter as if they were standing right next to him. Each was unique, recognizable. He knew Mini was unconscious, that Lorstad was fearful, and that Alexis piloted the craft and that her heart was racing.

He focused on that heart. He knew that he could slow it, even stop it. For a moment—a measure of his own heartbeats—he thought that he might. If he simply caused the involuntary contractions to stop . . .

Alexis's heart beat one, two, three times before Chuck shook himself free of the mesmerizing rhythm and let the copter go. They would not harm Mini and he would not harm her captors—the Hippocratic fine print would not be executed today. The aircraft pivoted and soared upward and westward. Chuck knew where it was going.

He turned his attention to his team. Lanfen lay on the ground in the clearing, unmoving. He started in her direction, calling her name, but a strong, sharp thought from her stopped him.

Eugene. The blue SUV.

He turned and ran to the SUV, where Dice beckoned. The engineer was already gesturing into the open hatch. "Sara dropped a tree on Euge. He has a nasty head wound and a couple of broken ribs. Maybe more than that."

Chuck climbed into the back of the SUV and knelt over Eugene's body. He gave the wounds a cursory check, then looked out at Dice. "Go help the others. The two guys who brought me here—"

"Yeah," Dice said and headed for the center of camp.

Chuck took a deep breath, put one hand on Eugene's head and another on his ribs, and dived. There were three broken ribs—none threatened any major organs. The head injury was more worrisome. The gash went nearly to the bone; the skull beneath it was cracked; the brain was swelling.

Chuck had seen such injuries in the OR at Johns Hopkins. He knew in what order things required doing. Seal bone, reduce swelling, knit flesh. He caused, in essence, a localized zone in which bone remodeling and tissue regeneration were greatly accelerated. He mended the cracked bone, soothed the swollen tissue, reduced pressure, sealed bleeders. He worked on the ribs next, gently massaging them, moving them, smoothing surfaces—having done this with Joey the first time, that went much more smoothly. He repeated the steps to increase blood flow, accelerate remodeling, and wick away excess blood.

When he finished—cold, sweating, and lightheaded—he knew that Eugene would remain unconscious for several hours and would take time to recover. But he *would* recover. From this. Losing Mini—even for the time it took to find her—would be harder.

He slid out of the cargo bay of the SUV to find half a dozen people looking at him. Dice, Brenda, and the two military men—Decker and Wood—stood in a semicircle several feet from the rear bumper, while Lanfen and Joey sat on the ground at their feet. Chuck dropped to his knees in front of Lanfen, taking her hands.

"Are you all right?"

She nodded. "Just mad. Frustrated. Furious. They got Mini." This last came out in a low growl. "Lorstad and Alexis. I tried to mess with the engine—to bring them down softly—but one of them decked me."

"Which one?"

"Alexis, I'm pretty sure. It didn't feel like Lorstad."

"What did she do to you?"

"I don't know. I just lost my balance and folded up."

"Wow—you *never* lose your balance."

"I *know*. How's Eugene?"

"He'll be okay. How long was I working on him?"

"About fifteen minutes, Doctor," said Decker, moving toward him a step or two. "I think we'd best be getting you all back to Spiderweb. Get the injured into the infirmary."

Chuck looked at Joey. The Sho-Pai engineer seemed a little groggy. "Are you—"

Joey raised his hand in a vague gesture. "I'm good, really."

"He has a concussion," said Brenda. "He failed math. Or I've grown some extra fingers."

Chuck reached reflexively for Joey's head, laying his hand alongside the young man's temple. Brenda was right; Joey did have a concussion, but Chuck was too depleted to do anything about it.

"Sir, I think we need to get everybody back to Spiderweb."

Chuck looked up at Lieutenant Decker and nodded. "Yes. Yes, there's nothing left to do here." His gaze swept the ruined camp again, lingering for a moment on the two bodies lying broken and bloodied in the clearing. "Nothing left."

He felt an overwhelming sense of failure. He had failed Sara and Tim. He had failed Mini. He could do nothing for the two dead Alphas; that failure was complete. But for Mini, he would move heaven and earth. He caught Lanfen's eye and heard a single word in his head: *We.*

We *will move heaven and earth.*

Chuck had no doubt that they could.

Chapter 23

MOVING HEAVEN

At Spiderweb, military doctors whisked Eugene and Joey off to their infirmary while Chuck and the others were escorted to a mobile unit roughly the size of their own habitat. Its spartan decor reminded Chuck of an anonymous waiting room—simple angular sofa, spare padded chairs in shades of gray and mauve, a low coffee table at one end, a tiny kitchenette, and a round table with a handful of straight-backed chairs at the other.

They found Mike there with Anton, the two guarded by a pair of uneasy MPs. Their unease was not obvious; Chuck felt it as a vague wriggling sensation at the nape of his neck. Anton, cuddled up tightly against his father's side, was absorbed in a game he was playing on an iPad.

Mike . . . Mike looked haunted. His eyes when they met Chuck's held a mix of wariness and despair. What had happened between now and the time they had parted company that had turned Mike into a cornered animal?

Lieutenant Decker saw to their creature comforts, showing them where there was bottled water, coffee, and food. Then he announced his intention to let the admiral know they had arrived safely.

"Where is she?" Chuck asked, mildly surprised that she wasn't here to meet them.

"She's over in the communications trailer, sir. Engaged in conversation with President Ellis."

"Ah." Chuck glanced at the men standing on either side of the door. "I wonder if we might have a moment alone with Mike and Anton."

The lieutenant's brow furrowed. "Sir?"

Chuck lowered his voice. "Mike doesn't know . . . what happened to the others. I think I should be the one to tell him."

"I'll post the men just outside then, sir. If you should need them—"

Chuck smiled wanly. "Yes. Thank you, Lieutenant."

He wondered what Decker imagined his two MPs could do against even one Zeta. He'd witnessed the destruction at the Beta base camp, after all. Chuck could only imagine that he was having trouble reconciling the new reality with the one he had lived with for his entire life. In Lieutenant Decker's old reality, people simply did not wreak massive destruction with their brain waves.

When the door had closed behind the soldiers, Chuck moved to sit across from Mike in one of the waiting room chairs. Lanfen, Dice, and Brenda arranged themselves around the seating group as well, their expressions neutral.

"You okay, Mike?" Chuck asked.

Mike didn't beat around the bush. "They want to get back inside the mountain, Doc. They want *us* to get them back inside the mountain—back inside the Deep."

"You destroyed the Deep."

"Yeah, I did. I blew the crap out of it. I buckled the floors and brought the mountain down on top of everything. I think there are still fires burning in there. But they think that if I brought it down, I can help them tunnel in." Mike leaned forward, hands knotted into fists between his knees. "Doc, no one should get back into that mountain again. Ever. I brought out some of the bots so all your work wouldn't be lost. I thought maybe they'd be interested in those. But they want me—us—to open the mountain up."

Chuck was stunned. Why in the name of God . . .

He realized that everyone, even Anton, was looking at him.

"Who proposed that?" he asked. "Was it Admiral Hand?"

Mike shook his head. "The mission commander. Name's Fredericks. He may have been speaking for Hand, but I'm not sure."

"Then we ask. I've experienced Admiral Hand as being a reasonable woman. We'll explain why it's important no one get back into Olympus."

Mike reddened. "Don't call it that, Doc. It's Deep Shield. It was always Deep Shield. Because when push came to shove, Sara wasn't that much different than General Howard. They were both monsters. She's just a more powerful monster."

Chuck felt the tug of other minds and looked up to meet Lanfen's gaze, then Dice's.

Mike didn't miss the brief interaction. "What is it? What happened with Sara and Tim? I figured since you're here, you got them both on ice—no?"

Chuck met Mike's eyes. "No, Mike. Things went from bad to worse."

"We'd gotten Tim into an immersion tank," said Lanfen, "but Sara killed our power and he escaped. They went after Eugene because he wasn't like us."

Mike's eyes grew wide with fear. "They didn't—"

"He's in the infirmary here," Lanfen reassured him. "He'll be okay, thanks to Chuck. But after Euge was injured, they went after Mini and she . . . she took them on pretty much single-handedly. She's a lot more powerful than any of us knew and they underestimated her. They were no match for her, in the end." She took a deep breath. "Mike . . . Sara and Tim are dead."

He sat very still for a moment, then looked down at Anton, who looked up from his game. Mike closed his eyes, pulled his son tightly to his side, and shook his head. "Sara stopped seeing reason a long time ago. And I don't think Tim ever did see it. I don't know how to feel about this, Doc," he added. "Dead. I don't know how to feel."

"None of us does, Mike," said Dice. "This is terra incognita for all of us."

"And for our hosts," said Lanfen. "I want to trust the president and her chief of staff. I want to trust Admiral Hand. But they're not the final authority when it comes to what happens to us. There's Congress to deal with—maybe more men like Bluth who just haven't exposed themselves yet. There are factions that will fight over us. People who will want something from us, even if it's an assurance that we're not like Sara and Tim."

"And me?" Mike asked, his expression guarded.

"Stop beating yourself up, Mike," said Dice. "No one should be put in the position you were in. Sara and Tim were actively trying to run the world. You weren't. You got caught with them when Deep Shield decided to go underground."

"They really thought they were doing the right thing, though," Mike said. "At least Sara did. Tim didn't give a rat's ass about doing the right thing. In his head, he was still playing a video game. I guarantee you that some people are gonna think we're all like that. And whether we are or not, some people are always going to think of us as inhuman monsters." Mike shook his head and forcefully exhaled. "And maybe we are. I drank the Kool-Aid, too, Doc. It wasn't poured down my throat. I took my seat on . . . the mountain. Can't just brush that aside, isn't right. The rightful pain I feel about this, all of this, is just about the only thing I can make sense of right now."

The sound of footsteps ascending the steps outside the cabin were the only warning they got before the door opened to admit Admiral Hand and the mission commander, Colonel Fredericks.

Hand had a laptop tucked under one arm, which she set on a side table and flipped open.

"The president will be joining us online momentarily. Obviously, we have questions for you. In the meantime, I'd like to answer any questions you have for me."

Chuck realized that, once again, all eyes were on him. He took a deep breath. "I think the most pressing question is what happens to us now? Especially Mike." He didn't miss the look that Anton gave his dad.

Joan Hand seated herself next to the side table and gave Chuck her entire attention. "I can't tell you that, Doctor. That will come out of our conversation with the president. What would you like to happen?"

"I think I can speak for all of us when I say that our first order of business is to get Mini back from the Benefactors. She did not go willingly. They took her—for purposes that I'm not sure I understand."

"Do you even know where these people are?"

"Yes," said Dice. "We do. And as powerful as they are as an organization, there's no way they can close down or move that facility quickly. They might abandon it if they suspected we knew where it was. But they were trying to hide that from us till the last. While we were there, we were never allowed to see anything more than just the immediate area. Lorstad brought us here one at a time using his ability to teleport. Even the outsiders who work at the Center are brought in blindfolded to live on-site. Joey didn't even know where it was until I hacked their system and mapped it."

Hand nodded. "How dangerous do you think these so-called Benefactors are? What's their agenda?"

"Frankly," said Dice, "they seem to have a massive superiority complex. They view themselves as the next step in human evolution—or did until they got wind of what we were doing.

Then they realized their own system of obtaining extraordinary talents had limitations."

"You mentioned that they have to undergo some sort of 're-charging' period."

"Yeah. And even for adepts as experienced as Lorstad—the man who took Mini—that can mean hours in an isolation unit. Their abilities are artificially maintained."

"I see," said Hand. "So if they're cut off from their technology—"

"They weaken," Chuck said. "They lose their abilities to some extent. I don't know to what extent because we've never seen them get that low. And it seems like they are able to do some fairly amazing things before they get to that point."

The laptop pinged just then, and the admiral answered the summons. In a moment, Margaret Ellis appeared on the screen. Chuck saw that she was not alone—there were a number of other people in the Situation Room with her. He recognized her chief of staff, Curtis Chamberlin, and two of the other men. They were Phalen Whitecross and Joseph Firestone, a pair of high-profile senators from opposing parties—both of whom had already made noises about running for president. That realization raised the hackles on Chuck's metaphorical spine. He hated to think their fate lay in the hands of anyone vying for public office or hoping to score points with a constituency.

There were introductions all around and Chuck tried to read the faces of the men seated around the table with the president. He saw unease, curiosity, suspicion.

It became apparent that the big-ticket item for the legislators was whether or not to come clean to the American people about what had really gone down in Michaux State Preserve. Were Sara and Tim homegrown terrorists who had been taken out by an elite paramilitary squad (Zeta Squad, appropriately), or was the whole story to be made public, now that the danger had passed?

"Wait," said Chuck, interrupting Senator Whitecross. "I'm sorry, but we don't know the danger has passed. These people calling themselves the Benefactors—or the Learned—have taken a member of my team. A young woman who they obviously feel will be useful to them in some way. I have no idea what they intend to do with her or to her, but I can tell you that these people have a worldwide network and have very little regard for those they feel are—are . . ."

"Inferior," finished Lanfen.

"They're not as powerful as the individuals you took out, are they?" asked Colonel Fredericks. "You said they were tied to their tech."

"Mini 'took them out,'" said Lanfen, "and they've got her. They've also got several very talented novice Zetas that we were working with before we came here."

"*And,*" said Dice, "they've got our equipment. They have two complete kinetic conversion rigs, which means that they could potentially manufacture more machines and raise up more Zetas."

"And do what with them?" asked Senator Firestone.

"I don't know," said Chuck, "but one thing is that the Learned are not all on the same page when it comes to their future interactions with—"

"Profanes," finished Dice. "That's what some of them call people they don't consider Learned."

"The two Benefactors that we interacted with the most," said Chuck, "were exemplary of that seeming divide within the group. Our initial contact, Kristian Lorstad, and his associate, Alexis Bruinsma, were at odds over how to regard our technology and what it portended for human evolution. I gathered that both of them are answerable to—and maybe even members of—some sort of guiding council. We never learned much about them. Lorstad seemed reluctant to discuss it—sidestepping our questions or giving minimalist answers."

"So what you're saying is," said President Ellis, "we have a virtually unknown organization with powers similar to your own whose agenda is also unknown."

"Not quite unknown," said Chuck. "They want to create a more robust society that will weather whatever happens to the rest of the world."

"Do you think they intend to recruit people?" asked Firestone. "Like a terrorist organization?"

"No. They most definitely do not want to recruit people. From what I gather, the organization started with a group of European families and has been restricted to members of those families for several generations, at least. Their numbers are relatively small—or at least that's what we were told—because not every member of every family responds to their technology." He shook his head—this had been going on long enough. Now it was time for some answers. "President Ellis, the admiral asked us if we had any questions. We do. Chiefly, what do you intend to do with us?"

There was, as Chuck suspected, no cut-and-dried answer to that question, so it was something they discussed at length—discussed, in fact, until the sun had begun to set. Sara's and Tim's bodies had a more certain destiny than the living did. They had already been transported to a military medical facility where they would be autopsied and studied. The thought of it made Chuck queasy, but he had to admit that it was the most practical thing to do under the circumstances. He shared his team's desire to take up their research again—to find a way to make zeta capabilities a boon to mankind.

"Zeta talent," said Chuck, "needs to be further studied. The potential is astounding. And we need to learn how to cultivate it for the benefit of humanity. By that, I mean the simple, practical things zeta waves can be employed to do that will enrich people's lives: allow a paraplegic to remain gainfully employed; allow surgeons to heal without cutting through tissue to get to an injury or disease-ridden organ or tumor; allow people engaged in dangerous work to do it in less dangerous ways. We'd like to go back to the beginning, before Deep Shield came into the picture. Before Olympus. I don't know if that's possible, but it's what we'd like. And we'd prefer to do it out in the open. In fact, I think honesty about what's happened would be the best policy for you to take."

"I tend to agree with that," Margaret Ellis said, "but you have to realize that I can't make the decision in a vacuum. Be patient with us, Dr. Brenton. We will try to move as swiftly as possible and keep you in the loop as much as we can. In the meantime, I think we need to move you to a more secure facility."

Chuck felt the sharp tang of concern from his entire team. "With all due respect, President Ellis, we've had our fill of secure facilities. Between Deep Shield and the Benefactors, we've been held against our will for far too long."

The president smiled wanly. "I promise we'll try to make it as painless as possible."

"And brief. We will submit for the short term in good faith, but, Madam President, our days of being locked away *for our own safety* are over." The severe tone of voice was foreign to Chuck but punctuated his declaration perfectly.

The president took in a breath and decided it was not in her best interest to turn Dr. Brenton into an enemy. "For now then?"

"As I said, a *very* brief now."

"What about the mountain?" asked Mike sharply. "There's been talk of making me open it up again. It should never be opened up, ma'am. Not ever. What's down there should just stay down there. That's why I blew the crap out of the place."

The president's fair eyebrows rose. "There's been talk of—? Whose talk?" Even from where he sat, Chuck could see that her eyes were on Joan Hand.

"Carl, you want to explain your ideas to the president?" the admiral asked Colonel Fredericks.

The officer cleared his throat. "Not in present company, ma'am. I think that's a discussion for another time and place."

"Let's have some of it now," said President Ellis. "Mr. Yenotov, I'm sure you can understand that there are things we don't know about Deep Shield that we might be able to find out by gaining access to the facility. If there are other cells or even stray operatives out there that Senator Bluth and Ted Freitag haven't yet revealed, we'd like to know about them."

"Yeah," said Mike. "I get that. *If* that's the real reason you want in there. There's a shitload of tech down there. War machines that would turn guys into supersoldiers. Weapons that would keep a sane person up all night just thinking about them. I hope I destroyed every last atom of it. I brought out some bots that are good all-purpose units. If your guys want to study those, great. I'd be happy to help them. So would Dice, I bet. I'd be less happy to tell you everything I know about Deep Shield—which is a lot—but I'd do it if it would help keep something like that from happening again. But Madam President, I'll be damned if I give anybody access to what might be left of those death machines."

President Ellis was nodding. "Yes. I see. And I understand. But again, the decision about what happens to the mountain doesn't lie entirely with me. I need *you* to understand that. All I can promise you is that when decisions are made, your input and special knowledge will be part of the process."

"What about Mini?" asked Lanfen. "Will you help us rescue her?"

In answer, Margaret Ellis turned her gaze to Admiral Hand. "Joan, find out where these people are and give me your best assessment of an approach to reaching them and extracting Ms. Mause."

"Ma'am."

The president logged out of the call then, leaving the Zetas no closer to knowing their fate than they were before. Admiral Hand and Colonel Fredericks went their way shortly thereafter to see to their separate duties. A corporal appeared not long after that to assign the team to a pair of barracks trailers next door to the common room—men and Anton in one, women in the other—then escorted them to the mess tent.

They were in the middle of dinner when they got the message that Eugene had regained consciousness and Joey was doing better and had been able to keep food down. Chuck bolted down the remainder of his dinner and headed for the infirmary, wondering how he was going to tell Eugene about Mini.

He was halfway to the medical facility when he felt the tug on his consciousness and heard Lanfen's light steps behind him as she ran to catch him up.

"I'm the one who saw it happen," she said. "I should be there."

Chuck took her hand. "I didn't much like the tone of that meeting," he told her. "I think the president was trying to tell us that what she'd like to do and what actually happens are two different things."

"Chuck, they're probably going to ship us off to some 'secure location' as soon as they've tidied up the base camp and Eugene is ready to be moved. If we go into a place like that, there's no guarantee we'll ever come out again. Sara put the fear of petty gods into the Senate, and fear is a deadly motivator. What should we do?"

"Find out what they've done with our wheels."

Lanfen chuckled. "Ooh. Very James Bond."

"Damn. I was going for James Dean." He sobered. "This is going to be hard."

Lanfen squeezed his hand.

EUGENE WAS SITTING UP IN his narrow bed when Chuck and Lanfen entered the infirmary's tiny prefab ward.

"Thank God, you're here!" Euge said the moment he saw them.

"No one will tell me anything except that you were all meeting with the president. Were you meeting with the president?"

Chuck nodded. "Except for Joey. He's still in the infirmary proper."

Euge paled. "What happened to him?"

"It's just a concussion, Eugene," said Lanfen quickly. She put a hand on Chuck's arm. "Which means he may need a little assistance from Chuck . . . again."

"Did we get them?" asked Eugene earnestly. "Did we get Sara?"

Chuck took a deep breath. "Not in the way we'd hoped. Sara was able to free Tim and . . . there was a confrontation. They're both dead."

Tears sprang to Eugene's eyes and his lips formed a silent "no." "What happened? I sort of lost track of things . . ."

"Mini happened," Chuck said. "When Sara dropped that tree on you, Mini just threw everything she had at Sara and Tim. And she had a lot. More than any of us realized."

"What about Mike?"

"Mike's with us now. So's his son, Anton."

"What? How did that happen?"

"Lorstad interfered," said Lanfen. "We're all fine. Bren and Dice got a little knocked around, but they're okay."

Eugene looked from Chuck to Lanfen and back. "Okay, but it strikes me that you're not telling me how Mini is. If she—if she killed Sara and Tim, then she's not going to be all right with that. Where is she? I need to go to her." He started to pull the blanket from his legs.

Chuck stopped him. "Eugene, listen to me. Mini is with Lorstad."

"What? She went with—"

"She didn't 'go with,'" Chuck said. "He and Alexis just took her. She passed out after she stopped Tim and Sara. Lorstad and Alexis swooped down in a stealth copter and zapped her away."

"I tried to take control of their aircraft," said Lanfen, "and I was having an effect, too. Then Alexis revealed a talent none of us knew she had. She basically short-circuited my brain—paralyzed me long enough for them to get away. There was no other way to stop them."

Chuck felt a wave of mixed guilt and shame rock him. "There was a way," he murmured. "I just couldn't make myself do it."

"What do you mean?" Eugene asked, his voice raw, his eyes glittering. "What couldn't you do to keep them from taking Mini?"

In answer, Chuck said, "Do you remember when I healed Joey in the lab?"

"Yeah. I remember."

"I did something similar for you. I went into your injuries and fixed them from the inside out. I've used it twice to heal and once to keep Decker from shooting down Lorstad's helicopter. I think you can imagine what might happen if I decided to use it less benignly."

Eugene's eyes widened. "God, Chuck, I'm sorry. It didn't occur to me. I would never ask that of you. Never. But we *have* to get her back."

"Yes. Right now the question is, will we have the government's help?"

Eugene blinked. "Why wouldn't we have the government's help?"

"Because the government isn't a monolithic entity. Different factions apparently have different feelings about what should happen to us. I gather they're in the process of duking that out as we speak."

Eugene's dark eyes flashed with swift anger. "We don't have time to wait for them to duke it out."

"Yes," agreed Chuck, uneasily. "I know. Dice can guide us back to the Center, but if they move her, we're screwed."

"No. No we're not." Eugene looked as if someone had passed an electric current through him. "Mini gave me something. Something we might be able to use to find her no matter where they take her."

He cupped his hands in front of him and stared at them intently, before opening them to reveal a gleaming doll-sized replica of Mini.

"Oh my God, it's Tinker Bell!" gasped Lanfen.

Eugene said, "Mini gave me this when we were at the Center. She wanted me to be able to know what she was feeling and thinking when we weren't together."

Chuck, amazed, peered at the tiny, light-filled golem. She was curled against the curve of Eugene's fingers, her eyes closed, her head tilted to one side, her features soft.

"Right now," Chuck said, "it looks like she's asleep. Apparently, they still have her sedated. How does she work?"

"I'm not sure, exactly. She's my projection. I mean, I make her appear, by thinking about her, but somehow she's also connected to Mini, so she reflects Mini's state of mind. So, maybe Mini's in touch with me somehow all the time. I don't know."

He licked his lips. "Chuck, this is weird, but I feel as if she's west of here. I mean, like, due west."

Chuck reached out a hand toward the sprite. "Is it okay if I . . . ?"

Euge nodded.

Chuck touched his fingertips to the radiant little construct. To his surprise, they tingled as if they had come into contact with an energy field of some sort. On a whim, he grasped Eugene's wrist with his opposite hand. The result was swift and definite. He felt as if his entire being had become a compass needle set to point from Eugene to the person at the other end of the connection.

"Do you feel it?" Euge asked. "I'm not just imagining it, right?"

"No, Euge, you're not imagining it." Chuck turned to give the puzzled Lanfen a wry smile. "They can knock her out and take her anywhere in the world, Lanfen. It won't matter. Eugene will be drawn to her like iron to a lodestone. She'll lead us straight to her."

Lanfen returned the smile. "That's the best news I've heard all day."

Chapter 24

MIDNIGHT

By noon the following day, the team knew that their fate was precarious at best. To say there was divergence in the opinions within the government about what should be done with them understated the case. That Leighton Howard had forced them first to compliance, then to flight, seemed to mean nothing in some quarters. Yes, they'd been taken advantage of and abused, *but* they were dangerous. As long as they were alive and awake, they were a threat to everything America held dear. That was one party line, at least. Other versions of it were less extreme, but still ran to some version of guilty until proven innocent and featured incarceration or sequestration, testing, and interrogation.

President Ellis proposed a process by which the Zetas would willingly and actively assist the government to pursue Kristian Lorstad and his associates, after which they would work within a system of government oversight to make their technology of benefit to the United States and the world at large. She was hailed as a hero by some elements within her government and pilloried by others. Only a handful of legislators felt that revealing the truth of the Pine Ridge debacle to the public was a good idea.

"The consensus is, we should keep you a deep secret," Margaret Ellis told them, "and restrict your movements."

They were alone with her telepresence in the common living area. Admiral Hand had set the laptop up, then withdrawn.

"You mean deep-six us," said Dice, his voice tight.

The president raked her fingers through her hair; it looked as if she'd been repeating the gesture all morning. "Ironic, isn't it? People who believe that your abilities make you ungovernable through an act of will imagine that they can govern you unwilling, or that you'll submit to force."

"The thing is," said Chuck, "we probably *would* submit to force if for no other reason than to prove that we're not like Sara and Tim. But I won't let my people be abused, Madam President."

"Margaret. No. Nor should you."

"And more important," he added, "we need to get Mini back before Lorstad does something irrevocable to her. The Benefactors' methodology imposes external stimuli on a quiescent mind. In Mini's case, they'll impose it on a mind that is not quiescent out of willingness to be part of the experiment. I have no idea what that would do to someone as brilliant and sensitive and powerful as Mini. I can't let that go, Margaret."

She didn't respond to that, but only gave him a look that expressed both understanding and regret. "The special forces guys have cleaned up your base camp and sent everything to DHS for disposition. The unit you're with is essentially ready to bug out with short notice and the thinking is that you'll be transferred to a secure DHS facility until—"

"Until we're disposed of, too?" asked Bren tartly.

"Until something can be worked out." The president hesitated, then added, "There are parties within government who see your talents as holding massive defensive potential."

Chuck and Dice traded glances. "Pardon me if we seem less than excited by that," Dice said. "We've heard it before."

"Out of the damn frying pan and into the fire," murmured Bren.

Chuck leaned close to the laptop's camera. "Madam President—Margaret—please don't do that to us. *Please.*"

"I have a meeting I need to prepare for," she said. "I'll keep you posted." She rang off, leaving the team staring disconsolately at the screen.

"That settles it," Lanfen said.

"The SUVs are in the picket line with the other vehicles," Dice said blandly.

"You have the keys?" asked Brenda.

His smile was tight. "We don't need keys."

"Are you talking about escape?" asked Mike from the corner of the sofa, from which he'd watched the entire exchange. Anton sat beside him, reading an Avengers comic.

Dice nodded.

"I need to get Anton home," Mike said. "I want to help you guys get Mini back, but I don't want him to be part of this."

Anton looked up, a frown furrowing his brow. "Daddy, I don't want to go home unless you're going, too. Mommy really misses you. She cries every night. I hear her. And now that I'm gone, there's only Darya to protect her. She needs us."

Chuck didn't have to guess what that simple speech did to Mike Yenotov's insides. *He* felt as if someone had just punched him in the gut.

Mike ruffled his little boy's hair. "Hey, Ant-Man, I can't come home until we rescue Mini. But if you go home and tell your mom I'm all right and that I'm helping a friend get out of trouble, I think she'll stop crying. What do you think?"

"Yeah. I think it would make her feel good to know you were okay and just, y'know, helping Mini. Mini is nice."

"What are we going to do?" asked Lanfen.

Chuck let himself sense what the others were thinking. It became easier to sort through the tangle of emotions with every attempt. If they needed to "bug out" before the unit did, then they would do it through stealth, not brute force. He hoped that would be duly noted by the various factions engaged in deciding their fate. At the moment, though, he couldn't really spend a lot of time caring how they were viewed. He could only think of two things: Mini, and maintaining his friends' freedom.

There was a rap at the door of the quarters and Admiral Hand stepped into the room. She was alone, which was a bit unusual. She scooped up the laptop and tucked it under her arm, then turned to face Chuck.

"We're bugging out in the morning. Right at sunrise. That way we won't be flashing headlights all over the place. You'll need to report to your drivers at oh-five-hundred hours. Your vehicles are parked right behind this building so you may wish to assemble here earlier than that. I'll send MPs to make sure you're all up and about at oh-four-thirty. Everyone clear on the timetable?"

Chuck looked at her speculatively and nodded. "Yes, I think we've got that. We'll be rounded up at oh-four-thirty. I guess we ought to turn in early in that case."

"It would be a good idea." Joan Hand moved to the door, then paused. "Smooth sailing," she said, then slipped out of the room.

The team exchanged glances.

"Was that what I thought it was?" asked Brenda. "Did she just make it *easier* for us to escape?"

"No one would ever be able to prove it," said Dice, "but it sure looks that way."

"Midnight," said Chuck, and everyone in the room knew exactly what he meant.

THE SURVEILLANCE CAMERAS WERE EASY. Mike, Joey, and Dice were all capable of making them see whatever was wanted, which, in this case, was nothing. The human guards were something else again. Lacking Mini's masterful illusions, Chuck was the only one among them who could remedy that. He knew it; they knew it. He had the ability to make the guards turn a deaf ear and a blind eye. The realization immersed him in a cold tide of dread. He had no question that he could disrupt the guards' brain function. His question was whether he could do it without causing them permanent harm.

There were any number of things he could do. He could switch the neurotransmitters at the base of the brain to the state that brought on sleep, but if he and his companions were tearing across America evading capture, he wouldn't be there to flip the switches on again, and so far, he'd had to be in close proximity to a subject to affect them. He might try ramping up the production of adenosine, he supposed. The neuromodulator built up in the blood during waking hours, causing drowsiness, then broke down in sleep. Theoretically, if Chuck could dose the MPs with adenosine, they'd awaken when it was depleted, if not before.

Theoretically.

He leaned back on the sofa, closed his eyes, and gently thumped his head against the wall.

"Oh, that can't be good."

He opened his eyes to see Lanfen looking down at him. In her black sweater and skinny jeans, he thought she looked like Catwoman or Emma Peel. The sun had set an hour ago. Everyone else but Eugene had gone to their quarters to rest.

I'm so tired.

She sat next to him on the sofa. "You're more than tired. What's wrong? You're spraying angst all over the place."

He glanced across the room to where Eugene was watching his Mini-pixie sleep. If he was spraying angst, Euge didn't seem to notice. Possibly because he had too much of his own. Chuck took a deep breath. "I'm afraid, Lanfen. I'm scared. I've juggled half a dozen ways I can deal with the guards and they all terrify me."

"Why? You've successfully and safely healed two people—"

"I've done more than that. I stopped Lieutenant Decker from shooting the copter down yesterday by creating a hiccup in his reflexes."

"Okay. And you did it without harming him."

"Lanfen, I came within a hair's breadth of stopping Alexis's heart yesterday."

"No, you didn't," she said. "Because you wouldn't. Chuck Brenton, you are probably the most decent human being I know."

"Lanfen, I *thought* about it. I considered it."

"Really. For how long?"

"Long enough. Too long."

Lanfen took his hands in her own and looked him in the eyes. She spoke to him in a voice that was like water over rock, like music, like wind in the cedars. "You thought I was injured. You thought Mini was in danger. You were panicked. *Breathe.* Tonight, every member of our team will do what we do best. No one will be in danger. You won't be panicked. *Breathe.* You'll be calm . . . cool . . . collected. Dr. Charles Brenton, neuroscientist. You'll have a goal, a mission. You'll breathe. You'll be focused. You'll know what you're doing, because you know how the human brain works probably better than anyone in the country.

"Breathe."

He smiled—and breathed. *What are you doing to me?*

Is it working?

Yes.

Then, why do you care what I'm doing?

Chuck laughed aloud. "You know, I thought you were Catwoman. Now I realize you're Obi-Wan Kenobi or maybe even Yoda."

"Yes, use the Force you must. Now, breathe . . . and listen."

He did both. She took him on a tour of his own head then, walking him through all of his thoughts on safely disabling the guards—or at least disabling their ability to tell reality from dream. It was a strange sensation, as if they were literally strolling hand in hand through his mental landscape, sifting through his stores of knowledge for an ideal state in which to leave the MPs' minds.

The realization no doubt came to Lanfen first, but Chuck experienced it as if it had come to them both simultaneously.

Meditation.

Neither of them spoke the word aloud.

Of course. Delta state.

"Can you do that?" Lanfen asked. "Can you initiate a delta state?"

Chuck considered it. "I think so. Yes. But it's potentially a more fragile state than sleep." He imagined something startling an MP out of his meditative state, foiling their escape.

"We'll just have to make sure we're especially sneaky tonight so it won't happen," said Lanfen.

"What won't happen?" Eugene had gotten up from the table and was standing in front of the sofa, staring at them.

Chuck came fully back into the present. "Startled guards."

"Okay, you two are officially weirding me out. Do you have any idea how hard it is to follow a zeta conversation?"

Chuck did have some idea. He realized that, more and more, communication between the Zetas was happening at the subvocal level. That was amazing. And it was unsettling. It meant the Zetas were going somewhere that non-Zetas like Eugene could not go—were communicating on a level he could not experience. Chuck marked that in his mind as a goal for another time—figuring out how to spark Eugene's brain into producing zeta waves.

Right now, he needed to know if he could induce a meditative state in a normal human brain. "Euge, are you up for a little science experiment?"

Chapter 25

GOING TO GROUND

Midnight.

The camp was quiet now, though there had been a flurry of purposeful activity until well after sunset aimed at being ready to break camp with morning's light. Dice, Joey, and Mike first told the cameras what they would see: guards at their posts, moonlight gleaming off every metallic surface, interior lights extinguished except in Admiral Hand's personal trailer.

There were a quartet of guards in the portion of Spiderweb that Team Chuck occupied. One was stationed in front of the men's quarters; the second, only yards away in front of the women's quarters. The third and fourth stood watch in front of the common room. There were others elsewhere in the compound, but none within sight of the vehicles or the path they'd have to take to reach them.

Chuck dropped the first MP into a delta state without even leaving their trailer. The man went into the meditative state every bit as easily as Eugene had done earlier. Chuck exited the trailer alone then, mentally biting his nails, and circled behind it to the women's trailer on its left. That guard went into delta easily, too. Chuck slipped back the way he'd come, bypassing the men's quarters to reach the common area.

The first guard there went silently into delta, but the second resisted, his brain rousing itself from meditation as soon as Chuck had initiated the state.

He tried again, a gentle push. The soldier visibly shook himself free, rotating his shoulders and shifting his weight. Chuck tried a third time with the same result. This time the MP stamped his feet as if to keep them from falling asleep.

"Hey, Garfield," the MP finally said to his partner, "I'm going to walk the perimeter. Getting sleepy. Need to move around."

Chuck, peering at the men from between the commons and men's cabin, felt panic leap to his throat. It leapt almost to the tip of his tongue when his target frowned and glanced at the silently meditating Garfield.

"Hey, Gar, I said—"

Chuck reached into the MP's head and shoved him down into delta, at the same time flipping the neurotransmitters at the base of his brain off. The guy's face went slack, his eyes rolled back in his head, and he sagged back against the building he was guarding, sliding down the wall until he sat hunched over his rifle, looking for all the world as if he were taking a nap.

Horrified, Chuck came out of hiding, his eyes on the already prone Garfield, praying that nothing would jar the man out of his meditative state. He reached the downed soldier and knelt beside him to check his breathing and pulse. A strange humming sound from Garfield made him freeze. He looked up at the other MP and gave his brain waves a tiny bit more of a nudge. Garfield fell silent.

Chuck shifted his attention back to the sleeping soldier, checking his breathing and his pulse. Both were steady and strong.

"Sorry," Chuck murmured, and rose as Lanfen and Brenda reached him.

What happened?

The thought was Lanfen's. "He was resistant," Chuck said quietly. "I put him to sleep."

"I thought you didn't want to do that," whispered Bren.

"Didn't. Couldn't be helped. Let's go."

They turned and made their way behind the commons cabin to where their SUVs waited. The rest of the team had already gathered there and were quietly arranging themselves in the vehicles. The tailgate of one of the SUVs was open and it looked as if someone in a shiny metal suit was just curling up inside. It took Chuck a moment to realize that it was Bilbo.

Mike threw a sleeping bag over the robot and turned to face Chuck. "Thought he might come in handy."

"Good thought," Chuck said, and Lanfen gave the construction engineer a kiss on the cheek.

"Thanks, Mike."

"Least I could do."

Dice came back to the rear of the SUV. "I just had a thought. If we start the engines here, it might wake up the whole camp—including your sleepers."

Chuck stared at him. None of them had thought of that. It reminded him again how ill-suited they were for this sort of subterfuge.

"Not a problem," said Mike. "I'm sure that between Lanfen and me we should be able to roll these babies out to the road before we need to turn the engines over."

"Good grief," murmured Chuck. "Of course, you can. Okay. Mount up."

They'd planned their route in advance. They'd drive through the night to get as far from Olympus and Spiderweb as they could. Then Mike would take one of the SUVs and head north to return Anton to Ontario while the rest of the team headed straight back to the Center . . . unless Mini's sprite dictated otherwise.

The two vehicles rolled silently through the woods toward

the firebreak road by moonlight, their lights off, the only sounds of their passage tires crushing dirt and forest debris. The wind in the treetops and the rush of a nearby stream were just as loud. When they were about half a mile from Spiderweb, they met the firebreak. Dice and Mike started their engines, turned on parking lights, and picked up speed.

Half an hour later, they came out onto an empty country road and moved yet faster. An hour after that, they met a major freeway and melted into the sparse flow of traffic. It was near dawn when they pulled into a truck stop for bathrooms, gas, food, and coffee. The air was chill and the parking lot lit by LEDs that faked sunlight poorly. There was a single large building that housed a restaurant, a convenience store, and a gas station.

Dice handled the gas pumps, electronically fooling them into thinking that transactions had been initiated with credit cards. Then they went into the restaurant/convenience store to liberate some cash from the ATMs. Again, Dice performed his particular magic, transferring money from his own bank account, while carefully erasing its electron trail. The debit would appear in his account, if anyone was watching—which they certainly would be—but it would be anonymous, and placeless.

"There were transponders on both vehicles, you know," Lanfen said conversationally when Chuck came out of the men's bathroom to find her looking out the window of the convenience store into the parking lot.

Chuck stared at her. "You disabled them, right?"

She nodded. "And then I moved them." She pointed at a semi with Mississippi plates that was idling at a diesel pump, then at a pickup with Wisconsin tags that was just pulling out of the parking lot. She smiled. "And then I turned them back on."

"I love you," Chuck told her.

She cocked her head to one side. "I know. Now prove it."

He blushed. "In front of everyone—"

"Feed me, Romeo."

They both laughed.

As their transponder trails disappeared in two different directions, they enjoyed a panic-free moment of relaxation before getting back on the road. Mike promised he'd rejoin them as soon as possible and headed north with Anton; the second SUV with its seven passengers—six humans and a robot—headed due west.

Joey was driving, Eugene riding shotgun with Mini's sprite on the dashboard, where he could watch her. Chuck shared the second row of seats with Lanfen and Brenda, while Dice dozed on the rear seat. Chuck was getting dozy himself, his head resting on Lanfen's shoulder, when Eugene said, "Oh God," in a voice that chilled Chuck to the soul.

He sat up on an ice-cold current of adrenaline and opened his eyes. "What? What's wrong?"

He saw what was wrong before the words had quite left his mouth. On the dashboard, Eugene's pixie had awakened. Her body was still and rigid, but her eyes were wide open. The expression in them was one of abject terror.

Eugene turned his head and met Chuck's gaze. "What are they doing to her?"

"I don't know," Chuck whispered. What he did know was that Mini was still due west of them, buried deep in Lorstad's subterranean fortress, and that she needed them. "We'll get to her, Euge. I promise you."

He left unsaid that getting to Mini was the easy part of their mission.

The fact that he had no idea how they were going to get her out was the hard part.

EPILOGUE

The video was titled "The Truth About Michaux State Preserve." Any and every Web search regarding the recent and unusual events in Pennsylvania found this clip perched at the top of the results. It began simply enough, a winding amalgam of symphonic colors and bright sounds. Then a tortuous digital glob morphed and warped into pieces of neuroanatomy. The display halted at a three-dimensional representation of a rotating neocortex.

"I won't bore you with the threadbare trope that we only use ten percent of our brains." The modulated voice pitched and yawed from guttural to elflike.

"I will say with certainty that our minds are capable of much more than we realize or have sufficiently explored."

The graphics gave way to a stock photo of Pine Ridge.

"Those of you who have looked hard enough have no doubt stumbled upon some very disquieting rumblings. Rumors leaked here and there about psychic telekinetic terrorists who seized Pine Ridge and were bent on world domination. Those of you who have stumbled upon this video by chance, stick around. I have a lot to say."

The screen popped black and a slow, undulating tone rippled forth.

"Listen very closely now. The outrageous, absurd, and flagrantly impossible claims concerning the Pennsylvania Triad are unequivocally and patently . . . true."

White circles appeared merging and linking into one another, growing as the perspective shifted outward to accommodate the enlargement. The wavy tone tightened.

"I'm glad that you are still here. What comes next is far from easy, but I have come to realize that its dissemination is necessary—crucial even."

The large circular lattice condensed into a single sphere.

"This is the first of many videos I will publish across the Web. Don't worry, no one on earth has the capability to erase or block my work. As long as the Internet is functioning these videos will be available to all."

The orb multiplied and the gumball shapes adhered together, spheres within a sphere.

"A small warning, once your thoughts and beliefs are tilted to the ideas I'm going to share with you, you will very likely experience some subtle and profound changes. Once we reach the end of our journey it is my desire and belief that you will be fundamentally transformed. Radically altered in ways that as of now you would neither believe nor comprehend. In my experience these changes are irreversible. Again this is fair warning."

The perspective pulled outward to reveal rotating electrons and a full model of an atom.

"It is important that you understand the origins of all this. I come to you as a scientist; I am not a guru or a theologian, at least not by education. This is not a self-help promotion. I am not promising a pot of gold at your doorstep. What I am attempting is nothing less than aiding and abetting the next stair step in our collective evolution. Before I delve into practical matters, first I am going to touch on the history and science of all of this so we can begin our time together with facts."

The video cut to the Forward Kinetics logo.

"It began with a neuroscientist, a man by the name of Charles—we call him Chuck—Brenton. He formed a company with mathematician Matt Streegman called Forward Kinetics . . ."

ACKNOWLEDGMENTS

The understatement of the century is to say that I am grateful for all the encouragement and support I have received. First, any author, artist, or serial dreamer could accomplish nothing without the support of their spouse. To my wife, a thousand pardons and a thousand thanks; this would not be possible without you by my side. To my agent, Emma Parry, thanks for going the distance for my work and giving me a path to attempt the same. David Pomerico, my intrepid editor, your ardor for *The God Wave* has been a source of inspiration for me, thank you. Scott Steindorff and Dylan Russel of Stone Village Productions, I'm honored by your interest and investment in *The God Wave*. I am eager and excited to take my novel into a new medium with you. Maria Silva and the public relations staff at HarperCollins, thank you for all your hard work. You've made my books more visible—I'm grateful. To Kim Yau and Dana Spector, a little serendipity can go a long way—I'm glad we met.

I'd also like to acknowledge that unseen factor: the mental current that causes ideas to seep into one's consciousness from the ether. This mother of stories cannot be defined as just imagination; there is purpose and dare I say a will behind its machinations. I know different people call this force many things; I have not coined a term for it. I simply acknowledge its presence and give due gratitude. If my work makes this dynamic more familiar even by one iota then I believe I have done some good.

ABOUT THE AUTHOR

PATRICK HEMSTREET is a novelist, neuroengineer, entrepreneur, special-warfare-trained navy medic, stand-up comic, and actor. He lives in Houston, Texas, with his wife and sons.